Jodi Taylor is the author of the bestselling Chronicles of St Mary's series, the story of a bunch of disaster-prone historians who investigate major historical events in contemporary time. Do NOT call it time travel!

Born in Bristol and educated in Gloucester (facts both cities vigorously deny), she spent many years with her head somewhere else, much to the dismay of family, teachers and employers, before finally deciding to put all that daydreaming to good use and pick up a pen. She still has no idea what she wants to do when she grows up.

JODI TAYLOR

A SECOND CHANCE

HEADLINE

Copyright © 2014 Jodi Taylor

The right of Jodi Taylor to be identified as the Author of
the Work has been asserted by her in accordance with the
Copyright, Designs and Patents Act 1988.

First published in Great Britain in 2014 by
Accent Press Ltd

This edition published in paperback in Great Britain in 2019 by
HEADLINE PUBLISHING GROUP

1

Cataloguing in Publication Data is available from the British Library

ISBN 978 1 4722 6439 8

Printed and bound in Great Britain by Clays Ltd, Elcograf S.p.A.

Headline's policy is to use papers that are natural, renewable and recyclable
products and made from wood grown in well-managed forests and other
controlled sources. The logging and manufacturing processes are expected
to conform to the environmental regulations of the country of origin.

HEADLINE PUBLISHING GROUP
An Hachette UK Company
Carmelite House
50 Victoria Embankment
London EC4Y 0DZ

www.headline.co.uk
www.hachette.co.uk

DRAMATIS THINGUMMY

Dr Edward Bairstow   Director of St Mary's.

Mrs Partridge   His PA and Kleio, Muse of History.

HISTORY DEPARTMENT

Madeleine Maxwell   Chief Operations Officer.

Tim Peterson   Chief Training Officer.

Kalinda Black   Liaison Officer at Thirsk University.

Mary Schiller   Senior Historian.

Greta Van Owen   Senior Historian.

Mr Clerk   Historian.

TECHNICAL SECTION

Leon Farrell   Chief Technical Officer

Mr Dieter   Technician

MEDICAL SECTION

Dr Helen Foster   Does not play well with others.

Nurse Diane Hunter   The object of Markham's affections.

Turk   Allegedly a horse.

SECURITY SECTION

Major Ian Guthrie	Head of Security.
Mr Markham	Security Guard
Mr Randall	Security Guard.
Mr Evans	Security Guard

RESEARCH AND DEVELOPMENT

Professor Andrew Rapson	Head of R&D. Should not be allowed to play with matches.
Dr Octavius Dowson	Librarian, Archivist, and matches hider.

IT DEPARTMENT

Polly Perkins	Head of IT.

OTHERS

Mrs Theresa Mack	Kitchen Supremo.
Mrs Mavis Enderby	Head of Wardrobe.
Mrs Shaw	Peterson's assistant and bringer of chocolate biscuits.
Miss Rosie Lee	A nightmare.

HISTORICAL FIGURES

Isaac Newton	Mirror-stealing troublemaker.
Irate Cambridge citizens	Self-explanatory, really.
Gloucester citizens	Possessed of a death wish St Mary's can only admire.
9lb Double Gloucester Cheese	An instrument, if not of death, then certainly of major concussion.
King Priam	King of Troy.
Queen Hecuba	His wife.
Kassandra	They should have listened to her.
Hector	Hero of Troy.
Andromache	His wife.
Astynax	Their Son.
Paris	Not as guilty as everyone thinks.
Achilles	Blond psychopath.
Ajax of Locris	Not a good man in a temple.
Helios	More trouble than everyone else put together – even in a world which contains historians.
Henry V	
Assorted Armies	English, French, Greek, Trojan …
Our ancestors	All of them. All 250 of them.

FROM THE FUTURE

Chief Farrell	Yes – him.

FROM THE PAST

Chief Farrell   It gets complicated. Don't sweat it.

Professor   Retired physicist.
Eddington   A good man in a fight.
Penrose

VILLAINS

Ronan   Trouble from the future.

Assorted raptors

A monolith   With a mind of its own.

PROLOGUE

Troy fell.

That's what it says in every record from Homer onwards. Just two words. Short and impersonal. Troy fell. Words which completely fail to convey, even slightly, the carnage, the brutality, the suffering, the horror, everything that must inevitably accompany the end of a ten-year war and the fall of a great civilisation.

Because I was there, on the blood-soaked sand, amongst the Trojan women lined up on the beach for export, all empty-eyed with shock and grief.

I was there.

I saw infants torn from mothers already grieving for dead husbands, sons, and brothers. Some were tossed carelessly aside as useless. Some were spitted there and then. Some were flung into the surf where they bobbed, wailing, for a few seconds. Now and then, a woman would find the strength to fight back and a frantic struggle would break out. All along the beach, men strode, cursing, shoving, and punching. Urgent to restore order, divide the spoils, and get away.

I crouched on the sand, head down, watching from under my brows. I saw Andromache led past, silent in her grief, to be handed to Neoptolemus and begin her days

1

serving the people who had hurled her tiny son from the city walls.

Somewhere, my people were safe – I hoped. I was the only one outside. I was the only one stupid enough to be caught. Any minute now, rough hands would drag me forward, pull down my tunic, assess what they saw, and allocate me to some grinning Greek. I would be loaded on to a ship with the others. If I was lucky. If I wasn't good slave material – and believe me, I wasn't – I'd be pushed onto the ground and raped repeatedly and violently until I bled to death in the sand. I was under no illusions. It was happening all around me.

This is where a passion for History gets you. Right in the front line. Up close and personal, while History happens all around you. And, occasionally, to you. I could have been a bomb-disposal expert, or a volunteer for the Mars mission, or a firefighter, something safe and sensible. But, no, I had to be an historian. I had to join the St Mary's Institute of Historical Research. Over the years I'd been chased by a T-rex, had the Great Library fall on me, grappled with Jack the Ripper, and been blown up by an exploding manure heap. All about par for the course.

More women were fighting now, clawing and shrieking. They were cut down without a second thought. There were so many of us that the Greeks could afford to be wasteful. The city had been emptied. Every Greek would go home laden with the spoils of war – weapons, temple goods, gold … and slaves.

Long lines shuffled towards the boats. I don't know why they were in such a hurry. It would take them days to clear the city. Maybe they feared the aftershocks.

Footsteps approached. I crouched lower and pulled my stole around my head. The two women in front of me were yanked away. I saw dirty feet in scabby leather sandals. Someone grabbed my hair and hauled me roughly to my feet.

My turn.

The city burned behind us. Black smoke billowed towards the heavens, sending out an unmistakeable message to gods and men.

Troy had fallen.

Before that, however, there was this …

'I really don't see how you can blame me for this, Dr Bairstow. I wasn't even here.'

And, of course, that was my fault too. Apparently, if I had been here, then none of this would have happened. I failed to see the logic of this argument.

'I fail to see the logic of this argument, sir. We both know if I'd been here at the time of the – occurrence – then I'd be blue, too. However, I wasn't, so I'm not. Blue, that is. But, until he regains his normal colour, I'm very willing to stand in for Dr Peterson on this assignment.'

I wasn't, of course. With so much to do for the upcoming Troy assignment, there was no way I wanted to spend a day with an elderly professor from Thirsk University, no matter how many Brownie points it would earn us, or how much Dr Bairstow would appreciate this favour to an old friend. However, the honour of my department – to say nothing of St Mary's – was at stake, so I really had very little choice.

Heads would roll for this. Starting with one in particular.

Back in my office, I requested the pleasure of

Dr Peterson's company.

My assistant, The Rottweiler, or Miss Lee if you want to use the name on her payslip, delighted at the opportunity to drop someone in it, replied smugly that he was already on his way.

Peterson, of course, was my primary target, but while I was waiting for him to materialise, a very acceptable substitute was also available.

I called Major Guthrie, Head of Security, supposedly cool and level-headed, and implicated as deeply as everyone else. He gave me no opportunity to speak.

'You can't blame me for this.'

'You underestimate me.'

'No, seriously, Max, by the time I realised what was happening, the damage was done.'

'They're historians, for God's sake. What did you think would happen as soon as my back was turned? That they all would sit down and crochet something?'

My voice started to rise.

'Yes, but …'

I gave him no chance.

'And as for those idiots in Research and Development – how could you not guess?'

I knew he was laughing at me. It didn't help.

'I turn my back for one day. Just one bloody day. And when I get back my department – my entire bloody department – is blue!'

'Not your entire department,' he said, defensively. 'Mrs Enderby and a couple of others from Wardrobe are still – pink. Or black in one case, of course. And a sort of brownish-coffee colour in another …'

I could hear Tim Peterson's voice in the corridor. I snarled, 'This discussion is not over,' snapped off my com link, and turned to face my prey.

He stuck a blue head round the door. 'Did you want me?'

Rosie Lee opened a file and pretended to read.

I drew a deep breath.

'Before you start,' he said, 'it's not my fault.'

'You're blue!'

'Well, so is everyone else. Why are you picking on me?'

'In my absence, you are supposed to be responsible for my department.'

'And so I was. I responsibly did a risk-assessment thing-thingy ...'

'Which took the form of ...?'

'I asked Professor Rapson if he thought everything would be OK and he said yes,' he said, with his *what have I done now*? expression. 'And then,' he continued, warming to his health and safety in the workplace theme, 'I performed a safety check ...'

'Which took the form of ...?

'I kicked the big rock and it seemed OK.'

I breathed heavily. 'Did you, at any point – any point at all – issue the instruction "do not paint yourselves blue"?'

'No, I can't say I did. I didn't see the need.'

'Why the fu – why ever not?'

'They were already blue, Max. It was too late. They were blue when they turned up. It seemed a good idea at the time.'

'So from whom did this idea originate?'

There was a bit of a silence.

I strode to the door, crossed the gallery, and thundered down to the blatantly listening throng of blue historians.

'Bring me the head of Mr Markham!'

He turned up about ten minutes later, continuing the blue theme.

'Hey, Max. How did it go?'

I'd been to Thirsk to see friend and ex-colleague, Kalinda Black, and attend a presentation. One day. I'd been away one day …

'Never mind that. Explain to me, in terms I will understand, just what the hell happened yesterday.'

'Well, it's like this …'

Disregarding the digressions, excuses, and ramblings, it went something like this:

Ignoring such previous disasters as the Icarus Experiment, (when Mr Markham had set the bar high by managing both to burst into flames *and* knock himself senseless), Professor Rapson had set up the Monolith Experiment. The idea was to transport a monolith across the lake to a pre-dug hole in Mr Strong's cherished South Lawn, taking the opportunity to investigate the methods used to transport Stonehenge monoliths while doing so.

Obviously, the entire history section had volunteered, together with a good number of technicians and security personnel, for whom anything was better than working. A decision they would later come to regret. Many of them had entered into the spirit of the thing by dressing in what they considered appropriate costume, and – the crux of the matter, as far as I was concerned – painting themselves blue (on no historical grounds whatsoever, it should be said).

Tragically, according to Markham, Chief Farrell, head of the technical section, and Major Guthrie had both rained on the parade slightly by insisting on non-prehistoric orange lifejackets, which everyone felt detracted slightly from the realism of the experiment.

As frequently happened with the professor's experiments, everything had started well. The monolith (represented by a large concrete block manufactured especially for the occasion), rolled down to the lake in a suspiciously well-behaved manner, but sadly blotted its copybook in the last few yards. An unforeseen *increase* in velocity led to a corresponding *decrease* in direction-control, and the whole thing, monolith, rollers, and those stupid enough to forget to let go of the ropes attached to it (which was all of them) hurtled down to the jetty, reached escape velocity, and crashed down onto the waiting raft, which immediately sank with all hands.

Permian-style extinction was only avoided by the Chief and Guthrie who managed to stop laughing long enough to fish bobbing blue people out of the chilly water with long sticks and deposit them on the bank, coughing up copious amounts of lake water.

It was at this point that the unwashable-offness of the blue dye had become apparent. Apart from that, beamed Mr Markham, it was generally agreed by everyone that this one had been a stonker.

Twenty-four hours later, most of the unit was still blue and likely to remain so. A variety of soaps and cleaning fluids having proved inadequate, it seemed dermabrasion might be the best way to go. I described a scenario in which Mr Strong's floor-sander and I played leading roles.

'Calm down, Max,' said Peterson, after Markham had departed, thereby reducing the number of Smurfs in the room by fifty per cent. 'What's the problem?'

'The problem is that the biggest assignment of our lives draws ever nearer. Our first big briefing is next week. I have a ton of stuff on Wilusa that I need to look through. I'm putting together a series of lectures to the technical and security sections on the fall of Troy and Chief Farrell wants to talk to me about Number Eight. Again. I really don't have time to escort an elderly professor around 17th-century Cambridge just because I'm the only non-blue person in the building. How long before this stuff wears off?'

'No idea. It's been over twenty-four hours now. I think it's starting to fade, don't you?'

'No.'

'What? Not at all?'

'No.'

He scrubbed his face with his sleeve and inspected the result. Along with the rest of the history department, he wore a blue jumpsuit so the general effect of blueness was overwhelming. The IT section, who wore black, looked like giant bruises. The technical section, with their orange suits and blue faces, could probably be seen from all three space stations.

'Not even just a little?'

'No. Just who is this Professor Penrose, anyway? And what does he have to do with us?'

'Oh, you'll love him, Max. He's a really decent old buffer. He did a lot of the background science stuff when the Boss was setting up St Mary's and now, finally, he's retiring, and the Boss is giving him this jump as a going-away present. Apparently, his big ambition has always been to meet Isaac Newton – a big hero of his – and the Boss said yes. So, tomorrow, a quick dash to seventeenth-century Cambridge and a glimpse of the great man. Nothing to it.'

'Aha!' I said, indulging in Olympic standard straw-clutching, 'I've already done that period. In 1666 I was in Mauritius chasing dodos, so I can't go. Oh, what a shame.'

'No problemo. The jump's set for 1668. No cause for alarm.'

I sighed.

'It'll do you good. You've been head-down in research for months. You could do with a break. It'll be a nice day out for you.'

'I've just had a nice day out. And look what that led to. God knows what will happen if I disappear again. I'll probably get back and –'

'Oh, come on. You're just miffed because you had to go to that presentation at Thirsk while we were all having fun here. You'll enjoy it. You know you will. And honestly, Max, he's a super old codger. You'll love him.'

He was right. I fell in love with Professor Penrose on sight. Actually, I think it was mutual.

He bounded from his seat as I entered the Boss's office, bright blue eyes sparkling with excitement. He

11

wasn't much taller than me, but had a girth which suggested many good university dinners over the years. His simple child-like enthusiasm for everything made him appear considerably younger than his actual age. I put him in his late sixties. I later discovered he was seventy-six.

Dr Bairstow, Director of St Mary's and a man who had certainly never bounded in his life, made the introductions.

'Dr Madeleine Maxwell, may I introduce Professor Eddington Penrose. Professor, this is Dr Maxwell, head of the History department, who will replace Dr Peterson who is sadly … indisposed.'

'Eddie, my dear, call me Eddie. I'm delighted to meet you. So much prettier than the other one, although he was quite charming, of course. I gather he's turned blue.'

Dr Bairstow said nothing in the way that only he can.

'I'm afraid so, Professor, so you have me instead.'

'Excellent, excellent,' he said, rubbing his hands together. 'I can't wait. Do you really think we'll see him?'

'I'm confident of it,' I said, confidently.

The Boss intervened. 'Dr Maxwell, I assume Dr Peterson has given you a full briefing.'

'Indeed, sir. We'll arrive around noon and hope to catch a glimpse of the great man either coming or going from his midday meal.'

Unless he was skulking in his rooms sticking pins in his eyes, of course. I probably shouldn't mention that.

'This is so exciting! I can hardly wait.'

His enthusiasm was infectious. I remembered my own first jump, now many more years ago than I cared to recall. I too had bounced around St Mary's, full of myself.

I pushed aside my reservations about taking a civilian on a jump and invited him to dine with me that evening.

We sat at one of the quiet tables in the dining room and got to know one another.

The food probably wasn't quite what he was accustomed to. Here at St Mary's, our needs are simple. So long as there's plenty of it and it's covered in gravy – or custard – or sometimes both – we're usually quite happy. We're an unsophisticated bunch.

We work for the St Mary's Institute of Historical Research, which in turn is loosely attached to the ancient and venerable University of Thirsk. St Mary's is shabby and battered and so are we. We have two main functions – to record and document major historical events in contemporary time (oh, all right, call it time-travel if you must) and not dying. We're pretty good at the first one. The second needs more work.

Eddie chatted happily through dinner. I asked him why Sir Isaac.

'Oh, he's a childhood hero of mine. The man was a colossus – the reflecting telescope, optics, mathematics, gravity … what a remarkable intellect. And now, I'm actually going to see him in person. It's wonderful, Max – a lifelong ambition about to be achieved.'

He chugged back his water. No wine. We don't drink the night before a jump. At least, not since Baverstock and Lower set the coordinates after a night on the pop and found themselves more involved in the Siege of Paris than they could have wished.

'So tell me, my dear. What about you? What's your lifelong ambition?'

13

'Well, short-term, Professor, to return my department to their original colouring.'

'Yes, Edward and I had a good chuckle over that.'

I tried – and failed – to imagine Dr Bairstow chuckling. Sometimes when he was pleased, he did display the satisfaction of an elderly vulture unexpectedly encountering a dead donkey. But chuckling …

Chief Farrell wandered past on his way back to Hawking Hangar, smiled just for me alone, and then said politely, 'Good evening, Max. Good evening, Professor.'

Professor Penrose watched him go, then turned to me, his eyes twinkling. 'Your young man?'

He didn't miss much, for sure.

'I'm not sure I'd call him young, Professor.'

He laughed. 'At my age, my dear, everyone is young. Should we have asked him to join us?'

'He won't stop. He's busy working on our pod. We're in Number Eight.'

Pods are our centre of operations. They jump us back to whichever time period we've been assigned. They're small, apparently built of stone, flat-roofed, and inconspicuous in any century you care to name. We eat, work, and sleep in them. They too, are shabby and battered. Especially my pod, Number Eight, which has seen more than its fair share of action over the years. Tim had given the professor an introductory tour so he'd already encountered the unique pod smell – overloaded electrics, wet carpet, hot historians, the backed-up toilet, and, for some reason, cabbage. Eau de pod.

'And your long-term ambitions, Max?'

He was persistent as well.

14

I had a bit of a think.

'Well, Troy has always been my ultimate goal, of course ...'

'Yes, so I understand, but what next?'

I fiddled with my fork.

'Well, Agincourt would be nice ...'

'Yes?'

'Well ...' I fiddled a bit more.

'Goodness gracious. I suspect some disreputable secret. I should, of course, murmur politely and change the subject, but other people's disreputable secrets are always so interesting.'

I laughed. 'Well, it's a secret, but not really disreputable, Professor. Sorry to disappoint you.'

He leaned forwards. 'Tell me anyway.'

My mind went back to that particular evening, just a few short months ago.

After all the Mary Stuart dust had settled, we – Leon Farrell and I – had gone on a date. A real one, I mean, with posh frock, heels, make-up, everything. ...

And it had been magical. Just for once, no one from St Mary's was around. It didn't rain. Nothing caught on fire. No one was chasing us. It was just a perfect evening.

I met him in the Hall.

He was studying a whiteboard with his head on one side.

'Did Marie Antoinette really carry on speaking after she'd been beheaded?'

'Well, the legend says her lips carried on moving for some time afterwards, if that counts as speaking. If the brain can function for three minutes without oxygen, I suppose it's possible her last thoughts could be articulated for maybe part of that time. I'm not sure whether her voice box would work though. I'd have to ask Helen.'

I realised too late that it might have been more appropriate on a date just to have said just *yes* or *no* and changed the subject to something a little less death-related. I was very conscious of being completely out of my social depth.

We set off for the village pub, The Falconberg Arms. Our date had to be within walking distance because I'd recently driven his car into the lake. Long story.

The evening was lovely – warm and velvety, and we took our time.

The landlord, Joe Nelson, met us just inside the door. I'd known him since I arrived at St Mary's. As a trainee, this place had been my second home. He was short, blocky, and his head of thick, dark hair could not disguise ears like satellite dishes. He had a sickle-shaped scar on one cheekbone. I knew he and Leon had been friends for years. Like obviously called to like, because here was another one who never said a lot.

'Leon.'

'Joe.'

The world's two chattiest men stood for a while, possibly exhausted by the effort.

Eventually, he stirred. 'I thought you might like some privacy, so I've arranged for you to be in here.'

He led us down a corridor to a door on the left.

'The breakfast room,' he announced and threw open the door with a flourish.

I stepped into Fairyland.

Only one of the three tables was laid. A crisp white cloth covered a small table near the fireplace. Gentle candlelight winked off crystal and cutlery. A low arrangement of golden roses in the centre of the table filled the room with their scent.

"The Moonlight Sonata" played quietly in the background.

'This way, please,' he said and led us to our table where a perfect Margarita awaited me. The years rolled back to a hotel in Rushford, when I'd worn this dress and he'd looked a sensation in that suit and we'd danced and taken the first steps towards a tentative understanding. Looking back over the last twelve months or so, we hadn't made a lot of progress. But he was trying and I had promised my assistant, David, just before he died, that I would try too. I still missed him every day.

'Leon, this is just perfect.'

'Thank you. Drink this.'

'What is it?'

'Alcohol.'

'Great. Why?'

'Because I want to talk to you.'

'In that case, alcohol might not be the way to go.'

'I want you to drink this and then listen to what I have to say.'

'You're plying me with alcohol so I'll say yes to something horrible?'

'No, I'm plying you with alcohol so you'll listen. I tried to talk to you about this after Jack the Ripper. And again after Nineveh, but there were more important things

17

to be said then. I don't want an answer from you now. I just want you to listen calmly and without panicking and alcohol seems the best way to go.'

'OK. Hit me.'

I sipped, felt the familiar warmth spread through my limbs, and sucked the salt off my bottom lip.

He peered at me. 'How do you feel?'

'Pretty damned good.'

'OK. I have a proposal for you.'

No, no, no. Not marriage. I really thought I'd made my feelings on marriage perfectly clear. Asked once what was the ideal quality in a husband, I'd replied: 'Absence.' No one ever asked again.

'No,' he said, hastily topping up my glass. 'Calm down. Drink this.'

I sipped again and felt my panic dissolve in the tequila.

'Get on with it, then.'

'What?'

'Well, this is me. One drink and I'm happy. Two drinks and I'm unconscious. You have a window of about eight seconds. Get on with it.'

'All right, here goes. I'd like you to leave St Mary's.'

I stared at him in dismay. 'What? Why? What have I done? Are you breaking up with me? Why should I be the one to leave? If you're uncomfortable having me around then that's your problem, not mine. I'm not giving up my job just because we're over. You leave.'

'Yes,' he said, removing my glass. 'Something tells me I may have missed the window.'

'What window?'

He sighed heavily.

'I have no sympathy,' I said. 'You gave me alcohol.'

'Yes, I brought this on myself. Let's just give it a moment, shall we? And then I'll have another go.'

The first course arrived – seafood platter.

I concentrated on my food. Something that comes easily to me. 'These prawns are delicious. Do you want yours?'

'Yes. You look very pretty tonight.'

'Thank you, that's very kind. I wore this dress to that hotel in Rushford. Do you remember?'

'I do. I think that was quite a night for both of us.'

'And at the end of it, you walked away.'

'I had to,' he said, matter-of-factly. 'You have no idea of the effect you have on me, do you?'

I swallowed. 'Or you on me.'

He took my hand. The room swayed a little. My heart rate kicked up.

The door opened and they brought in the next course. 'Everything all right in here?'

'Yes, thank you,' said Leon.

I nodded, speech being beyond me just at that moment.

We ate in silence for a while. The food was delicious. The setting perfect. Nothing even remotely like this had ever happened to me before. That he could go to such trouble, just for me … I looked around at the candles, the roses, the man sitting opposite me …

He caught me looking. Nothing was said. In fact, nothing was said for quite a long time. I broke his gaze and fumbled for my glass. I must be ill. My appetite had completely disappeared. My breathing was all over the place and I was suddenly hot. Very hot indeed.

Looking at his plate, he said softly, 'We've had a rough year and I wanted this night to be special.'

I took his hand and, looking him firmly in the eye, stepped out over a yawning chasm and said, 'It will be.'

He caught his breath, pushed back his chair and reached for me …

Joe Nelson stuck his head around the door. 'Ready for dessert?'

I said, 'Yes,' and Leon sighed. Again.

We settled down, but the moment was gone. He was wise enough not to push it.

'Perhaps, instead of thinking so much about the past, we could take some time to talk about our future.'

I made myself smile politely and clutched my glass in a death-grip.

'I'm just going to say this straight out. All I ask is that you don't say no without giving it some thought.'

'What's this all about?'

'Well,' he said slowly. 'Have you given any thought at all to what you're going to do after Troy?'

'I'm an historian. We don't do planning ahead.'

I was avoiding the issue because, actually, I had. The downside to achieving your life's ambition is – where do you go from there? What do you do afterwards? Where's the challenge? I must admit, the thought had been troubling me. 'I'm not sure what you mean.'

'I have a proposal for you.'

He saw my panic.

'No, no, calm down. Poor choice of words. I should have said proposition. I have an idea.'

I breathed a little easier.

'Go on.'

He eyed me. 'It might not be easy. In fact, I know it won't be. It might be the most difficult assignment you've ever had. You may not survive. I almost certainly won't. And even if you do, things will certainly never be the same again.'

Now he had my attention.

'I know you've made no plans for a future you never expect to have. I know you love your job and you're good at it. I know you don't pay a lot of attention to what goes on outside St Mary's, but I'd like to make a suggestion.

'No,' he said, as I opened my mouth to panic again. 'Please hear me out. Sometime in the future – when we both want to – I'd like us to leave St Mary's and start another life. No – please, let me finish. One day this job will kill you. It might be years in the future, it might be tomorrow, but one day you won't come back. Or one day I'll open the pod door and you'll be dead and I won't want to go on living in a world that doesn't have you in it somewhere. So what I'm saying is – before that happens – we both leave and start a new life. Together. I'm an engineer. We get a place with a work area and I can take time to work on some ideas I've had. And you, Max, you could paint to your heart's content. You can have half the workshop – or your own space if you want – and spend some time doing the other thing you're really good at. You can take the time to produce a body of work, build a reputation … We could walk together, hold hands, feed the ducks, go to the cinema, learn to cook, make new friends, watch TV; there are so many things we could do together. I'm sorry if it sounds corny and dull, but I don't

21

think it would be unexciting. And we'll certainly never be bored because I've seen you cook. I just want to spend my life with you. Now, more than ever. Please don't say no straight away. Promise me you'll think about it.'

I didn't have to think about it. I had a sudden blinding flash of clarity and from way back I heard Kal say "One day this won't be enough". At the time, I never thought it would apply to me, but now I realised exactly what she'd been talking about. On the other hand, this was scary stuff. This was about relationships, sharing, domesticity, and all the things I really regarded as the inventions of the devil. I took a very deep breath.

'No.'

I hope never to see that look again.

'Can't you take some time to think about it?'

'No.'

'It doesn't have to be now. It could be years away.'

'No,' I said. 'I don't want to wait for years. After Troy – however long that takes – you and I give in our notice, move away, and make a new life. Doing those things you said. And God help you, because if we don't live in perfect peace and happiness, I'll make your life a living hell.'

He took both my hands, glass and all. 'I can wait.'

'It might be some time. Troy could be a two-year assignment, at least.'

'I can wait.'

I took a huge breath for a huge step. 'OK then, is that a deal?'

He couldn't look at me. He swallowed and nodded.

'It's a deal.'

22

I relayed some of this to Eddie who nodded thoughtfully and, surprisingly, changed the subject.

'Compared with Troy – and Agincourt – tomorrow's jump must seem very tame to you.'

'Not at all, Professor. Dr Bairstow once said "It's not always battlefields and blood." and he was right. For instance, I've seen the Hanging Gardens and they are stupendous.'

No need to tell him how that one ended. Or the Whitechapel jump. Or the Cretaceous assignment.

This is the bit we never really discuss. Not even amongst ourselves. These days, the attrition rate is nowhere near as high as it used to be. Almost as if an uneasy truce has been worked out between us historians, who really do our best to behave ourselves as we jink up and down the timeline, and History, who, these days, seems slightly less inclined to slaughter us wholesale for any minor infractions.

This is really not something you want to explain to a civilian who is accompanying you to the seventeenth century in less than twenty-four hours.

I consulted with Doctor Foster the next morning, just on the off-chance Eddie had contracted something serious overnight. She sat on the windowsill and puffed her cigarette smoke out of the window.

I looked pointedly at the smoke alarm. She looked pointedly at the battery, which was lying on the table. Where it always was. I sighed. Leon, fighting the good fight over batteries and losing on all fronts, would not be happy.

'Professor Penrose. Is he fit?'

'Fitter than you, Max. On the other hand, of course, I've seen 10-day-old corpses fitter than you. That knee of yours is going to let you down one day.'

'No time before Troy.'

'We'll get it fixed immediately afterwards. Before it gets really serious.'

It didn't really matter, although I couldn't tell her that. I hadn't told anyone, apart from Eddie. I couldn't even bring myself to think about what Ian, or Tim would say.

'To return to Professor Penrose …'

'Yes, fit as a fiddle for his age. This is not to be construed as permission for you to bounce him around Cambridge. We all still remember what you did to Mr Dieter.'

Dieter and I, escaping from a landslide in the Cretaceous period, had once had a bit of a bumpy landing. They'd practically had to demolish the pod to get us out. But after a couple of days in Sick Bay each and a major refit for Number Eight, everything was fine, so I really don't know why people can't let that go.

We were off.

'Right then, Professor. If you'd like to take a seat. No, not that one – the right-hand seat. That's it. Make yourself comfortable. I'll be with you in a minute.'

He seated himself, wriggling a little in the lumpy seat, staring around, taking it all in. And possibly trying not to breathe in the smell.

We were inside Number Eight. The console was to the right of the door in this pod and two uncomfortable seats were bolted to the floor in front of it. Above the console, the screen showed an external view of orange techies, scurrying around the hangar outside, doing last-minute techie things. Around the pod, lockers held equipment for long-term assignments and our own personal effects. Thick bunches of cables looped around the walls and disappeared up into the ceiling. A partitioned corner contained the toilet and shower. A small chiller held life's essentials and on a shelf, by the enormous first aid cabinet, stood a kettle and two mugs. We're St Mary's. We run on tea.

The locker doors were dented. The console was scratched in some places and shiny in others. Some of the stains on the floor could have told an interesting story.

The toilet rarely worked properly and often not at all. I think I've already mentioned the smell. But they're our pods and we love them.

Leon winked at me. 'It's all set up, Max. Co-ordinates are laid in. I believe you're straight in and straight back out again.'

'That's the idea.'

He pulled his scratchpad from his knee-pocket and leaned over the console, bashed in a few figures, and straightened up. 'I'm done. Have a good trip. Good luck, Professor.'

The professor bounced again, speechless with excitement.

'Take care,' said Leon, looking at me. As he always did.

'We'll be fine,' I said, inaccurately.

The door closed behind him.

I checked the console one last time.

'Not too late to change your mind, Eddie.'

He laughed.

I said, 'Computer, initiate jump.'

'Jump initiated.'

And the world went white.

We were tucked away in some smelly alleyway off Trinity Street, so I was able to give Professor Penrose the traditional two minutes to get his head around when and where we were. He stuck his head out of the door, exclaiming, 'Bless my soul. God bless my soul,' over and over again, while his senses got to grips with the sights, sounds, and, especially, the smells of

17th-century Cambridge.

He pulled himself together eventually.

'Sorry, Max. That was unprofessional of me.'

'Not at all, Eddie. On my first jump I was turning cartwheels.'

We set off for Trinity College, where a young Fellow named Isaac Newton was, with luck, about to make an appearance.

Cambridge was every bit as wet and dreary as I thought it would be. I shivered inside my cloak as we picked our way carefully along Trinity Street, easing our way through the crowds. The place was packed as students, townspeople, tradesmen, and livestock noisily shoved their way along the uneven cobbles.

Eddie was staring around. 'Do you know, I think the Tourist Information Centre might be just down there. One day.'

I didn't reply. I was picking my way through something pink and blobby. Apparently well ahead of its time, Cambridge had implemented proper street-cleaning services as far back as 1575. God knows what it had been like before, because today we were up to our ankles in piss, rotting vegetables, dog turds, unidentified innards, vomit, puddles of dirty water, horseshit, mud, and things I didn't even want to think about. Even more alarmingly, packs of foraging dogs roamed everywhere. I wished I'd brought a stick. The town itself had been described, I forget by whom, as low-lying and dirty with badly paved streets and poor buildings. I had no argument with any of that.

Trinity Street, with its inns and merchants' houses,

was handsome enough, but, behind the main streets, a network of squalid alleyways and dirty yards led down to the river. As always, the pod was parked in one of these squalid alleyways. Show me a squalid alleyway – any squalid alleyway – and I'll point to the pod parked in it.

As we drew closer to Trinity College itself we could see a number of people streaming in and out of the Great Gate. Worryingly, none of them were women.

We stood quietly in a doorway and watched the crowds go past. I wanted to take some time before actually entering the college. There shouldn't be any difficulties at all with this jump; we were, after all, about to visit one of the world's premier colleges, not the Battle of Waterloo. But we're St Mary's and we have been known to have the odd problem occasionally. Eventually, I gave the nod to a quivering professor and off we trotted.

Eddie went first, neat and respectable and scholarly in black. I was dressed as his servant and also in black. I walked one step behind him at all times, so I could keep an eye on him.

He marched confidently through the smaller doorway in the ornately decorated Great Gate. I looked up at the statue. Henry VIII clutched his sceptre. At some point in History, students would substitute a chair leg. The current whereabouts of the sceptre are unknown.

'It'll turn up one day,' said the professor confidently, following my gaze. 'You know what colleges are like. It'll be somewhere, propping someone's bedroom door open. Or someone's using it as a poker.'

We knew Newton's rooms were off to the right,

between the gate and the Chapel. A wooden staircase led from his rooms to the enclosed garden and there was no other exit so he had to leave through the front door. We were fortunate not to have to penetrate too far into the college. Accordingly, we looked around for somewhere quiet to tuck ourselves away and wait.

I'd never even visited Cambridge before, far less Trinity College, and I was gobsmacked at the size and scale of my surroundings. It had been called the finest college court in the world and I could easily believe it. The buildings were magnificent. Time to look later. First, we had to park ourselves somewhere out of the way while we waited.

I pulled up my hood and kept a respectful pace behind the professor. I saw no other women on the premises and had no idea whether I should actually be here at all. This is where a too-hasty briefing gets you. However, I'd had what seemed at the time to be a brilliant idea and brought a small mirror so I could stand inconspicuously behind the professor, keep my eyes averted so as not to contaminate any men, and still be able to see what was going on around me.

I don't know why I ever thought that would work.

We were prepared to wait for several hours, although with luck we wouldn't have to. We wore stout shoes and warm, waterproof cloaks and could stand all afternoon, if necessary. The air was wet, but it wasn't actually raining and the afternoon was mild enough for early autumn. Away, in the distance, I could hear crows calling in the still air.

There were plenty of people around – all of them

men – mostly dressed in black. Everyone was either wearing or carrying a hat. I saw a variety of wigs, mostly of a dull brown colour. The grey afternoon leached all colour from the scene, but, even so, I doubted it was ever a riot of colour. They walked to and fro in small groups, heads bowed, discussing, presumably, the secrets of the universe. Everything was exactly as I had hoped it would be – quiet, peaceful, and non-threatening.

My plan was to wait quietly, watch the great man walk past, either on his way in or out of his rooms, restrain Professor Penrose from accosting his idol, and then return him, safe and sound, to Dr Bairstow and St Mary's for a celebratory drink.

Things didn't turn out that way at all.

Eddie, who had been here before, pointed out the various buildings and their functions to pass the time. From there, it was only a small conversational step to discussing other and (according to Eddie) lesser colleges. Queens, for instance, founded by the Lancastrian queen, Margaret of Anjou, whose sharp tongue and high-level paranoia were two of the reasons for the Wars of the Roses.

Since Eddie was a Yorkist and I had Lancastrian leanings, we whiled away the time with a discussion that was brisk and not always to the point. I was busy slandering the entire Yorkist line when the door opened and a tall, thin figure slipped out. I'd been a little worried we might not know him, but, trust me, the Newton nose was a dead giveaway. He pulled the door to behind him, settled his papers more firmly under his arm, and stood for a moment, looking up at the sky. Given his habitual vagueness, he was probably trying to work out where he was.

Professor Penrose stiffened like a pointer scenting a game-bird and involuntarily took several steps forward.

The movement attracted the figure's attention and he turned towards us. My first thought was that he was far too young to be our man. Mid-twenties at the latest, with a long pale face, a wide mouth, and a determined chin. A very modest wig hung down either side of his face – like spaniel's ears.

I was completely taken by surprise. The three of us froze – Professor Penrose with his arm outstretched as if to shake his hand, me with my mirror, and Isaac Newton still clutching his thick sheaf of papers tied with ribbon.

We all stared at each other for a long moment.

Completely forgetting my careful briefing – this is why we don't let civilians do this – Eddie stepped forward, saying, 'My dear sir. This is an honour, a very great honour ...' and stopped as it became apparent his idol was ignoring him and looking at me.

Oh God, I shouldn't be here. They probably had very strict rules about letting in women and I was about to be burned at the stake. Or stoned. Or flogged. Or impaled. Historian on a stick. I knew this would happen. This was why Peterson had originally been selected for this assignment. There was no doubt the sight of a woman within these hallowed halls of learning had seriously discomposed the great man who stood, open-mouthed, staring at me.

Confused, Eddie turned to look as well. 'What ...?'

I was conscious of the harsh sound of the crows again,

ominous in the silent court. What sort of trouble were we in now?

The two of them stared at me and I still hadn't a clue what was going on. Nothing new there, then. I actually looked down at myself to check I was correctly dressed. What was happening here?

Isaac Newton made a hoarse sound and stretched out a trembling hand. I still didn't get it. He was obviously in the grip of some strong emotion, but what? Slowly, the truth dawned. It wasn't me at all. It was the mirror. He was staring at the mirror. Why? Did they have some rule about mirrors? I know it sounds odd, but clump together large numbers of male academics unleavened by a little female intelligence and practicality, and all sorts of bizarre behaviour patterns and phobias can emerge.

'Of course,' he said and I was startled at the strong, rural burr in his voice. His appearance was quiet and gentlemanly and I suppose I'd expected his voice to be the same.

'Of course,' he said again and it was apparent he wasn't talking to either of us. 'A mirror.'

And before I knew it, he'd taken several long steps forward and snatched the mirror from me, turning it over in his hands.

'Yes ... yes ... of course ... replace the lens ...'

He backed away, turned, and before I could stop him strode swiftly towards his rooms. With my mirror. Isaac Newton had stolen my bloody mirror!

Now we were in trouble. That was a modern mirror and there was no way I could leave it here. This was more important than Professor Penrose and certainly more important than me. I'd be breaking every rule in the book if I left that here. It's not that as a mirror it was anything special, but you just can't go littering the timeline with anomalous objects. History doesn't like it. That's History as in Kleio, daughter of Zeus and immortal Muse of History. Or, if you prefer, Mrs Partridge, PA to Dr Bairstow and pretty formidable in either incarnation. I'd have to lead a team to get it back. And if we couldn't find it … or he'd already incorporated it into something important … like the bloody reflecting telescope … there would be hell to pay.

If I was going to get it back, it would have to be now, before he could re-enter his rooms. But I had Professor Penrose to think of as well. I couldn't just go off and leave him to his own devices.

Newton was several yards away and picking up speed. I said to Eddie, 'Stay here. Don't move.'

Too late. The professor had already started after him in a kind of lurching hobble that still wasn't bad for someone his age. So I set off after the pair of them.

Isaac Newton, looking over his shoulder and seeing us racing towards him, did what anyone would have done; shouted for help and broke into a run.

I muttered some dreadful curse, hurtled past Professor Penrose, and, before he knew what was happening, tried to snatch the mirror back from an astonished Newton. Who wouldn't let go. For long seconds we tugged back and forth, both determined not to relinquish our hold.

People were turning to watch. I cursed again, offered up a silent apology to the greatest mathematician the world had ever known, and kicked him hard on the shin. I think he let go of the mirror out of sheer surprise. I turned, grabbed the professor's arm, shouted, 'Run!' and we set off for the gate.

I heard a voice behind us shout, 'Stop. Stop them. Thieves.'

Oh, shit. Our little incident had been witnessed by others in the Great Court, wrong conclusions drawn, and now we were in trouble.

It's that easy.

The cry was taken up by other voices and the next moment half a dozen burly young men were on our trail.

Bloody bollocking hell! How could so much go so wrong so quickly?

I cast caution to the winds, shouted, 'Come on, Eddie. Move!' and we shot out of the gate and into the busy street.

If I'd had Peterson with me, we would both have slowed down so as not to attract attention, split up, and discreetly made our way back to the pod. But I had Professor Penrose, so that was out of the question. We put our heads down and buffeted our way through the crowds. Cries of protest marked our progress. We apologised and excused ourselves as best we could, but the young men pursuing us showed no such restraint, pushing people aside in their eagerness to get to us. They were gaining.

Help came from an unexpected source.

I didn't notice, to begin with, but our progress became easier. People stepped aside to let us pass and then closed again behind us. I thought I was imagining it to begin with, but, no, the noise behind us increased as the crowds hampered our pursuers.

I knew there was no love between town and gown. In 1630 the colleges had refused to give aid to victims of the plague, even going so far as to lock their doors against the sick. Maybe relations between them were still a bit iffy.

For whatever reason, we were drawing away from them and slowed down. What a pleasant change to have someone on our side for once. I began to regret my possibly too-hasty opinion of beautiful Cambridge and its lovely inhabitants.

I could still hear uproar behind us. A familiar sound. People shouted at us, at the pursuing students, at the barking dogs. The pursuing students and the dogs barked back. You never heard such a racket.

Definitely time to go.

I picked up my skirts and ran again. Beside me, Professor Penrose ran quite nimbly for someone his age. I fumbled inside my cloak for my pepper spray, just in case.

A group of scruffy young men lounging outside The Black Bear, alerted by the shouts behind us, turned and, seeing us running, spread out across the road to prevent our escape.

Avoiding this bunch of alcohol-soaked ne'er-do-wells – or students, as they're generically known – we turned right. Bloody students. Why were they always hanging around pubs when they should be at their studies? I never did that. We swerved down an alleyway, fortunately going in the right direction. Because I knew where we were. We were behind Holy Trinity church, somewhere in the maze between Sidney Street and Trinity Street and luckily hurtling the right way. A hand grabbed my cloak. I turned, closed my eyes, and squirted. He fell back with a cry, both hands to his face. The shouting intensified.

At the bottom of the alleyway, we should go right. I could see a corner of the pod, just to the left of an archway.

Someone seized me again. The professor spun around and delivered a left hook that sent him reeling. My assailant fell sideways onto three stacked boxes of fruit. They and he fell across the alleyway.

'College boxing champion in my day,' panted the professor.

The alleyway was full of people, all shouting at us. But our way ahead was clear. I pulled over two barrels, fortunately empty, and sent them rolling down the alley.

'Go, Professor, go.'

He didn't argue, he knew he was the slower. I could catch him up later. The alleyway was lined with all sorts of useful detritus. Broken chairs, crates, piles of rubbish, the odd dead dog … I threw everything I could in my wake. Anything to slow them down. I'm not a bad sprinter and all I had to do was stay ahead of them.

A huge, red-faced man wearing a stained leather apron stepped out ahead of me, his mighty arms outspread. He should be so lucky. I gave him a quick squirt and he bellowed with pain and, as he covered his face, I managed to squeeze between him and the wall.

Eddie stood by the pod at the end of the alley. Bless him, he'd armed himself with a stick and, from the look on his face, was prepared to use it. Ignoring Major Guthrie's careful training, I cast a quick glance over my shoulder. Not a good idea. I could hear the Major's voice now. 'Never mind what's going on behind you. You'll find out soon enough if you stop to look.'

There weren't as many of them as I had thought from the noise. But they were close. I couldn't afford to be caught. Without me the professor wouldn't be able to get into the pod. And in the seventeenth century the penalty for theft was hanging. In my case, they'd probably chuck in a few charges of witchcraft as well. I really should get an office job.

Something whizzed past my ear. Great! Now they were throwing stones.

No, they weren't. Professor Penrose was throwing stones. And old vegetables, bits of wood, pots, anything he could lay his hands on. He'd probably bowled for his college as well. The threatening shouts behind me became warning shouts.

Ignoring everything going on around me, I ducked my head and raced for the pod.

And then, just as I thought we were safe, two more men appeared from behind the pod and seized the professor's arms. He struggled. They weren't gentle and I feared for his ancient bones.

Time to bring out the big guns.

I reached behind me for the stun gun under my cloak. We're really not supposed to do this. I zapped one man and he fell backwards, twitching.

I tossed the pepper spray to the professor, shouting, 'Point it away from you, Eddie,' because he was a physicist and you never know.

Hands seized me. I twisted away and zapped blindly. I heard another cry and clatter as someone else crashed to the ground in a convulsing heap. It was only a matter of time now – yes, here we go – 'Witch! Witch!'

You couldn't blame them, I suppose. From their point of view, I stretched out an arm and a man fell to the ground. Predictable, but given that this was supposed to be a world-famous seat of learning in the Age of Reason, I was a little disappointed. On the other hand, I'm a Thirsk graduate myself, and nothing other universities do surprises me very much.

We were within about ten feet of the pod. So near and yet so far. Some citizens had drawn back, leaving four or five of their braver brethren to tackle the woman and the old man.

If I'd had Peterson, or Clerk, or Van Owen, or any of them, it would have been a piece of cake. This sort of thing happened so often it was practically the standard end to most of our assignments.

I heard the professor shout, heard another shriek as someone got a face full – with luck not the professor himself – jabbed an elbow into someone's midriff, swung a fist, and caught something hard. And, once again, I'd forgotten to untuck my thumb, and, once again, it hurt.

It really wasn't one of those nice, clean, carefully choreographed Hollywood fights where the stunningly beautiful heroine – that would be me – tastefully attired in skin-tight black leather and impractical heels, destroys an entire platoon of heavily armed opponents without even breaking a fingernail.

I slipped and slithered in whatever the good folk of Cambridge had been happily tossing into their streets that morning, aimed punches that missed, got tangled up in my own cloak, was nearly sprayed by an excited Professor Penrose, zapped another one, and worried I would run out of charge.

Then, suddenly, I was free. Two men lay on the ground. One still stood but had his hands to his face, moaning. Two men still had hold of the professor and as I looked, the nearer one let go and reached for me. I zapped him and twisted past. At the same time, Eddie let loose with the spray. All the other citizens had fallen well back by now, but I could hear distant shouting and running footsteps.

I shouted, 'Door!' and seized Eddie, who squirted again, following through with the classic knee to the groin. I made a note never, *ever* to mess with a septuagenarian theoretical physicist.

I whirled him into the pod before he could victoriously trample on his fallen foe. Someone caught my cloak again and tried to drag me back out. I lashed backwards with my foot and caught him, painfully, I hoped, on the shin. But we couldn't get the door closed and in a few seconds there would be others and once they were inside the pod, we were finished. I reached up to my hair and pulled out a wickedly sharpened hairpin. Always my weapon of choice. I jabbed viciously – once, twice, and someone cursed.

The professor knotted his hands in my assailant's hair and tried to pull him off me. We all staggered backwards and fell heavily across the console.

Which was not good.

Lights flashed. Alarms sounded.

The computer said, 'Emergency extraction requested.'

I shrieked, 'No. Abort. Abort.'

I yanked the man off the professor and shoved him towards the door, all the time screaming, 'Abort. Computer, abort extraction,' and completely forgetting the authorisation code.

The door was open. We can't jump with the door open. We shouldn't be able to jump with the door open. And we certainly didn't want emergency extraction. We were about to be ripped out of Cambridge at nose-bleeding speed …

I heaved the man out of the door – although actually, I don't think he could get out fast enough. None of his friends had followed him in and here he was, alone in this talking box … he took to his heels.

I slapped the manual switch. The door closed cutting off the noise of the angry citizenry of Cambridge baying for our blood, albeit from a safe distance.

'Professor, hold on tight! Brace for impact!'

Too late.

The world went black.

I rolled over. Every bone in my body hurt. I'd done this before and it still wasn't any fun. That's why emergency extraction is for emergencies only.

I remembered I had a passenger.

'Professor Penrose?'

He stirred.

'Lie still, Professor. Don't try to get up just yet. They'll open the door in a minute and we'll get you up to Sick Bay.'

I was wasting my breath.

'My goodness me,' he said, delightedly. 'That was exciting. Can we do it again?'

'Are you injured at all, Professor?'

'I don't believe so. A little winded, of course. It's been a long time since I had to exert myself to that extent.'

He seemed in remarkably good nick for an elderly academic who had been pursued through the muddy streets of Cambridge by a baying mob before being hurled through time and space like something in a welly whanging contest. I scanned him anxiously. I didn't want him having a heart attack.

I helped him sit and, suddenly wondering what was

41

taking Chief Farrell so long to get to us, turned to look at the screen.

Never have the words *now we're in trouble* been so appropriate.

'Oh dear,' said the professor. 'This doesn't look good.'

He was right. The view from the screen definitely didn't look good at all.

That wasn't what he was talking about. He held up his hand, which was red with blood.

And the day just got worse.

'It's OK, Professor, I'm trained for this. Can you lie back down on the floor for me? Does anything hurt? Is there any pain?'

'No. Although now you mention it, I do feel a little giddy. It must be the excitement.'

It was probably blood loss. Somehow, he'd been stabbed. High up on his left shoulder. He hadn't noticed in the excitement and I hadn't noticed because of his dark clothing. He wasn't gushing, but he had a narrow, deep wound from which blood oozed unspectacularly but steadily. I bound him up, elevated his feet, and, at his request, made him some tea.

'It's like donating blood, Max. They always give you a cup of tea.'

I sat beside him on the floor. 'I have to hand it to you, Eddie. You're bleeding all over the floor and clutching your tea like a pro. We'll definitely have to make you an honorary member of St Mary's.'

He chuckled.

'I'm just going to leave you for a moment and sort out a few things with the controls.'

A splendidly ambiguous sentence that could mean absolutely anything. I really didn't like the look of this. We might have been better off in Cambridge.

The screen showed nothing. And I really mean nothing. Not black, not white, not electronic snow. The screen showed nothing. I checked the controls. There was no fault with the equipment inside or the cameras outside. The screen showed nothing because there was nothing to show.

I looked at the chronometer. Baffled. It read zero. I watched for a few seconds, but the read-out was unchanging. I flicked it on and off, but the result was the same. According to the chronometer, no time was passing. The read-out said zero and zero it remained.

I checked the outside sensor readings for atmosphere, temperature, all the usual stuff.

Nothing.

Again, all the instruments were working perfectly. There was simply nothing for them to read. There was nothing out there. Nothing at all. We were surrounded by nothing.

'What is it, Max? What's wrong?'

I couldn't explain because I didn't know. My instinct was to say something comforting, but that wasn't fair on him. He was an intelligent man – a leader in his field. And a good man to have around in a scrap as well.

I shook my head. 'I don't know, Eddie. Computer – verify date and location.'

The reply was usually instantaneous, but now there was a very definite time lag of some four or five seconds.

'Unverifiable.'

'Computer, please confirm date and location of previous jump.'

'Cambridge, 1668.'

'Computer, confirm date and location of current jump.'

'Unable to comply.'

'Computer, why?'

'Specify.'

Bloody thing.

'Computer, why can you not identify our current location?'

'Current location unidentifiable.'

'Why?'

'Rephrase.'

I gritted my teeth.

'Why is the current location unidentifiable?'

'There is no current location.'

'Why is the current date unidentifiable?'

'There is no current date.'

'Computer, what is outside?'

'Nothing.'

'Define nothing.'

Now there was a very long pause.

'The absence of anything.'

'Is that what is outside? The absence of anything? Confirm.'

An even longer pause.

'Confirmed.'

Right. We were out of here. This was definitely not a place to be.

'No cause for alarm, Eddie,' I said, resetting the coordinates for St Mary's as fast as I could go. We'll soon have you home. You'll get the traditional bollocking from Dr Foster for having got yourself stabbed and then you really will be one of us.'

I threw the final switch. 'Off we go. Computer, initiate jump.'

Nothing happened.

'Computer, initiate jump.'

Nothing happened.

Oh ... shit.

'I think,' said Eddie, struggling to sit up, 'that I should have a look.'

No, he shouldn't. He should remain on the floor, conserving his strength. On second thoughts, what for? A longer and more lingering death? And I was clueless. I had no idea what had happened. Or where we were. The giant brain of Professor Penrose might just have some answers.

I helped him up and got him into a chair. We studied the read-outs, which didn't take long. Everything was either blank or read zero.

He said, quietly, 'Give me a minute, Max, will you?' and sat thoughtfully sipping his tea.

I stowed the pepper spray and stun gun. The cause of all the trouble, my little round mirror, lay on the floor. One or both of us had obviously trodden on it, because it was cracked.

Seven years bad luck.

I should live so long.

'The mirror crack'd from side to side;
"The curse is come upon me," cried
The Lady of Shalott,' intoned Professor Penrose, which

45

I could well have done without.

I sat down again and stared at the console. Nothing had changed.

I'm not religious. On assignments I tend to place my faith in any local gods hanging around, Osiris, Odin, Athena, Marduk, whoever, because there's no point in tempting fate. At any other time I just tend to drop everything in the lap of a vaguely believed-in god of historians, with instructions to sort everything out as soon as possible, so I don't know what made me think of that bit in the Bible:

And the earth was without form, and void; and darkness was upon the face of the deep.

From the King James version, obviously. Only Christians could replace the majesty and awe of the King James Bible with something as dreary and uninspiring as a directive from the English Egg Marketing Board and then wonder why no one takes them seriously any more.

I pulled myself together. I could hear the usual background electronic hum of the pod, but otherwise everything was horribly silent.

Eddie stirred. 'Well, let's put together what we know, shall we? We don't know where we are because, according to out instruments, we're not anywhere. We're nowhere. We don't know when and, according to our instruments, no time is passing outside. We don't know what's out there because, again, according to our instruments, there's nothing out there. This is fascinating, Max. Absolutely fascinating.'

He was as bad as us historians. Faced with impending catastrophe, an historian will always pause in the

46

headlong dash to safety and think – *Oh, that's interesting. The Spartans didn't always tie up their hair, after all.* Sometimes, of course, that's the last thing they do think. Professor Penrose was obviously made of The Right Stuff. Historian stuff.

'In what way, Professor?'

'Well, look at us. We're inside this little box – pod, rather, and we're all right. We can move and speak, so obviously time is passing for us. In here, everything is as it should be. It's out there that's the problem.'

We had problems in here too, actually. For a start, Eddie was turning very pale. He waved me away. 'No, no. I'm fine. Just thinking,' and stared thoughtfully at the screen.

And secondly, not immediately, but soon, it would start to get very stuffy inside the pod. We don't carry oxygen. Why would we? We're supposed to be able to open the bloody door and step outside.

I sat quietly because Eddie was thinking. And because sitting quietly conserves oxygen. Of which we would soon have very little.

Just for something to do, I reset the co-ordinates. Again, the jump failed.

'I don't understand this, Professor. Everything is working. It's just – not working.'

He put his hands over mine.

'I've had an idea. Let's not try to get back to St Mary's. Let's go back to Cambridge. We'll be quite safe there, so long as we don't open the door. Let's keep it simple, Max. Just throw it into reverse gear and go back to Cambridge.'

'Excellent idea, Professor.'

And it was.

It just didn't work. Once again, the jump failed.

He sat back, suddenly looking his age. I found him a blanket. He declined another cup of tea. His pulse was very erratic. I feared for him again.

'How about ...' I said, a little reluctant to expose my ignorance to such a giant intellect. 'How about, Professor ... we just switch everything off and then back on again. Always works for me when my data-table's got itself into a tangle.'

He brightened. 'Excellent idea, Max. We'll make a physicist of you yet.'

'Before you get too excited, Eddie – there's a possibility that not only will it not work but we won't be able to power up again and then we'll be even worse off than we are now.'

'No, I don't think so,' he said, confidently.

I crossed to the trip switch, looked back at him, and said, 'Ready?'

He nodded eagerly.

I tripped the switch and we were plunged into the darkest dark I've ever known. After a few seconds, the battery-operated emergency light came on over the door.

'Count to twenty-nine,' said Eddie, in the dim glow, 'then throw the switch on again.'

'Why twenty-nine?'

'My favourite number.'

So, feeling rather foolish, I counted steadily to twenty-nine, took a deep breath, and threw the switch.

A click, a rising hum, and with a couple of electronic

beeps, the console lit up again.

And nothing had changed.

We were still trapped in the middle of nowhere, with a dwindling supply of oxygen and everything was working but not working.

I returned to the console, sat down, and had a bit of a think. I was in charge of this assignment and it was balls to the wall time.

'Well, now,' I said, quietly. 'We have choices.'

'We do indeed,' he said, heavily. 'Shall we discuss them?'

'I don't know where we are, but I don't think we're going to get out of this.'

'Don't you?'

'Don't I what?'

'Know where we are.'

'Of course not. According to our instruments, we're not anywhere.'

'No,' he said, thoughtfully. 'We're not, are we? Sorry. Continue.'

'We can end this sooner or we can end this later. Your thoughts, please.'

'Well, in my case, it doesn't make much difference. I'm beginning to feel very cold and weak. I suspect I'll lose consciousness soon and I'll never wake up. It's you who has the decision to make, Max. Do you want to spin it out for hours and die, frost-covered and gasping for your last breath, or go on your own terms and in your own time?'

'I don't want to spin this out, Eddie.'

'No.'

49

'But then again, I don't want to die, either. I have a future waiting for me. I won't give up yet.'

'I'm glad to hear that. I rather had the impression you were … undecided about one or two things.'

Once again, he saw more than was comfortable. 'Now,' he said decisively. 'I'm going to have a bit of a think. Give me a poke in five minutes in case I've dropped off.'

I took the time to have a bit of a think myself. I thought about Leon Farrell. Then Troy. Then I thought about how pleased I was to have done that in the right order for once. I reviewed my life and then went back and replayed some edited highlights. There were a lot more of those than I once thought there would be.

Professor Penrose stirred. 'I have an idea. It's a very bad one.'

'They're often the best sort, Eddie. Tell me.'

'We open the door.'

What? Was he out of his mind? Had blood loss affected his brain? I stared at him. 'The benefits being …?'

'Out there is nothing. In here is something. Matter exists. Time is passing. We open the door. Something collides with nothing. That collision may – may – kick-start the jump. It's not a solution, Max. We almost certainly won't survive. All I'm offering is uncertain death rather than certain death.'

I considered.

'It'll be a hell of bang.'

'It certainly will.'

'I'd have to override the safety protocols.'

'Can you?

'I think so.'

'We'll only need a tiny, minute fraction of a second. Just enough for an infinitesimal amount of something to … escape. No more. Can your computer handle something that small?'

'No idea. Doesn't matter really, does it?'

'No, not really.'

I considered how to phrase this.

'Computer, on my mark, disengage safety protocols. Point zero zero zero one of one second later, re-instate protocols, close the door, and make the pre-set jump to St Mary's. Authorisation Maxwell, five zero alpha nine eight zero four bravo.' I crossed my fingers. 'Confirm.'

'Confirmed.'

'Well, there you are, Eddie. It says it will. Whether it can, of course … Will we survive this?'

'If it helps, Max, if it doesn't work, it will all be over very quickly.'

'Understood.'

We were silent.

'Max, I'm sorry to have got you into this.'

'Eddie, the fault is mine. I should have looked after you better.'

'If it's any consolation, I don't regret any of it. I regret very little in my life. Do you?'

I considered. 'I'd like to skip the early years, but on the whole, no.'

'That is always the sign of a life well spent.'

I fell in love with him all over again.

'We'll do it together, Eddie.'

'Very well.'

I took his hand and guided it to the controls.'

'Got it?'

'Yes.'

'I'll give the word and then …'

'It'll be very quick, Max. We'll never know anything about it.'

'Eddie, if I wasn't already spoken for …'

'Max, if I was forty years younger, it wouldn't matter if you were spoken for or not …'

'You're a bad boy, Eddie. Just my type.'

I felt, rather than heard his little chuckle.

We held hands, tightly.

'Computer – on my mark, disengage safety protocols. Mark.'

Light seared through my eyes and boiled my brain.

The blast stripped the flesh from my bones.

Heat coalesced.

We were burning …

We were falling …

We were dying …

If only I could shift this nagging feeling that something was important …

I could hear faint electronic beeping. That was good. Something was working. Obviously, the console had fired up. Everything was operating. All I needed to do was … If I could just open my eyes … Or move my hands …

I struggled. Something important.

A fuzzy voice came and went.

I strained to move something – a finger – anything. Important. The beeping increased. Another fuzzy voice said something else. The beeping faded away … for a long time …

I opened my eyes and everything was black. I slid away …

I opened my eyes and people spoke. Now they slid away …

I opened my eyes and Nurse Hunter said, 'That's better, Max. Try and stay with me this time.'

I smiled because I liked her and … something important … she slid away …

To be replaced by someone for whom sliding away was never an option.

Her voice had harmonics that could raise the dead.

'Maxwell? Stop lazing around and open your eyes. Now, please. This is Dr Foster.'

I said thickly, 'Are you really from Gloucester?' And slid away. Which probably saved my life.

Finally, I opened my eyes and took in the bed, the beeping equipment, the dim lights, and Hunter. I remembered the thing that had been so important and croaked, 'Professor Penrose?'

She bent over me. 'Safe.'

Now I could sleep.

They told me I should be grateful to be alive. I didn't feel the slightest bit grateful. Actually, I didn't feel the slightest bit anything. I was enjoying that pink fluffy cloud feeling associated with strong medication and the euphoria of not being dead. A pleasant sensation I was determined to prolong as long as I could.

Because now, of course, I knew I was in real trouble. There's nothing like taking your boss's old friend, embroiling him in a back-alley brawl, getting him stabbed, and hurling his aged bones across time and space before precipitating him across Hawking in a flaming pod, to further one's career.

Dr Bairstow was going to have a great deal to say to me.

I knew he was there. I thought about lying still and feigning death, possum-like. Perhaps I could pretend I'd lost my memory. I could definitely get away with claiming I'd lost my mind. I was warm. I was comfortable. I could lie here for ever if I had to.

No, I couldn't. Just the knowledge that he was there, waiting …

I opened my eyes.

He stood at the foot of my bed, dark against the window, his expression difficult to read. We regarded each other for quite a long time, which was unnerving. Telling myself I was too ill to get a proper bollocking, I waited.

The silence went on and on.

Finally, he shook his head and said simply, 'Words fail me,' and limped away.

I closed my eyes again.

Next up was Leon, who had to be getting pretty tired of sitting by my sickbed and listening to my bones knit. I know I was. No wonder he wanted us out of St Mary's. And after being trapped, alone, in the dark, wherever and whenever we'd been, I was inclined to agree. No need to tell him that, though.

I knew the signs. The best thing to do is let him get it off his chest.

'The jump was to Cambridge. In the middle of the Fens. It's one of the wettest cities in the country. How did you manage to set fire to your pod? We build them so that even historians can't set fire to them. For God's sake, tell me Isaac Newton is still alive. That you haven't incinerated one of the greatest scientific figures of all time? And what about Professor Penrose? He's seventy-six and you bring him back with a stab wound, second-degree burns, and concussion. You were visiting an educational establishment, for crying out loud, not the sack of Constantinople.'

'1204,' I murmured, helpfully.

'You melted your pod!'

'I'm fine, thank you.'

'We had to close Hawking for a day. Residual radiation.'

'And the professor. He's fine, too, thank you for asking. He had a great time.'

'There was a fireball!'

'And I think we may have kick-started the invention of the reflecting telescope.'

'I've no idea where to start on Number Eight. The outer casing looks like grilled cheese!'

'So, quite a successful jump, I think.'

He drew a deep breath and made a huge effort at staying calm. 'How are you?'

'I melted my pod? Cool!'

Communication – the cornerstone of St Mary's success.

I went off to see Eddie as soon as I was fit. To reassure myself. He laughed when he saw me. Both of us were as red and shiny and bright as new fire trucks.

He sat in his borrowed pyjamas, his bed strewn with papers, printouts, and God knows what, happily accepting Nurse Hunter's attentions. She winked at me as she left.

'What ho, Professor!'

'Max, my dear. How are you?'

'Up and about and absolutely fine. How about you?'

'Well, I still feel as if I had been through one of those old-fashioned mangles, but that lovely young lady tells me I'll be up in no time. Tell me, did you notice the temporal read-out?'

'No,' I said, very carefully. 'We were on fire at the time.'

'Ah well,' he said, jovially. 'As Joan of Arc probably said: "Build a girl a fire and she's warm for a few minutes. Set a girl on fire and she's warm for the rest of her life."'

I stared at him, suspiciously. 'Joan of Arc should have known better than to misquote Terry Pratchett. The great man might not like it. But are you sure you're not an historian?'

He chuckled his dirty chuckle. 'If I'd known that I would meet you ...'

'Seriously, Professor, the heat, the blast, the radiation – we should be scattered all over the universe.'

'Yes,' he said, a little regretfully, I thought. 'Just think, Max, our atoms would have been part of the most spectacular galaxies, the biggest black holes, the strangest and most beautiful worlds ...'

He sighed. 'But we're not and I have no clear idea why. Our pod protected us to some extent, of course, but I am really at a loss to account for it. I gather our arrival was spectacular.'

'The word fireball is figuring prominently in Chief Farrell's vocabulary these days.'

'Another miraculous Maxwell escape. Maybe the universe has something else in mind for you.'

I laughed. If I was being kept alive, it was only in the way they keep turkeys alive for Christmas.

'Professor, where do you think we were?'

He looked thoughtful for a moment. 'Tell me Max, what do you know about the River of Time?'

I rummaged in my head for one of Chief Farrell's faint and far-off lectures.

'Um, well, that was Einstein's definition of Time. That Time moves like a river, meandering around galaxies, speeding up or slowing down as it's caught in backwaters or eddies. That there are places where Time flows differently. As in a river.'

'Exactly. Well, one explanation is that we were trapped in some quiet backwater in the River of Time. Somewhere Time had slowed to a standstill. Stagnant water. Or, we were marooned, so to speak. Left high and dry by the River of Time. Or, still continuing the River analogy, if Time flows smoothly from one second to the next, there is the possibility we were trapped between two seconds. I don't know.'

He threw me a cheerful look. 'Or, I may have a really outrageous and impossible theory.'

'More outrageous and impossible than being trapped between two seconds?'

'Oh yes. Are you familiar with the other definition of Time?'

'Yes.' I nodded. 'Newton's Arrow of Time. Time can only move in one direction. Forwards. Never deviating from its path. Never speeding up or slowing down. Just like an arrow.'

He watched me intently as he spoke. 'Well, if I really wanted to be controversial, then I would ask you to imagine what will happen when the Arrow of Time finishes its flight. As it must. When Time no longer moves forwards. When everything stops. When everything, everywhere, is cold and dark and dead. All the stars have burned away to Nothing. The never-ending story has long since ended. Time has stopped because there is no longer anything for it to measure. There is no change from one moment to the next. Entropy has won. The universe is dead.'

I shivered. I couldn't help it.

'Is that where we were? At the end of everything? At the end of the universe? How did we get out?'

'Again, I think I know what may have happened, but not why it happened. I think opening the door allowed something to escape. A tiny, fleeting moment of time. Time was free. Time escaped. Something met Nothing. Nothing was no longer Nothing. There was a bit of a bang. And here we are.'

He twinkled at me again, waiting for me to catch up.

I said this very carefully, so he wouldn't think I was completely stupid. Or insane. 'Eddie, if there was no time and no space ... Are you saying – was that – did we witness The Big Bang?'

He laughed. 'Oh, no. No, no, no.'

I felt the most complete idiot. Good job my face was already red.

'No, no. That wasn't *our* Big Bang ...'

He looked up, suddenly serious, waiting for me to get it. Why had I never noticed how very penetrating his bright blue eyes were?

I felt the challenge, but I was ... I was afraid to put it into words.

'Professor, did we just witness the ... re-birth of

59

the universe?'

He looked over his shoulder although we were the only people in the ward, and lowered his voice.

'Well done, but not quite right, Max. I don't think we witnessed it – I think we caused it.'

I'm not often stuck for words. Sex renders me speechless sometimes, but not usually for very long.

When I could speak again, I said, 'What does Dr Bairstow say?'

'Oh, he holds you completely responsible.'

Before I could panic, however, he was flapping round under his bedclothes.

'Eddie, what are you doing?'

Now he was rummaging under his pillows. 'Where is it? Ah!'

He handed me a piece of paper. 'Do you ever read P G Wodehouse?'

I took the paper. 'Yes ...'

He nodded. 'There you are, then.'

Helen came in and looked at us both severely. We were obviously contravening some rule about patients not enjoying themselves. I got up to go. 'I'll see you later, Eddie. For dinner.'

'Looking forward to it, Max. It's a long time since I've dined with a lady in my pyjamas.'

I rocked with laughter.

'Sorry, that was badly expressed. You know what I mean. Make sure you make full use of that.'

Out in the corridor, I unfolded the paper.

I read the one word written there and grinned to myself.

Revenge is sweet!

I clattered off to see Dr Bairstow and get myself back on the active list. Rather surprisingly, he didn't try to deduct the cost of recreating the universe from my wages. Encouraged by this unexpected benevolence, I showed him Eddie's slip of paper and explained what I had in mind. He snorted but didn't actually say no, which was good enough for me.

Mrs Mack was directing operations in the kitchen.

'Max! Good to see you up and about again.'

'And so shiny!'

'Well, I wasn't going to say anything, but now you come to mention it … What can I do for you? Mint choc.-chip sundae? My killer chocolate mousse? An artery-clogging McMack burger?'

'Actually,' I said, 'I'd like to hire some butter.'

She frowned. 'I think you may still be a little confused. You don't hire butter.'

'I do. I want to be the sole owner of every inch, pound, pat, whatever, of butter in this unit. But not for ever. That's why I cunningly used the word "hire".'

'And I'm going with the cunningly used word "why?" '

I explained.

When she'd stopped laughing, I said, 'We'll split the proceeds between us. I shall donate to the animal shelter round the back of St Stephen's Street. How about you?'

She thought for a moment. 'That children's holiday organisation.'

'Excellent.'

She chuckled evilly. 'I'll go and have a word with my team and lock up the cold store.'

'And I,' I said, heading for the door, 'will call a meeting.'

I gazed down at them all. Shinily.

They gazed back. Bluely.

There are probably all sorts of jokes in there somewhere, but I wanted to move on quickly to the money-making part of the scheme.

'Good morning, everyone. Just a friendly heads-up. I've just come from Dr Bairstow who, not surprisingly, is pretty pissed off with presiding over a bunch of Smurf look-alikes and has asked me to announce the following:

'From this moment onwards, anyone remaining blue will be charged for the privilege. In other words, people, the longer you remain blue, the larger will be the fine incurred, with a corresponding decrease in your pay packets at the end of the month. That's it. Dismissed.'

No one moved. I tried hard not to gloat. Then gloated anyway.

'But Max,' said Schiller. 'We've tried.' She licked a finger and rubbed uselessly. 'It won't come off.'

I held up the professor's scrap of paper. 'Yes, it will. I have in my hand a piece of paper which should ensure peace in our time.'

They squinted.

I clarified.

'Butter.'

They blinked.

'The application of the substance known as butter will speedily dissolve and remove your unwanted blueness. I've checked with Mrs Mack and she has a more than adequate supply. Enough for all of you. However ...'

I was so enjoying this.

'However, owing to a previous transaction, ownership of this more-than-adequate supply has been transferred. From this moment on, every single scrap, scrape, and dribble of this liquid gold belongs to – me.'

I made a move to leave, apparently deaf to the gabble behind me.

Markham planted himself in front of me. 'How much?'

I did a rough calculation. There were twenty blue people in this unit.

'£50 for four ounces.'

'*What*? But that's ...'

'Daylight robbery,' I said, helpfully.

'We can get butter from the village shop, you know.'

'Be my guest. Don't forget to sign out. Oh, no, that's right. Blue people not allowed out of St Mary's. How could I have forgotten? Ah well ...'

'But ...'

'Yes, Mr Markham?'

He lowered his voice. 'Some of us ...'

'Yes?'

'It's not just hands and face.'

'Sorry, I don't understand.'

'You know. Some of us ... all over.'

'No. Still not with you. Some of us – what – all over?'

'You know ...'

'You don't mean ...?'

He nodded miserably. 'It was a dare.'

'Oh my God,' I said, delighted. 'You're going to have a hell of a rash. Hope you're not allergic to dairy.'

'You're an evil woman.'

'And shortly to be a rich, evil woman. Pay up or develop something horrible. *And* you'll still have to pay Dr Bairstow. At least I'm trying to help. How can you be so ungrateful?'

He reached for his wallet.

'I'm paying now, but one day I'll have my revenge.'

I looked at the cash. 'A hundred pounds?'

'Yeah, well, you know … Don't want to boast, but it's going to take a lot more than four ounces … Where are you going?'

'Dining with Professor Penrose. Although I may have lost my appetite.'

I was sad when Professor Penrose finally left us. We sat together for a while, waiting for his car to arrive. Once again, he was telling me how much he'd enjoyed every single moment.

'Even the really exciting bits?'

'Especially the really exciting bits. I have to say, Max, if I was at the other end of my career, I'd be taking a quick course in History for Beginners and signing up at St Mary's as fast as I could. As it is …'

I took his hand. 'I hope you have a long and happy retirement, Eddie. Filled full of incident and adventure.'

He looked around and lowered his voice. 'And you, Max. Are you looking forward to your long and happy retirement?'

'Of course,' I said with enthusiasm and conviction and he wasn't fooled for a minute. He really didn't miss anything at all. He knew more about what I was thinking than I did. Still, I suppose if you've spent your entire working life probing the secrets of the universe, then the thoughts of one small, ginger historian must be a bit of a doddle.

I smiled, uncertainly.

'Is it possible, Max, that you have some reservations?'

'No. And yes.'

'Well,' he said comfortably, 'I often find it useful, when making a difficult decision, to look at the situation in reverse.'

I raised my eyebrows.

'For instance, how would you feel if his offer was withdrawn? That the option of this scary new life was no longer available? Or, how would you feel if he made that offer to someone else? How happy would you be about that?'

'Not happy at all, Eddie.'

'Now consider this. Is it leaving St Mary's that's the problem? Or starting a new life somewhere else?'

'I ...'

I stopped, suddenly very unsure.

'It's understandable, Max. You joined St Mary's before you'd had any real experience of the world. You are in the strange position of leading a hazardous but sheltered life. Now you can look forward to a safe but unpredictable life. Who knows what each new day will bring you? Are you, for instance, likely to get halfway to Tesco and suddenly find yourself fighting monsters?'

'Not that often, I should imagine.'

'So if it's not the new, safe life that concerns you, then

is it, as I suspect, having to share that new, safe life with someone else?'

'Eddie you're far too smart for my peace of mind.'

'Well, you may as well tell me. I'm very discreet.'

'I don't know whether … whether I … I don't know if he …'

I stopped, floundering. Words had obviously taken the day off.

'You don't know what's going to happen next, is that it? You've spent all your working life knowing the Persians will attack, the Pharaoh will die, the earthquake will occur. You've had control over everything that happened in your life. But now, your life is about to happen to you.'

I nodded.

His eyes twinkled. 'Welcome to the real world, Max.'

I had to laugh.

'It is, I think, comforting to know that you are not approaching this new phase of your life with unconcern or an unrealistic assessment of the problems of living closely with someone. Somehow, though, I think the two of you will find a way. It may not be the conventional way or even the way you expect, but, having met the two of you, I have no fears.'

He paused. 'However …' he said, suddenly serious.

'Yes, Professor?'

'If it does all go horribly wrong, you must promise me one thing.'

'What's that?'

'You must promise me first refusal.'

I loved this man.

'Eddie, if it all goes horribly wrong, I promise I'll be all over you like a rash.'

He patted my hand.

'I don't think yours will ever be a conventional life, Max. And I think you will find your happiness in an unconventional way. Ah – here's Teddy.'

Teddy Bairstow?

'And my car.'

I stood. 'I'll say goodbye now, Eddie. Take care of yourself.'

He kissed my cheek and murmured, 'Don't forget – if it doesn't work, my bedroom door is always open!'

And on to Troy. Our next assignment.

This was my favourite moment – everything stretching out in front of us, gleaming with promise and excitement and we hadn't yet had a chance to screw it up.

They were all there, except for the Boss, absent on a punitive visit to Thirsk. Which would keep them both quiet for a while.

I gazed at the sea of expectant faces in front of me. The history department had seated themselves down one side of the Hall. The security and technical sections were spread across the other, with small pockets of R&D staff scattered around. Their people, wise in the ways of their leaders, had carefully arranged for Professor Rapson and Doctor Dowson to be as far away from each other as possible while still actually being in the same room.

Mrs Enderby and her team from Wardrobe were chatting excitedly to Mrs Mack and the kitchen staff nearby. The medical crew sat at the back, possibly estimating potential casualties, but more likely playing Battleships.

Everyone had scratchpads, blank data cubes, sticks, files, and even old-fashioned scribblepads laid out in front of them. We were all ready to go. I took my usual deep breath and plunged straight in.

'Good morning, everyone. Thank you for coming. As anyone who isn't actually dead must know by now, our next assignment is Troy. The purpose of this briefing is to get a broad outline of the mission, allocate responsibilities, and discuss the proposed schedule.'

Using the big screen, I brought up such maps as we had been able to find. Plus a few artists' impressions, just to give everyone an idea.

'This is our objective – the city of Troy and its surrounding areas. Situated on the coast of north-west Turkey and flanked by the two rivers Simoeis and Scamander, Troy's position on the major east/west trade routes and guarding the entrance to the Black Sea has ensured it has become the most important and richest city in this part of the world. Troy has accumulated massive wealth by collecting tributes and tolls and generally skimming everyone's profits.

'The ruling family is headed by King Priam. He has a large family, mostly sons, nineteen of whom are legitimate. His official wife is Queen Hecuba and the most notable of their offspring are Hector, Paris, Deiphobos, Helenus, and Kassandra. Hector is Priam's heir, favourite son and hero of Troy. His wife is Andromache and their infant son is known as Astyanax, Lord of the City. So that's Team Troy.

'Shortly to be ranged against them – Agamemnon, high king of Mycenae, leader of the Greeks. His brother is Menelaus, king of Sparta and husband of the supposed cause of all the trouble, Helen. Then there's a whole host of followers to be identified – that cunning bugger

Odysseus, Big and Little Ajax, the tedious Nestor – and Achilles, of course. Forget the tall, blond hero – he's a cross-dressing psychopath. Achilles is the first warrior to wage total war. Not the traditional, familiar, ritualistic fighting of the time, but all-out-slaughter-everything-in-sight-in-a-berserker-rage war. Not that anyone ever complains – either because they're happy to be on the winning side, or because they're too dead.

'I shall refer to the attacking force as Greeks, even though this is long before Greece actually existed as such. Homer gives them many names – you'll find them referred to as Hellenes (nothing to do with Helen) or Achaeans or Argives. The Trojan forces also consist of Thracians, Phrygians, Lydians, Carians, Lycians, and many more. For simplicity, we will be calling them Greeks and Trojans.

'Any questions so far?'

Nope.

'Right. This is the last great Bronze Age struggle. A struggle between east and west. But, whatever the cause – and we'll be identifying that – Troy will fall. And we'll be there to see it.

'There will be two parts to the assignment. The first part is pre-war. The city of Troy existed for a good long time before the war and for a good long time afterwards. So the first visit is the control visit. We will familiarise ourselves with the city – getting to know it well will enable us to evaluate the impact of the war. That done, we return ten years later, to witness the end of the Trojan War.

'The Pathfinders will establish the dates. Dr Peterson

will oversee this part of the mission. We'll be looking at the period between 1250 and 1180 BC. All co-ordinates will be worked out by the IT section and laid in by Chief Farrell. Once we have the dates sorted, we'll make a quick pre-visit to select locations for the pods. That team will consist of me, Chief Farrell, and Major Guthrie. We may be there overnight while we suss things out, but it's unlikely.

'There will be two sites, designated, with startling originality, A and B. Site A is to be inside or as near to the upper citadel as is deemed practical and Site B will be in the lower town. Miss Van Owen will supervise Site A and Miss Schiller will supervise Site B.

'The Rule of Threes, people. Three pods on each site containing three people who will each spend three weeks on site before returning for one week's R & R. There will be no more than nine people on any one site, of whom at least three will be security.

'Pods Four, Six, and Seven will be located at Site A and Three, Five, and Eight at Site B. One and Two will operate as shuttles, ferrying people and supplies under cover of darkness. Our transport pod, TB2, will not be used on this assignment.

'Our second visit will enable us to record the end of the war and assess the impact on the city.'

I paused. Everyone stopped writing or typing and looked at me.

I grinned. 'Yes, and to see the Trojan Horse, of course.'

They heaved a sigh of relief and we continued.

'On to individual responsibilities – I've tried to

accommodate people's preferences and specialities as much as possible, but, as usual, there's a lot to do and not many to do it.

'Major Guthrie. You and your team will be responsible for mapping and surveying the city. I want a detailed street-plan. The lower town has been lost over time and the upper town had its top sliced off later to accommodate the new Temple of Athena, so this will be important. Please can you try to get most of it done on the first visit. It's probably not a good idea to be seen surveying a city while there's a war on.'

He rolled his eyes. 'This is all in addition to preventing historians from damaging themselves, each other, and/or the timeline?'

'Of course. Are you anticipating any difficulties?'

'Surveying the city – no. Preventing damage to our current crop of historians – yes.'

'You'll cope,' I said, heartlessly. 'You always do.'

He sighed. 'I can feel the traditional pre-assignment depression settling around me.'

'Look on the bright side, Ian,' said Leon. 'If they do manage to kill each other off then we can all come home early.'

He brightened. 'True.'

I swept scathingly on.

'Mr Clerk, I'd like you to be responsible for the study of religion and ritual. This should include the pantheon of gods, and rituals pertaining to births, death, and marriage. All the usual stuff. Select your own team. You'll be based at Site A. Any questions?'

He shook his head, still scribbling away.

'Culture – Miss Prentiss. I'd like you to take this on board, please. Language and writing, if any, legends, stories, the usual. Please include entertainment – public and private. Art, pottery, ceramics, statues. You know the sort of thing. You'll be at Site A with Mr Clerk. I imagine there will be some overlap. Any questions?'

'How many can I draft into my team?'

'Not more than three. All team leaders – be aware you can mix and match. Borrow each other's people by all means, but don't forget to give them back. There aren't enough of us to work on all these projects simultaneously, so work out a schedule. No one team has priority and the work does not have to be completed in any particular order. We can have up to nine months on site, which should be more than enough. Understood?'

You have to tell historians these things; otherwise there would be more conflict inside the walls of Troy than outside.

'OK, the next one's the biggie. Dr Peterson and Doctor Black, who has returned from Thirsk to be with us on this assignment, will head this one. Social Structure. Tim, I want medicine and health, including diet. Daily life, family structure, housing, clothing, all that sort of thing. Please also look at ethnicity and gender roles.

'Kal, I'd like you to take on actual society structure – kings, priests, soldiers, tradesmen, slaves, and everything in between. And, most importantly, the structure of the royal family. We'll need you to identify as many of the main players as possible. We may even get to see Helen herself.'

I doubted it. While I had no doubt the war itself was

74

real, along with Achilles, Menelaus, Hector, and all the others, I had strong doubts about whether Helen ever went to Troy. Anyone who's read Herodotus is familiar with the casual attitude towards the abduction of royal women. You snatched Princess A, made off with her, and a few months later you lost Queen B – kidnapped in retaliation. It was almost a ritual.

According to the world's first historian, it was inconceivable that Priam would risk his city and the lives of his people for a woman whom Paris had stolen from his host. A breach of the rules of hospitality that should have resulted in both of them being returned to Menelaus with Priam's compliments, apologies, and an invitation to dispose of them as he pleased.

No, I was convinced the Trojan War was about money and power, not a queen, no matter how beautiful she might have been. Troy was the most important city in that part of the world, strategically placed to control the maritime trade routes of the time. Mycenae coveted that role. Hence Agamemnon's move against them and the massive following he was able to muster. It was a power struggle. We would see this again with Rome and Carthage.

I continued.

'Doctor Black will be at Site A and Doctor Peterson at Site B.

'Mr Roberts, you'll be at Site A. I'd like you to study commerce; trade, shipping, and the harbour – if there is one. Look at the shops, markets, warehouses, and associated trades. Please pay particular attention to coins – if they have any, together with the barter system and how it's managed.'

He was overjoyed and terrified all at the same time. He was the most recently qualified of all my historians and, as I had been at the time, both desperate for some responsibility and scared of messing it up. I glanced at Van Owen who nodded slightly. She'd keep an eye on him.

'Major, I'm back to you again. I'd like you to liaise with Miss Morgan to report back on military politics. The army, the navy – they must have one, for heaven's sake.' Why weren't they deployed when the black ships turned up? The structure of the government, city defences – you know the sort of thing. Walls, watchtowers, gates, water supplies. Please pay particular attention as to whether the siege was complete or whether they used the eastern routes to supply the city. How did they withstand a ten-year siege? You'll both be at Site B.'

I paused for a glug of water.

'Right, team leaders, start organising your people. I want them to become specialists in at least one area but remain flexible enough to cross groups if needed.

'All personnel are to undergo medicals. See Dr Foster and get your appointments sorted out. Everyone is to update their Field Medic training.

'Report to Mrs Enderby and get yourselves kitted out. Everyone wears tunics – chitons – linen in summer and wool in winter. Ladies' are full length; men's finish around the knees so now is the time to tone those calf muscles, gentlemen, and deal with the vexing question of unwanted hair. And while I think about it, wear everything in before we jump. I don't want to see a bunch of people running around in shiny new tunics and sandals.

'The shift pattern is three weeks on and one week off. Miss Lee, please organise the shift rota, liaise with Mrs Mack over food supplies, and with Chief Farrell over the shuttle rota.

'Dr Dowson will provide the background info. See him with your lists of material to upload.'

I paused for another glug.

'Please be aware that in one instance at least, we have been misled. In the *Iliad*, the Trojans speak Homeric Greek. In reality, they spoke Luwian, which is similar to Lycian and closely related to Hittite. Dr Dowson will be issuing everyone with a list of basic words and phrases. Learn as much as you can, but remember that while the Greeks have a more or less common language, sometimes the Trojan allies have difficulty understanding each other. So don't panic if you can't make yourself understood.

'Dr Peterson, as head of the Pathfinders, please liaise with Dr Dowson about establishing the dates. He and Miss Lee will set up the usual rota.'

When you have people coming and going, trying to narrow down a set of co-ordinates for a specific time and place, you need to monitor things very carefully indeed. Therefore, we set up a data-stack, to be maintained by someone who inspires terror in the ranks. In other words, Rosie Lee, my assistant, with whom no one ever argues. Ever. To keep it simple – we're historians after all – there's just one rule. No jumping about all over the place. Everyone moves in one direction. Forwards. They'd start in 1250 BC and slowly move forward until they established the dates for the Trojan War. Mr Markham was accepting bets. My guess was 1184 BC as stated by Eratosthenes – a bloke who really knew what he was talking about. I had quite a lot of money riding on it.

'Chief Farrell, all pods to be serviced and ready to go. We're using all of them except TB2 – too big. We don't want to attract attention.

Ian Guthrie snorted. 'A bunch of historians all together in a war zone? We'll not only attract attention, we'll be lucky to last a week.'

'Less than that if the security section operates to its usual deplorable standards,' said Kalinda.

I cleared my throat.

'It's going to be a huge amount of work. We're going to need to go like the clappers to get it all done. But one thing – and this applies to everyone, so pass it along. This is a once in a lifetime event. No one has ever had this opportunity before and maybe never will again. Work hard, but don't forget – lift your head occasionally and look around you. Remember where you are. And enjoy it.'

And so it began. I'd done this before and I knew from experience that the lead-in to an assignment was often more strenuous than the mission itself.

I spent hours in the Library, building data-stacks and assembling info packs with Dr Dowson.

I ran a series of lectures on Troy and all matters Trojan, tailored to the special needs of the technical and security sections.

I spent a lot of time arbitrating between Dr Dowson, our librarian, and Professor Rapson, head of R & D, as they fluctuated between their normal states of armed neutrality, frigid formality, and bull-headed hostility.

I spent even more time avoiding Major Guthrie, who wanted to talk to me about latrines, which was a subject I found considerably less fascinating than he did. He pointed out most people had a colon that worked more than twice a year.

I commiserated.

Everywhere I went, glassy-eyed people with earpieces wandered around muttering, 'Kuis – who. Kuwari – where. Kuwati – when.' Only to bump into a group of people wandering back the other way, intoning, 'Isarwilis – right. Ipalis – left.'

As I expected, I spent a considerable amount of time adjudicating between team leaders as they selected their teams. Phrases like, 'I'll swap you half of Miss Yilmaz if you let me have the use of Spencer and Travis every second day,' were common. Whole peace initiatives were worked out more easily than this. I stayed well out of it, intervening only when things looked like getting bloody. We had eleven historians, for heaven's sake. Back in the day, it had been just Kal, Tim, Sussman, and me and we managed.

They got themselves sorted out eventually, but it was hard work and I was anxious we didn't wear ourselves before we even started. I remembered the three months lead-in to our jump to the Cretaceous Period. This was very similar with the same enormous amount of information to assimilate. And even if I didn't have to compile my own *Dinosaurs for Dummies* guide this time, there was still another language to learn, customs and traditions to remember to observe, fractious historians to soothe, and the latrine-fixated Ian Guthrie to avoid.

I'm not paid anything like enough.

I ran lectures for everyone, liaised with Leon over the shuttle schedule, discussed our wardrobe with Mrs Enderby, listened while Mrs Mack talked at me about supplies, and tried to remember to meet Leon for lunch. Not always successfully.

But we inched our way forwards. Teams were selected and agreed upon. I laid down the historian rules and regs. Leon did the same for the pods and Major Guthrie left no one in any doubt over what would happen if anyone even thought about not complying with his security protocols. Helen terrified us all with a series of illustrated medical lectures that put even St Mary's off its collective lunch.

One day, however, I woke up and every box had been ticked. Every eventuality prepared for.

We were ready.

I stood outside Number Three, running through things in my mind. Even though this was only the pre-visit – a quick in and out to decide on our two sites – the excitement was still there.

I was going to Troy. *The* Troy. The Troy of legend. The Troy of Priam and Hector and Andromache and all the rest of those never-dying characters whose deeds and voices still reverberate down the ages.

I was going to see the legendary city of Troy.

Whether the Trojan War did or did not happen – or Achilles – or Odysseus – or the Trojan Horse – no one can deny the impact the legend has had on western civilisation. And now ... no matter how many times I did this, I never, ever lost the excitement. The anticipation. The eagerness to see ... to be there ...

And then I remembered that this was the beginning of my last mission. That I wouldn't be doing this for much longer. I felt a little twist inside. But I wasn't finished yet. The end of this mission was still a long way off.

Hawking was packed. All of St Mary's hung over the gantry or waited behind the line. The Boss wished us luck. We stepped inside.

The coordinates were all laid in. I took the left-hand

seat. Leon seated himself alongside. Guthrie checked his weapons and waited. Leon ran his eyes over the console and nodded.

This was it.

I said, 'Computer, initiate jump.'

And the world went white.

We were set to land about a mile from the city. And we did. Not in a swamp. Or at the bottom of the river. Or two miles out to sea. We were exactly where the Pathfinders had intended us to be. Excellent work.

Leon shut things down while Guthrie checked the screen. I preferred to get my first view from outside. I swung a faded woollen cloak around my shoulders, shouldered a wicker basket, and waited by the door. Farrell and Guthrie both carried stout sticks and, in Guthrie's case, any amount of hidden weaponry.

'All set?'

They nodded.

'Door.'

They let me go first, which was wise of them. They must have guessed I'd have trampled both of them into the dirt in my haste to get outside and *see* ...

We'd landed near a small copse, on the western bank of the Scamander. I turned slowly, keeping Troy for last. To the west, the Aegean glinted, bright in the sunshine, and a forest of masts dipped and swayed with the breaking waves. The harbour was on the western coast with direct access to the sea. Turning back to the north, I could see that the sheltered bay, which must have seemed such a benefit to the city many years ago, was badly silted. Small boats weaved their way up and down the narrow channels, but nothing big could ever get that far inland now.

Well-defined cart tracks led from the cluster of haphazard buildings around the harbour, across the dust plain to the ford. We could cross there too and then it was just a hop, skip, and a jump to the city.

To Troy.

I took a deep breath and lifted my eyes.

Troy stood about a mile away, although the heat haze made it difficult to judge distances accurately. Rising from the flat plain around it, the city dominated the entire area – the Troad, the Aegean, and access to the Black Sea. Standing foursquare on the plain, it made the statement. *Fear me, for I am Troy. I am mighty and powerful, and you are as dirt beneath my feet*. Just as it had been designed to do.

And it was so much bigger than I expected. The extent of the lower city was far greater than modern-day archaeology had suggested. Estimates had put the population between five and ten thousand. I put it at ten thousand and possibly more. And although I could see defensive ditches and fences, the lines of the city had blurred to some extent. Small clusters of buildings dotted the plain. Patches of cultivated land nestled between olive groves and small areas of woodland. I saw fields and livestock, especially horses.

From where we were standing I could see streams of people moving along the tracks, dragging carts or driving livestock. Traffic moved both ways, in and out. This was good news. We could join this stream of humanity and not be noticed.

We'd stood long enough. Guthrie went first, with Leon. I followed along behind with the basket. In my experience, the only time women get to go first is when walking through a minefield.

Heads down, we joined the trail of people streaming towards the South Gate. In front of us an elderly woman and a young boy drove three goats who had their own ideas about forward progress. We sidestepped them and tucked ourselves in behind a family group, purpose unknown.

This was the Bronze Age. There would be no papers for us to show. I ran through my carefully prepared Luwian words and phrases. Not that I would be called upon to speak, but, in an emergency, I could stand behind Guthrie and mutter the words he needed. It might not matter. Language in those days was a very local affair and it was perfectly possible that someone living as little as ten miles up the road would speak a very different dialect. Possibly a completely different language altogether. If all our attempts at communication failed, we would revert to Plan B – looking stupid. For some reason, that never fails for St Mary's.

We approached the South Gate – the city's first line of defence from the south. If archaeologists had guessed right over the years, there should be a primary ditch and wall with one gate. Enter through that and we would find ourselves in an area dominated by warehouses and storage for goods on their way to and from the harbour. Passing through this we would have a choice of two gates cut into the outer walls and from there into the lower part of the city itself.

Here goes.

I could see Ian had a firm grip on his staff, the other casually resting on his belt from where he could get to his stun gun. This part of the mission was under his control and his instructions were clear. 'In the event of trouble, I'll cover your escape. You and Farrell get away and meet me later at the pod. Understood?'

I did understand but we all knew the possibility of us leaving him to cover our escape, alone against ten thousand Trojans, was never going to happen. I sent a quick request to the god of historians that we wouldn't ever have to put it to the test. Apparently that notoriously bubble-headed deity was on the job today, because none of the guards even looked at us. Nor in my basket. In fact, they couldn't even be bothered to emerge from the vine-covered shelter, in which they were lounging, into the hot sunshine to check people over. Finally, we stepped through the second gate, the people ahead of us melted away and we were inside Troy.

We were inside Troy!

As per standard operating procedure, we drew aside, standing in a doorway, while the foot traffic flowed past us and we could get our bearings.

It wasn't my first experience of Mediterranean life lived outdoors and I know I'd put the population at about ten thousand, but for one moment I really got the impression that all ten thousand of them were here in this street with us.

Everything happened outside. Narrow streets were made even more so by old women squatting on their heels, holding up goods for sale. Vegetables, clumps of greenery, squawking chickens tied by their feet; they shouted the virtues of their wares at the tops of ancient, cracking voices. Everyone seemed to have something to sell. Small children raced through the crowds, shouting and laughing. Inevitably, one of them tripped over the uneven paving and went sprawling. A man bent and set him on his feet again, not even pausing in his conversation with someone standing out of sight in a doorway.

People shoved and shouted. Livestock bleated, neighed, or clucked. A cat slunk past with something twitching in its mouth. Somewhere high up behind an open window, a woman scolded and a child cried.

A group of soldiers shouldered their way through the crowd. They all wore swords, their light, ceremonial armour was burnished to a high shine and the cream-coloured horsehair crests on their helmets nodded and swung as they moved. Abruptly, they turned off through a curtained doorway. A man shouted for service and a group of women laughed and shrieked. Ah, that sort of service!

The houses were built of mud-brick and whitewashed to dazzling brightness. Such windows as they had were small and set high up, probably to deter thieves. Clay tiles covered flat roofs. I was pleased. The pods would fit right in here. All we had to do was locate appropriate sites.

We set off.

It was hot. The sparkling sunshine and cool breezes of the plain hadn't made it as far as the city, and the narrow streets were stuffy and airless. The smells of dust, animal manure, cooking, people, and wood smoke were overwhelming and it was with relief that we got to the end of the little street and found ourselves in an open space.

We were to discover that the lower city was by no means as densely packed as the upper citadel. Sometimes quite large areas of land separated small clusters of houses and workshops. These semi-rural environments contained olive and fruit trees, cultivated land, pasture, cattle-yards, stables, and smithies.

'Let's try down here,' said Guthrie and we followed a well-rutted path past three or four squat houses, a shop with a lean-to and what looked like a tiny tavern. The path led through a small olive grove and out the other side. A half-demolished wall stood to our right. I suspected it had fallen down of its own accord and then been plundered for building materials. However, judging by the tangle of undergrowth, no one had bothered for a while.

Pausing, I looked back. I could just make out the backs of the buildings through the trees.

Close, but not too close.

I turned to Leon. 'What do you think?'

He paced out the area. Guthrie began investigating behind the wall. I sat on a rock and looked around.

Not bad. A little close to the southern gate and a little close to existing inhabitants, but it was flat, mostly rock-free, not swampy, and, in this crowded city, comparatively quiet. There were no signs of winter floods – this whole area is prone to flash floods even in modern times. Best of all, we could orient the pods north which would help to keep them cool in the harsh summer heat.

Guthrie reappeared. Now he was pacing away as well.

The two conferred then joined me on my rock.

'Max? What do you think?'

'Very promising. Quiet and secluded. Firm underfoot. No one close by. Good orientation. And most importantly, it looks deserted. These olives haven't been pruned for a few years. And if it does belong to someone – well, we'll think of something. Bribery is usually good. Chief?'

'Agreed. We can get three pods in here quite easily. The usual configuration – a three sided square. We'll throw up awnings of some kind that will give us shade and cover. And there's room for the shuttle pod around the back, too. So long as it comes and goes under cover of darkness, we should be fine. I like it.'

'I like it too,' said Guthrie. 'Flat land all around. We can see everyone coming. But still private. We can dig the latrines over there. One man on the roof as lookout. I don't think we'll do better.'

'Me neither. Just give me a minute.' He pulled out his scratchpad, cast a swift glance around, and began to type. Guthrie walked off again and I pulled out a recorder and began a slow three-sixty degree sweep. That done, I swept back the other way.

The whole thing took about twenty minutes and in all that time, we saw no one, which was encouraging.

Stowing away the electronics, we prepared to depart. We did a quick FOD plod (Foreign Object Drop. Leaving anything behind is punishable by death, to be painfully inflicted by me), followed by a quick check that we hadn't inadvertently picked something up, known as the POD plod. Satisfied we were clean, we retraced our steps. Our little cluster of buildings still looked deserted. Maybe they were all at the market.

We were definitely in a working-class area. I could hear the sounds of hammers on metal. Horses neighed in the distance. Troy was famous for its horses. Hence the Wooden Horse of Troy. We saw leather workshops. And carpenters. I inhaled a sudden smell of fresh wood as we walked past an open doorway.

Everyone seemed to keep livestock; either tethered or restrained behind piles of old brushwood to make a temporary pen in the corner of a yard. Small greasy sheep hobbled around on skinny legs. They had to be raising them for wool because I've seen more meat on a chip. Evil-eyed goats balanced precariously on top of low walls and glared. One of them reminded me of Rosie Lee.

As we moved away from the South Gate, the buildings grew larger and less commercial. Streets were wider and most were paved. Houses were more tightly packed together, but there were signs of organisation and planning. Things weren't anything near as higgledy-piggledy as the more southern end.

The streets were jam-packed with people, with no signs of traffic management anywhere. Everyone from high officials to mangy dogs claimed right of way. Those who made the most noise seemed to take priority.

Again, we paused to take a look up.

Making an unmistakeable statement, the citadel walls towered over everything. They were quite unlike anything I'd ever seen before with large blocks of limestone at the bottom, smaller as the walls increased in height and finished with the ubiquitous mud bricks at the top. They sloped inwards and appeared to have been built in irregular sections with vertical insets. For decoration, maybe, or to accommodate irregular contours.

I knew there would be two main gates. The Dardanian, more or less in the centre and the infamous Scaean Gate; the one the Trojans would dismantle to admit the Wooden Horse. I was speculating on the likelihood of that ever having happened when Guthrie nudged me back to the present and we moved on.

There was plenty more to see. The colossal north-east bastion dominated the citadel, serving the dual purpose of protecting the water cistern and acting as lookout tower, with uninterrupted views over the town and all the surrounding area.

We strolled casually towards the Dardanian Gate. And that's when we realised how easy we'd had it so far, because they wouldn't let us in. Not that we tried. It would have been a complete waste of time. Smartly dressed guards in full armour were turning nearly everyone away. Would you believe it? Bronze Age Troy: the first gated community.

We did what we could, strolling unobtrusively past the gate a couple of times, including a period of about ten minutes when Leon pretended to fiddle with the shoulder straps on my basket, which now contained my cloak. Because it was hot. It was bloody hot. Trapped heat was reflected from stones and bricks. You could have cooked eggs on the road. Guthrie sighed in pretended exasperation, leaned against a wall in the shade, picked his teeth, and watched the gate through half-closed eyes.

I took the opportunity to have a good stare as well.

The structures through the wide gate were large and

porticoed. Unlike the lower city, where most buildings were added on as required by the family unit, these were freestanding. Many had second floors, supported by pillars. And, tantalisingly obscured, I could just make out a complex of some kind. It was easily the biggest structure there – the palace perhaps – and maybe combined with a temple and treasury as well. Something else to check out.

Finally, Guthrie heaved himself upright and we wandered away, keeping the walls to our left.

I thought at first we'd have no luck at all in finding a site. Conditions here were very crowded. Obviously, being near the water supply, the area between the Dardanian Gate on the inner wall and the Eastern Gate on the outer wall was a very desirable place to live. There were probably good schools and plenty of parking for those off-road vehicles, too.

We turned and trudged back the way we'd come, keeping the walls to our right. This time we had more luck. In the north-west shadow of the walls, we found a tiny patch of land. Nowhere big enough for the three-sided square layout, but we could do three pods in a row. They could face the walls, too, making them easy to defend and north facing. The downside was that not only was it far too busy to risk a shuttle pod even at night, there wasn't the room, anyway. Site A would have to lug everything up from Site B. Well, it wouldn't do them any harm and there's a price to be paid for living in desirable residential areas. Maybe we could find them a donkey.

Leon and Guthrie went through the pacing and

muttering routine again and I stood, casually rotating (and that's not nearly as easy as it sounds) getting the details filmed for study back at St Mary's.

Guthrie called a halt at last. 'The shadows are getting long. We've been here hours. Time to go. They probably close the gate at sunset and we don't want to be stuck here.'

We set off. I heaved my basket into a more comfortable position and followed my menfolk back through the town at a respectful distance.

I could hear them laughing.

We landed at night. In stages. First, just one pod. When there was no reaction, the second one arrived a day later. Quietly, under cover of darkness. Again, no angry mob descended upon us. We crossed our fingers when the third one arrived but there were no problems at all. Site B was established.

We followed the same procedure for Site A. Van Owen reported a certain amount of curiosity from children, dogs, and old women, but no hostility of any kind. People came and went all the time.

I ticked off the personnel.

Site A consisted of Van Owen, Kalinda, and Prentiss in Number Four; Roberts, Dieter, and Clerk in Number Six; with Randall, Weller, and Brooks in Number Seven providing the security.

Site B consisted of Schiller, Morgan, and me in Number Eight; Farrell, Guthrie, and Peterson in Number Three; with Markham, Ritter, and Evans operating out of Number Five. A good mix of historians and security staff, with a techie on each site should we manage to break anything.

We gave everyone a few days to become acclimatised, although everyone had mission experience. We set up the camp. Major Guthrie indicated the site for the latrine, although his enthusiasm didn't lead to him actually doing any of the digging.

At Site B, the pods formed the traditional three-sided square, with rickety and patched canvas awnings stretched over the central area to give us some shade and privacy, and to make us look more temporary and even scruffier than we actually were. We appointed fire-monitors, wood-choppers, water-getters, cooks, and unskilled labour. Actually, the unskilled labour was me. I'd once nearly amputated my own feet with an axe and no one in their right minds would eat anything I cooked.

Life is lived outside in this part of the world, so we laid down coarse mats, lugged the non-tech stuff out of the pods, and scattered it casually around. Two days later, under a thin film of gritty dust, it looked as if we'd been there for years.

Of course, just about the first thing that happened was that Markham and Roberts were nearly arrested for chicken stealing, temple desecration, and, if I'd had my way, just being Markham and Roberts. I've often suspected that Markham's ambition is to have an arrest record in every century but I was somewhat surprised that Mr Roberts, unusually quiet in an unusually noisy organisation, was included in this particular felony.

Major Guthrie and I were out, ostensibly for a pleasant evening stroll, but in reality to suss out the areas to be surveyed over the next few days. The sun was sinking behind us as we picked our way around the maze of streets in the lower city. Most people cooked outside and tantalising smells wafted past us. I sighed. Whatever we were having was unlikely to be anything like as good.

We heard it before we saw it.

The unmistakeable hubbub of outraged citizenry. Up and down the ages, whether they're complaining about the Huns, the poll-tax, the weather, the king's latest mistress, the bad harvest, the difficulty of getting good pre-school care under Herod the Great, the French, the price of petrol, the losing chariot team, the noise is always the same. Some poor sod would be getting it, somewhere …

Discretion being the better part of valour, we instinctively wheeled into a deserted side street, well away from whatever was happening around the corner. Unfortunately, the uproar followed us.

Guthrie drew me into a convenient doorway and we prepared to wait out whatever it was.

Whatever it was turned out to be Markham and Roberts, trotting down the street (never run – it draws attention) and casting anxious glances over their shoulders. (You should never look back, either, just concentrate on running away.) The sounds of enraged citizenry were faint, but still pursuing.

Guthrie cursed horribly, stepped out of the doorway, seized them both, and before they knew what was happening, yanked them both into our sheltering doorway.

Both of them looked hot, dusty, and worried. Markham appeared – lumpier – than usual.

Guthrie opened his mouth, but was forestalled by a small phalanx of temple guards trotting past, heads swinging right and left, hands suggestively on their sword hilts. They drew level and then passed on before any of us had time to move.

We gave them a few minutes, and then as the sounds of uproar moved away, emerged back into the street.

'You,' I said menacingly to Mr Roberts, 'belong to me. And I can do with you as I please.' I turned to Guthrie. 'Shoot him.'

'What?' said Roberts, shocked. He hadn't worked for me for very long.

'I'm a woman on the edge. We've been here nearly a month. There's no chocolate left and I'm down to one cup

96

of tea a day. How far do you want to push me?'

Markham, experienced in this sort of situation, plucked at his sleeve, shook his head, and made *shut up, shut up,* gestures.

I continued. 'But for the purposes of this exercise, I am abandoning you to Major Guthrie. You ...' turning back to Mr Markham, 'already belong to him body and soul, so I shall leave you both to his tender mercies.'

Markham shifted his feet. 'Can I transfer to the history department?'

Guthrie stared coldly. 'Even the history department is never going to be that desperate. What's under your tunic?'

With some difficulty, he hauled out a chicken. Who but Markham would have a dead chicken down his tunic? A fine specimen, too. Snowy-white feathers and, in this age of skinny, muscular, long-legged, aggressive chickens – nicely plump.

'You stole a chicken?'

They said indignantly that they had found it.

'So you came upon a lone chicken and it died, right in front of you, and you picked it up to give it a proper burial?'

'Nearly right, sir. It was dead when we found it.'

A nasty feeling enveloped me. You didn't just find dead chickens lying around. Particularly not chickens of this quality.

'Where did you find it?'

'Outside that big white building in the square where the leather worker on the corner sells those things with the ...'

'It's a temple offering, you pillocks! Someone left it as an offering to the gods. Which you have stolen. Even if Apollo isn't nocking an arrow even as we speak, there's any number of hungry temple officials wondering where their supper's gone. Those guards were looking for the offering. And you. And probably not in that order.'

They looked, if possible, even more dejected than the chicken.

'Shall we put it back?'

'You will not, under any circumstances, venture near that temple – any temple at all – clutching a dead chicken.'

Especially one that had been dangling down the front of Mr Markham's tunic. The phrase 'The last dead chicken in the shop' refused to budge from my mind.

Major Guthrie was made of sterner stuff.

'Your irresponsible behaviour has endangered this mission and everyone here. If either of you could be spared, you would now be on your way back to St Mary's for Dr Bairstow to deal with.'

They quailed. Roberts, on his first major assignment, looked terrified.

'Sorry, sir. We didn't realise. We thought it was just a dead chicken.'

'We did it for the team,' added Markham, a past master at averting personal retribution and attempting to stuff the chicken back whence it came.

I averted my eyes. Some sights are not meant to be seen.

'Latrine duties,' said Guthrie, a past master at dealing with Mr Markham and unmoved by this personal appeal.

Latrine duties involved emptying the toilets daily, conveying the contents to the latrine pit, carrying out a close inspection in case anyone had dropped anything anachronistic down there (you'd be surprised), and then covering the day's offerings with a layer of dirt to keep the smell down.

'For a month,' I added, getting into the spirit of the thing.

They sagged.

Something unmentionable dipped briefly below Markham's hem and he hastily hauled things back into place.

I stared intently at a wall and counted the bricks.

With a restraint I could only admire, Guthrie commanded them to leave his sight with all speed.

'And if either of you are caught, Dr Maxwell and I will disavow any knowledge of your actions.'

They fled. Something I could only hope was the chicken made another unscheduled appearance, swinging briefly between Markham's legs and then, thank God, they turned a corner and we were finally able to let go.

I dried my eyes on my sleeve and we pulled ourselves together.

'Did you see their faces?' said Guthrie with satisfaction. It wasn't often he got the better of Mr Markham.

'You have an unsuspected streak of cruelty, Ian.'

'Yes,' he said complacently. 'Yes, I do.'

'And,' I said, happily, 'chicken tonight.'

He stopped dead.

'Do you think he was wearing shorts under that tunic?'

'Yes. Almost certainly. Probably. Maybe. No.'

'So, just bread and cheese, then?'

'Oh God, yes.'

We worked our socks off. I'd once spent three months in the Cretaceous Period and, up until now, that had been my longest assignment. We were six months down and slightly ahead of schedule. I estimated another six weeks or so. Six more weeks of solid, unspectacular observation and then, when that was completed, it would be back to St Mary's for a month to consolidate our data. After that, we'd be back again for the really Big Job. The end of the Trojan War. I experienced a shiver of excitement every time I thought about it. Which was often.

The assignment was going well. Living here was no hardship. Life was good. The gods smiled on Troy and its people.

The inhabitants were prosperous and hard-working. Wealth poured into the city, resulting in fine public buildings and temples, a reliable water supply, clean (ish) streets and always, towering above everything, keeping us all safe, the walls of Troy.

These intimidating walls encircled the city. Walls so tall, so formidable that, even after a ten-year war, the greatest soldiers of the age would be unable to breach them. Walls behind which the Trojans were safe as houses. And yet, for some reason, they would tear them down and let in their enemies. Why would they do that? We would find out.

We lived quietly and happily. We established our daily routine. Up with the sun, breakfast on the remains of yesterday's bread dipped in oil to make it soft and one – just one – precious mug of tea.

After that, there was housekeeping – and that took time. Wood gathering, going to the markets for what we could scrounge or exchange, shaking out the mats, and sweeping the pods clear of the all-pervasive gritty dust, and fetching water – lots of it. We got through gallons of the stuff, washing clothes and keeping the pods and ourselves clean.

We couldn't leave the pods open because Trojan livestock appeared to be fearless and frequently wandered in and made itself comfortable. Shifting them could be perilous and in a battle of wills with a small flock of geese Markham had come off considerably worse. Small but determined, he'd rattled in again, eventually driving them from the pod, emerging not only triumphant but badly bitten and covered in goose shit as well.

After an early lunch, usually of bread and the local wet, salty cheese, we scattered to our real jobs. Having no set function, I seconded myself wherever needed, or went up through the busy streets to Site A for a bit of a catch-up.

The rule was that everyone was back by sundown, when we would prepare our evening meal. Meat or fish if we had it, and usually we hadn't, bread, cheese, eggs (which seemed to be some kind of currency in Troy) a vegetable broth, and some fruit. Sadly, Markham had invented some kind of dreadful grey stodge, which he merrily doled out and people *ate* it. I can't cook and therefore I can (and frequently do) eat pretty well anything put in front of me. But not Markham's porridge.

In vain did he protest its authenticity. Other people ate it – and lived. I made polite excuses.

We cooked and ate outside, sitting on our coarse mats, and afterwards we would report on our day's findings for an hour or so and then I would make them stop. Historians can go all night if they have to – and that refers to discussing their findings, as well.

We would sit around the crackling fire, under the stars, chatting and laughing. Sometimes, Roberts would produce his guitar. Everyone had been allowed one personal item: a book, musical instrument, whatever. We would have a bit of a singsong; just like every other Trojan household across the city. It was certainly easy to become assimilated on this assignment. We had no troubles with the locals in any way. Except for being ripped off and robbed blind by the tiny, terrifying, elderly Trojan women in the markets, of course.

I looked up from the fire one night to see two small, curious faces peering through the trees. I'd seen them before. It was the little girl from the tavern and her brother. I'd often seen their father, serving customers outside under the trees. Sometimes he would wave. These were his children. Seeing me stare, Leon twisted around and, after a moment, held out his hand.

Guthrie, who had stiffened, relaxed, and Markham withdrew his hand from under his cloak.

The two children came forward and stood hesitantly, just outside the firelight. The little girl regarded us steadily and without fear. The little boy scraped the inside of his nostril with a grubby finger and held out the result for inspection.

Leon said nothing, but cut an old, wrinkly apple in two and silently offered them half each.

They took it and then fled.

They were back the next evening and we got a better look at them. The boy, Helios, was around three or four, skinny and looking as if he had been put together with the unwanted pieces of other people's bodies. His sister, Helike, angel-faced and graceful, was a year or so older.

Again we said nothing and, as Leon reached out his hand, the boy offered a small bowl, containing a dozen figs.

We all sat around the fire and munched away. Apart from Leon, none of us had any experience of children and were slightly at a loss. They were here. Now what should we do with them?

They solved that problem themselves. The little girl pulled out a roughly carved doll with a rag dress tied around it, clambered onto Guthrie's lap, and began to chatter away to him. His face was a picture. No one dared laugh.

When I looked back, Leon, Markham, and the boy were playing jacks together in the dust and getting on like a house of fire. I heard Markham say, 'Stop picking your nose, kid. Your head'll cave in.'

Markham took them back to the tavern after an hour or so. He fussed around them, making them hold his hand as they set off into the night. Their father seemed very relaxed about the whole thing. It's small events like this that bring home the differences in various cultures.

When you have a small population, children are valued – they are the future, after all, and, for the kids themselves, this manifests itself in a careless confidence. Who would hurt them? Why would anyone hurt them? They wandered happily wherever they pleased. In this era of extended family groups and nosey neighbours, someone, somewhere was always watching out for them. They never came to any harm. I remembered my first day here, the running child who fell over and the man who, without breaking his conversation in any way, picked him up, dusted him down, tousled his hair, and sent him on his way again, unharmed.

They seemed to regard us as their second home after a while, coming around in the evening, playing hand games, singing their own songs. Markham took them back every night. It paid off. He was offered work and paid in wine and half a cheese.

In case you've ever wondered, Trojan wine, Greek wine, all wine from that era, was ghastly. Seriously awful, tasting of liquorice and sulphur. Invented a couple of millennia before battery acid was required, they called it wine and drank it instead. Strong enough to strip paint, it was always served with water, which, believe me, did not help in any way. Mixing wine had evolved into a ceremony. In the *Iliad*, Achilles, receiving the Greek delegation of Odysseus, Phoenix, and Big Ajax, did them the honour of mixing the wine with his own hands.

I allowed them all a drink on what would have been Saturday night. If we had any honey cakes or anything special, we saved that for Saturday nights as well. Sometimes people came down from Site A as well, and we had a bit of a knees-up. The kids tried to teach us to dance. So Roberts strummed away as the men stamped, more or less rhythmically in the dust. Women danced separately. Probably because we were considerably better at it.

There was a lot of laughing. Life was good.

The city was thriving. There was no hint of the conflict to come. If Priam was aware of the Greeks massing over the water, no word had yet filtered down to street level. The rich got richer and even the poor didn't do that badly. Priests distributed food from the palace and from public and private sacrifices. Once or twice – in the spirit of historical research – we queued up ourselves.

Our neighbours were congenial and couldn't care less about the new people suddenly living two fields away. Houses went up and down all the time as family needs dictated. No one was bothered about a couple of scruffy shacks on the far side of the olive grove. In fact, we were joined briefly by a small family plus grandmother and two goats, who camped twenty yards away, waved and smiled cheerfully, sent their children across to steal anything that wasn't nailed down, and then disappeared as mysteriously as they had come.

One of the men got a small job of some kind occasionally, picking olives or grapes or stacking lumber for a day. The payment of eggs or olives or, once, an old boiling fowl was greatly appreciated.

We lived quietly, established our daily routines and noted what went on around us. The war was over a year away.

Life was good.

It would have been very good, but the gods rarely allow perfection.

Kal and her team had spent weeks observing and identifying all the members of the royal family and their household, and, unless Paris had her locked in a cellar somewhere, reluctantly we had to accept the fact – Helen of Sparta never came to Troy. There was absolutely no trace of her anywhere.

It was a stunning disappointment. At her request, I drafted more people to Kal's team, but even after a month's intensive observation we could find no trace of her. She simply wasn't here.

Maybe she did have an affair with Paris. Maybe he had persuaded her to run away with him – but even if he did he never brought her back to Troy. There is a story that she spent the duration of the war safely in Egypt. Something else to check out one day.

Every day I hoped some piece of evidence would become known. Or someone would catch a glimpse. Or that she might still appear in one of the many ships that docked daily.

But, logistically, it was impossible. We'd been at Troy for six months now, with only a few more weeks left, and, apart from hunting trips, when he was always accompanied by at least five or six of his brothers, Paris, son of Priam, never left the city. He had no opportunity to travel to Sparta and abduct Helen. And it was far too late now. The war would begin in a little over a year from now and it would take Agamemnon all that time to put together his forces. He needed to summon his allies, build and equip ships, manufacture weapons, and arrange his lines

106

of supply and communication. On the other side of the Aegean, the High King of Mycenae was assembling the greatest army of the age and none of it was anything to do with the most beautiful woman in the world.

As always, it was all about the money.

As for Paris, far from being the pretty, weak, besotted boy of legend, in reality he was short, tough, and probably the best archer in Troy. As a skilful hunter, he went out almost daily and never came back empty-handed, driving through the streets in triumph, displaying his kills to cheering crowds. Next to Hector, who was almost worshipped as a god, he was the most popular member of the royal family. But in all our time there we never once saw him in the company of any woman other than his mother or his sisters. In fact, his sister-in-law, Andromache, seemed to be the only female in whom he ever showed any interest whatsoever, and even that appeared to be on brother/sister terms.

'Camouflage,' said Kal. 'If you must attach yourself to a woman, who better than the most happily married woman in Troy?'

We were standing in the crowd, watching. A religious ritual had been completed and grey-haired King Priam had paused to exchange a few words with favoured priests. For this public occasion, he wore a magnificent purple chiton, patterned with gold at the hem. A blue chlamys or cloak hung from his right arm, ostentatiously casual. As he turned his head, the sun glinted on his ornate golden headdress. He wasn't tall – it was obvious from whom Paris had inherited his stocky build, but he spoke and people paid attention. The three or four priests being addressed all stood with their eyes politely lowered, listening attentively.

Hector, on the other hand, obviously took after the queen. Tall and still slender after all that childbearing, Hecuba stood with her women, patiently waiting. She too wore royal purple – a peplos in her case, beautifully draped and hanging in folds to the ground. In an age where women wore their wealth in public, she was festooned with gold. A wonderful torque-style necklace flashed in the bright sunlight – as it was obviously designed to do. She wore many heavy bracelets and rings. The light veil she would have worn during the ceremony was caught back, allowing glimpses of her intricate gold headpiece to be seen. The weight must have been incredible, but, under her mask of make-up, her face gave nothing away. Even at this distance, as she stood under her sunshade quietly awaiting her husband, her air of authority was tangible.

It was all about display. About gold and jewellery and rich fabrics. About the wealth and power of Troy. About being seen. The walls of Troy made their statement and, periodically, the royal family came down into the lower town and made theirs.

Paris and Andromache stood a little apart. To honour the occasion, he was a little more smartly dressed than usual, wearing a simple, dark-red chiton and neatly tied sandals. He was, however, vain enough to draw attention to his well-muscled arms with two golden armbands, each in the shape of a snake.

Andromache's simple pale green robe fell in graceful folds. Unlike Hecuba, she had bloused hers over her belt.

I wondered – was she pregnant again? No one had ever mentioned this possibility. Maybe it was just the style of her dress. She too stood under a sunshade held by two women. Obviously a suntan was not a fashion statement. In fact, right up until the twentieth century, no woman with any pretension to fashion at all would display a complexion anything other than milk white.

Paris said something to her and they both laughed. Hector approached, taller and fairer than both of them. He had obviously taken a little more care over his appearance than his careless brother. His purple-bordered robe proclaimed his royal status. Bronze and gold cuffs encircled his wrists. Unlike his bareheaded brother, he wore a simple gold circlet.

Paris appealed to Andromache, gesturing at his brother and the three of them laughed again. A happy moment in the sun.

Hector gently took his wife's arm and she smiled up at him. For a brief, intimate moment, even amongst all these people, at this public event, there were just the two of them, and then they fell in behind the king and queen. Courtiers, soldiers, and priests made haste to join them. Brazen horns and trumpets sounded. People cheered, and the procession moved slowly off towards the palace. A kaleidoscope of glittering colour. Seeing and being seen.

No woman walked at Paris's side.

I sighed. 'There's no Helen, is there?'

'Well, that's what you've always said, isn't it? And it looks as if you were right.'

'I know, but even so ...'

'Oh, I agree. I would have given a lot to see the face

that launched a thousand ships.'

I looked around at Troy. Prosperous, powerful, and seemingly unassailable.

I looked at the vanishing royal procession. No pretty-boy Paris. And no Helen.

'What else do you think Homer got wrong?'

'We'll have to wait and see.'

We'd finished. Seven months had flown by. Like everyone else, I was weary, covered with ingrained dust and grime, and desperate for a long, hot bath, my own bodyweight in chocolate, and a plateful of sausages. And yes, all three simultaneously. Why not?

I stood with Guthrie and Peterson in the cool pre-dawn air as we took one last look at Site B. Our home for nearly seven months.

I knew every stick, every stone, and every last blade of coarse, brown grass here, and now we were leaving. Part one of the assignment was finished. We had a huge amount of data on Troy and its citizens. An almost complete map of the city. Several holos of daily life. Number Eight was stuffed full of wonderful, unique, priceless data. Boxes full of sticks, cubes, disks, films, even scribbled hand-written notes and sketches. Half of me couldn't wait to get at it and the other half was reluctant to leave. When we returned, the city would be at war.

We'd spent some time discussing whether to leave at least one pod on site. To mark our territory. Both Leon and Dieter had been reasonably confident that even after nearly ten years it would still be functioning on our return, requiring nothing more than a major re-alignment to make it operational again. We'd decided against it on the advice of Guthrie. While the Trojans posed no threat – there was no way they could even get inside it – that bastard Clive Ronan was still out there somewhere. Waiting for any opportunity. Alone and desperate. An unattended pod was asking for trouble. In the end it seemed easier to cope with suspicious Trojans than lose another pod to him.

In an effort to prepare the ground for our return, we'd told our neighbours we were leaving. They nodded. We told them we would return. They nodded again, uninterested. The chances were that they wouldn't be here when we returned, anyway. When we returned, they would have been fighting the Greeks for ten years. Ten years of war would wreak enormous changes.

We withdrew in stages. Number Three had gone first. Number Five followed soon afterwards. Just the three of us left, now. When we returned, all this would be different. None of it would ever be the same again.

I watched the mist burning off as the sun rose and smelled wood smoke on the air.

Guthrie stirred. 'We should go, Max. People will be up and about soon. And they'll be waiting for us back at St Mary's.'

'Ready when you are.'

The world went white.

Peterson bumped us on landing. He always did.

I activated the decon and the cold, blue light took care of any nasty Trojan viruses we might have brought back with us. In fact, since we'd lived there so long, I did it twice, just to be sure.

Peterson and Guthrie fussed around, picking up their kit. Peering through the screen, I could see an orange army of techies, ready to swarm over the pods the second they could get us out of Hawking. They would be itching to get on with it.

We stepped outside. St Mary's seemed strangely harsh, noisy, smelly, and unfamiliar.

I took a deep breath and looked around. Dr Bairstow stood on the gantry, as he always did, looking down at me. I smiled and nodded.

He nodded and – did he? No. No smile. On the other hand, any mission that doesn't end in death or my P45 is a good one.

The rest of the team were waiting for us. We always finish an assignment together. I insist on it. Van Owen and I assembled the troops and pointed them more or less in the direction of Sick Bay. Wise in the ways of historians, Dr Foster had sent advance troops to divert us from the bar. Which was a shame, because after months of the choice between Trojan rotgut or nothing at all, I was really ready for something blue and potent and with a little umbrella.

Helen, in a white coat and stethoscope, effortlessly achieving the sort of discipline for which lesser women would require black leather and a hunting crop, indicated we should form a line.

Being St Mary's, we formed several clumps and a rhomboid.

I could hear Markham informing Nurse Hunter he had a septic goose bite.

'Really? Was the goose septic before or after it bit you?'

'I think you need to check me out in one of the examination rooms.'

'No need. You're septic, but the bite's fine.'

'Actually, I think I may have cholera. You really need to check me over. Fast.'

'Do you actually have any symptoms at all? Of anything? Anything medical?'

'Yes. Yes, I do. I've got that thing that makes you feel funny. You know. All over. Requires immediate and urgent attention.'

'What are you talking about?'

'You know. Four letter word. Begins with L. Ends in E.'

'Ah, lice! Come with me.'

Schiller appeared. Apparently, she'd already been cleared because she was wearing blues and a worried expression.

'Max. We have a problem.'

'Give me a break. We've only been back ten minutes.'

'It's Professor Rapson. He's – not himself.'

'Well, thank God.'

'No. Max, you really need to come. And Dr Dowson is …'

'Is he not Professor Rapson, either?' I said, lightheaded with the anticipation of sausages.

'He's – upset.'

I stared at her. 'What's going on?'

Her glance flickered to Major Guthrie standing close by and listening.

'Can you come and have a look?'

I started to ease out of the line.

'Where are you going?' said Helen, sharply. I swear she has eyes in the back of her head. 'You've not been cleared yet.'

'So clear me.'

She sighed and punched up a fresh screen on her scratchpad.

'How do you feel?'

'Fine.'

'Off you go, then.'

'What? That's it? What happened to *have I been flinging my body fluids around? Or contracted scrofula? Or lost a leg?*'

'Despite Markham's best efforts to present with cholera, everyone's fine. Including you. In fact, I've never seen you so unscathed. I think this is the first assignment ever when you haven't returned with some sort of injury. Are you sure you haven't just been hiding in a cupboard for seven months?'

'Very funny. I'll be off, then.'

'And me,' said Peterson, always wanting to know what's going on.

'And me,' said Guthrie, also always wanting to know what's going on, but for different reasons.

'Oh, there's no need, Major. You'll have a lot to do here.'

'Actually,' said Schiller, 'that may not be such a bad idea.'

My plate of sausages would obviously have to wait. We set off on reconnaissance.

115

'Where is the professor?'

'In the stacks.'

'Has Dr Dowson banned him again? Is that what this is about?'

The stacks are behind the Archive. It's where we keep details of our older assignments and some of the more obscure stuff. Huge, high racks of shelving contain less-used records. The shelves reach from floor to vaulted ceiling. One of those big library ladder things could be wheeled around to reach the rarefied atmosphere of the top shelves. St Mary's, however, observing custom and practice rather than health and safety, generally scrambled up and down and swung around the shelves like Tarzan of the Apes, but noisier and more hairy. When I was a trainee, we'd had competitions.

The stacks themselves were in chaos. Not historian chaos – the other kind. A blizzard of papers lay everywhere. Boxes were overturned and their contents scattered. The place looked rather like St Albans after Boudicca had happened to it. Without the severed limbs and mutilated corpses, obviously, but the effect was the same. We picked our way through the devastation.

Overhead, I could hear a voice. Singing. Apparently, Timothy Leary was dead.

No, no, no, no.

On the outside.

Looking in.

Cutting across this tuneless lament, I could hear Dr Dowson shouting. This wouldn't be good. I'd once come across the two of them in the professor's office, where a scholarly debate on the sinking of the White Ship had rapidly spiralled out of control and they were facing off and on the verge of breaking out the traditional academic chant of 'Come and have a go if you think you're hard enough.'

We rounded a corner, following the noise.

Dr Dowson stood, literally wringing his hands, staring upwards into the gloom.

'Oh, Max. Thank God. I can't get the old fool to come down and I just know he's going to fall. What did he think he was doing? I've always said that one day … and now look what he's done. We must get him down.'

Guthrie slipped past me.

'What has he done, Doctor?'

I stepped forward to get a better view upwards and skidded on something. 'Oh, yuk. What have I just trodden in?'

Dr Dowson waved his arms. 'All of you. Stay back. Don't touch anything. Put your hands in your pockets.'

'Why is everything sticky?' demanded Guthrie. He sniffed his fingers. 'Is this …?'

Dr Dowson caught his arm. 'Stop, Major. Don't lick your –'

Too late.

'It *is* honey,' he said in amazement. 'I thought it was. Why is everything covered in honey?'

I turned slowly. He was right. We had honey everywhere. And we had a Professor Rapson who was high in every sense of the word. I had one of those foreboding things. I turned to Peterson who obviously was having similar thoughts.

'Xenophon,' I said.

117

'Pompey,' he replied.

Guthrie tried to wipe his hands on his tunic. You can't shift honey that easily. 'What are you two talking about? What's going on here?'

Peterson sighed. 'Toxic honey.'

Guthrie stared at his fingers in horror. 'What the hell is toxic honey?'

'It's all right, Major. It's just a touch of mad honey disease. It's not fatal. Usually. You'll feel a bit wobbly for a bit, maybe see a few things, but you'll be fine.'

'I only tasted a tiny bit.'

'That's all it takes, sadly.'

'But what is toxic honey? And since I'm talking to the history department, tell me in less than one hundred words.'

I marshalled a few facts. 'Toxic honey. Made by bees using pollen from rhododendrons growing by the Black Sea. Causes disorientation, uncoordinated movements, nausea, and hallucinations. Both Pompey and Xenophon's armies were infected with the stuff and were defeated. Not fatal. Wears off in a couple of hours. You'll get a bit giggly. And high. High as a kite, actually. Although not as high as the professor, here. We need to get him down before anyone sees him.'

'There's a ladder somewhere,' said Peterson and disappeared into the gloom.

I turned to Dr Dowson. 'How did he manage this? In the absence of rhododendrons, bees, hives, and even the Black Sea, how the hell has he managed this?'

'He was looking for modern equivalents. I understand ragwort can sometimes –'

'I can hear my hair grow. Oh, wow, I can actually hear my own hair growing.'

'Yes, you might want to sit down for a bit, Major.'

Doctor Dowson grabbed my arm. 'Max, we really need to persuade him to come down. Delusions of flying are very common in cases of this sort. Imagine if he tries … We must get him down.'

'Why would he do this?'

'Well, who knows, Max? Who knows why the old fool does anything? I used to think that so long as we kept him away from matches we had a reasonable chance of getting him through the working day intact, and now it turns out he can't even be trusted with a jar of honey.'

He was distraught. Given that he and the professor existed in a state of almost perpetual warfare, an observer might have been surprised at his distress. But I'd seen the two of them standing back to back at Alexandria, facing their enemies together. With nothing more than a converted vacuum cleaner and a milk churn, they'd sprayed flames and defiance, shouting ancient war cries, their sparse hair standing on end, covered in soot, and far more formidable than anything Clive Ronan had been able to throw at us that day. They'd been together, in one capacity or another, nearly all their working lives. I suspected that each would be astonished at the affection he really felt for the other.

And not only that. While Dr Bairstow was able to take a moderately relaxed view regarding St Mary's *joie de vivre*, especially after a major assignment, he had zero tolerance for drugs and the use of drugs. Any drugs. At any time. By any one.

119

And it wasn't just the professor soaring into the stratosphere. Major Guthrie was leaning against the stacks, singing gently to himself. I thought that was one of the scariest things I'd ever seen. Until a white coat drifted gently down from above. Followed by a tie.

'Oh, God! Put your clothes back on, you old fool. There are ladies present.'

'Don't worry, Doctor, we'll get him down.'

'How?'

'Ian!' I shook his arm. 'Concentrate. Do we have some sort of cherry-picker?'

'Mmm?'

'Some sort of cherry-picker? How does Mr Strong change the lights? Paint ceilings? Prune trees?'

'Tree fellers.'

I let my arm fall, mystified.

'Tree fellers?'

'Yes. Well, four sometimes, but usually only two,' and collapsed, giggling, against the shelves.

I stared at him coldly. 'Not helping.'

His face changed. 'Elspeth? I looked for you.'

'Major ...?'

'I looked everywhere for you.'

'Don't give in to the dark side, Major.'

'What's going on here?' demanded Helen, turning up to make things worse.

Above our head, a voice rose in song again.

'Well I can fly.

'High as a kite if I want to.

'Faster than light if I want to.'

'Don't touch anything, Helen,' said Peterson, returning

120

at last, wheeling the library ladder.

'Why not? What is this stuff?'

'No!' we shouted in unison.

Too late.

'Why is everything covered in honey?'

'Long story,' said Peterson. 'I'm going up. There's a little platform at the top of the ladder. A bit like one of those airplane embarkation stairs. I'll get him off the shelves and persuade him down the ladder. You scoop him up at the bottom.'

'Don't be an idiot,' said Helen, brusquely. 'There's no room for two people up there and I love you so much.'

Silence. No one caught anyone's eye.

'Right,' I said. 'Tim, you take Helen. Dr Dowson, you keep an eye on the galloping Major, and I'll go and talk to the naked man up there. Miss Schiller, where's Dr Bairstow?'

'In his office, as far as I know.'

'Watch the door. No one comes in.'

Peterson heaved Helen onto the other shoulder. 'You can't go up there, Max. You won't have the strength if he takes it into his head to do something stupid.'

'Well, you can't go. You're wearing the unit's medical officer.'

'Yes, did you hear what she said? I have witnesses.'

'Fat lot of good that'll do. If she remembers any of this, she'll never let us live. We'll all have to join a witness protection programme somewhere.'

'Someone's coming,' said Schiller from the door, because the day just wasn't bad enough.

'Quick,' said Tim. 'Everyone look normal.'

121

Guthrie's legs folded beneath him like wet string.

Oh, great.

Leon had come looking for me. Discharged from Sick Bay, he'd gone to my room and I wasn't there. He'd gone to the dining room, expecting to find me in a close relationship with a plate full of great British bangers and I hadn't been there either. After that, of course, he'd just followed the noise.

We regarded him with all the dismay of a politician who has suddenly remembered the existence of the electorate only ten minutes before the polls close.

I wasn't sure whether his arrival was a good thing or not. We all tend to forget he's actually second in charge at St Mary's. Mostly, I think, because he never needs to make the point. What people like Barclay never understood is that the louder and longer you shout, the less people listen. That doesn't mean, however, that he can't shout if he wants to.

He summed up the situation at a glance.

Dr Dowson, alternately exhorting the professor to come down at once for the love of God, and then threatening him with some blood-curdling fate should he actually choose to do so.

Ian Guthrie, collapsed in a badly folded heap on the floor and singing something incomprehensibly Caledonian, no doubt involving banks, braes – whatever the hell they are –, and Bannockburn.

And the Chief Medical officer, who appeared to be eating the Chief Training Officer who had a stupid grin on his face and was putting up no sort of resistance at all.

We must have been back all of twenty minutes.

122

I got a long, slow look. The words *seven months* could not have been more clearly conveyed, even if they'd been set to music. I got the message. There's no sex on assignments. That would be stupid and embarrassing. And our shifts hadn't coincided. So he'd waited seven months and I suspected he wasn't going to wait very much longer. However, we had other things to deal with first …

'*Speeding through the universe.*
Thinking is the best way to travel.'

Correctly categorising everything happening at ground level as irrelevant, he threw his head back and, in a voice in which failure to comply was not an option, called, 'Professor Rapson, if you would be good enough to join us down here, please. You are causing some alarm and Dr Dowson is distressed.'

Obviously, something got through. The overhead singing ceased.

'Octavius, my dear fellow …'

I said urgently, 'He shouldn't try to get down alone.'

'He won't. I'll get him down. Go and see Dr Bairstow who is looking for you and none of you want to be found here. Dr Peterson, please help Major Guthrie to his quarters. Miss Schiller, if you could assist Dr Foster to hers, please. Go now. Dr Dowson, you will remain.'

He began to climb the library ladder.

As I sped thankfully away, the last thing I heard was the professor's faltering footsteps on the metal staircase. 'Occy, my friend, what is all this?' and then I was out of earshot, never doubting for one moment that all would be safely resolved.

I raced up the stairs, arriving, hot and sticky in the

Boss's office. Mrs Partridge frowned disapprovingly, but she always did. I flashed her a grin, just to annoy her, and bounced in to see him.

'Good morning, sir.'

'Dr Maxwell, welcome back.'

'Thank you, sir. Nice to be back.'

He looked me up and down. 'You appear to be remarkably unharmed.'

'I am.'

'If a little sticky.'

'Honey, sir.'

'Of course,' he said, as if chatting with a honey-covered expat from the Bronze Age was the most natural thing in the world, which, of course, at St Mary's, it was.

'I understand that in addition to a successful assignment, you have managed to prevent Mr Markham contracting cholera.'

'My talents are limitless, sir. Something I was planning to bring up at my next performance appraisal.'

'Really? Why?'

'Well, it wouldn't be appropriate to bring it up at someone else's, would it?'

'Since I feel certain that by then, any credits you may have earned will be more than outweighed by corresponding debits for damages incurred, I remain unalarmed by this threat.'

'I'll leave you to enjoy your false sense of security, sir.'

As I was oozing out of the door, he said, 'Very satisfactory work, Dr Maxwell.'

Beneath my outer layer of honey and dust, I glowed.

'Thank you, sir.'

'Twelve hours.'

'Sorry, sir?'

'The usual recovery period. Twelve hours to sleep it off and then complete recovery. Please convey suitable reassurances to Dr Dowson.'

I gaped. How does he know these things?

I dithered outside the Boss's office. I could smell sausages. And fish and chips. And all the other favourites so carefully chosen to welcome us home. There would be chocolate mousse. And pancakes. And Mrs Mack's chicken tikka masala. The noise from the dining room was as tempting as the smell. Oh God, I really wanted a sausage. And no, that's not a metaphor.

But …

Heroically, I made my way to my own room, where, with luck, something nearly as good would be waiting for me.

Everyone has their fantasies. Some of them quite wide-ranging and varied.

Comprehensive.

Imaginative.

Detailed.

I was looking at about eight of mine all at once.

The room was dim. Somewhere in the background I could hear *Lucy in the Sky with Diamonds*. That was for me. In private moments, he always called me Lucy. The girl with kaleidoscope eyes.

He'd pulled my old table to the foot of the bed and laid it with a cloth I could barely see, the table was so stacked with good things.

Not one, not two, but three boxes of my favourite chocolates sat invitingly open. Behind them, two (because one is never enough) tall sundae glasses of chocolate mousse. Plates of smoked salmon, pink and curling. A plate of sushi. A jug of margaritas stood next to two frosted glasses. And in the centre, the second star of the show, a colossal plate of crisply roasted sausages, done just the way I like them, with all the scrummy black bits still attached.

I say second, because the real star of the show lay stark naked on the bed, grinning like the naughty boy he intended to be, and monumentally, magnificently pleased to see me.

He linked his hands behind his head and leaned back on the pillows.

'Well, Lucy, what shall we do now?'

Later – much later, actually – when I could finally string two words together, I asked, 'Who's Elspeth?'

He was silent for a little while and then said, 'You must know the name. Elspeth Grey?'

I did know the name. Elspeth Grey was the very first name on our Board of Honour. The names of those who have died in the service of St Mary's. She'd gone off to 12th-century Jerusalem and never come back. That bastard Ronan had got her.

I nodded, unsure whether to say any more. This was Leon's nightmare – that one day I wouldn't come back, either. This why he wanted me out of here. I thought of the quiet and contained Ian Guthrie. All those years and

I'd never guessed. I heard again the pain in his voice.

'*Elspeth?*'

And I shivered.

Like the Windmill in WWII, St Mary's never closed – always humming with activity and, occasionally, strife. Well, now it didn't so much hum as roar. Historians raced from the Hall to the library and back again, dragging printouts or clutching data-sticks, reviewing and organising our data, identifying areas for further study. Trying to pull the whole shapeless mass of information into something useable was a bit like eleven bickering historians stuffing a duvet into its cover while wearing boxing gloves. In the dark.

Tired-looking techies swarmed all over the pods, complaining their typical techie complaints because we'd actually used the things instead of leaving them pristine and virginal on their plinths. (The pods, I mean, not the techies.)

I reported daily progress to the Boss, as did Leon.

Apart from the first twenty-four hours when we hadn't left my room (and why would we?) we didn't have a lot of time together. It didn't seem important at the time. We had a whole future ahead of us.

We did talk occasionally of our new life together. Since he'd already borne the revelation that I couldn't cook with equanimity, I gave him the rest of the bad news.

'Not that keen on housework, either.'

'We'll get someone in.'

'Really? You'd be all right with that?'

127

'I've seen you fashion a weapon out of two pieces of toilet paper and a paperclip. There's no way I'm going to be trapped in a small flat with an angry woman who has access to a vacuum cleaner.' He put his hand over mine. 'It really will work, you know.'

'I know,' I said. 'I do know that, really. And if you changed your mind and didn't want to do it then I'd be really disappointed. It's just ... I'm ...'

'Of course you are,' he said, following this without difficulty. 'But everything will be fine. Yes, there will be days when doors will be slammed and pots will be thrown. But I promise you now, you'll never have to hide in a wardrobe again.'

As a child, I'd spent a lot of time at the back of my wardrobe, eyes squeezed tight shut, hoping and praying that this time – this time – I would open them to the snow-covered trees of Narnia and safety. It never happened.

I nodded. 'I am looking forward to it. Not leaving St Mary's – that's not going to be fun, but ...'

'You're not saying goodbye for ever,' he interrupted. 'We'll still see them. They can come for Sunday lunch. Not all of them at the same time, of course, we won't have enough chairs. We can meet them in the pub. You're not cutting them completely out of our lives. Remember, they're my friends too.'

'You're right. I don't know why I'm worrying because I do have a fall-back position. If things don't work out for us, Professor Penrose has offered to take me on.'

He regarded me severely.

'Is it not enough that you bounced that poor man all around the universe without threatening his declining years as well?'

'You can't blame me for setting up a first reserve.'

'I'm so glad to see you're approaching this new phase of your life with total commitment.'

'He was very keen.'

'He was very concussed.'

I glared at him.

'One day you really must tell me why you think I'm so unattractive to other men.'

'It would take much longer than one day.'

'It's not just Professor Penrose, you know. The world is full of men who find me irresistible.'

'Really? Well, I'll be blowed.'

'After that last comment – unlikely.'

Everything had changed on our second visit. By our calculations, the war was well into its tenth year now and the Trojans were suffering. Long years cooped up behind their own walls had taken their toll. The arrival of their allies had more than tripled the population. The streets were packed with Lydians, Carians, Phrygians, Lycians, Thracians, and many more, all noisily pushing their way through the crowds and filling every roadside tavern and eating-place.

The rural areas were much less haphazard than during our first visit. Almost every square inch was under cultivation. Livestock no longer roamed free, but were confined and carefully guarded.

Our olive grove was still there, but someone had assumed ownership, pruning the trees and scything the grass. Three haystacks, carefully built around central poles, now stood between the tavern and us.

We had thought long and hard about returning to our original sites. Surely our sudden reappearance would provoke at the very least, gigantic curiosity, if not outright hostility. We were foreign – we left – the war came – and now we were back. It wasn't hard to imagine their suspicions.

We abandoned Site A as being too public. Too near the heavily guarded citadel. And we needed to be closer together. Just in case.

We eased back into Troy very carefully. First one pod, with me, Guthrie, and Peterson. We waited a day. No one tried to kill us. The second pod, Number Five, landed late at night, so in the morning, there were two of them.

Nothing happened.

We repeated ourselves three days later with Number Three, twenty yards away to the west, on the other side of the grove. No reaction. Finally, and with a certain amount of trepidation, we introduced a fourth, Number Six. So that was twelve of us here and I'd fretted over nothing because it was two days before anyone even turned up to investigate and then it was only a short, scrawny, grubby boy with a shock of dark hair and ears like the wing mirrors on an old Beetle I'd once owned. Helios had grown up.

And if Helios had grown, then so had his sister Helike, who must now be around fourteen or fifteen years old. Rather old to be unmarried, especially as she was such a pretty girl. Helios, poor lad, had been behind the door when good looks were being allocated. We discovered later, mostly through the medium of mime, that she had been briefly married to a soldier, an archer I think, who had been killed around six months before and, as was the custom, she had returned to her father and both children now worked full-time in their father's tavern.

There were a number of soldiers billeted at the tavern but they never bothered us. In their world, people came – people went. People lived – people died. There was a war on. No one cared. There were other things to worry about.

There was sickness in the city, for a start. With so many people jammed so tightly together, of course, there would be. And food was short. It was there, but never quite enough. Water was not rationed, but soldiers stood at every well. It was all good-natured enough, but no one took more than their fair share.

The old women had disappeared from the streets. They had nothing to sell. People hoarded any surplus food they happened to have. No one was starving, but the children had that pinched look. There was no running around now. They and everyone who could be spared from fighting or manning the walls worked in the fields, wringing every last mouthful of food from the exhausted soil.

But if the Trojans were suffering, the Greeks had it even worse. They were in the tenth year of a siege that was going nowhere. Where was the promised plunder? The spoils of war? The women?

I think the tenth year marked some sort of watershed for them. They didn't want to play any more. They just wanted to take their toys and go home.

We heard it every night. Their shouted arguments drifted over the city walls in the still night air. And with the rising sun, one, maybe two ships would up-anchor and, accompanied by jeers and insults from those remaining, row silently away.

I don't actually know how Agamemnon kept them there. Apart from the lack of any military progress of any kind, their campsite was filthy. There are only so many latrines you can dig over ten years. Broken gear and piles of stinking rubbish littered the shoreline. The shallows were thick and oily with sewage. When the wind was in the right direction, we could smell it from Troy. The conditions must have been appalling.

They'd built their own famous wall – the ditch with sharpened stakes to protect themselves from the Trojan chariots – and they squatted sullenly behind it. The days slipped away – as did Agamemnon's troops.

The Troad, that once fertile plain, was devastated. Gone were the small farms, the huddles of houses, the neatly tilled fields, the olive groves, the woods. Everything had been flattened under the enormous weight of the opposing armies. The trees were long gone. The crops trampled back into the soil. The herds driven back to safety inside Troy itself.

Yes, the Trojans were suffering, but they were on their home ground. The Greeks, trapped on their narrow beach and with their backs to the sea, were becoming desperate.

Something had to give.

Blame Homer with his long descriptions of aristeia – personal combat – in which admiring soldiers from both sides supposedly took a break from the fighting to watch their champions duke it out. In fact, the old boy was a bit of dead loss. Wonderful poet – crap war correspondent. For a start, there was very little formal fighting. The Greeks, far from home, were more concerned with keeping themselves supplied, spending long periods further and further away from Troy as they stripped the Troad and surrounding areas of everything they could find.

So nine years had drifted by in inconclusive sea raids and the odd skirmish outside the walls, with nothing to show for it.

But now, now we were well into the tenth year and, suddenly, everything changed.

It came out of the blue. One day we were on the walls, lethargically watching the ten-year stalemate – and the next day, all hell broke loose.

We were moving into the season of the hot winds. Winds that blew dust into every last nook and cranny. Dust that stuck to sweating skin and drove us insane. Dust that got into our clothes, our beds, our food, and under our eyelids. Winds that blew hot air into our faces no matter in which direction we faced. Winds that irritated and niggled and maddened and we all became snappy and fractious, even with each other. Nothing personal. It was just that time of year. The nearest equivalent is blowing a hot hair-dryer into your face twenty-four hours a day.

Whether the winds were a contributing factor, I don't know. Probably. But today was the beginning of the end. Today, although we didn't yet know it, Achilles would finally emerge from his tent, insane for blood and revenge, and all hell would break loose.

As Homer describes it, Agamemnon and Achilles had quarrelled over the division of their booty. Achilles had a massive strop and withdrew to his tent, from whence he refused to budge. Think petulant teenager. The war was going badly for the Greeks, so Patroclus, his friend and countryman, had stolen his armour and led Achilles' Myrmidons into battle himself. He was immediately engaged and killed by Hector, who, along with everyone else, was under the impression he had killed Achilles.

135

Sadly, we'd missed those events, but today Achilles' need for revenge would overcome his grief and remorse. Today, he would re-join the battle.

We didn't know it yet, but a lot of people were going to die today.

It was a normal day. I was on the walls with Peterson. Kal and Markham were further along, trying to estimate how many more ships Agamemnon had lost during the night. At this rate, the Trojans didn't need to do anything but wait it out. So what took Hector and his army outside the walls was anyone's guess. Homer puts it down to godly intervention. And for all I know it may have been.

Trumpets sounded around the town and voices were raised both inside and outside the walls.

Within the city, excitement boiled in the streets. People raced to the walls. Something was happening. And it was happening now.

It was as we were jostling for position on the walls that Roberts nudged me.

'Look up.'

I glanced up and to my right.

There, on the walls above the Scaean Gate, exactly as Homer had recounted, Hector, the Trojan hero, was talking quietly to his wife, Andromache, who carried their infant son, Astyanax. They stood a little apart from everyone else, their heads close together. We were too far away to hear the words, but their body language was eloquent.

They were saying goodbye.

For me – for all of us – it was the most amazing moment. Legend springing to life right in front of our eyes. Because, if Homer had got this bit right … then this was the day when man-murdering Achilles left his tent to do what he did best …

I let my imagination roam …

With his back to the sea, Agamemnon would be issuing his final orders.

Armoured Achilles would be emerging from his quarters, intent on avenging the death of his friend Patroclus.

Up on Mount Olympus, home of the gods, Zeus would be informing them they could fight for whichever side they pleased. There were no holds barred today.

And here, in Troy, Hector was taking leave of his wife and son, both of them knowing in their hearts that this day would be his last and that Troy was doomed.

She clung to him, unable to let him go. He touched her cheek – a small gesture of comfort and courage.

The trumpets sounded again. Hector pulled on his helmet with its unique dyed red horsehair plume and his little boy cried out in fear. Gone was the loving family man and in his place stood Hector the warrior, the hero of Troy, magnificent in his bronze armour, decorated with intricate gold patterns.

The gate opened. Long lines of Trojans marched out. The Greeks lined up to meet them.

It had begun.

Achilles led his screaming Myrmidons directly at the main body of Trojan soldiers who raised their shields and spears. The two sides met with a roar and crash of metal that shook the ground.

Battles are nowhere near as neat and tidy as Homer

137

would have us believe; and most of the time we had no idea who was who. All we could do was discreetly record as much as we could and sort it all out later with the aid of slow-motion replays. I'd been strict about this. The temptation is to forget the recorder and just watch events unfold. I'd described, in horrible detail, what would happen to anyone who forgot why we were here. I had people stationed up and down the walls and two more at the Scaean Gate, as well. I could do no more.

The slaughter was horrific. Vicious and violent. Brutal. Massive. It was hard to see how anyone could survive. Men fought hand to hand, face-to-face, swinging swords, stabbing with spears, even throwing rocks. They clubbed each other with stones and when they ran out of weapons entirely, punched, kicked, and head-butted.

The tide of battle swept across the plain, first one way, and then another. Clouds of dust hung in the air, catching in our throats and making our eyes sting. I've fought. I know how thirsty combat can make you. I could only try to imagine how those shrieking, roaring soldiers must feel, baking in their armour under the pitiless sun, choking in their own dust and sweat.

Not that it appeared to slow anyone down. Everywhere, arms rose and fell tirelessly. Some discarded their shields and fought with a sword in either hand. Others used their shields to protect the archers, giving them time to pick their targets.

Occasionally, very occasionally, someone would pull themselves out of the melee and limp back to their own lines, but only very occasionally. In this sort of fighting, you were on your feet or you were dead. There was no halfway house today.

I heeded my own instructions – for once – and kept my attention rigorously on what was happening in front of me, but all the time I was waiting … waiting for some event – big or small – that I could recognise, say 'there' – and use this as a starting point to identifying those around me.

And then I did.

A huge skirmish was taking place across the plain, to the south-west. A handful of Greek soldiers were laying ferociously into a larger Trojan force. If this was who I thought it was, then this was the man-killer, himself.

Terrified and overwhelmed, the Trojan force split, half of them racing back towards Troy and the other half falling back into the River Scamander itself, maybe hoping to find some safety there.

Not so. A magnificently armoured figure roared commands and urged his men on. Could this be – please let it be – it must be – Achilles. I'd always pictured him as a giant. A colossal killing machine in golden armour, but even with his distinctive black horsehair crest, he stood no taller than anyone else. And his armour was of bronze, just like everyone else. He was just a man. But he fought like a god. Roaring like a bull, he plunged into the water after the fleeing Trojans, striking left and right.

No one escaped.

They say: 'The river ran red with blood,' and it did that day. So many bodies lay in the water that they blocked the flow of the river, which backed up, flooded its banks, and began to change its course.

Nor did the killing stop there.

Back on the dry and dusty plain, tireless Achilles once again gathered men to himself and set off in relentless pursuit of more Trojans. And Hector.

I didn't know where Hector was. Or Paris. Or Deiphobos, or any of the Trojan generals, but the whole world could see Achilles in his fury, slaughtering Trojans by the truckload and working his way ever nearer to the Gate of Troy.

One brave warrior stepped forward – it might have been Agenor, Antenor's son – and threw his spear, which caught Achilles a glancing blow, just below his well-armoured knee.

Whoever it was, he wisely didn't hang around and was off like a deer with a roaring and completely uninjured Achilles in hot pursuit. What happened to Agenor, if indeed it was he, I couldn't see in all the dust, but a hundred Trojans used Achilles' absence to try to cram themselves in through the gate as fast as they could go. There was no dignity. No chivalry. No honour. They fought and elbowed and shoved in their eagerness to be within the safety of their own walls. To be as far as they could from the big, blond killing-machine outside.

All except one.

I'd found Hector. Exactly where Homer said he'd be.

In the distance, Achilles abandoned the pursuit of Agenor and raced back across the plain, still on fire with his need to avenge the death of his friend.

With one voice, the people along the walls shouted a warning. Even Priam, the king himself, rose to his feet and gestured.

But Hector stood firm. His ornate bronze armour was

heavily dented and his red horsetail streaked with dust. But he hefted his bronze and wicker shield, planted his feet firmly. And waited.

It's not easy to stand quietly and watch someone die. Because that's what we do and I wonder about us, sometimes. We were about to witness one of the greatest duels of the Ancient World. Hector and Achilles. The hero of Troy against the greatest killer of the age.

Silence fell.

The thud of Achilles' footsteps was plainly audible even from my distance.

I craned my neck for a better view. The woman next to me, whose breath reeked of garlic and had the worst teeth I'd ever seen, pushed spitefully and said something nasty, but I was in no mood to give way. I jabbed back and muttered something very rude in German. One of the best languages there is for a really good curse.

Priam was joined by his wife Hecuba and then by Andromache, who turned her head and spoke. The nurse took Astyanax away. He wouldn't see his father die today. It didn't matter. He had only days left to live, anyway.

Troy's time was running out.

That was when it hit me. Hard. This was not some remote event to be studied, picked over, and analysed. This was real. These were people's lives. These people existed. They loved. They suffered. They were all about to die. And we were going to watch.

Whether the sight of his family, standing together, and pleading for his return was too much for even Hector to endure, I don't know. He turned his head to look at the fast approaching Achilles, then back to his family again.

141

His wife lifted her arm as if to plead with him, then let it fall. Hector looked back to Achilles and then suddenly took off, back towards the gates.

Which had closed.

All around the walls people screamed a warning, but there was no time to get them open.

Unprepared, no weapon drawn, and with Achilles close behind him, Hector did the only thing he could.

He ran.

He did not run three times around the walls as legend claims. He ran away from them, racing across the plain, hurdling the bodies of the slain, and dodging broken bits of chariot and discarded armour, as Achilles, roaring his fury, chased along behind.

Who knows how far and how fast they would have run? Achilles could not catch Hector and with his opponent between him and the walls, Hector could not get back to Troy.

He skidded suddenly to a halt, sliding in the dust and raising a cloud of it around him. Another figure stood nearby with two precious javelins. Now he had a fighting chance. Deiphobos had not abandoned his brother.

In the *Iliad*, Deiphobos is really that grey-eyed bitch, Athena, who leads Hector on and then abandons him to the wrath of Achilles.

The encounter was short and brutal. There were no fine speeches. No godly interventions.

Achilles threw his spear.

Hector ducked and it sailed harmlessly over his head.

Straightening, he threw his own spear. Achilles caught it square on his famous shield with a clang we could hear all the way back in Troy and deflected it away.

Hector turned for his second spear. But Deiphobos, maybe fearing for his own safety, had disappeared. Hector was abandoned and completely alone. Just as the *Iliad* describes.

The groan could be heard all over Troy.

Did he know? Did Hector know in his heart that he could not escape? In his last moments, did the gods grant him that knowledge? That his city could not escape? That his people could not escape?

He didn't hesitate for one moment.

Casting aside his heavy round shield, he pulled out his sword, flourished it above his head, threw back his head to shout his last defiant battle cry, and hurled himself straight at Achilles ...

... who stood his ground, head on one side, considering ... then slowly, lazily even, lifted his spear and stabbed Hector a great blow in the neck.

A huge fountain of bright red blood arced through the air.

The champion of Troy fell on his back in the dust.

Not a sound could be heard on the walls. Not even from the watching Greek lines.

Hector lay in the dust in a spreading pool of red, twitching slightly. Not yet dead.

Achilles tilted back his head, clenched his fists, and roared his triumph to the gods, to the ghost of Patroclus, to the city of Troy, to the whole world.

With Hector still not dead, he stripped him naked, slashed his ankles and threaded them through with leather thongs. He tied the ends to his chariot and set off around the walls of Troy, with Hector's still-living body bumping along behind him, leaving a long scarlet trail in the dust.

A great cry went up. The whole city gave voice to grief. The women sent up a wailing lament and Andromache dropped like a stone.

Her women rushed to her aid. Homer has her working her loom at the moment of Hector's death, but she wasn't. She was there. On the walls. She saw his death. She didn't see her husband's slowly disintegrating body being dragged time and again around the city of Troy whose walls, unfortunately, were not high enough to spare its occupants the sight of their hero's humiliation. They wept.

All except one.

Paris, Hector's brother, bare-chested but wearing an archer's leather wrist guard, stepped carefully around the wailing women without even seeming to see them. Taking up his great bow, slowly and with great care, he selected a perfect arrow. Below, Achilles was approaching for yet another circuit of the walls. The thing bouncing off the rocks as it was dragged behind the chariot was no longer recognisable as a man.

Racing ahead of his own dust, Achilles approached at speed. Somewhere along the way he'd shed his helmet and his long, fair hair streamed behind him. Still he roared his victory at the Trojan forces, the words indistinguishable over the rumbling wheels. Galloping flat out, his black horses thundered across the plain, manes and tails flying. Foam flecked their flanks and flew from their bits. They looked as out of control as their driver.

I said softly, 'Kal, your team is to stay with Achilles. My team – focus on Paris. Above the Scaean Gate.'

144

Because, unseen by most, with their attention fixed on the approaching Achilles, Paris had climbed on to the wall. Bracing himself with one knee, he leaned far out – almost too far – and slowly drew back his bow, seeking his spot. His face showed nothing but an intense concentration as he took aim. The sun was not low enough in the sky to dazzle and, as if the gods had spoken, the wind dropped.

I felt the world pause.

And then, smoothly, perfectly, he let loose his arrow.

I didn't see the flight but I saw the impact, god-driven, straight into the famous heel. In his chariot, Achilles staggered, lost his balance, and control of his horses.

The chariot swerved wildly. One wheel hit a rock and the light vehicle bounced high off the ground.

Limbs flailing, Achilles flew through the air to land head-first and with massive impact onto the rocks. With a crack that could be heard from the walls of Troy all the way to the furthest of Agamemnon's ships, his head burst open.

The world stopped. Silence fell.

The Greek ranks stood in stunned disbelief. The moment of their greatest triumph had become their greatest disaster. Even on the Trojan walls, people stood frozen in shock, while down on the plain, lacking their master's hand, the horses had come to a halt.

By some freak of circumstance, or even the gods' sense of humour, the broken bodies of the two greatest heroes of their age lay not ten feet apart.

Up on the Scaean Gate, Paris lowered his bow, spat over the walls, and walked slowly away.

We were up all night, transcribing that lot. We ran the tapes repeatedly, identifying the main protagonists, trying to bring order out of our chaotic recordings. We didn't have time for leisurely interpretations. We needed to be perfectly clear what had happened that day so as to ensure we were in the right place for the next day's events.

I got about an hour's sleep and then was awoken by Kal, yammering in my ear. That really shouldn't happen to anyone first thing in the morning.

'Max! Wake up. They've gone. Get your people to the walls. They've gone. The Greeks have gone.'

I'm really not that good in the morning. I rolled off my mat, struggled to my feet, staggered a little as my limbs sorted themselves out, and blinked while my brain got itself into gear.

Others were stirring around me, banging their shoes together to dislodge scorpions and reaching for their equipment.

'Right,' I said, before they all scattered. 'Stay in pairs. No one goes anywhere alone. Take a minute to check your equipment is working before you go. There won't be any action replays so we have to make sure we get it right first time.'

I grabbed a waterskin and a recorder.

Guthrie was barking orders at his team. Every historian was to have an escort. Leon and Weller were to remain behind with the pods.

'Move,' I said, impatient at the delay and terrified of missing something. The Greeks had gone and standing on the beach should be one of the most widely recognised objects in all the world. In all of History.

The Trojan Horse.

The actual Trojan Horse.

Finally.

'Remember,' called Leon after me. 'Check under the tail.'

Old joke.

We scattered to our tasks. Everyone knew the area for which they were responsible. We'd been over this so many times and now ... now, finally, the moment was here.

I was going to see the Wooden Horse of Troy.

I flew through the streets, hardly caring whether Guthrie was with me or not, making straight for the western wall. Along with everyone else in Troy. I fought my way through the excited crowds. Guthrie stuck with me and it was a good job he did or I'd have been trampled half a dozen times. It wasn't an ill-natured crowd. They just wanted to *see*.

As did I.

I had to see ...

We struggled up a stone stairway and out on to the walls. The breeze tore at my hair. The walls were jam-packed with excited people. I bobbed up and down in frustration. In the end, Guthrie used his elbows and we fought our way to the front. I stood on tiptoe, craning my neck left and right, trying to take it all in at once. All around me, Trojans pointed and exclaimed.

Kal was right. They were gone. The Greeks were gone.

I could imagine the night they'd had. With Achilles dead, I guessed the heart had gone out of most of them. Their greatest fighter was dead. They were still on the beach. Ten long years had passed and they were no closer to taking the city than the day they arrived. The walls of Troy still stood strong. They'd had enough. They hadn't even waited for the dawn.

I imagined them, one by one, pulling silently away into the night, eager to leave this cursed place behind them. And rather than let the world witness the humiliation of seeing his forces abandon him, Agamemnon had gone with them. I couldn't blame him for not wanting to be left alone to face the mockery of the Trojans. Or even worse – the entire world. Everyone would know what had occurred here. The failure of his great venture. Ten years wasted and nothing to show for it. News of his shame would fly around the known world.

The Siege of Troy was over.

I heard a loud scraping noise and to my right the Scaean Gate was dragged open. A troop of heavily armed soldiers marched out. The Trojans cheered. The gate closed again behind them. They were taking no chances. These were war-hardened, cautious people. The legend that they had knocked down their own gate to give entrance to a giant wooden horse was suddenly completely unbelievable.

Because there was no Trojan Horse.

I could see pretty well the whole plain from where I was standing, up and down the coast, right down to the shoreline, and there was no Trojan Horse.

No giant wooden construction of any kind.

I felt a huge cold wave of disappointment and disbelief. First no Helen and now, no Trojan Horse. It shouldn't make any difference, of course, but it did. To me, it made a massive difference. There never was and never had been a Trojan Horse.

I could hear excited chatter all around me. Next to me, an old man in a stained ochre tunic was shouting excitedly and pointing. I shut it all out and tried to concentrate.

The plain was far from empty. The shoreline was littered with debris left behind by the retreating Greeks. Useless pieces of armour, broken gear, chariot wheels, spars, pieces of ships that had been cannibalised, the smoking remains of campfires – all the unwanted detritus of war littered the plain.

There were even a number of horses, standing here and there, their heads down, thirsty, their manes and tails ruffling in the breeze – obviously too old to make the return voyage. They looked sad and abandoned on this long and lonely beach.

I could see no sign anywhere of the Greeks and their ships. The sea was empty and the horizon clear.

A swelling murmur ran along the walls. A man shouted. A horn rang out. The wind picked up again and, above me, flags and pennants streamed sideways, snapping in the wind. I blinked dust out of my eyes.

Another horn sounded a reply down on the plain. The

soldiers broke ranks and began to poke around the remains, kicking over old pots and rubbish, looking for anything of value.

With no signal given that I could see, the Trojans left the walls. The Scaean Gate dragged itself open again and the citizens of Troy, confined behind their own walls for ten long, long years, streamed out across the plain.

We watched them go. I preferred to stay on the walls. The view was much better from up here. I pulled out my little recorder. Guthrie, as he always did, watched my back. I panned up and down the shoreline a couple of times. I got shots of the walls, and then turned back into the town, to record the last of the near hysterical exodus from the city.

That done, I stood resting my arms on the wall and had a bit of a think.

I called Van Owen, who confirmed she and Ritter were safe and working. I called Leon, who reported there was no one around – Helios and his family had gone to the walls, along with everyone else.

Peterson reported that he, Kal, and Evans were out on the plain and all was well. In fact, if I screwed up my eyes, I was pretty sure I could see Markham out there as well, turning over a broken javelin and talking to Roberts.

So what was making me so uneasy?

Beside me, Guthrie stood quietly, alone with his own thoughts, as usual.

The Greeks were gone. The Trojans liberated. No Trojan Horse. Was I confusing unease with disappointment? Disappointment that one of my favourite moments in all of History just hadn't happened?

This was stupid. When you sit down and think about it – how likely was the Trojan Horse? That they would find enough wood to build such a huge structure in the first place? That men could conceal themselves inside and not be discovered? That the Trojans, after a ten-year war that had cost them so dearly, would actually bring down their own walls?

There never was and never had been a Trojan Horse.

I remembered my own, special little Trojan Horse, made for me by Leon all those years ago. Our arguments over where the trapdoor had been. He always maintained it couldn't have been in the belly as so often depicted. He favoured under the tail. I had rather looked forward to seeing Greek heroes wriggling out from the Horse's backside like so many giant tapeworms.

But it was not to be.

There was no Trojan Horse.

And then, thank the god of historians – I woke up.

Yes, there was!

Right here in front of me. I was looking at it. And another one over there. And two more over there. And a whole group of them over there. There wasn't just one Trojan Horse. There were nine, ten, eleven – at least twelve that I could see, and maybe more.

My thoughts were tumbling all over the place. I let them. I let them wander wherever they wanted to go. They knew what they were doing.

I had part of the picture. Not the whole thing, but I had a beginning.

But, first things first. I called Van Owen. 'Who's with you?'

'Ritter.'

'Send him back to your pods. And Roberts and Evans. Get them to fill every available container with water. Fill the tanks. Get as much as they can. Secure all food supplies. From this moment, we are self-contained. We eat and drink nothing – nothing, do you understand? – from contemporary sources. I'm up on the west wall, under the pennant with the blue horse. Can you meet me here? Soonest.'

'On my way.'

I called Leon, faithfully guarding the other pods, and gave him the same instructions. 'Weller and Ritter will assist. I'll explain later. We're a bit busy, but it's important.'

'Understood,' he said calmly, and now I could relax a little.

I called in Peterson as well and he, Guthrie, Van Owen, Kal, Markham, and I sat under a shady tree in the small square next to the fish market. We kept our voices low, but we needn't have bothered. The city was empty. After ten years, only those who couldn't actually walk were still inside the walls.

Peterson had liberated a couple of flat loaves since no one had had breakfast.

'What's this all about?'

'Well, firstly – no Trojan Horse.'

People nodded. They were disappointed as well. It's always important to know the truth, but we all need our stories.

'Although, that's not true. There isn't one Trojan Horse. There are twelve of them. Think about it.'

153

Kal said, 'There are a dozen horses out there. Is that what you mean?'

'Yes. Horses are valuable. Very valuable. Trained chariot horses almost beyond price. They've left twelve behind. Why?'

'They're old. Or injured. Not worth space on the voyage.'

'So why not slaughter them, cut them up, and eat them on the way home? No one in this part of the world has seen much meat go by recently.'

Van Owen said, 'Because there's something the matter with them. There must be.'

'Yes,' said Peterson, in sudden excitement, 'if you read Homer, the *Iliad* opens with a plague. First, the dogs fell sick, then the horses, then the people. They put it down to the wrath of Apollo. These are some of the sick horses.'

I continued. 'And the Trojans, who are hungry and without the benefit of Homer and hindsight, will take them inside the city. They'll be slaughtered. There will be offerings to the gods – which the priests will eat afterwards. The soldiers will get the lion's share and the rest divided amongst the people. A modern cow can feed over a thousand people.'

Don't ask me how I know these things. I just do.

'One of these admittedly rather stringy horses could feed, say, six hundred. Minimum. That's over seven thousand people directly contaminated. Most of them soldiers. And it won't stop there. The blood runs off into the gutters. Dogs and cats will lap at it and then roam the city and spread the sickness. No one will wash their hands

154

properly. A baker will handle contaminated meat and then go on to bake his morning loaves. Which people will eat. Years of warfare and a restricted diet will have made these people vulnerable. In twenty-four hours, virtually everyone in the city could be puking and shitting uncontrollably. All right, some will hardly be affected and maybe not many will actually die – but they'll be in no condition to defend themselves.'

I stopped and pulled off another piece of bread.

Kal said, 'And then what? All right, it's Shit City for a couple of days, but how is that a problem?

'Because if the Greeks come back, barely anyone will be able to lift a sword.'

'But why? Why would the Greeks come back? Are you saying they left these horses deliberately? To poison people? And then they'll come back and take the city?'

'I don't know,' I said, suddenly grinding to a halt. 'I just don't know.'

'No.' said Guthrie. 'It doesn't matter whether or not the Trojans can defend themselves. Even if the Greeks turn up, the Trojans will nip back inside their walls, shut the gates, and everyone's back to square one. The one thing we do know is that the gates and walls make this city almost impregnable, whether manned or not. They could certainly hold out long enough for people to recover.'

'True, Major. So you think the Greeks have gone for good?'

'Yes. I think they've gone for good.'

I could hear people's brains turning, still trying to reconcile the legend with the facts. And if we were having trouble, imagine how reluctant the rest of the world would be to learn there was no Helen, no Trojan Horse, no heroes, no gods, just an undetermined skirmish that lasted for ten years and then just petered out. People like their stories – their legends. They don't give them up easily.

I sighed. 'Well, we have a job to do. So long as we don't eat or drink anything contemporary, we should be fine. Warn your people and let's get on with it.'

We went back to the walls.

They were already leading in the horses. To modern eyes, they were scrawny-looking things – typical horses of the day. Big heads, barrel bodies, and thin legs. Their heads hung low, but they didn't look sick.

So, this part of the legend was true. The Trojans themselves voluntarily brought their downfall into their city.

And the next part was true as well. Above the Scaean Gate, a lone figure raised her arms. Unlike the rest of the royal family who, with the exception of Paris, ostentatiously dressed in every shade of the rainbow and glittered with gold and jewels, she was simply dressed in white, as if personal appearance was of no importance to her. In contrast to the women around her, with their intricate hairstyles dressed with combs and pins of silver and gold, her red-gold hair exploded around her head like a sunburst.

Her voice, clear as a clarion, cut through the racket. I couldn't make out the words, but we all knew whom this was.

This was Kassandra, daughter of Priam, one of only two people in Troy who warned against bringing the

Trojan Horse into the city. And no one listened to her.

Her beauty supposedly caused the god Apollo to fall in love with her, and when she spurned his love – which you just don't do to a god – he cursed her twice. Firstly, with the ability to know the future. And secondly, and most cruelly, that no one would ever believe her.

They didn't believe her now. King's daughter or not, she was just that mad bat Kassandra, the one who was always ranting on about something or other. They laughed and pointed. And laughed again.

She redoubled her efforts.

They redoubled their laughing.

And then, in mid-rant – she stopped. She lowered her arms, turned her head and, for one moment, I thought she looked directly at me.

I couldn't look away. I wanted to. But I couldn't.

Then Guthrie spoke and the spell was broken.

Considerably shaken, I stepped behind him, out of her sight, just to give myself a moment.

The horses were followed by cheering crowds. All over the city, butchers would be sharpening their knives. Priests were lighting fires. Troy was preparing to party. Party until it dropped.

We were out there, of course. We'd have been mad not to be. So long as no one ate or drank anything, we'd be fine.

The party started as the sun slipped below the horizon. The last carefully hoarded supplies were broached as people flung years of restraint straight out of the window. After ten long, bitter years, they finally had something to celebrate.

And celebrate they did. The entire city was one giant street party. Every lamp was lit. Drink flowed. The smell of roasting meat was everywhere. Long lines of people danced along the streets, picking up and discarding others as the fancy took them. Many couples peeled off into dark doorways and a whole new generation could have been conceived that night.

Every square had at least one bonfire and winding queues of waiting people. Roasting horsemeat smells quite good, but none of us was tempted. I'd made it a hanging offence, anyway. I'd personally checked our supplies and I knew Kal had done the same on the other side of the olive grove. We would only ever have this one opportunity and I wasn't going to squander it by having half my team on the sick list.

So we moved among the crowds, laughing, dancing, recording, and, in my case, wondering what the hell would happen next.

I'd never actually been on an assignment where this had happened. We jump to specific events, already having a fairly clear idea of what will happen. Sometimes minor details are wrong, but if we jump to Hastings 1066, we know the Normans will win. We might not know how, and the arrow in the eye is something we're going to have to sort out one day – but the point is – we know the Normans win. As Professor Penrose had once pointed out to me, our work was hazardous but predictable.

Now, we had no idea how this would end. Anything could happen. It was quite exciting. I said so and Guthrie rolled his eyes.

I called a halt at midnight, expecting some muttering

about party pooping, but we were all exhausted. We'd been at it since dawn.

And starving, too. I ate nearly two mouthfuls of Markham's ghastly stodge before I realised what I was doing.

And then we all went to bed.

I woke early the next morning and lay for a while, staring up at the fading stars and still thinking about yesterday and what I was missing. Around me, I could hear my team moving around. I sat up. Roberts and Markham were tea monitors this morning. I took mine a little way off, sat with my back against an olive tree and thought.

And got nowhere. I just couldn't see how this would end. By now, of course, most of Troy would be groaning in the gutters and pebble dashing every available surface. Even those who had escaped food poisoning would have the hangover from hell. Some – possibly many, given their weakened state – would die, but not enough for Troy to fall.

I was still missing something.

We had bread left over from yesterday, which we ate with some cheese and made plans for the day.

Peterson and his people were deployed around the lower town. I was going back on the walls. Guthrie was to accompany me.

Leon, bless him, volunteered to remain behind and secure the two sites.

'Non-historian,' he said cheerfully. 'Slightly less useful than the fifth wheel on a bike. Go, my children. Flutter forth. Make your way in the world and do whatever it is historians do all day long. I shall remain here, feet up in the shade – but vigilant. Always vigilant.'

Peterson snorted and we all set out. I had Guthrie again. Silent, as usual.

It was a funny sort of day. The wind had died away but there was no relief. Everything felt close and airless. Sounds seemed muffled and distorted. I hoped for a breeze off the sea later. Even the hot winds would be preferable to this stifling heat.

My God, there'd been a hot time in the old town last night! Never mind the Greeks – Troy already looked as if an invading army had put it to the sword. People lay in shady corners, white-faced, their garments stained with unspeakableness. A naked man sprawled face-down in a pool of something. The smoke from neglected cooking fires drifted across litter-laden streets. Hardly anyone was around. Some poor sods – slaves, probably – were out in the hot sun, drawing water. They looked reasonably all right, as slaves go. They probably hadn't been partaking of last night's tainted meat. From somewhere nearby, I could hear the sound of vomiting. And then another, even more unpleasant sound. Someone groaned and cursed.

A few guards stood on the walls, leaning heavily on their spears. The one I passed had his eyes closed. Fat lot of good he was going to be, asleep in the hot sun.

And it was hot. It was very hot indeed, especially since we weren't yet much past mid-morning. I felt the perspiration roll down my back. Even Guthrie, normally as cool as they come, had sweat beading his brow. By unspoken consent, we moved into the shade of a high wall.

I stared out across the plain to the empty sea. A few people were out there, picking over the remains.

The city slowly woke up behind me. More people emerged on to the streets. There were tasks that must be performed – livestock to be fed, water to be drawn. The city trundled painfully back into life again.

The morning passed. I listened to the chatter in my ears – nothing out of the ordinary.

We moved slowly, following our patch of shade along the wall. We'd brought water, but limited ourselves to a sip every now and then. Because, when it was gone – it was gone. I wasn't going to risk any Trojan water.

I was about to suggest finding somewhere cool for a spot of lunch around noon when I glanced at Guthrie. He was very pale. A bead of sweat ran down his cheekbone.

In sudden concern I said, 'Major, are you all right?'

He pulled himself together with an effort that was painful to watch.

'Yes. Yes, I'm fine.'

He swayed and even more colour drained from his face.

'Ian, you're ill.'

'No, I can't be. I haven't eaten or drunk anything that someone else hasn't had. And I don't feel sick – I just feel – strange.'

He looked strange, too. A kind of otherworld look about him, as if he wasn't quite here.

'Can you hear that?'

'What?'

'We need to get off the walls.'

'Why?'

161

'Don't know.'

He wasn't looking at me. He stared blindly at his feet and spoke very quietly through clenched teeth.

'Off the walls. Now.'

I didn't argue. I'd known him too long. I guided him to the staircase and we stumbled down to street level. I tried to get him into the shade, wondering if he had sunstroke, but he insisted on standing in the wide space by the fish market and I couldn't budge him.

It really was no day to be standing in the hot sun. And it was so, so hot. My tunic was drenched. My eyes stung with salty sweat.

He caught my arm. Hard. I could feel his fingers digging into my flesh.

'Tell them, Max. Stand in open ground. Get away from the buildings. Get them away from the buildings.'

I'd heard of this before, but not really believed it.

I opened my com. 'This is Maxwell. Code Red. Code Red. Code Red. Get away from any buildings. Find an open space and stay there. Immediate action. Now. Maxwell out.'

Dogs began to howl across the city. First one, then another, took it up. I looked round, but could see no cause. A flock of shrieking birds shot high into the air, wheeled once and disappeared.

I stared around. Ian was holding his head. A tiny, stifled groan escaped him.

The silence was deafening.

The weight of the heat was unbearable.

The world held its breath.

The gods were poised.

162

And then, from deep, deep beneath my feet, I heard a dreadful sound. Like a bellowing bull.

Poseidon, the Earth-Shaker had awoken.

Oh God, I knew what this was.

This was not my first earthquake.

I just had time to shout, 'Earthquake. Everyone get down,' when the earth moved. And for all the wrong reasons.

Just a small shudder initially, and I thought this might not be too bad after all, and then the ground began to shake, harder and harder, increasing in volume and strength.

I crouched and struggled to keep my balance. The noise was tremendous. The earth groaned and then groaned again. Around me I could hear crashing pots, breaking crockery, then louder crashes and bangs as items of furniture moved or fell over. As the tremors got stronger and louder, the buildings started to fall. Small mudbrick huts went first, collapsing in a cloud of dust and then the bigger buildings started to go, just dropping in on themselves with a roar of collapsing stones.

As suddenly as it started – it stopped.

There was a moment's breathless silence.

And then the screaming began.

I picked myself up off the ground and crossed to Guthrie. He, like me, was covered in brick dust.

I pulled him to his feet. 'Are you hurt?'

'No. Are you?' The old Ian was back.

'No.' Although my little heart was pounding away nineteen to the dozen. We tend to take solid ground for granted and it's a bit disconcerting when suddenly it isn't so solid any more.

He wiped his face, which did absolutely no good at all and looked around.

'Bloody hell, that was a big one.'

He was right. Buildings or parts of buildings lay in heaps of rubble. Trees leaned at crazy angles. A huge split zig-zagged across the square, missing us by only a few feet.

'Ian, did you know that was going to happen?'

'No. I just knew something wasn't right. The pressure in my head … I couldn't see. Couldn't hear anything except the noise. It's gone now.'

I'd heard of this. Some people are sensitive to thunder storms so I suppose there's no reason why others shouldn't be sensitive to earthquakes. Theseus of Athens, son of Poseidon himself, was able to foretell earthquakes. And I had heard tales from America – before the borders closed, obviously – of people who claimed to be able to do the same thing. Mind you, that same person also told me that over there they actually pick up the ball and run with it when playing football, and how believable is that?

I stood quietly, brushing the dust from my clothes, waiting for him to collect the reports. He finished, closed down his com and nodded. 'No major casualties.'

The sun beat down upon us. I looked up at the sky, washed of all colour by the oppressive heat.

People were emerging from buildings around us, cut, bruised, dazed, dragging out their children, their family treasures, or whatever they happened to have in their hands at the time. Their faces reflected shock and bewilderment and then, as they saw the devastation to

164

their city, outright fear. Uncomprehending children wailed for their parents. Women screamed. Men shouted, clawing vainly at the rubble.

I stared. Every instinct is to help. But what could I do? Guthrie solved the problem for me. Seizing my arm, he pulled me across the square.

'Come away, Max.'

Years ago, I'd been in a wartime hospital in France when it caught fire. I still remember the panic and confusion as helpless people staggered from the smoke and flames out into the thick mud, only to run in hopeless circles, endangering themselves and others. This was no different. I'd tried to help on that occasion – I should do so again.

'Ian …'

But he was ruthless. I was dragged away. He was right. I had a duty to my own people first, but to run past helpless and broken people – children – when they called out to us as we passed …

Somehow, we got back to the pods.

Leon came forward. He broke our self-imposed rule and gently rubbed my arm. 'Everything all right?'

I nodded and did a head-count. Everyone was present and nearly correct, which, with St Mary's, is about the best you can ever hope for. Markham had a field dressing on the side of his head. It looked as if he'd been caught by falling masonry, although knowing him, he might well have been bitten by another irate goose.

We called it quits for the day.

The aftershocks continued throughout the night, varying in strength and duration. We sat outside in the breathlessly hot night, pod doors open, in case we needed to make a quick exit and listened to the sounds of terror in the already stricken city. In the distance, we could hear furious waves thundering down upon the shore.

No one got any sleep and about an hour before dawn we went out again.

I was in constant contact with Van Owen, who had taken a team into the city. There had been damage throughout, she reported, but the buildings in the citadel, although more tightly crammed together, were better constructed and had suffered less damage.

Guthrie and I had returned to the pods around mid-morning to pick up new disks when it happened again.

Guthrie, who had been perfectly normal up to that moment, suddenly clutched his head and groaned.

I just had time to shout a warning when the big one struck. And this time it was a big one and it did not stop. The ground trembled and jerked. The earth groaned in pain. We were all thrown to the ground. Inside the pods, I could hear equipment falling out of the lockers.

These things usually only last a few seconds –

although it often seems much longer.

Not this time. The ground heaved violently. On the other side of the olive grove, I could hear buildings coming down.

Terrible noises came from the city. Screaming people. Terrified livestock. The seemingly never-ending crash of collapsing buildings as the topless towers of Ilium swayed and fell. And then, over everything, an almighty rumbling that swelled in intensity until we couldn't hear ourselves shout.

Already on the ground anyway, I curled into a ball, protected my head, and, like everyone else in Troy, endured as best I could. This was how I always imagined the end of the world.

The earth gave one last shudder and was still.

No one moved. I could still hear things clattering to the ground around us. And then – if you discounted all the screaming – everything was quiet …

I uncurled and brushed dust, dirt, and debris from my tunic.

People nearby were pulling themselves and each other to their feet. Injuries were miraculously few. Schiller had sprained a wrist as she fell. Markham now had several new cuts and bruises to add to his almost permanent collection.

I coughed and spat dust.

'Chief, please run a full check on all the pods.'

He nodded, rubbed dust, and God knows what from his hair and stepped into Number Three.

'Miss Van Owen, How are things with you?'

'Astonishingly, we're fine. A bit dusty and knocked

about, but yes, we're OK.' She moved on to matters we both considered much more important. 'Max, you've got to get up here. It's gone. Completely gone.'

'What has? What's gone?'

'The Scaean Gate. It's completely demolished. And its fall has brought down the sections of wall on either side. There's nothing left but rubble. There's massive damage to the upper city too – the western part of the palace has collapsed. The statue of Athena has fallen. The big tower is down and it's damaged the cistern. There's water everywhere. Fires are breaking out all over. You have to get more people up here now. Just a minute. What?'

I could hear shouted voices in the background.

'Say that again. What? Oh, my God!'

'What?' I shouted, very nearly beside myself. 'What's happening? Report.'

'Max, there are ships approaching. Hundreds of them. It's the Black Ships. The Greeks are coming back.'

Of course they would. The probably turned back yesterday, after the first earthquake. With the possibility of tidal waves, they would seek a safe harbour and this was the nearest.

'How long?'

'Before they get here? Maybe half an hour or a little longer. They're riding the waves and the wind is behind them.'

'Your priority is keeping your people safe,' I said. 'But I want as much of this as possible.'

'You've got it,' she said, calmly and closed the link.

I deployed everyone. Leon to stay with the pods. Schiller, bandaged but functioning, Guthrie, and Peterson

169

to the Scaean Gate to cover the Greek landing. Markham, Prentiss, and me to the citadel.

'We have less than thirty minutes. As soon as the Greeks land – get back to your pods. That goes for historians, too. I don't care if you discover that Agamemnon was a woman and Helen has been shacked up with Odysseus these last ten years. As soon as the first Greek sets foot on Trojan soil – you move. Understood?'

They nodded and we scattered.

Leon caught my tunic as I passed. 'For God's sake, be careful.'

A bit like telling water to flow uphill, but I nodded anyway. I was in such a hurry that I don't think I even took the trouble to look at him properly.

The trumpets sounded as we set off. First one, then others took up the call.

All over the city, they were calling out the men to fight. Any man. Every man.

I saw young boys with swords as big as they were. Everyone had a cudgel of some kind. Women snatched up their children and locked them in cellars or hid them in outhouses, standing guard outside with hastily snatched up household implements.

All of Troy was arming itself. To defend themselves and their homes. It wouldn't do them the slightest bit of good.

My heart bled for them. A ten-year war. Sickness. Earthquake. Devastation. And now they were defenceless and the Greeks were back. Truly, the gods had deserted them this day.

This would not be the glorious victory or heroic defeat

of legend. This would be a slaughter. Too weak to resist, taken unawares, feeble with hunger and sickness, they stood no chance at all. It was as if all the Horsemen of the Apocalypse had gathered here today in this one spot, to oversee the razing of that most powerful of cities – Troy.

We pushed our way through the crowds of screaming people. Many buildings were still upright or partially so, but the street patterns had disappeared under the rubble.

We scrambled over the wreckage of people's lives.

The Dardanian Gate was unguarded. Soldiers had more important things to do. We entered the citadel, where the panic was no less widespread than in the lower part of the city.

Men ran past on their way to what was left of the walls. Fires bloomed everywhere. Ash and dust floated on the wind.

Markham insisted we stay together, arguing he wasn't Solomon's baby and couldn't cut himself in half. A small corner of my mind registered that our Mr Markham was not only extremely good at his job but also considerably more intelligent than he would have us believe.

We filmed the broken buildings, especially the Temple of Athena, now badly damaged, with one side completely cracked away and leaning dangerously. Somewhere in there, if legends were true – and after the last few days, who could say what was true and was not? – Kassandra and other noble Trojan women and priestesses would seek sanctuary. That would not end well.

We filmed as much as we could, with Markham chivvying us along like an anxious sheepdog. I could hear

Prentiss dictating into her recorder. We found a gap in the buildings and climbed over tumbled stones to try to get a view of what was happening on the plain.

Van Owen was right. The Greeks were back; flying on the crests of powerful waves crashing on to the shore. A thick, black wall of ships, hundreds of them, were followed by hundreds more. Their sails billowed fatly in the same stiff wind that flung dust and ash in our faces.

Prentiss recorded the ships. I filmed the ruined city. Markham, ignoring historical accuracy in the way that only the security section can, clutched a stun gun in one hand and a thick wooden staff in the other and shifted anxiously from foot to foot.

'Max …'

'Yes. We're finished. Come on.'

I don't know how it happened.

Prentiss slipped.

Her foot skidded sideways. She gave a cry of pain and fell heavily and awkwardly, dropping her recorder.

Markham was there in an instant.

'Can you get up?'

'Yes, of course. Aaaah! No.'

'Let me lift you.'

'It's not that – my foot's stuck.'

Markham handed me his gun and I kept watch although no one was taking any notice of us. They were all far too busy trying to get themselves to safety.

He crouched awkwardly and investigated.

'Does it hurt?'

'No. It's just wedged in there.'

In there was a gap between two white limestone blocks

that had once been part of a grand house to the south of the palace.

He wiggled her leg.

'How's that?'

'No bloody good at all.'

'Can you get your sandal off?'

'No.'

'Well try, will you? I really don't want to have to amputate your foot. I haven't had breakfast yet.'

I stood up and looked out to sea. The ships were very close now.

'Guys …'

'Hold on,' said Markham, wedged the end of his staff under the smaller rock and heaved. Good old Archimedes and his lever.

The rock shirted an infinitesimal inch and then settled back again.

The ships were almost within touching distance of the beach. The noise in the city grew to a roar. Many people were scrambling over the rubble of the walls and streaming across the plain in a vain effort to escape the oncoming invaders.

I said to Markham, 'Try again. I think we nearly had it that time.'

Prentiss said, 'Go. Both of you. I'm stuck. You'll never get me out in time. Better only one dead than three.'

'Shut up,' said Markham. 'Only those who don't actually have their foot in a hole are entitled to a vote.'

He shoved his staff in again, spat on his hands, and heaved. There wasn't very much of him, so I joined in. The rock lifted again.

'A bit more,' shouted Prentiss. 'Nearly.'

Markham grunted with the effort.

Away to my right, the first Greeks, desperate to reach land had driven their boats far up on to the beach and were leaping onto the sand.

That they had no clue what had happened to the city in their absence was clear from their demeanour. They hadn't returned to attack. They had sought only a refuge from the Earth-Shaker.

Now, looking around them at the fallen walls, the shattered city, and its disorganised populace, they could hardly believe their luck. They had been prepared to establish and defend a disputed beachhead. It could never have entered their wildest dreams that the city would drop into their laps this way.

All might not have been lost for the Trojans. The Greeks were as confused and bewildered by events as they were. If they could have mustered a force and got down to the old Greek ditch, and held firm, they could still have pushed the Greeks back into the sea.

But they were sick, shocked, injured, and disorganised and they were lost. I don't know where their generals were. Hector was dead, Priam taking refuge somewhere, and Aeneas would soon be on his way out of the city to Carthage. They never stood a chance.

I heard one voice, bellowing orders like a bull. That would be the High King, Agamemnon, directing the attack. Trumpets sounded, and with a mighty roar, the whole Greek army swept up the beach towards the fallen gate, hacking down everything in their path.

People screamed and fled back into the city.

'Come on,' said Markham. 'We've got to do this.'

We heaved again. The block shifted again.

'Yes,' shouted Prentiss.

I seized her under her arms and pulled. Markham let out a hoarse cry. 'Hurry. Can't hold … much … longer.'

'Nearly there.'

'Nggaahh! It's slipping. Get her out. Get her out.'

I heaved. Prentiss braced herself against the rock with her free leg and pushed.

'Bloody get her out, will you?' cried Markham. 'I want to have kids some day.'

I pulled so hard we both fell over backwards. Markham let the stone drop and stood panting.

I said, 'So, to sum up. One historian with a damaged foot and one security guard with a hernia. Could be worse.'

She grabbed her recorder and we ran. We had to move fast. The pods were at the other end of the city. We stared in dismay at the lower part of the town.

'You should have left me,' said Prentiss, angrily.

'Fine,' said Markham. 'Do you want us to put you back?'

We needed to get away as quickly as possible. From up here on the citadel, we had an excellent view of the Greeks, streaming across the plain and heading straight for the Scaean Gate. Or rather, where the gate used to be.

The Trojans had rallied. They were weak, but they weren't giving up. Everyone had seized a weapon. A small group of soldiers held the gate with reinforcements moving in.

'We'll go out through the Dardanian,' said Markham,

175

pushing us both along. 'We'll make our way along the east wall and then cut across to the pods. If they can hold the gate for ten minutes or so, we'll have a chance. Move.'

We clattered along the streets, pushing our way through hysterical people running away from the fighting. I don't know where they thought they were going to go.

The ground was rough with tumbled buildings to scramble over or try to get around. Fires bloomed with orange flames and I could hear the crackle of burning all around us. Acrid smoke caught in my throat and stung my eyes. All the time, I was listening for the sound of approaching soldiers. For how long could the Trojans hold the pile of rubble that used to be the Scaean Gate?

Not long was the answer to that one. We all knew how this was going to end. But maybe they could hold it long enough for us to get away.

A group of men, clutching shields and swords but with no time to don armour, raced past us, shouting to one another. Whether they dislodged something, I don't know. The already leaning building to my left leaned even further. The front portico crumbled. Markham seized Prentiss and pulled her one way. I jumped the other. The building collapsed in a welter of stone and timbers and dust.

Coughing, I became aware of Markham shouting. 'Max? Can you hear me?'

'Yes,' I said, brushing off loose pieces of stone and picking myself up.

'Where are you?'

On the other side of the house. I'm fine. Nothing broken.'

'I'm coming to get you.'

'No! Stay back. None of this lot is very stable. You go on. I'll work my way around to the next street and catch you up.'

'Max …'

'That's an order, Mr Markham. Go.'

They went.

I shook out my stole – one of the most redundant things I've ever done – and looked for a way out. Squeezing between two wooden beams that held up a second floor, I found myself in a room open to the sky. The walls had sagged, but the door lintel was intact and, being very careful not to dislodge anything, I eased my way through and into what I thought might have been a small porch. Pillars lay criss-crossed on the ground. Looking around I could see lots of sky – it was simply a case of wriggling out through the most stable-looking gap. I looked up. There was an awful lot of house still to come down on me if I was too hasty.

For God's sake – there were fifty thousand murdering Greek soldiers on their way here and it really didn't matter whether I died under a pile of rubble or at the end of someone's spear, did it?

I threw myself at the largest gap I could see and wriggled. Sharp edges dug into my ribs. I cut and scraped my hands, trying to pull myself through. My tunic was caught on something. No time to fiddle about. I yanked. Somewhere behind me, I heard the ominous clatter of falling stones.

177

I had nothing to lose. I heaved myself forward – much too hard – and tumbled, head-first down a pile of rocks to land, sprawling, on a comparatively rock-free pavement.

I raised my head and looked around. The Temple of Athena stood opposite, still with one crazily leaning wall, although the wooden vestibule and main part of the building still seemed intact.

In the other direction was the Dardanian Gate and even as I looked the first Greeks piled through, weapons drawn, ready for anything.

I hoped the god of historians had seen Markham and Prentiss safely down into the lower city. They would stand a better chance there.

I pulled myself up and, keeping as much as I could to the shadows, flitted across to the Temple. The wooden front was still intact. The doors stood open.

I slipped inside.

I took a moment to adjust my eyes to the cool, dim, silent interior. Glancing behind me, I could see soldiers fanning out across the square. They would be here in seconds, eager to plunder.

And to rape.

I remembered, too late, the fate of Kassandra and possibly all the other women taking refuge here in the temple. This was not the place to be.

Far too late.

They were already clattering up the steps.

I edged along the wall to a far corner, sliding my feet silently across the smooth marble floor, crouched, and pulled my stole around me. Perhaps – just perhaps – they would take the treasure and the highborn Trojan women and leave a poor slave in peace.

I really was kidding myself.

Now, they were through the door.

If the legends were true then the first one in – the leader – was Ajax of Locris – Little Ajax. Although if he was little then God knows how big the other one, Big Ajax, could be.

They piled in. And stopped.

Now that my eyes had adjusted, I could see more clearly.

The statue of Pallas Athena stood at the far end, bathed in a shaft of dusty sunshine. Not the big public statue, destroyed in the earthquake. This was a smaller, more intimate representation of the dual nature of the goddess, with a lance in her right hand and a distaff and spindle in her left. The statue was surrounded by broken lamps, hastily reassembled and lit. Pools of oil and shattered earthenware lay on the floor where they had fallen in the earthquake. Apart from the pool of flickering light around Athena, the rest of the room lay in deep shadow.

There are many contradictory stories about what happened next.

Some say Kassandra was torn from the Palladium itself, the symbol of Troy's indestructibility, but I can say now that that ancient statue was not there. Maybe had never been there, since the current statue looked as if it had been in place some considerable time. The Palladium, if the legends are true – and why wouldn't they be? – was even now being smuggled out of Troy by Aeneas, to make its way, eventually, to Rome. And maybe ... maybe ... if other legends are true – and why wouldn't they be? –

from there to Britain. Taken to Britain by Brutus, his descendent, who gave his name to the island. Maybe, deep down, we're all Troy's children.

This is what actually happened.

Kassandra and her women are clustered at the foot of the statue. Great Athena stares unblinkingly over their heads.

More Greek soldiers clatter into the temple, into this inner room, this domos. Their echoes reverberate off the marble, but no matter how much noise they are making as they enter, they fall silent in the presence of the goddess.

Nothing happens for a long time. From where they stand, they cannot see me. But they can see Kassandra and the other women. They can see the statue and the temple treasures. They can see what they have come for.

Only the presence of the goddess holds them back.

What will they do?

One woman steps forward. From her air of authority, I would say this might be Theano, priestess of Athena and daughter of a king. She is royal in her own right. Years ago, she and her husband, Antenor, spoke out against the war.

She speaks now and her voice, trained for ritual and ceremony, carries effortlessly around the big space.

No one moves.

She speaks again. She gestures at Kassandra who stands like the goddess herself, brilliant red hair blazing in the lamplight. For the first time, I see her face clearly. She is indeed beautiful, but it is an intense, a heart-breaking beauty. I once stood close to Mary Stuart and she too had that same air of tragic destiny.

Kassandra lifts her chin defiantly at their scrutiny but does not, even for one second, let go of Athena's foot.

For that is the law. The law of sanctuary. And it applies to everyone. From the lowest slave in the land to the king himself. So long as she can touch the goddess, Kassandra is under her protection. That is the law.

Except today. There is no law today. Today, many things will change for ever.

There is still silence in the great Temple. Finally, Ajax jerks his head. I know Theano is spared. Legend tells us that she and her husband sail away with Aeneas and the Palladium.

Not everyone is so lucky. At this moment, Priam is being hacked to pieces in the Temple of Zeus. The baby, Astyanax, is being torn from his mother and hurled from the walls. Hector is already dead. I had no knowledge of the fate of Paris.

But Theano is spared.

Not so Kassandra.

She watches the other women trail from the Temple. Only Theano looks back and then she too is gone. From Troy and History.

Kassandra is alone.

I know what will happen now. As does she. As does everyone here. I wish there was something I could do. But I can't. I can't do anything. I don't even want to watch. I remember again that shared moment on the walls. When she looked at me.

Ajax walks slowly forward and speaks to her. Some sort of command.

She laughs at him. Defying him.

He cannot afford to lose face.

He steps forward again, knots his hand in her hair and pulls.

His men gasp.

Such sacrilege in the presence of the goddess.

She tightens her grip on the statue.

He pulls. Her head is wrenched back. I can see the tendons in her neck, but she will not let go.

He seizes her hair with his other hand as well. Now he pulls really hard. Her scalp tightens. Slowly, her left hand begins to slip. And then her right.

Still no word is spoken. The only sound is Ajax's harsh breathing. Both Kassandra's hands are slowly sliding off Athena's smooth feet.

And then ... then ... she turns her head the few inches she can manage and looks at me.

Straight at me.

Again.

Again, I can't look away. She speaks. In *English* ...

'*I see you,*
Golden-eyed girl.
Watcher of time's brave pageant.
Beloved of Kleio.
Weep for your dreams
For today they die.
Your heart will grow cold.
And as the leaves fall
The golden-eyed girl
Will leave this world.
Never to return.'

As she says the last words, her hands slide away and

she is no longer under the protection of the goddess.

Who does nothing to prevent this outrage. This sacrilege to her temple. Which is typical of any bloody god you care to name. It doesn't matter whether it's the small, local gods who live in the hollow tree outside your village: the ones who knew you, your mother, and your mother's mother back to the beginning of time. Or the big, male, sky gods with their intolerance and cruelty. All gods are the same. They're big on the worshipping and the ceremonies and the imposing buildings, but when you really need them – they're never there.

Athena certainly wasn't. All right, she later drove Ajax mad for his desecration, but where was she when Kassandra needed her? Where was Apollo, who loved her? Where were any of them?

I crouched in my dark corner as Kassandra's words reverberated around my head. Her curse was that no one ever believed her. But I believed her. Today, she finally had a believer. She would go on to foresee both her own death and that of Agamemnon – and still no one would ever believe her. Only me.

Ajax dragged her outside. Even he wasn't prepared to go that far inside a temple. Her screams went on for a very long time.

His men started to strip the temple.

I was undecided. Stay or go?

No one had seen me yet. Maybe they would miss me completely.

A small man with bad skin and reeking of onions and goats found me. He wandered over to take a leak and tripped over me.

Thanks again, Athena.

I was very careful to make no trouble. Not to resist. Not to give them any excuse. Our instructions are always very clear. Keep quiet. Keep your head down and your mouth shut and wait to be rescued.

They shoved us outside, along with the other temple goods and a few other women, all as dishevelled and coved in brick dust as I was.

Kassandra, naked, was being pulled across the square towards the gate. Greedy Agamemnon would claim her for himself. It would be his undoing.

In my ear, Markham said, 'Max? What's happening?'

I carefully reached up and tapped my ear. A sign I couldn't talk.

'Are you in trouble?'

Tap.

'OK. Hang on. We'll get you.'

The soldiers lined us up, clearly making their choice. Ajax however, despite having had his, was in no mood for anyone else to get theirs and shouted irritably at them. An angry, red scratch showed on one cheek and he kept touching it. He couldn't leave it alone. He looked unsettled and angry. What had Kassandra said to him? Or had the seeds of his madness had already been sewn?

I heard Guthrie's voice in my ear. 'Are you still in the citadel?'

Tap.

'Just keep your head down, Max. Do not get into any trouble. We'll get you. Just stay safe. I mean it. You've got form.'

The temple goods were piled in the courtyard, along

with other spoils looted from nearby buildings. Ajax cast it only a cursory glance and us women not at all. In fairness, we were a pretty ropey-looking lot – dishevelled, bloody, and so covered in dust it was practically impossible to tell we were women at all, let alone pick out the pretty ones.

Time passed. The heap of treasure grew larger – to Ajax's obvious satisfaction. More women were added to our group, which was good. Always try to get lost in the crowd. Some of them wrapped their arms around their bodies, rocking and keening.

With my own safety assured – at least for the time being – I turned my attention to the rest of my team. I tapped my ear again.

'Max? What's the problem? We're on our way.'

I hugged myself, rocked, and began to wail. 'Report.'

'Everyone is safe. We have casualties. Some serious but not life threatening. Three and Five have jumped with the wounded. Black is prepping Six. Markham, Ritter, and I are getting to you.'

'No. Bottleneck. They'll take us to the ships. Pick me up there.'

'Unacceptable.'

I knew what he meant. I might not make it to the ships.

'An order, Major.'

He paused, but I was right. It made no sense at all for them to fight their way up here, snatch me up and then fight their way back again to the pods. Let the Greeks get me down there and they could just grab me as I passed.

'Understood.'

*

185

We sat there all day in the hot sun. The occasional aftershock brought more walls down, but we were safe enough in the middle of the square. I hunched my shoulders and made sure I stayed behind everyone else. At first, I tried to watch what was going on around me. I even considered activating my little recorder, but that was just asking for trouble. I stowed it carefully away in my hidden pocket because the last thing I wanted was for some future archaeologist to dig up a three and a half thousand-year-old, state of the art, digital 3D recorder with my initials illegally scratched on the bottom.

As I say, at first I tried to watch, but as the hours passed the sights and sounds of so many people dying were just too much. The old, the sick, the wounded, anyone they didn't like the look of were just executed on the spot. A quick spear thrust, and down they went into the blood-soaked dust. The streets echoed to the screams of the terrified and the dying.

I did as the other women did. I drew my stole across my face and apparently gave myself up to despair.

They moved us as the afternoon thought about becoming evening. The stifling heat had not let up for one second. I was parched, and, when the moment came, not at all sure I could get my stiff legs to work.

A couple of pokes with the butt end of a spear convinced me that I could.

I said softly, 'We're on the move.'

A voice said, 'We're ready.'

And off we went.

The trouble began at what was left of the Dardanian Gate.

I was at the rear and couldn't see clearly, but, as we approached the gate, the leading women suddenly broke their silence and set up a keening wail that lifted the hairs on my arms. Other women took up the cry. I craned my neck to see what was going on.

Our guards, obviously anticipating difficulties, waded in, using their spear butts to prod and club us onwards, shouting all the time.

It was no use. Our ragged line shambled to a halt. Wailing women tore their garments and scratched their faces.

Spread-eagled against the gate hung the naked body of Paris. They'd hacked off his genitals. He had been impaled by over thirty arrows, including one through each eye. They'd used him as target practice. Judging by the fly-infested pools of blood at his feet, he'd taken a long time to die.

Not a warrior's death.

Bastards.

One woman broke ranks and ran to dip her stole into his blood. For a moment, it looked as if our little procession would end in chaos. Other women surged forwards, too. Ajax barked an order and they were cut down without mercy. They lay like broken dolls, their blood hideously red against the grey dust.

We huddled together in shock. The girl next to me was trembling violently. She was only very young. Her dust-covered hair hung around her face and her huge dark eyes were jerking wildly. Her breath came in short, sharp pants. Any minute now she would succumb to hysterics. Others would follow suit and then we'd all be in trouble.

I took her hand and pinched the webbing between her thumb and first finger. She jerked violently, caught her breath in a kind of gasp, and then, to my relief, the tears started to fall. She pulled her stole across her face and turned away.

I never saw her again. I sometimes wonder what became of her.

We edged our way past the bodies, out through the gate and along the main street, heading towards the gap in the walls.

I've never seen a city die before. I never want to again.

The lower town was almost gone. Fires still burned and we coughed our way through the smoke. Half-burned bodies sprawled everywhere. One woman hung out of a window, her upper torso completely untouched and her legs burned away to the bone. I remembered women locking their children in outhouses or cellars and wondered how they had fared. Dead and dismembered soldiers lay everywhere. I could smell the metallic stench of blood. We climbed over bodies. I could hear buzzing flies. Away off to my left a woman screamed repeatedly. I kept my eyes forward, watching where I put my feet. What I had to stand in.

The smoke made us cough. The air was thick with ash and dust which settled in the folds of our clothes and coated our hair. I had no spit with which to swallow and the taste in my mouth was of burning metal. Everyone, everything, was coated in thick layers of grey grime.

Apart from other lines of women and children, I saw no other living person anywhere in the lower city. I began to fear for my team. All around me, the other women were crying and wailing. I used the noise.

'Major?'

'Max, we can't see you. You all look the same.'

He was right. Apart from bloodstains, there was no colour in our clothes. Everyone was covered in dust. Even our hair was grey. Our faces were thick with it. I could see the tear tracks on the faces of those around me.

'Where are you, Major?'

'I'm at the Scaean Gate. Ritter's out on the plain and Markham's down by the South Gate.

'I'm at the Scaean now.'

And at that moment, my luck ran out, because the same runty little soldier who found me in the first place took exception to my murmurings and hit me hard with his spear butt, right across the face.

I thought I'd gone blind. I definitely thought my nose was broken. I staggered sideways and would have fallen, but the two women on either side grabbed me and held me upright. I guessed that if you couldn't walk then you were dead.

I tried not to panic. This was Ian Guthrie. He would find me. I was tagged – we all were – and if he could get close enough then they could trace me, whether I could see or not. So despite everything I felt reasonably optimistic, until I staggered out on to the plain and as my sight cleared, I saw, for the first time, the scale of Troy's defeat. There were thousands and thousands of people, women mostly, sitting, lying, standing in shuffling lines … thousands and thousands of them.

How would they ever find me?

I could feel my eye swelling and my nose felt like a football. If I ever got my hands on that little runt ... although actually he'd done me a favour because now I could bunch my stole and use it to mop up my nose and cover my mouth at the same time.

'Leaving gate. Moving west. About 30 women. Three guards.'

We trudged on a little further. The two women with me wouldn't let go and I didn't push it. I was familiar with this. In a crisis, help someone else. It's a kind of defence mechanism for the mind. Something else to think about. I patted their hands to thank them.

We halted at the top of the beach. Our guards leaned on their spears and picked their noses. Occasionally, one shouted to another. This was the dangerous time. No supervision from higher up and they would soon get bored. They would want a little fun.

'Max, sit down.'

I sat.

A pause.

'Stand up again.'

I stood, looking around me.

'Now sit.'

I sat, but I'd attracted attention. Little runty man lifted his spear, but before he could get to me, we were on the move again.

Now they meant business. We formed a line. Around me, passive despair was giving way to desperation as women fought for their children, their babies, their freedom. It was suicide, but that didn't stop them. Many preferred to die here on the beach, outside their own city rather than be taken away by the Greeks. More soldiers piled in, punching and kicking and, in extreme cases, despatching the troublemakers without a second thought. The sand was stained with blood.

It was hot and they were impatient and thirsty. Occasionally, someone would be singled out as an example to the others ...

Our own line shunted slowly forwards. Towards what, I couldn't see. But I had only seconds. If they didn't find me soon ... once I was on a ship ... if I got that far. Not everyone made the cut. Where was St Mary's? The two women in front of me were yanked away.

I stared blearily at a pair of dirty feet in scabby sandals. Someone hauled me to my feet. Not gently. A hand grasped my chin and turned my head this way and that, looking, inspecting. I was turned around. Someone's hands were all over me, assessing my worth.

A voice said, 'It's me.'

I couldn't see much, but I knew that voice.

'This will hurt. I'm sorry,' said Guthrie. 'Go limp.'

He slapped my face – which began to throb all over again. I had no difficulty going limp and he heaved me over his shoulder like a sack of coal. Shouts of advice and encouragement followed us off the beach.

'Report,' I said, from upside-down, arms dangling.

'Van Owen's team has jumped. Markham and Ritter returned with them. All personnel correct and accounted for. Number Eight with Peterson is still here. Waiting for you and me.'

He stopped talking.

Leon wouldn't go without me. Something was wrong.

'And Chief Farrell?'

'Will probably be waiting for us when we get back.'

I said no more. He had other things on his mind. Like getting us through a burning city filled with drunken, violent soldiers exacting revenge for a ten-year siege.

It wasn't easy. Every other Greek soldier, laden with looted gear, was heading for the shore. He shoved and cursed his way through the crowds like a salmon swimming upstream. A group of men caught his arm and voices were raised.

He slapped my rump and replied in purest Caledonian. Everyone laughed. Except me.

I hung as limply as I could, trying to look unattractive so they wouldn't want their turn too, and obviously I was successful because after one last laugh, they went on their way.

The gate was just a pile of rubble and twisted timbers. Guthrie clambered awkwardly over the wreckage. I lifted my head and watched, covering our retreat. Smoke drifted across the rubble and caught in my throat.

Hanging upside down made my head throb unbearably. His armour dug into my rib cage. I could barely breathe. My eye had closed and ribbons of blood

193

and snot hung from my nose, mingling with my hair. However, I was alive and, if not safe, at least I was safer than I'd been ten minutes ago.

He found a sheltered corner away from the shouting and lowered me to the ground. I sat with my eyes closed as he carefully cleared my nose and wiped my face with more gentle care than I would have expected.

'I don't think your nose is broken, but you already have a world-class black eye. Can you see? How many fingers am I holding up?'

'Seventy-three.'

'Close enough. Does it hurt?'

'A little. My face feels as if it's going to explode.' I could be the first woman in History to be killed by her own nose.

'It'll be quicker if I carry you. But painful.'

'Whatever it takes, Major.'

The streets were unrecognisable from the Troy I had known. Bodies sprawled everywhere like broken puppets. None of them had died easily. Many had been trampled, either by incoming Greeks or by fleeing townspeople.

A little pink hand lay in the gutter.

I could see orange flames everywhere and caught the smell of burning meat on the wind.

The streets were thick with the detritus of war. Household goods, dead livestock, shattered roof tiles, and discarded weapons. I could see arrows lodged in the walls, broken javelins, smashed pottery, dead people – everything here was either broken or useless. Or dead. Anything with value was on the beach, waiting to be shipped.

194

Far-off voices rose occasionally in anger, or song, or fear, but Guthrie guided us surely through the smouldering remains of Troy.

Navigating the open spaces was nerve-wracking. Anyone could put an arrow through us.

'Put me down. We can run faster.'

'Not likely. Having you draped all over me is better than a shield.'

Our neighbours' little group of houses were well ablaze. I could see two charred bodies in the doorway. I remember thinking how loud the crackling sounded in the evening air. The shop had been looted. A few broken pots lay on the ground, but everything else was gone.

And the tavern – the little tavern where Helios and Helike had lived …

Guthrie lowered me to the ground and we looked on.

'I hope you're getting all this,' he said harshly and turned away.

Pieces of people lay everywhere. Except for Helike. They'd kept her intact.

We heard a shout behind us. Two Greeks appeared around the corner, each clutching a wineskin and prepared to defend their territory against all comers. Their eyes lit up when they saw me.

Guthrie indicated that he would be delighted to share his prize in return for a drink and pushed me towards them.

I took the one on the left. Guthrie dropped his in seconds and then zapped mine for good measure. We're not allowed to kill people. It's never a good idea to start decimating your ancestors.

'Come on,' he said, seizing my arm and we threaded our way through the smoky olive grove. The heat was fearsome and the fumes made my eyes run. We turned constantly, trying to cover all the angles, but there was no one else around. Rural areas aren't anything like as exciting to plunder as urban ones. You can't uproot olive trees and take them back with you.

Number Eight was intact. After what I'd put it through over the years, it was going to take more than a few flames and rioting soldiers to cause it any concern. The door slid open and Peterson covered our approach.

Now that I was safe, I couldn't wait to get inside and busy myself. The last thing I wanted to do was think about that beach and what was happening there. And what would have been happening to me if not for Guthrie.

I said, 'Thank you, Ian,' and touched his forearm.

He pulled off his looted helmet and breastplate and dropped them on the ground with a clatter. His face was smoky and sweat-streaked.

'An honour and a privilege, Max.'

I grinned at him. 'Worst helmet-hair ever,' and he thumped me on the shoulder.

Peterson checked us both over. 'No foreign objects.'

We entered the pod.

No Chief Farrell.

I passed Guthrie some water, had a good glug myself and said to Peterson, 'Report.'

'Everyone got away safely. Just waiting on the Chief and then we're off, too.'

'Where did he go?'

He shifted uneasily. He didn't know.

196

What the bloody hell did Leon think he was playing at?

I opened the locker doors and peered at the cubes, sticks, tapes, disks, written notes, maps and in my own case, sketchpads. Every single, priceless little fact we'd been able to gather about the Trojan War. Enough data to keep Dr Dowson happy for years and years to come.

I gave myself a second to feel the satisfaction of a job well done. But only one second.

'In case we have to, can we go at a moment's notice?'

'Yes. FOD and POD plods done.' The words, 'Just waiting for Chief Farrell, who has suddenly and inexplicably disappeared,' were not spoken.

I felt a sudden cold hand on me and heard again Kassandra's words.

'Weep for your dreams,
For today they die.'

This was the end. Our last assignment. I was safe. Where was he? Was it all going to be snatched away at the very last moment?

'Here he is,' said Guthrie suddenly. Huge relief washed over me like a wave. The door opened.

It was Leon and he wasn't alone.

Clamped to the front of him, like a tiny, terrified monkey clinging to its mother, was young Helios. His eyes were screwed tight shut and black blood crusted the side of his face.

The door closed behind them and for a while there was no sound but Leon's heavy breathing.

'Weep for your dreams.
For today they die.'

I think I knew, at that moment, how this was going to end.

I said, tightly, 'Report.'

He caught his breath and then said, 'They're all dead over there. I couldn't save his sister but I managed to get Helios out.'

He stroked his hair and went to put him down, but the little lad clung on even more tightly.

Peterson and Guthrie stood like statues.

I knew how this was going to end, but I tried anyway.

'Guthrie and I came that way and it's all clear now. You can let him go.'

'Are you mad? He wouldn't last an hour.'

I was conscious of something building inside me.

Fear. Because he wanted to lift Helios out of his own time. Not just save his life and then leave him to take his chances – we'd done that before and got away with it. Or rather, History had allowed us to get away with it. But this – this was deliberately taking someone out of their time – which was bad enough – and then what? Drop him in another time? In another life? Or bring him back twenty years hence? To pick up where he left off? What did he think he was playing at? The consequences to the timeline ... History would not permit this and she wouldn't mess about. Her solution would be swift – and final.

And anger. How could he do this? How could he put me in this position? How dared he make me the one who had to condemn this little boy to death? And I would. Make no mistake about it. I would. I wouldn't like it, but if I had to, I would do it.

And a terrible grief. For everything I had just lost and for what I was about to lose. I was going to lose it all.

The long silence had given him my answer.

'Max, you can't. You're condemning him to death. Or worse. You can't just abandon him. You've saved people before.'

No. I'd picked people up off the ground and given them the chance to die another day. In their own time and in their own place. This was not the same thing at all. This was so wrong. Every little bit of historian inside me was shouting – screaming – a warning. They say women don't know how to say no. In fact, men have been saying that for centuries. That when women say no, they mean yes. Well I've got news for you, busters …

'No.'

No more. No less. No explanations. No reasons. No excuses. Just say: 'no'.

'He won't last the night. You're sending him to his death. If he's lucky. Look at him. He's not old enough to be a slave. They'll take him on a boat, use him on the voyage home, and then toss him overboard as they make land. That's what you're condemning him to.'

'No.'

Guthrie picked up his weapon, and he and Peterson left the pod. They were giving me the opportunity to sort this out before it went too far. They didn't want to be involved and I didn't blame them. I didn't want to be involved. How could he do this?

'Max, I'm begging you. Even if he survives tonight, Troy isn't going to be safe for years. Do you know what life here is going to be like?'

Of course I did.

'No.'

Helios, still too terrified to know what was happening, tried to bury his head in Farrell's shoulder. Farrell gently rubbed his back.

'Max, I've never asked you for anything, but I am now. I just want to find him somewhere safe.'

There was nowhere safe for Helios. And if I didn't stop this, there would be nowhere safe for any of us.

'No.'

His voice cracked in desperation. 'I'm begging you. Please. Just save this one person. Just save Helios.'

'No.'

The finality in my voice must have got through to him. He tightened his grip and planted his feet. The challenge was unspoken, but it was there.

'I'm second in charge at St Mary's. I can order you …'

And I was mission controller.

I crossed to a locker, pulled out a handgun, and slapped home a clip.

'Open the door, Chief, and put him outside.'

'You …' he stared. Shock, betrayal and hurt all chased each other across his face. 'I can't believe you would …'

I raised the gun.

'Open the door, Chief, and put him outside. Do it now, please.'

'So that's it, is it? It's all right when you pick soldiers out of the mud or a woodcutter out of the snow? But for everyone else …?'

I said nothing. I wouldn't debate this.

'You … bitch.'

Yes, Leon, that's what you've made me. And this is what I'll do to keep all of us from catastrophe. And I couldn't expect Guthrie and Peterson to stay outside for ever. If I didn't end this now, then Guthrie would.

Or History.

'You heartless, hypocritical bitch! I can't believe … you'd leave this boy to die. This is Helios, for God's sake. You gave him chocolate. You played hopscotch with him. You have a chance to save him and you're telling me to just turn him out? Out there? Do you actually know what's happening out there? Or are you so caught up in History and yourself that you're too stupid to notice? Well, I'm not you, thank God. I won't do it. Shoot me if you dare.'

'I'm not going to shoot you, Chief Farrell. I'm going to shoot him.'

I levelled the gun at Helios.

'Or you can open the door and put him outside to take his chances. They're better than if you try to keep him in here.'

He didn't move. He didn't believe me and it was vital that he did.

I clicked off the safety. Would I do it? Would I kill a child? Most importantly, would he believe it? He must. It was our only way out of this.

I hated him for what he was making me do.

The silence dragged on and on. Finally, he turned his head and said, 'Door.'

Only then did I realise I'd been holding my breath.

Without looking at me, he said, 'Twenty minutes.'

'Agreed.'

Then he was gone.

Peterson and Guthrie re-entered the pod. Guthrie raised his eyebrows when he saw the gun but said nothing. I made it safe and put it back.

Tim checked over the console. I washed my face and hands, dabbed at my nose again with shaking hands, tried to tidy my hair, and straightened my clothing. I'm an historian and we never go back looking scruffy.

Without seeming to, I watched the clock, wondering what the hell I would do if he wasn't back within twenty minutes.

But he was.

Guthrie said, 'Here he comes,' and as he spoke the door opened and Farrell tumbled in.

I wasn't the only one staring at him in shock. He looked exhausted and even through his two-day stubble his cheeks were grey and hollow.

Without looking at anyone, he took himself off to a corner and sank to the floor.

I said, 'Whenever you're ready, Tim.'

'Jump initiated.'

And the world went white.

That night, I partied harder than I ever had in my entire life.

I drank. I ate. I drank. I danced. I drank.

Markham and I participated in the infamous tray race and nearly broke our necks.

My attempt to drink a yard of ale nearly drowned Miss Prentiss.

Kal and I sang "Blow the Man Down" in a way that

gave sea-shanties a bad name.

I caught Guthrie or Peterson looking at me occasionally, so I smiled, waved, and partied even harder. I knew that if I never spoke of it then they wouldn't either. I'd lifted the incriminating tape from the pod's internal security system and destroyed it. If Guthrie noticed the gap, he never said anything.

No one ever knew what Leon Farrell had tried to do. I didn't write him up. That was the most I was prepared to do for him.

We never spoke directly to each other again in this life. We communicated through com links or third parties. I avoided him if I could. I never forgave him.

Whenever he looked at me, his eyes were ice-blue and empty. He never forgave me.

We never left St Mary's. Our new life together died, stillborn.

I should have been devastated but I wasn't. I was buoyed up on a wave of righteous anger. That he, of all people, could have tried to do such a thing was almost past belief. And so I took my rage and my fury and I nursed them. I could never forgive the man who had forced me to choose between him and my job. Because, in the end, with my back to the wall, I had chosen my job – as, I think, we both always knew that I would.

Of course, that wasn't the end of the story of Troy. Legend tells us that the cause of all the trouble, Helen, returned to Sparta with her husband and, typically, the pair of them lived happily ever after, while for everyone else the bloody aftermath rumbled on for decades.

Odysseus struggled to get home for twenty years. Kassandra and Agamemnon would both be murdered by his wife, Klytemnestra. Him in his bath, naked and vulnerable; and her, stabbed in Agamemnon's bed-chamber as she quietly awaited her self-predicted fate.

We left Odysseus and his problems for another time and another jump. That would be a major assignment in its own right, but both Kal and I jumped to Agamemnon's palace at Mycenae because we wanted to see the end of Kassandra's story.

We went as bath slaves. We landed well ahead of the actual event, slipping into the deep shadows and spending hours waiting, unmoving and silent. We witnessed what we had come to see and slipped away in all the confusion and upheaval that follows a mighty king's murder.

Troy was the end of many things and the beginning of others.

For everyone in that part of the world, after Troy, nothing was ever the same again.

Or for me at St Mary's, either.

It was a measure of our growing independence and prestige that, for this presentation, Thirsk came to us.

We wined and dined them and then sat them down in the Hall. I gave my usual introduction, outlined the mission parameters, and described the methodology. The streamers came on-line and suddenly we were there – on that small hill outside Troy, panning across the fertile plain that was as familiar to me as yesterday.

I felt my heart contract and, under the guise of watching the holo, moved back into the shadows.

We took them through the city, showing brief glimpses of daily life. Not too much – we didn't want them descending into vigorous academic debate – or screaming and hair-pulling as lesser mortals might call it – before we'd finished.

We gave them shots of the upper and lower city – a brief look at the royal family – a very brief glimpse of Achilles and Hector as they faced off for their fatal confrontation – a fabulous shot of the Black Ships piling up on the beach and finally, a far-off shot of the devastated city burning – all black smoke and ash and the long lines of people on the beach.

They were speechless. We had to show it twice and even then they wanted more.

Afterwards, the Chancellor asked me if I would publish. 'The ending of the war. The Trojan Horses. You should publish.'

I shook my head. I'd left it a little late to start publishing now. I could imagine the reaction to my paper. I'd rocked enough boats in my time. Leave the world its stories.

I shook my head.

'Publish or perish,' she reminded me.

For a member of St Mary's there are many more imaginative ways to perish than simply failing to publish regularly.

I thanked her and declined.

She regarded me over the rim of her glass.

'Could I interest you in joining us at Thirsk?'

I paused, my own glass halfway to my lips. Could she? That was a thought. A very flattering thought. After all, I had been prepared to leave St Mary's. Mentally, I'd already made the jump. Now I was being offered somewhere to jump to.

A new beginning. In new surroundings. Somewhere I wouldn't remember, every day, how Chief Farrell had poisoned the Troy assignment for me.

I could see Kal regularly. And Peterson and Dieter when they visited.

I could cut my bloody hair.

She was watching me carefully. 'Think about it,' she said, and walked away to re-join Dr Bairstow.

Actually, I did. I thought about it a lot.

The next evening there was a knock at my door. I'd been dozing in front of the TV. I shambled over in sweats and with my face imprinted by the pattern of the cushion. One day I'll be sophisticated. I opened the door to see the Boss standing there. I woke up in a hurry.

'Dr Maxwell, may I come in?'

'Of course, sir.'

At least I didn't have to rush around tidying up. I learned at a very young age not to leave any trace of my passing. The bed was made and everything tidy.

He sat on the saggy couch.

'An excellent presentation, Dr Maxwell. Please pass on my thanks and congratulations to everyone involved.'

I said, 'Thank you, sir,' and waited for the real reason for his visit.

'Am I going to lose you?'

I decided to be honest. 'I don't know, sir.'

He nodded. 'The Chancellor, in what she imagines is a gesture of courtesy, has informed me she is doing her best to poach a leading member of my staff. Tell me, Max, if you do leave, would you be running from – or running to?'

'That's a very good question, sir. I don't know. To tell you the truth, I don't like myself very much at the moment.'

'Do you think that by removing yourself from St Mary's you can escape this self-dislike?'

'Well, a change is as good as a rest, they say. I don't know. I'm sorry, sir, these days, I don't know what I do want.'

He got up to go. 'While you're thinking about it, may I offer a word of advice?'

'Yes, sir.'

'Paint. I remember a young historian returning from WWI, some years ago now, a little younger and lot less wise than she is today. She resolved her own unsettled thoughts by dragging them out into the open air, plastering them across the walls in Sick Bay, and daring anyone to object. I rather liked that young historian and I wouldn't like to think she's gone for good.'

I swallowed hard. 'Yes, sir.'

'I'd like you to clear away the Troy material as soon as possible, Dr Maxwell. I have a new assignment lined up for you.'

'Yes, sir.'

He paused at the door. 'That's three consecutive *yes sirs*, Dr Maxwell. Your docility is unnerving. Kindly desist.'

'Yes, sir.'

I brooded for a day or so. As Dr Bairstow had said, once, long ago, I'd come back from the Somme with a head full of images that wouldn't give me peace. This was very similar. I had to get this down somehow. If I ever wanted peace of mind, I had to get this down. I planned two pictures, the first showing Agamemnon, dead in his bath, and the second, the death of Kassandra.

Once started, as usual, I couldn't stop. I painted it all.

The hollow, wet slap of water echoing around the bath chamber. The jerking, jumping light from the flickering lamps reflected in the restless water and bouncing back on the walls and the ceiling. Puddles of water everywhere. The sweet smell of oils and perfumes. Agamemnon's naked body rocking gently in the choppy water. Squat and blocky, criss-crossed with scars, with gaping wounds that trailed separate scarlet ribbons across the turquoise water.

And standing above it all, tall and straight, wet hair hanging, her sodden clothing clinging to her body, heavy but strong, cold-eyed and implacable, another Lady Macbeth, two thousand years ahead of her time. Her blood-red shadow fell across the body of her husband like a curse.

Even while I was getting that scene down, I was thinking of the next. The other half of the story. This murder would be different. The first showed the accomplished deed, the second would show the other murder as it actually happened.

I wanted to show the contrast between the two women. Kassandra the girl, tall willowy, ethereal, other worldly, powerless now, and Klytemnestra the matron, the queen, heavy with childbearing, supplanted, past her best and dangerous because of it.

Kassandra in robes of turquoise, the same colour as the water in Agamemnon's bath, red hair exploding around her head, Medusa like; and Klytemnestra in royal purple, her fading hair escaping its intricate knot. Both women's faces are inches apart, eyes locked in hatred, jaws tense, each knowing the other for what she is, and it is only as you look down that you see she has plunged the dagger deep under Kassandra's breast, up into her heart. Kassandra is already dead but these two will remain locked in hatred until the end of time. Shadows from every corner reach across the room and every single one is pointed at Klytemnestra.

I did paint both pictures – and I finished them. I don't often paint people but this went like a dream. They were big too. Peterson had to stretch the canvas for me. I left them propped up against the wall and wondered what to do with them, and after a week or so they were just part of the furniture until Dr Dowson approached me one day and asked if I would be prepared to let him have them for the Archive. I watched them go with no emotion as they disappeared with the rest of the Troy material.

And I still couldn't make a decision.

People think we historians are stuck in the past and have no idea what's actually going on around us. That's not true. Sometimes we're very aware of what's going on around us. Sometimes we even participate.

We were attending another all-staff briefing from Dr Bairstow and he really wasn't happy at all.

'Good morning, everyone.

'I'll put all this in simple terms for the hard of understanding. As those of you who take the trouble to keep abreast of current events will be aware, the latest attempt by the government to implement a form of poll tax to pay for their current crop of stupidities has been meeting with the same levels of success as those achieved in 1381 and 1990. There is countrywide unrest and, even in Rushford, I understand a politely worded letter of protest was delivered to the council yesterday. I personally become very depressed by mankind's inability to learn from its mistakes. However, any of you thinking of venturing out into the world this weekend should be aware of current events.

'Please also be aware that your contracts specifically require political neutrality, so if any of you were thinking

211

of indulging in matters riotous, you will be in breach of contract and liable to disciplinary proceedings. Since none of you ever have, or ever will, pay one single penny in poll tax or its equivalent, I will be particularly unsympathetic to anyone attempting to emulate the exploits of Messrs Tyler, Ball, and Straw. I trust I have made myself clear on this matter.'

Disappointed, his unit nodded.

'Dr Maxwell, may I see you in my office at your earliest convenience, please.'

Shit! How does he know these things? He couldn't possibly know that Peterson, Markham, and I, full of civic indignation, were off to add to the turmoil in Rushford at close of play today. Markham even had our banners ready. The polite NON AD CAPITAGIUM (No to the poll tax), the hopeful MAGIS STIPENDIUM HISTORICI (More money for historians) and the always accurate POLICITI NOSTRAE OMNEC WANKERS SUNT (Most politicians are not very good).

We suspected he'd obtained the wording from an online translation site. No one had the heart to tell him.

Mrs Partridge was tight-lipped.

'He's already had telephone calls from Thirsk, the bank, and the Chief Constable this morning. Please try not to irritate him, Dr Maxwell.'

'Of course not, Mrs Partridge.'

Fat chance.

'Good morning, sir. Are we staring at bankruptcy again?'

'It's never that bad, Dr Maxwell. There are always areas where – adjustments – can be made.'

212

I made haste to distract him before he thought about adjusting me.

'What happened about The Play, sir? I thought we were going to be rich for ever.'

Some five hundred years ago, Dr Bairstow had commissioned a play from the man himself, Bill the Bard, concerning the life of Mary Stuart and buried it at St Mary's for us to find and become financially independent. This inspired plan had fallen at the first fence when Professor Rapson, sneaking a quick preview, discovered that in this version, the sixteenth century had executed Elizabeth Tudor instead. We'd had to nip back and sort it all out. That part of the mission had been extremely successful. Sadly, the part where we were supposed to bring back that murdering bastard Clive Ronan had gone less well. He'd given us the slip. Again. He always got away. But one day …

However, back to the present. Dr Bairstow hadn't finished.

'And then, of course, our collection of sonnets, the incalculably priceless sonnets revealing the identity of the Dark Lady, were somehow – given away, Dr Maxwell.'

Now that was a little unfair. I'd offered them to a future, damaged St Mary's whose need was far greater than ours. And he'd reburied the sonnets himself for them to discover in the future. How was I to blame?

'In some nebulous manner which I cannot be bothered to explain, Dr Maxwell, I hold you completely responsible for our current predicament. However, I am giving you the chance to redeem yourself.'

He surely didn't expect me to nip into the future and

ask for them back?

He handed me a file.

'The Gates of Grief.'

I know this sounds like one of those violent computer games to which the security and technical sections are always challenging each other down in Hawking, but the Gates of Grief is actually the narrow stretch of water in the Red Sea, where the Horn of Africa nearly touches the Yemen, and, according to the latest research, it's the place where our ancestors made their second and only successful crossing out of Africa, to spread across the rest of the world.

I stared at him. Even after all these years, he still had the power to surprise me.

'But sir … How …' and then remembered he wasn't in the best mood and was unlikely to appreciate a member of his senior staff bleating at him like a confused sheep.

He raised a discouraging eyebrow but I battled on anyway.

'Establishing the coordinates will be nearly impossible, sir. Estimates vary between 130,000 and 60,000 years ago and …'

'You've been back further than that, Dr Maxwell.'

'Yes, but that wasn't event-specific, sir. That was just bimbling around in the Cretaceous. The Gates of Grief is just one tiny event in a vast ocean of time and without …'

'Not a tiny event, Dr Maxwell. One of the most important events in the development of the human race.'

'Agreed, sir. But the point I am trying to make is that without specific coordinates …'

He handed me a piece of paper. 'Specific coordinates.'

I stared at it. If Dr Bairstow said these were the coordinates, then they were. I wasn't going to argue.

'How …?'

'I want a mission plan by this time tomorrow. You may select your own team.'

I drew breath to speak again but I was obviously destined not to complete a sentence this morning. Without knowing quite how it happened, I was on the other side of the door and Mrs Partridge was regarding me with her habitual look of mingled exasperation and suspicion.

I had the freedom to select my own team. I stood in the gallery and looked down at the history department, milling noisily around the Hall, swilling tea and arguing. Some of them were still pretty battered after Troy. Schiller and Van Owen were worn out. Prentiss still limped. Roberts and Morgan were on light duties.

I went to see Peterson.

'Have you got any fully functioning Pathfinders?'

'Nope. They're all still hobbling, bruised, bandaged, and/or knackered.'

'That's what I thought. Is it me or do young people today have no stamina?'

'Says the woman whose black eye actually encompassed her ear as well.'

'What about you?'

He was instantly suspicious. 'What about me?'

'I've got a jump. Want to come?'

'Why me?'

'Last time I left you in charge, my department went blue.'

'Oh, we're not back to that again, are we? You must

215

learn to let go, Max.'

'OK, if you're not interested …'

'I didn't say that.'

I waited.

'All right. What is it?'

'The Gates of Grief.'

'That sounds cheerful. What particular disaster are you leading me into now?'

'The second and only successful migration out of Africa. Sunny climate. Beach views. No crowds. Simple observation. No interaction of any kind. Anything from two days to two months. Cheap holiday.'

'Sounds good, actually. Yes, sign me up. Anyone else?'

'No,' I said, maybe a little too quickly, but he said nothing.

'When?'

'Day after tomorrow?'

'Fine.'

We met outside my pod, Number Eight, two days later. Peterson surveyed it critically.

'I can't believe this old heap is still working.'

'It'll hold together long enough for you to bump us clear across the Yemen and into the Red Sea.'

'Says the person responsible for turning her pod into a fireball.'

'Are you ready?' enquired Dieter. 'Or shall we all go and sit down while the two of you thrash out which of you is the worst driver? Trust me – there's nothing to choose between you.'

Having effortlessly offended both of us, he

disappeared into the pod. We followed him in. Peterson ran through the pre-flight checks. I stowed our gear.

Two minutes later, the world went white.

We landed on the eastern side of the strait on a wide plain – part sand, part coarse grass. To the west, an island-dotted sea reflected a deep blue sky. It's only when you jump back to a time before the industrial age and air travel that you realise how dirty our world has become. In the distance, the coarse sea grass gave way to low, undulating, green hills. A soft breeze blew. Waves lapped gently.

'Well, this is nice,' said Peterson, lugging out the cam net. 'Give us a hand.'

We spent the next hour setting up camp. A cam net stretched over the pod rendered us not invisible, but certainly inconspicuous. And gave us some much-needed shade. There wasn't a tree in sight. We set up a campfire, made a brew, and settled down to wait.

And wait.

And wait.

We were still waiting two weeks later.

Tim had a glorious tan. I had a peeling nose. We'd practised our swimming, read a few books, explored the coastline, written our logs, and just generally loafed around. Just like being on holiday. We had provisions for three months. We could afford to wait. It did cross my mind that Dr Bairstow had sent us here to get us out of the way for some reason. When I mentioned this to Peterson, he laughed and accused me of paranoia. Which is ridiculous because of course I know the whole world isn't really out to get me. I'm pretty sure Switzerland is neutral.

Another week passed, but life was pleasant so I didn't care. The sun was hot but the breezes were cool. Sea levels were a good one hundred and fifty feet lower than today and a series of humps and small islands stretched across the Red Sea like a herd of Loch Ness monsters.

'Shouldn't be too difficult,' said Peterson, following my gaze. 'Presumably they just island hop.'

I nodded. He was right. From here, it looked easy. Even from the other shore, they would be able to see across the straits to the low, green hills of the Yemen. They had something to aim for. They weren't just blindly setting out into the unknown.

As living conditions became harsher in Africa, small groups of people set off to make new lives for themselves. Initially, they had travelled north and settled in the Levant. And eventually died out. That line failed. As the Sahara grew even harsher, people began to look east for a way out. Which would bring them here – to the Gates of Grief. To perhaps one of the most important events in all the long story of mankind. Because DNA evidence is quite clear. There was only ever one successful migration out of Africa and every one of us – every single person outside of Africa – is descended from one of the people who made that one crossing. Estimates put the number at around two hundred to two hundred and fifty people. That's how closely we're all related. Something we should remember sometimes.

And we were here to witness that single, successful crossing.

We hoped.

We rarely took our eyes off the shoreline, waiting to see the people – our ancestors – emerging from the sea. If everything went well for them, it could all be over in minutes – they'd be off and away and we'd have missed it. Time ticked by.

We didn't bother guarding our campsite. Old habits die hard and it took some getting used to, but the fact remained. There were no modern humans anywhere outside of Africa. Which was, of course, the whole point of our being here.

Sometimes, however, especially at night, with this huge emptiness all around us, stretching out in every direction, the thought was just a little overwhelming.

Just after we'd cleared away our midday meal one day, Tim was tightening the cam net when he looked across the water and said urgently, 'Max. They're here. They're coming.'

And they were.

I jumped to my feet. Far out in the water, I could see bobbing dots. A lot of bobbing dots. They were here.

We grabbed our kit and settled in our carefully chosen site. Somewhere we could see them and they couldn't see us.

Tim was correct. They were island hopping. We set up the recorders and got stuck in.

'Look at that,' said Tim, softly. 'Who says our ancestors weren't bright?'

He was right. They were wonderfully well organised. A series of rafts were strung together, piled high with bundles and carrying what looked like the old and the very young. I've heard it said that you can judge a civilisation by the treatment of its old people. In an age where people were a scarce resource, every person was valued. There were not so many people in the world that they could be careless with each other.

The more able-bodied – women as well as men, ranged up and down the rafts, checking, pushing, pulling, encouraging.

Some carried long staffs, not to punt, as we initially thought, but over the deep places one person would extend their staff horizontally, someone would grasp the other end and the shorter people and those who couldn't swim would work their way, in perfect safety, hand over hand, from one staff to the next.

Some half dozen men led from the front, poking with their staffs, finding the way.

'Pathfinders,' said Peterson, smugly.

Some people carried tiny children on their shoulders and all the time they shouted to each other. They had language. They shouted instructions, advice, and encouragement. They urged each other on. No one was forgotten.

Occasionally, someone clung to a raft, either guiding it or having a rest.

They were swimming one minute, then they were splashing through shallow water. Then back to swimming again as they hopped from island to tiny island.

But the longest and most difficult stretch was the final stage. The last tiny piece of land was some way from the eastern shore. And the currents ran swift here. And they would be tired.

Their leaders struggled to keep their feet, gave it up,

and began to swim, dog-style, heads held high out of the water. And then, even as we watched, they weren't swimming – they were floundering. Two or three lost their staffs, which were immediately whirled away from them. People shouted from the rafts. Some tried to stand up and the rafts wobbled. Packs fell over the side and floated away. More people shouted. Someone made a grab for one and fell overboard. Someone else screamed. The men at the front, who should have had all their attention on finding their way forward, looked back. Another of them was whirled away by the current.

The line of rafts began to separate. Either because the lines had snapped or they were being cut so that if one sank, it wouldn't take the others with it.

Men and women shouted incomprehensibly. Panic was beginning to spread. The convoy was breaking up. One raft began to float away. There were children on it …

They still had some way to go to shore. They weren't going to make it. This crossing was going to be as unsuccessful as all the others.

I felt a kind of despair. They'd come so far. They'd so nearly made it. They deserved to make it. Surely we could do something. We had ropes. We could help.

I scrambled to my feet in the sand.

Peterson pulled me back down again.

'Where do you think you're going?'

'Rope. We can help.'

'No, we can't.'

'Tim, for God's sake …'

'No, you can't, Max. Not this time.'

'They're not going to make it. We must do something.

This is one of the most significant events in human History.'

'And that's why we can't interfere. Not this time. Don't you see? It's far too important. If we interfere we're changing all of human History.'

I struggled against him.

'Stop it,' he said sharply. 'I'm not letting go and you'll just hurt yourself.'

'Tim, these people are dying.'

'Then they're meant to. You know that. You're an historian, Max. You've got away with a lot in the past and you probably will again in the future. But not today.'

'Let me go, Mr Peterson. Now.'

'No,' he said, simply.

'I'm ordering you ...'

'No.'

'Tim ...'

'I'm not doing it, Max, so give it up.'

I was still struggling. We were kicking sand everywhere but he held me in a grip of iron. I had no idea he was so strong.

'They're dying out there. '

'And we'll be dying here if I let you go.'

'They're our ancestors. They're us. What is the matter with you?'

'Do you think I'm happy about this? But someone always has to keep their head. It was you at Troy. Today, here and now, it's me. You can't do this, Max. You can't wipe Chief Farrell out of your life for what he did at Troy and then turn round and do exactly the same thing yourself.'

'It's not the same thing.'

'It's exactly the same thing. I won't let you do it. Now stop struggling. I'm warning you, I'll write you up and that would finish both of us.'

He stopped and took a deep breath. 'It's all in the lap of the gods, Max. As it should be.'

I was suddenly still. He was right. Reluctantly, I nodded and slowly, an inch at a time, he let me go.

I rolled away from him and busied myself with the equipment. Doing what I was here for. Watching people die. Raging silently at History. At injustice. At the futility of it all. For all the people everywhere who quietly and patiently build their lives, only to watch them being knocked down by war, famine, earthquake, or just plain bad luck. I was so finished with this bloody awful job. I would go to Thirsk, work in a clean office, participate in learned debate, and never, ever, have to stand helplessly by and see people die again.

I stared at the equipment so I didn't have to watch this tiny group of people whirling away, lost in the currents, disappearing one by one, as the waters closed over their heads. Children, old people, all of them.

But why had Dr Bairstow had given us these coordinates? Surely not to witness yet another failure in a long line of failures. And here was an interesting question. Was this the successful migration to which Dr Bairstow had given us the coordinates? Or was this the successful migration *because* Dr Bairstow had given us the coordinates?

Then, suddenly, maybe it wasn't going to be another failure.

'There,' said Tim, with sudden excitement. 'Further up. No, to your left.'

I looked.

One of the rafts, swirling wildly in the current, was within a few yards of the shore. The two adults aboard were standing and literally hurling small children into the water. As close to the shore as they could get them. Around them, their raft was breaking up. They had only seconds.

Tiny dark heads bobbed in the water, scrabbling, puppy-like in the surf. One went under. I didn't see him come up.

They were nearly there. They were so close. Only a few feet to go.

I could see their faces; watch their frantic struggles as they fought their way to land.

So tantalisingly close … Someone on the beach could just reach out a hand … They touched land, struggled to get out, and were pulled back into the surf again. They'd made it. They were here. They just lacked the strength for those last few feet and the waves wouldn't let go.

'Go,' said Tim and I went like the wind.

I raced into the surf, seized the first child I could see and pulled him out of the waves. Another appeared in front of me, head high in the water, kicking for all he was worth, his little face grim with fear and determination. I caught at his arm and held him safe while he found his feet and climbed out of the water.

Another, older child was about six feet away and she had hold of a bundle. A struggling bundle. She pushed it towards me. I let a wave carry it forward and deposit it on the beach. I swear, all I did was just nudge it with my foot as the next wave tried to pull it back again. That surely didn't count.

I picked up the crying bundle and handed it to one of the children. The older girl was clambering out of the sea, panting and exhausted. I waited until she was clear and then helped her to her feet. We both stared out to sea.

The two adults were clinging to the remains of the raft, which was being pulled back away from us.

What could I do? What could I possibly do?

The problem was solved for me. While I'd been busy here, the rest of the group had been struggling to land back along the beach. Some three or four people raced past me with their long staffs.

They were so organised. They had a plan. One stood up to his knees, and extended his staff. A second man took hold of that and extended his. A woman took his and extended hers. They were nearly there. A fourth man began to work his way along the line, calling to the people on the raft.

They were elderly. Maybe they wouldn't have the strength.

Strength or not, they could see that every moment was taking them further and further away from any chance of rescue. They kicked out for the shore as the last of the raft disintegrated. Hide-wrapped packs bobbed around them in the water.

Everyone got the same idea at once. The bundles floated! I had no idea what was in them, but they floated. Shouts rang out as everyone yelled the same thing in their own particular language.

'Grab a bundle and kick!'

They did.

The woman on the end was shouting and waving her staff. An elderly man, his white hair vivid against his dark skin, grabbed the end and began to work his way along. Hand over hand, just as they'd obviously practised. The other man was not so lucky. I caught one last glimpse of his terrified face as he went under, his arms raised high in the air.

Everyone wailed. Every person was important.

The woman on the end let go of her staff, struck out and seized his arm. Two men splashed past me and into the sea. One of them was Peterson.

An excellent swimmer, he reached them first, pulling the man to the surface, just holding him and the woman above the water, nothing more, until other rescuers arrived and they all struggled back as a group, helping each other before collapsing, exhausted onto the sand.

The old man's eyes were closed and it wasn't looking good. Peterson lay face down on the wet sand, shoulders heaving.

Everyone else was crowding around the old man and he wasn't moving.

In a bad situation, the secret is to make it worse. As far as History was concerned, we were dead men walking, anyway.

I moved a woman gently aside and went to look.

He was still alive. My relief was overwhelming. I pulled him carefully into the recovery position, feeling his birdlike bones under my hands, cleared his airway and just left him to rest. He had a pulse. He was breathing. He coughed up some seawater. And then some more.

I stepped back and looked up the beach. Everywhere, people were wading through the shallow waves. Many were collecting up bundles, staffs, everything that had been washed up with them. Nothing would be wasted.

They hadn't all made it. I could see bodies, face down, being swirled this way and that in the current as they were pulled away from land. Some of them were very small. But a good two hundred people had pulled themselves out of the sea and taken those first steps out of Africa.

Since we'd rather blown the concealment side of the assignment, we stepped back and both sides appraised the other.

They weren't tall, but they were upright, with the natural, graceful deportment that walking all day can bring. Nor were they skinny. They were lean and well-muscled. Men and women were similarly dressed in short hide loincloths with a kind of apron at the front. At this moment, their feet were covered in wet sand, but if their calloused hands were anything to go by, they would be covered in thick skin.

And their skin was beautiful. They were black but a black made up of many colours. I could see olive-green and purple shadows under their eyes and a glistening gold where the sun caught their cheekbones. They painted their bodies and although the sea had washed off most of them, I could see the remains of dots, squiggles, lines – complex patterns all carefully drawn in a thick, white pigment.

They adorned themselves with necklaces of shells and feathers. Nearly all the adults wore at least one strip of hide tied around their wrist. Many had several, and one, a large man, wore them nearly up to his elbow. A mark of status. Maybe he was their leader. Or the most successful hunter, with a strip of hide awarded for every kill.

Their closely curled hair was mostly dark, although many showed threads of white. They all, men and women, wore it piled up on their heads and held in place with what looked like thick mud, which even immersion in the Red Sea hadn't been able to shift. Eat your hearts out, L'Oreal. Some even had bedraggled feathers and braids still in place.

A number of dark, watchful eyes quite openly surveyed us, taking in our strange garments and our much less stylish hair. Not a few smiles flickered in amusement. I wondered what they were making of us.

Still, no one seemed particularly hostile. Curious, yes – I suspected natural good manners prevented them from touching us, exploring our strange hair and light-coloured skin – but not hostile. We'd helped them, after all.

I was wondering what would happen next when one of the old men and some of the children we'd fished out of the sea turned up. There was a great deal of communication and not all of it was language. After a while, I noticed certain sounds accompanied certain gestures. The position of the head seemed to be important. And only those actually speaking looked at each other. Everyone else respectfully dropped their eyes.

I was quite fascinated. These were our ancestors and they were as intelligent and articulate as we were ourselves. Although switching on the TV and catching a glimpse of the antics of our political, financial, and religious leaders would almost certainly revise my opinion. And not in our favour.

As the sun started to sink below the horizon, they busied themselves gathering their possessions together, lighting fires, and searching the waterline and rocks for seafood and fish. We dined well that night.

All down the beach, small fires blazed. Their only protection against the terrors of the night. Little circles of light to guard against what must sometimes seem to be overwhelming darkness.

Since, if you wanted to be accurate, we were the hosts, we felt we should bring something to the feast. Peterson disappeared back to the pod, returning a few minutes later with my entire chocolate supply, which he broke into tiny squares and distributed. They hesitated. Both Tim and I took a small piece each and ostentatiously put it in our mouths, chewed, swallowed, and smiled.

Heads swivelled towards an old woman, sitting quietly by the fire. She stared at it suspiciously. I suspect that small, brown objects closely resembling coprolite were not on the menu every night. Heaven knows what she would have made of fruit and nut.

Fascinated, we watched her examine the chocolate closely, turning it repeatedly in her hands, then she sniffed, apparently finding it harmless. Of course by now, in the warm night and so close to the fire, her little lump was getting soft. Slowly, she raised one smeared finger to her lips and tentatively licked it.

Everyone watched closely.

She made a small sound and licked another finger.

229

Surviving this, she popped the rapidly melting square into her mouth. We watched her face. As did everyone else. They had an official food taster. I'd heard of this. Encountering new plants and fruits every day, one member of the tribe took it upon herself (or himself) to taste leaves, seeds, berries, unknown fish, or animals, while everyone else watched to see if it was safe. She must be very good at her job to have lasted so long. A young girl sat beside her, watching her every move. I wondered if she was the apprentice.

Anyway, the chocolate passed muster and soon everyone was munching away. Sounds of enjoyment floated across the fire.

'Now you've done it,' I said to Peterson. 'It's you who's responsible for mankind's insatiable desire for the brown stuff.'

Our hair fascinated them. Even Peterson's, which, admittedly, looks like a badly made haystack on a windy day. I pulled out my hairpins and let it fall. Immediately, three or four women surrounded me and began to braid it.

Despite his protests, the same was happening to Peterson.

'Relax,' I said. 'Just go with the flow.'

And so we sat under the slowly darkening sky, listening to the waves wash the shore as our relations – and they were our relations; we were their children – laughed and chatted and arranged our hair into this season's fashionable look. It took a great deal of mud to keep mine piled on top of my head and the weight of it was astonishing.

'Never seen you look so tall,' said Tim, from the other

side of the fire.

While this was happening, all around us songs and chants drifted across from the other fires. They had a culture. Our own hosts joined in, clapping their hands and making odd clicking noises with their tongues. We did our best, but I'm tone deaf and Peterson has all the rhythm of a paralysed stoat. They laughed again, but it wasn't unkind laughter.

To show willing, Tim and I sang "Stairway to Heaven", the only song to which we both knew most of the words. They were very unimpressed, but very polite.

I tried to get their names. Several times I pointed to myself and said, 'Max,' and then, 'Tim.' They responded, but I couldn't make out what they were saying. Did they make names for themselves? Or did they just call each other *tall woman who hunted with me last year when we killed the antelope at the water's edge?*

But some things are universal. A sense of friendship. Of kindness. Of welcoming. You don't need words for any of that.

Stars came out and dotted the sky. I watched their faces in the flickering firelight. Large, clear eyes regarded their world without fear or hostility. Their faces were unlined and their smiles stretched from ear to ear.

I wanted to learn so much from them, but they were settling themselves down for the night and I could feel my own eyes growing heavy. Rather like my head. I looked forward to the next day and the chance to spend more time with them.

Completely ignoring rules and regs about returning to the pod, I made myself comfortable, spent a little while listening to the gentle rhythms of sea and speech around me, and then fell asleep.

I opened my eyes to an empty beach.

They'd gone. They'd left us.

The sun wasn't up and yet they'd gone.

We weren't anything like as important to them as they were to us. They'd risen, packed up their gear, and departed without even waking us. I struggled with the disappointment.

I stumbled to my feet and staggered a little, as my arms and legs sorted out which was which. Peterson stood at the top of a sand dune, staring into the far distance.

Shading my eyes, I could just make them out in the dawn mist. Walking into the future.

'Well,' said Peterson, quietly. 'There we go.'

'Do you think that's the group that makes it?'

'Yes, yes I do.'

I found I couldn't speak. I had a huge lump in my throat as we watched them walk off into what was yet to come for all of us. They'd split up into groups of fifteen or twenty, walking single-file down the beach. This group wouldn't go that far, but their children would go further and their children further still. Until one day …

We watched until the last figures disappeared into the haze. There we went, indeed. A young race, with its entire future ahead of it. I envied them. I wondered if they'd been as impressed with us as we'd been with them. Somehow, I doubted it. Not impressed enough to wake us before they left. For one last look at each other. I'd wanted so much to … and they'd just departed. Without even a farewell.

I was struggling not to cry.

Peterson turned away and walked back to the fire. Smoke drifted across the beach.

'Max. Come and look.'

Wiping my eyes, I scrambled down the dune.

'They've left us a gift. Look.'

They had. They'd left us one of their shell necklaces, carefully placed nearby on a flat rock and weighed down with a small stone so it wouldn't blow away.

My heart soared. They'd left us a gift. They hadn't just walked away after all.

I would have loved to take it back with me, but I couldn't. Peterson photographed it while I found three flat stones, placed one carefully on top of the other and laid the shell necklace on the top. A gift to the gods of this place with a request to keep them all safe.

Today, it's a hundred feet or so beneath the sea.

We stood for a while, each with our own thoughts, and then Peterson said, 'You and me. Are we all right?'

I nodded. 'Yes. At least, I hope we are. You were right to stop me. I nearly made a terrible mistake.' I stopped, swallowing hard.

He sighed. 'They didn't need us at all, did they? We're nowhere near as important as we think we are. A lesson we needed to learn, I think.'

'Well, I certainly did. I should say thank you.'

'No need.'

'Every need, I think, Tim.'

He smiled slightly. 'I wonder what they thought of us.'

'Not a lot, I suspect.'

I saw us through their eyes. Over-dressed. Over-fed. At odds with the world around us. Vain. Noisy. And that was just me …

How much less impressive than those quiet, assured people who fitted so perfectly into the world around them and who strode off into their unknowable future with less fuss and drama than most of us make just going to the shops.

I looked along the beach. Already the wind and sea were dispersing the ashes and blowing away the footprints. In less than a day there would be nothing to show they'd ever been here. That any of us had been here.

'Tim, I'm sorry.'

'Hey, I told you. No need to apologise.'

'Yes, there is.'

'It's OK. No harm done.'

'Thanks to you.'

I went to turn away but he pulled me back.

'Sit down a moment. I want to talk to you.'

We sat at the top of a low rise and I listened to the sounds of the sea.

'Are you leaving?'

'What?'

'Are you leaving St Mary's?'

'What makes you think that?'

'Well, I heard the Chancellor offer you a job and I know you're not very happy at the moment. Can I do anything?

'You just have.'

'I didn't do anything and you didn't answer the

234

question. Are you leaving?'

Was I? Was I really going to leave St Mary's?

'No, of course not. In what other job do you get to see the face of your ancestors? I couldn't do another job even if this one kills me. Which it probably will.'

He was silent for a while, poking the coarse sand with a stick.

'Glad you're staying.'

'Me too.'

He put his arm around me. First time ever.

We sat in silence while I had a bit of a think.

'Tim, did he do all this just to keep me here?'

'Dr Bairstow? Wouldn't be at all surprised.'

'Tim …'

'Yeah, I really wouldn't mention that to anyone, if I were you. Let's get our stuff. We should be getting back. Mission accomplished.'

'And we didn't really interfere that much.'

His face brightened.

'That's right. This time, we'll hardly have to fudge the report at all.'

Six months later, I was in my office getting ready for one of my favourite tasks. This was when I sorted out the assignments for the coming year.

Forget computers, data-stacks, and high-tech. The easiest way to plan for the coming year's assignments is to push the tables together in a U-shape, send your bitterly complaining assistant out for three rolls of lining paper, and get stuck in.

Miss Lee had marked off the centuries and I started laying things out.

Firstly, on pink sheets, there were the assignments from Thirsk. Since they paid our wages, they had priority.

Secondly, on green sheets, anything carried over from the current year. This didn't happen often, fortunately.

And thirdly, on blue sheets, suggestions and requests from people at St Mary's. And what a varied lot there were. Major Guthrie wanted Bannockburn. Again. He never seemed to realise he'd stand more chance if he selected a battle that England actually won. There was a request for The Great Exhibition at Crystal Palace. That would be from Kal, impervious to my argument that anything that recent was practically yesterday and didn't actually qualify as History at all.

I'd got as far as the Famous Assassinations assignment. This was one from Thirsk. In no particular order, we had Archduke Ferdinand at Sarajevo, whose death was a major cause of the First World War, Abraham Lincoln, and Julius Caesar. I rather fancied that last one for myself. One of the worst things about my job is that I don't get out and about in History as often as I used to. One of the best things about my job is that I can cherry-pick. I definitely fancied Caesar. I wondered if Peterson did as well. A nice little trip out for the pair of us.

There was a tap at the door and Markham and Roberts sidled through. Miss Lee, scenting entertainment, abandoned whatever task she was engaged upon, and I braced myself.

'You asked for suggestions,' said Markham, 'but we were out on assignment and missed the deadline. Is it too late?'

Technically, yes, but I couldn't be bothered to argue.

'Show me what you've come up with.'

Roberts stepped forwards. Smart, alert, and polite – I was instantly suspicious.

'Well, we thought we'd go for something a little different. You know, less battlefields and blood and more refinement and culture. So we've given the big boys a miss and put together three nice, quiet jumps that encapsulate the rich origins of –'

'Just get on with it,' I said.

'OK. Bohemia, 1265. Belgium, 1366 and Munich, 1385. As you can see, not the most obvious choices, but areas which, we feel, would benefit from a rigorous and thorough examination into the –'

I said, flatly, 'Bohemia, 1265. King Otakar sets up the new town of Budweis and grants them a license to brew. 1366, the Stella Artois brewery is founded, and 1383 is, I believe, a very important date for lovers of Lowenbrau everywhere.'

Markham stepped back in astonishment. 'Good gracious. What an extraordinary coincidence. I had no idea. Did you?'

Thus appealed to, the other musketeer shook his head and indicated his own surprise.

I tried hard not to laugh.

They regrouped.

'Well,' said Roberts, 'what about 1374 – the Dancing Mania of Aix la Chappelle?'

I was tempted. Who wouldn't be? A massive and widespread outbreak of spontaneous dancing. Probably caused by ergot poisoning, but nevertheless …

I looked at the two beaming, guileless faces in front of me and couldn't find it in my heart to reject them.

'Leave the details and I'll consider it.'

They scampered from the room.

I laid out the last sheets and stepped back, frowning. There were the usual clumps around Ancient Greece, Egypt, and Rome. Someone wanted the Battle of Hastings. That might be a good one – sort out the controversy over the arrow in the eye, once and for all.

There was another clump in the sixteenth century. The Tudors and Stuarts were always popular. I'd have to be careful whom I assigned. Schiller, Peterson, and I had already been there, sorting out Mary Stuart.

And I had various search and rescue operations to fit in around this lot. The Great Fire of London in 1666 and the destruction of St Paul's Cathedral. We would nip in, (well, I wouldn't – I was in Mauritius in 1666, but someone would), save what treasures we could find – and nip back out again. With luck before an entire cathedral fell down on top of us. If the god of historians was with us.

I was wandering around the tables, muttering and moving things around, when the phone rang. Without taking my eyes off twelfth-century France, I groped for the handset.

'Max?'

What did he want?

The line was terrible. He was obviously in Hawking and they were running some piece of equipment that made him sound as if he was on the other side of the universe.

'Chief Farrell?'

'Where are you?'

A burst of static hurt my ears.

'In my office.'

'You've forgotten, haven't you?'

'Apparently, yes.'

'Lunch?'

'What? What did you say? I can't hear you.'

'I'm waiting.'

The line went dead.

Well, that was odd.

I set off down the stairs, wondering what was going on. The Hall was deserted. Half a dozen historians had obviously decided to be somewhere else.

The dining-room was similarly deserted. Mrs Mack gave me a palms-up *where is everyone?* shrug and I responded with my palms-up *search me.*

A morning of oddities. We're St Mary's. It was lunchtime. I should be up to my withers in people clamouring for sustenance. It was Wednesday, too. Toad in the hole day.

The corridor to Hawking was deserted. I met no one. There should have been an advancing orange tsunami of famished technicians who hadn't touched food for anything up to forty-five minutes. And yet, nothing.

I let myself quietly through the hangar doors and knew at once that something was wrong.

Silence.

Complete silence.

Hawking was never quiet. There was always the hum of electronic equipment, techies shouting to each other across the vast space, the tinkle of dropped tools, and, over everything, a tinny radio playing housewives' favourites.

There was none of that. Just sound-sucking, heavy silence.

At least I'd found everyone. What seemed like the entire unit was standing around in twos and threes, all facing towards Number Eight.

No one spoke.

Without thinking, I let the door slip from my grasp and it banged behind me.

Heads turned.

Someone said, 'Here she is now.'

Peterson weaved his way through the crowd.

He stood directly in front of me, masking whatever it was from my sight. And me from them.

His eyes were red and wet. He said, very gently, 'Chin up, Max.'

I nodded.

He took my hand and threaded it through his arm.

We walked slowly towards Number Eight.

People fell back on either side.

No one spoke.

I saw Dieter sitting on the Number Seven plinth.

He was crying. Dieter was crying. His face was red and blotchy.

Polly Perkins had her hand on his shoulder. She was crying too.

I stepped carefully up onto Number Eight plinth.

Peterson ushered me into the pod.

Dr Bairstow stood in the back corner, his hands crossed on his stick.

I couldn't see his face.

Helen was kneeling on the floor, packing up her kit.

My world did not end. It exploded. Exploded soundlessly into a million tiny fragments, spinning silently through space. And I suddenly realised I didn't hate him. Had never hated him. And that it was now far, far too late.

He lay on his back, arms outflung. I could see his tool roll nearby. The console panel was off, exposing the innards.

Helen finished stowing her kit and began to speak. I heard only the words 'sudden,' and 'massive'.

242

After she had finished speaking, the silence dragged on.

I felt nothing.

Dr Bairstow lifted his head.

I couldn't look at his face.

'I know that you and he were not ... but I thought, perhaps, you might like a moment ...'

How does he know these things?

They left, taking Peterson with them. I was alone. In every sense of the word.

Stiffly, I knelt beside him.

His eyes were closed. He looked asleep.

I took his hands and gently placed them on his chest. For the first time in living memory his hands were colder than mine.

I straightened his clothes and smoothed his hair.

I leaned forward and laid my head on his chest. There was no strong, steady heartbeat.

I don't know for how long I sat beside him, holding his hand while he made his final journey. While he finally went somewhere I couldn't follow. To some place from which I couldn't bring him back.

Time disappeared.

Either a few minutes or a hundred years later, Tim touched my shoulder.

'We have to let him go now, Max.'

Maybe he was expecting me to protest.

I said nothing.

He helped me to my feet.

They'd cleared the hangar.

Helen and her team waited at one end.

Tim took me through the doors.

I turned towards my office, but he stopped me. 'Not today.'

He took me upstairs to my room.

I said my first words in this new life without Leon.

'I'm fine, Tim.'

'If you could see what I could see, you wouldn't say that.'

The tea tasted odd. Very odd.

I closed my eyes.

I could see nothing.

I slept.

I did not dream.

Whenever it was that I awoke, Tim was still there.

He handed me a mug of tea.

'Drink this. Then you need to tidy yourself up a bit. The Boss wants you. And Kal is on her way.'

'Kal?'

'Burning up the motorways as we speak.'

'She should see Dieter. He's not going to deal well with this.'

'She'll want to see you first.'

'I'm fine.'

And I was.

No huge red rose of grief bloomed inside me.

No aching sense of loss.

No bitter regret for lost opportunities.

No guilt.

No self-recrimination.

No – nothing.

Tim said, 'Max,' and looked more distressed than I could ever remember seeing him.

It occurred to me that I should say something to help him.

I said, 'Tim,' and put my hand on his.

Tears slid down his face.

'Tim, my dear old friend. Don't cry. He wouldn't want that.'

'I'm not crying for him, stupid.'

I'm shallow. I've always been shallow. Whether naturally or because of my up-bringing, I don't know and it's not really important. When Bad Things happen, I just shut down. Other people don't like this. *He* didn't like it. Hadn't liked it. But it's a godsend. It keeps my head clear. It allows me to function. Somewhere inside me is a locked room where the Bad Things lie deeply buried. My childhood, the child I carried and lost, Sussman's treachery, the murder of Isabella Barclay – it's all there, safely locked away. No trouble to anyone, least of all me. This was just another Bad Thing to be locked away and forgotten.

All things pass.

'Max, I don't know what to do for you.'

'You don't have to do anything for me, Tim. I'm fine. Let me make you some tea.'

He tried to protest, but I overruled him. He looked dreadful. Of the two of us, I was in far better condition.

He didn't finish his tea, getting up to go after just one sip.

'What's the matter?'

'I have to go.'

'Why?'

'Because I can't bear it any longer. Maybe Kal will know what to do.'

Then he was gone.

I finished his tea as well, showered, and was about to leave my room when Dr Bairstow turned up.

'Sir, am I late? I was on my way.'

'No, no. I thought I would come to you.'

'Please, come in.'

He limped straight to the window and drew the curtains. But not before I had glimpsed movement in the room across the roof.

They were clearing out Leon's belongings.

I appreciated the thought, but it was unnecessary. I was absolutely fine.

'Would you like to sit down, sir?'

He sat heavily, placing a bottle of wine, two large brown envelopes, and my personal file on the scarred coffee table in front of him.

I put two glasses on the table, sat down beside him and waited for him to begin.

He didn't ask how I was, which I really appreciated.

Like an echo from the past, he said again, 'Am I going to lose you, too?'

I responded cautiously. 'Not as far as I know, sir.'

He picked up the first envelope.

'I ask because I found this amongst L – Chief Farrell's personal effects.'

I opened the envelope. Property details. Small flats in Rushford with workspace. For the two of us. To live together. His dream. The one I'd trampled over with all the brutality of someone stamping a fluffy kitten into a field of daffodils.

'Would you like to have these, Max?'

No. I wasn't going to torture myself with what might have been.

'No, thank you, sir.'

He carefully replaced the contents and laid the envelope back on the table, saying, with difficulty, because he really didn't do this sort of thing well, 'If you think it would help, I can easily arrange a temporary transfer to Thirsk. If you think a change of scenery would be beneficial.'

I shook my head.

'Thank you, sir, but unless you object, I'd prefer to stay here. We have a lot on at the moment.'

'I understand.'

And actually he did.

He began again.

'I've sent him back. In his pod.'

I didn't get it to begin with. Then I did.

He was from the future. He couldn't stay here. Nor could his pod. It wasn't of this time. So the Boss had sent them back.

I'd lost him twice.

Again, he seemed to read my thoughts.

'It's his home. They'll put him with his family.'

Yes, his mother and his sons, who had died in some dreadful future epidemic. A loss from which he never quite recovered. Finally, they would all be together.

And I would be alone again.

He continued. 'There will be a service, of course.

Tomorrow. We'll put up a stone to remember him by. And his name will go up on the Boards of Honour.'

I nodded.

'I have his will here.'

We all made out wills. With our lifestyle, it was only prudent. They were all lodged with Dr Bairstow. He and Thirsk were our executors.

'He left everything to you.'

He passed me a piece of paper and pointed to a total.

'Sir, you do know we weren't …?' I stopped, unable to think of the right word.

'Yes, I know. It makes no difference. He never changed his will.'

'It doesn't seem right, somehow.'

'Nevertheless, you are his beneficiary.'

I looked at him. How much did he know?

'It will take a while, of course, but you will be quite well off, Max. Independent, perhaps. So, I ask again. Am I going to lose you too?'

I shook my head.

'You should be so lucky, sir.'

He smiled, slightly, and put the second envelope away.

'I was rather hoping you might be able to solve a small mystery for me. Would you like to hear a short story?'

I nodded, mystified.

'A long time ago, in the future, shortly after we had qualified, L – Leon was summoned to the Director's office. We both knew we were being groomed for something different. With his engineering background, Leon's training had been technical, and mine was administrative. I'd been shadowing the Director for six months.

'Anyway, we thought that we were finally going to get some answers, but it turned out to be something completely different. A couple of small jumps.

'Firstly, to a set of co-ordinates that no one knew anything about. Apparently, there was a Standing Order, which had been handed down from Director to Director over the years. On this date, send this historian to these co-ordinates and render whatever assistance is required. That was it. That was all we had to work with.

'The second was even more ambiguous. Another set of co-ordinates and an object to be delivered. Again, that was it. No further information.

'I should perhaps say that Leon, in those days, was a most unhappy man. Still grieving, sullen, and resentful. I don't know if he ever spoke to you about his early days at St Mary's, but the wounds of his family's death were still very raw. Every day, every moment, I think, was painful for him. He certainly gave me the impression he was only there because he had nowhere else to be. Anyway, he was very unimpressed with these assignments. Apparently, he was still muttering as he climbed into the pod.

'I don't know what happened on that jump. Nobody knows what happened on that jump and he's never spoken of it. He'd been damaged before, but when he came back he was defeated. Finished. You could see it in his eyes.

'I attended his de-briefing with the Director. Using the fewest possible words, he described how he'd gone, done what was needed, and come back again. That, as far as he was concerned was that. He had reached the end. He was looking for an opportunity to leave. Not just the room, but St Mary's as a whole. And possibly life itself.

'I think that must have been what prompted our Director to move the schedule up a little and start the initial briefing for the mission to send us back to this time. Leon reached for the first file, which just happened to be yours, Max, and opened it up.'

He opened my file as he spoke. In a clear pocket on the inside cover was my official photo – a larger copy of the one on my ID card. He pulled it out and looked at it thoughtfully.

'This is the photo that Leon saw. The Director was speaking, but he wasn't listening. He took this out, looked closely, turned it over, and read something on the back. And from that moment on, he was a changed man. Something lifted. He couldn't wait to start on the assignment.'

He turned it over. Nothing was written there.

'Do you have any ideas?'

I was mystified. 'None, sir.'

'Ah well.' He tucked the picture back in its pocket. 'I just wondered. I daresay we shall never know now.'

He paused. 'And finally …'

I stiffened. And finally … what …?

'I have a proposition for you to think about. I do not require an answer at this stage. You may take your time and consider your options.'

He sighed. 'I shall not be here for ever. It is time I started to give thought to my successor. Please do not be alarmed.'

'Too late, sir, I am alarmed. I can't imagine St Mary's without you. I certainly can't imagine working at St Mary's under another Director.'

'Let me reassure you on both counts. I do not intend to leave St Mary's for some time yet and you will have no difficulty working with my successor. It would have been Leon, of course, but that's not possible now. I have in mind, when the time comes, to appoint Dr Peterson.'

'An excellent choice, sir.'

'You could work with him?'

'I could indeed. So could everyone.'

They could, too. Peterson was a brilliant choice. His management style was far enough from Dr Bairstow's for him to have his own identity. Everyone liked him but he still commanded respect. He would be perfect.

'As for you, Max – I would like you to consider accepting the post of Deputy Director. Now. Or at least in the very near future. You would, in effect, be responsible for the day-to-day running of the unit, while I, and then my successor, can concentrate on bigger issues. You would act as a bridge between the old regime and the new. Dr Peterson will supply the leadership required, but you, you will provide the continuity.'

I sat stunned. Deputy Director? Me? And Peterson? The new Director one day? Did he know? Was this imminent?

'Not for a few years yet,' he said, reminding me yet again that I don't have a poker face. 'Please, take some time to think about what I have said.'

I shivered. Suddenly, it was all too much. Leon's recent death. This sudden revelation. In less than twenty-four hours, everything was up in the air. The chill wind of change was blowing through St Mary's.

'I'm sure I know the answer to this one, Dr Maxwell,

but do you have a corkscrew?'

Does the pope shit in the woods?

He held up his glass. 'To absent friends.'

'To absent friends.'

It was good stuff. Leon would have approved.

I sipped carefully. Something was required of me and I wasn't sure what.

And then I was.

He wanted to talk. He wanted to talk to the only other person in this time who knew who and what Leon Farrell was. Someone who could comprehend the depth of his own loss. I imagined Peterson and me, on a long-term assignment, just the two of us, out of our own time for possibly the rest of our lives. How it would be if one of us died and the other had to carry on? Alone …

I said carefully, 'So tell me, sir, what was he like when you met him? He once told me you knocked seven shades of shit out of him. Did you really?'

He barked something that wasn't quite a laugh and topped up my glass. 'You don't know the half of it.'

I listened. The bottle slowly emptied.

Two hours later, he looked exhausted, but better. He'd talked almost non-stop, his memories, brought out for my inspection, drifting insubstantially around my room before dissolving away in affectionate silence.

I saw him to the door.

He paused and put out his hand. 'Max.'

I took it. 'Dr Bairstow.'

Nothing more was needed.

The next day was Leon's service, which I attended, along

with everyone else in the unit. The Boss spoke. I can't remember what he said. I remember only the rainbow light streaming through the Chapel's stained-glass windows, falling in multi-coloured pools on the stone floor and the tears on Dieter's cheeks. He'd asked for Leon's tool roll – partly because he'd always coveted it and partly to remember him by. Kal sat on one side of him, Helen on the other, then Tim, then me on the end. The sense of loss filled the tiny Chapel. Tears were shed. But not by me.

I excused myself immediately afterwards and went back to my office. The tables were still laid out exactly as I had left them. When he'd still been alive. Filled with uncomfortable energy, I set up the schedules and assigned personnel. That done, I turned to my in-tray. I worked my way steadily through everything. Even the dross at the bottom, some of which had been there for months. I built data stacks, dictated reports, and caught up on my emails. I even did my filing because I was as sure as hell Miss Lee wouldn't.

When that was finished, I turned my attention to my desk. Rarely opened drawers were turned out and ruthlessly dealt with. I rearranged my working area. I tore down old or out-of-date papers from my notice board.

When I finally finished, dusty and worn out, it was very late. Well past midnight. The building had fallen silent. I'd been at it for hours and hours. There was a mound of stuff on Miss Lee's desk for her to deal with. Dr Bairstow was going to get a hell of a shock when he saw the number of reports I'd sent him, but my desk was clear and my in-tray empty.

I switched off the light and made my way along dim corridors, back to my room.

Tomorrow was a new day. A new beginning. A whole new life.

I threw myself at my work. I threw everyone else at their work, as well. I don't think anyone sat down for a month.

We cleared the old schedule and embarked upon the new. Tim and I earmarked Julius Caesar for ourselves.

Dieter became the new Chief Technical Officer. I was pleased for him. Tim came to me and told me they'd offered him Leon's old room and how did I feel about that? I don't know how he thought I would react, but I'd always knew it would go to someone, and knowing that it would be Tim on the other side of the roof was – acceptable.

Helen dragged me in for my six-monthly medical, sat on the windowsill, and lit a cigarette. I stared up at the smoke detector and then realised I didn't care any more. There would be no more battery battles.

She told me to slow down, that I'd lost too much weight too quickly. I pointed out she'd been telling me to lose 10lb ever since I walked in through the gates, and told her to make up her mind. Views were exchanged, culminating in instructions to sleep more and do less. We both knew that wasn't going to happen.

She sighed heavily, chucked her dog-end out of the

window, and continued with the questions.

'How are you feeling?'

'Absolutely fine.'

'Getting out much?'

'Julius Caesar coming up and Dr Dowson says he has something for us next week.'

'Not what I meant.'

'I know.'

'Anything even remotely resembling a social life?'

'Talked to Kal on the phone last night.'

'Still not what I meant.'

'I know.'

'Any sort of sex life?'

'She's not my type.'

She sighed and came right out with it.

'Are you sexually active?'

'No. I usually just lie back and think of the Spartans.'

'Ticking the box marked 'extra enemas' and moving on ...'

I should have been researching Caesar and Ancient Rome. Instead, I'd spent the last twenty minutes in the library, alternately looking out of the window or staring blindly at the half-completed data stack swirling in limbo in front of me.

'Cheese-rolling,' said Dr Dowson taking the seat opposite me as I struggled to get to grips with the day.

'What?' I said, confused. Understandably, I think.

'Cheese-rolling,' he said again.

Enlightenment failed to happen.

I dragged my thoughts back from where they'd been

and said again, 'What?'

'I need details for my current project. I'm looking into the Phoenician influences in early Britain.'

I decided to stop saying 'What?'

'Why?'

'Tin mines,' he said, with the air of one making everything crystal clear. 'Trading links with the west country. They took tin – what did they leave behind?'

A whole generation of half Brit/half Phoenician offspring was the most likely answer to that one.

I sighed and flattened my data stack.

'Cheese-rolling?'

He nodded, pleased at my lightning grasp of the subject in hand.

'Yes, it happens in several areas around the West Country, but the main event is in Gloucester.'

'Is?'

'Yes. Since the early 1800s at least.'

'There weren't that many Phoenicians around then, surely?'

'That's when they started keeping records. It's been going on since the 1500s. Probably even long before that.'

'So, just to be clearing – this cheese-rolling – you want us to investigate?'

'Yes.'

'When? Ancient British cheese-rolling? Sixteenth-century cheese rolling? Nineteenth-century cheese-rolling? Current cheese-rolling?'

'Oh, Nineteenth century, I think. Current is no good. The authorities have been trying to put a stop to it for years on health and safety grounds. Unsuccessfully, I'm happy to say, but I don't think they use a proper cheese any more and there are always delays while they have to wait for the ambulances to return from ferrying casualties to the hospital and we want to be in and out as quickly as possible. So, I thought if we go back a couple of centuries, we could experience the authentic cheese-rolling …. experience. Any Whit Sunday will do.'

'We? Are you intending to accompany us, Doctor?'

'Of course, Max. It's my project. Sadly, the old fool upstairs wants to come as well. We'll have our work cut out making sure he doesn't break his neck, of course.'

'Hold on. How can cheese-rolling break his neck?'

'Oh, dear me. Have you never …? This is from last year. Watch this.'

He brought up a data stack and I sat and watched. Appalled. And fascinated.

I suppose I had imagined – in my innocence – a couple of elderly ladies gently laying aside their parasols and decorously tossing a pretty little cheese – underarm, of course – at a row of girlie skittles while possibly wearing bonnets decorated with flowers and ribbons. I should have remembered fertility rites don't really work like that. Fertility rites involve blood …

This particular rite involved some kind of enormous, homicidal wheel of cheese, rolling and tumbling down a one-in-three hill – or cliff, as those outside of Gloucester would probably call it – obliterating everything in its path and closely pursued by similarly rolling and tumbling young men in proud possession of a death wish St Mary's could only stand back and admire.

A row of burly men were stationed at the bottom of the

258

cliff – sorry, hill – to catch those still on their feet and prevent them from crashing into each other, the scenery and – in extreme cases – Cheltenham.

A couple of years ago – maybe even last year, I would have sat back in amazement and said, 'Cool! Is there a ladies' race? Where do I sign up?'

Now, aware that at my age the bones don't heal always heal quickly, I wasn't so sure.

'Dr Dowson, is Dr Bairstow aware …?'

'Oh yes. Have no fear. It's all been cleared. Just a brief jump, of course, since we don't have a client and this one is for our own personal consumption, so to speak.'

I replayed the data stack and watched the devastation again. Dr Dowson insisted on slow-motion replays in case I missed some of the finer points of bone-breaking.

'Marvellous, isn't it? You can see the primitive influences. Fascinating. Quite fascinating. I thought you could put together a small group and we'll pay them a visit.'

I'm an historian and a regard for personal safety has never figured that prominently in my working life but I do have an occasional twinge of conscience about the personal safety of others. I called a meeting and showed them the data stack – every bone-busting moment of it before calling for volunteers.

Several hectic minutes later, Guthrie restored order.

We had to limit the contestants to six, but compensated with unlimited spectators.

'What about you, Max?' said Peterson. 'Are you going?'

'Of course. I'm the still, small voice of sanity.'

I could hear Guthrie laughing all the way down the stairs.

Once they'd all gone and just the history department remained, we held a meeting to discuss strategy. Which took about twelve seconds.

'Right,' said Peterson. 'The honour of the department is at stake. We're not having some techie or security oik win this. Right Max?'

'Absolutely. Your instructions are clear, gentlemen. Come back with your cheese – or on it.'

In the end, we took the big pod, TB2. It was ridiculous – everyone wanted to go. I did wonder, briefly, if the Boss had lost his mind, but, as usual, he knew exactly what he was doing. This was a St Mary's day out.

The history department was represented by Peterson, who'd pulled rank, and Roberts, who had medals for running. Why we thought that might be useful is a mystery to me. Security was fielding Markham and Weller, and the techies had entered Dieter (who was big enough to flatten any and all opposition – and possibly the 9lb Double Gloucester cheese as well), and Cox.

Helen headed medical support. Dr Dowson and Professor Rapson festooned themselves with recording equipment, all of which I knew they would forget to deploy once the races started.

And we were ready.

'Right,' I said as we assembled at the door of TB2, prior to unleashing ourselves on 19th-century Gloucestershire. 'Standard rules apply. No one goes anywhere alone. Don't drink the water. Try out the gurning, by all means. Many of you have a natural advantage there. Watch out for pickpockets and cutpurses. Gentlemen, raise your hats and bow if speaking to a member of the opposite sex and ladies should bob a curtsey. Any questions?'

I stepped aside lest I be trampled and off we all went.

The fair was great fun. We watched the gurning, and the shin-kicking, and the wrestling, inspected the goods laid out for sale, avoided some of the more dubious-looking booths, refused the offer of a tasty animal-product pie, evaded the more obvious con artists, and slowly followed the chattering crowds to the site of the main event.

I nearly killed myself getting up that bloody cliff. Or Cooper's Hill, as I should probably call it. Quite honestly, Edmund Hillary himself and a team of Sherpas would have nearly killed themselves getting up that bloody cliff.

I gave it up half way, telling everyone I'd get a better view from here rather than the top – which was true, because in addition to being nearly vertical, Coopers Hill is concave so the only thing you can see from the top is the bottom.

We – Schiller and I – settled ourselves in the sunshine, on a moderately comfortable tump of grass and discovered we could only maintain stability by clutching at a handy tree root and hanging on for grim death. Around us, happy families all dressed in their Sunday best were doing exactly the same, clinging on to saplings, odd fence posts, each other, and busily unpacking their refreshments. A good many flagons were being passed around.

We smiled at our neighbours, straightened our mobcaps, rearranged our shawls, and primly tucked our skirts around our ankles.

Mrs Mack had provided pasties and we got stuck in, because, as far as I could see, given the lack of safety procedures, health and safety restrictions, medical provision, or organisation of any kind, the event would only take just long enough for the four races to be run, the dead and dying scooped up and the cheeses awarded.

At the top of the hill, a large number of stalwart but possibly not too bright young men had assembled. I could see our guys among them, blending in nicely with their leather breeches, stout shoes, gaiters, and thick frieze jackets. They seemed undaunted. We're St Mary's. We don't daunt.

It is important, they told me later, to watch the cheese until it passes you, because cheeses don't care and often bounce into the crowd, maiming the innocent and those too slow-witted to duck. Once the cheese has gone past, *then* you switch your attention to the hill and can fully appreciate the carnage occurring there.

The first race was excellent. The cheese was unleashed and a second later so were the contestants. Most of them managed to stay on their feet for nearly two or three giant strides and then gravity won and down they went, tumbling down the steep slope, head over heels, to the cheers and jeers of their supporters. They pulled themselves to their feet, got their bearings, and set off again. And fell again. And rolled again. Some cartwheeled spectacularly through the air, arms and legs flailing, receiving a special roar of approbation. Some fell and didn't get up. The hill was littered with young men in various states of dilapidation. Coats were ripped or had come off altogether. Shoes lay everywhere.

'Good God,' said Schiller, awestruck.

I have no idea who won the first race. The survivors limped away, all with foaming tankards to aid convalescence. Several young men lay sprawled on the ground and had to be carried away. Astonishingly, deaths were rare.

Our guys were in the second race. St Mary's spectators, distributed evenly around the battleground, waved and cheered as they lined up with the other competitors. They waved back. Precariously. The slightest movement caused people to lose their footing. The Master of Ceremonies, bright in his red coat, called everyone to order.

'One to be ready,
Two to be steady,
Three to prepare,
Four to be off!'

The crowd roared encouragement and I woke up in Sick Bay.

What the hell?

Helen was going ballistic. I could see her mouth opening and closing. If I bothered to listen, I would probably be able to hear what she was saying as well. Whatever it was, it can't have been that serious, because Hunter was bashing away at her scratchpad with a huge grin on her face.

Finally, I said weakly, 'What happened?'

Helen unhooked the chart from the bottom of the bed and held it up. I focused with some difficulty.

'CBBC? What the hell is CBBC?'

'Concussed By Bloody Cheese.'

Hunter gave up the struggle and snorted her way out of the room. Such unprofessional behaviour. She was definitely off my Christmas card list.

'What the hell …?'

'You forgot to duck.'

'When?'

'Five seconds before a 9lb Double Gloucester smacked you between the eyes would have been the best time.'

The bloody cheese-rolling!

Peterson stuck his head round the door. 'Hunter says she's awake. Can I come in?'

'If you must.'

First things first. 'Tim, did we win?'

'Inconclusive, sadly. The cheese veered off into the crowd, causing a certain amount of consternation and was never seen again. Two farmers carried you down the hill. They dropped you twice. The crowd loved it. Almost as good as the race itself. You joined the heap of St Mary's incapacitated at the bottom.'

'Oh God. What's the damage?'

'Three broken bones,

Two gammy knees,

And a particularly painful dislocated shoulder,' he warbled to the tune of "The Twelve Days of Christmas". 'Oh – and a nasty case of CBBC. Don't you remember anything?'

'No. Not after the first race. Didn't any of you stop to help me?'

'How? Trust me, once you start, you can't stop. A bit like you and chocolate. I had a vague glimpse of you on your back, legs akimbo and then I'm afraid I had to concentrate on my own personal difficulties. Dieter took you off the farmers and carried you back to the pod and we laid you out with the other casualties. You were the only one who actually lost consciousness. I should warn you – Markham took photos. Oh, and you'll be thrilled to hear, Dr Dowson, although too excited to remember to record the first race, definitely got the second – what little there was of it – but it quite clearly shows you head-butting a giant cheese and falling flat on your back and showing your drawers. There's talk of putting it on YouTube. Unless you cough up. I believe the going rate is about £50.'

'What?'

'Per head.'

'But that's ... daylight robbery.'

'No, it's revenge.'

'For what?'

'You know, the butter incident. Oh – and there's a T-shirt as well. *I've chased the cheese.* Except for yours. Yours just has a large duck on it. Because you didn't. Duck, I mean. You do know you're never, ever going to live this down, don't you?'

'You bastard!'

I threw back the covers but Helen had him out of the room before I could get to him.

I cursed them all, but there was no choice. I paid up. Several charities did very well out of St Mary's that year. And once again, Dr Bairstow had known exactly what he was doing. The Great St Mary's Day Out was a huge success. Unless you were suffering from post-CBBC trauma, of course. Even I felt my mind lighten as we put Troy behind us and moved on.

16

I was hanging over the gallery, waiting for Peterson and watching my department argue their way through the day when Rosie Lee approached, waving a yellow telephone message.

'Can you see Mr Strong at the stables, this afternoon? About three?'

'Do you know why?'

'What am I? Psychic?'

'Did you even ask?'

'What am I? Your assistant?'

'Would you like to be? I don't actually have one.'

'It was a bad line and he was in a hurry. I could barely make him out. Have you let your side-saddle hours lapse again?'

'Of course not,' I said, indignantly, when a more accurate answer would have been yes.

Along with self-defence, running, and target practice, we're supposed to log a certain number of side-saddle hours every month. I'd let mine lapse for a number of reasons. I didn't like riding side-saddle, I didn't have the time to get out much these days, and, most importantly, I was a Head of Department – the rules didn't apply to me. They hadn't applied much when I wasn't a Head of

Department, and they applied even less now.

Peterson collected me and we made our way slowly downstairs, narrowly avoiding being mown down by a couple of trainees who were late for lunch.

'I can remember the day,' said Peterson grumpily, 'when we were the fastest things in this building.'

I laughed but it was true. Age had crept up on us when we weren't looking. On paper we weren't that old, but do a month in a different time here, three weeks there, nine months somewhere else, and it all mounts up. I'd worked it out once and I was actually about three years older than my official age. And those three years were taking their toll.

Thankfully, we lived long enough to finish lunch and afterwards, it being Friday, Peterson disappeared to supervise his trainees' weekly examinations. Most of the technical and security sections disappeared to kick the living daylights out of each other on the football pitch and I wandered off to the stables, wondering what on earth Mr Strong, our caretaker, could possibly want to see me about. He wasn't there, so I whiled away a few minutes talking to my old adversary, Turk. I'd done my side-saddle training on him and he'd done his best to maim me in return. He was semi-retired now, his head lean and bony with a lot of white hairs showing. I tossed him a carrot or two and he must have mellowed with age because he graciously didn't try to rip off my arm. I rested my elbows on the fence, feeling the sun on my back. It was a warm, sleepy afternoon and Turk was standing, slack-jawed, ears drooping when I heard something behind me.

He flung up his head and snorted a warning but it was too late. Something soft and smelly covered my mouth and nose. I tried to struggle but none of my body would do as it was told. I was vaguely conscious of being lugged round the corner. Someone said, 'Door,' and I was flung, not gently, inside.

I lay face down on the worst-smelling floor ever and tried to work out what was going on. I was in a pod. I knew that with my eyes shut. The smell was unmistakeable – and bad. In fact, the smell was terrible. Musty and rank, with top notes of sour person and really, really bad breath.

While I got to grips with this, the world went white. We'd jumped.

The supposed message from Mr Strong had been a trap. Even I'd worked that one out. I lay very still, eyes closed, waiting for some clues as to what was happening here.

A long-unheard voice said, 'You're not fooling anyone, Maxwell. Open your eyes.'

So I did.

Clive Ronan.

I hadn't seen him for some time. Once, he'd been the focus of practically my every waking thought and now I'd nearly forgotten about him. How stupid am I?

I said, 'Oh, there you are. How have you been?' and rolled over.

He said sharply, 'Steady. No sudden moves. I don't want to shoot you, but I will.'

Oh God, that didn't sound good. I sat up slowly, hoping I would throw up. It could only improve the smell.

I looked around his pod first. It was the stolen Number Nine right enough, and like me it had seen better days. The flooring was filthy and stank. The locker doors were dull and dented and two were missing altogether. Some ceiling panels were gone and bunches of wires hung down. Everything was dirty and greasy.

Just like Ronan himself. He looked unkempt and malnourished. I don't know where he'd been since I last saw him. I suspected he'd been jumping around History, stealing what he could and then getting out quickly before being hanged for thieving, burned as a witch, or shot for spying. The glamorous world of time travel.

I'd encountered him on several occasions in the past: Alexandria, the court of Mary Stuart, the Cretaceous period, even in the future, and every single time he'd come off worst. But on every occasion I'd had St Mary's with me in one form or another. This time I was alone and no one even knew I was here. This time I was in real trouble.

Looking at him closely, I could see he was ill. In addition to his puckered burns and melted ear, his skin was bad. Clumps of his hair had fallen out and I could see scabby scalp underneath. His hands trembled and his eyes shifted constantly. He coughed occasionally and more gusts of bad breath wafted around the enclosed space. He and his pod were dying hard.

This was not a comforting thought. I'd been snatched by a dying madman who hated me and had nothing to lose. The good news was that he didn't want to shoot me. The bad news was that he would have something much worse planned for the afternoon.

I stood up slowly and sat in the second chair. His gun wobbled away. I wished he'd point it somewhere else. It would be just my luck to be shot by accident. I leaned forward to look out of the screen, casually putting my hands on the console, which was greasy and unpleasant. A number of lights were on that shouldn't have been. And vice versa.

'I'll tell you once. Put your hands in your pockets. I won't tell you again. I'll just shoot you.'

I believed him. He wasn't one for empty threats. Usually, when he pointed a gun at you, you were dead five seconds later. He must be in a good mood today. I put my hands in my pockets and looked around me.

'You've let things go a bit, haven't you?'

'You can shut up, too.'

'Where are we?' I asked so he wouldn't know I'd already clocked the coordinates and was having a quiet panic.

He raised his gun again, but even without my glimpse of the coordinates, I knew that unmistakeable light outside. I was back in the Cretaceous. Again. Did I have a season ticket? Was it some sort of curse?

He was switching things off – or on. His pod was in such a state that it was hard to tell. We don't keep armies of techies around because we like the colour orange. Pods need regular attention. They need frequent re-aligning or they start to drift. I had a brief hope we were in the wrong place and he was going to try again, but it was misplaced.

He finished with the console and gave me his full attention.

'Well,' I said, affably, because the longer I was talking

271

in here, the less I was dying out there. 'Here we are again.'

'Did you kill Isabella Barclay?'

Whatever I'd expected, it hadn't been that. But there was no point in denying it. We both knew the truth. He just wanted me to say it.

'Yes.'

'Why?'

I had nothing to lose.

'She was an evil bitch. She was a traitor. She stood by while you tortured and killed to get what you wanted. And she left four men to die in the Cretaceous.'

'And now, I'm going to do the same to you. Get up.'

'No.'

'I shan't tell you again.'

'I shan't listen again.'

'Get up, Maxwell. You're going to pay. For everything you've done. And for the murder of Isabella Barclay. You're going to pay in full. Get up and move to the door.'

'No.'

'Walk to the door.'

'No.'

He flourished the gun again, but I was beginning to wonder. The pod was empty. The lockers were empty. I wondered if the gun was empty too.

He caught my thought. 'It's loaded. Don't kid yourself. Go and stand by the door.'

'No.'

I mean, what could he do? Shoot me twice?

'I'll shoot you and drag you out by your hair.'

I shrugged my shoulders, leaned back, and folded my

272

arms. If I was going to die then I might as well make it as difficult as possible for him. He kept threatening, but he still hadn't shot me. And I definitely wasn't going out there.

'If I shoot you in the knee you'll die out there. In agony. Either from the gunshot wound or worse. Walk out unscathed and you might survive a few hours. I know you, Maxwell. You'll take every chance you can get to live a little longer. So, on your feet.'

The door jerked open. I hadn't realised how cold and dark his pod was until the bright sunshine flooded in. The familiar, never-to-be-forgotten Cretaceous stink overcame even Ronan's rancid smell. Wet foliage, wet earth, wet shit and sulphur, all borne on a thick, muggy heat. I felt every pore open.

I stood slowly, trying to think. He stood with me and retreated behind his chair to maintain the distance. I had to get him outside with me. If he stayed inside then I was lost.

Major Guthrie's voice drifted down the years.

Always do the unexpected.

What did Ronan expect me to do?

He expected me to move slowly. To take as much time as possible. To put up some sort of struggle. To make a grab for the gun … The last thing he would expect me to do was go outside voluntarily. And the door moved so slowly …

I took one very reluctant step towards the door and then stopped.

He motioned me on with the barrel. I pretended to stumble. Thinking I was about to make a grab for the gun

273

he drew back, increasing the distance between us. While his weight was still on his back foot, I ran straight out of the door, skidded in the mud, turned left, and raced around the corner of the pod.

Without stopping to think – typical historian behaviour – I sprinted around the pod, appearing from the other direction just as the door was slowly jerking itself closed.

Praying the sensors still worked, I stuck my hand in the gap and the door stopped moving.

Keeping my hand on the half-open door, I flattened myself against the side of the pod and waited, panting slightly, feeling the sweat rolling down my back.

The pod couldn't jump with the door open. And the door couldn't close with my hand there.

His voice sounded very close. 'Move away or I'll fire.'

No, he wouldn't. He wouldn't risk damaging the door. I was the one supposed to end my days here – not him. And I still reckoned the gun was empty.

I was actually in quite a strong position. To shift me he was going to have to venture some part of his body outside the door. Either gun first, which I could grab or –

He took a leaf out of my book, moving with a swiftness I would not have expected in one so physically frail.

Suddenly, he was in my face – gun levelled.

'Step away from the door.'

And that was his mistake. He left me with nothing to lose.

If someone has a gun then you either want to be ten miles away or right up close. And I was right up close. I didn't make the mistake of going for him. I went for the weapon. I got both hands on the gun and concentrated on keeping it pointed at the ground.

And he still hadn't shot me. The gun *must* be empty.

We staggered across the clearing, both gripping the gun for dear life, slipping in the wet mud and, as we rolled on the ground, the bloody thing went off after all!

There was a one-third chance the bullet would miss both of us, a one-third chance it would hit him, and a one-third chance it would hit me. I lay suddenly still, eyes squeezed tight shut, gasping with exertion and fear, waiting for the pain, the blood, the knowledge of imminent death.

Nothing happened.

I opened my eyes.

Still nothing.

I rolled away, got to my feet, and patted myself down, still not quite believing I was undamaged.

Maybe I wasn't destined to die in the Cretaceous after all.

Oh yes I was.

Ronan pushed himself up, half sitting, half kneeling, blood spreading a bright, wet patch on his stomach. The hand holding the gun was unsteady and his face twisted in pain and hatred. That was a fatal wound. He really was dying now. He had nothing to lose. I was less than ten feet away. He couldn't miss. He lifted a trembling arm and pointed the gun at me. The wandering muzzle was doing figures of eight in the air but, at that range, he couldn't possibly miss me. And he hated me. I took a deep breath and waited for the end.

'Just one … bullet … left. Let's make it … count.'

My world contracted. There was just me. And the gun. The only thing I could hear was my thudding heart. The only thing I could see was his gun. I braced myself. The moment went on and on, and then, just when I couldn't bear it any longer and was about to hurl myself at him in desperation, he shifted his aim a foot to the right and fired, straight-armed, through the open door, directly into the pod.

The bullet thunked into the console. Hard on that sound, I heard a crack, saw a flash, heard another crack, and a cloud of black smoke billowed up from the console. The trip box flashed in response and went bang. Inside the pod, everything went dark. I could smell the burning-fish smell of shorted electrics.

He sagged to the ground, laughing up at the sky. Because he'd won. He was dying but he'd still managed to take me with him. He would be dead in minutes, but I was stranded here. Alone. With no hope of rescue. His was the final victory.

Something moved among the trees.

Oh God, I'd forgotten where I was. That the real peril here was not Clive Ronan.

On my original assignment here, some years ago, I'd had it drummed into me. Never, ever, *ever* go outside alone. Never, ever, *ever* go outside unarmed. And if you injure yourself and there's blood, get back to the pod as quickly as possible because otherwise you're as good as dead.

The Cretaceous Period was home to the world's greatest and most fearsome predators. From the great

Tyrannosaurus Rex who hunts alone, to the smaller Velociraptors who hunt in packs, they're all deadly. Years ago, I'd watched my partner, Sussman, being ripped apart by a pack of Deinonychus. And they hadn't waited until he was dead before feeding.

A shadow flickered on the other side of the clearing. Then another. Things were gathering. Attracted by the blood.

I looked down at Ronan. Still alive. For a moment, I considered dragging him back to the pod.

I heard a sound behind me.

Instinct kicked in.

I left him. I left him there to die alone.

They were closer than I thought. As I sprinted towards the pod, two erupted from the trees to my left. Another one from the right. The classic pincer attack.

I heard Ronan scream something.

I had forgotten how fast they moved. And how agile they were. Because, just as I was running towards the pod, and only feet away from safety, another came over the roof of the pod, straight over my head, landing just behind me.

I don't think it saw me initially. All its attention was on Clive Ronan. And then it did, swerving and slipping in the mud and coming straight at me.

I swear I flew into that pod. I don't even remember my feet touching the ground, expecting at any moment to feel the sharp claws digging into my back as they brought me down, its hot breath in my face as they tore at my flesh, ripped out my guts …

I slapped the manual switch as I hurtled through the

door, praying battery power was one of the few things still working in this fatally damaged pod.

It was. The door jerked, stopped and jerked again.

Screaming was not the right word to describe the sounds coming from Clive Ronan. Three shapes were closing in.

But there had been four. Where was the fourth?

As if in answer, just as the door was about to close a big, blunt head suddenly thrust itself into the closing gap between door and jamb.

Deinonychus.

Shit.

The shock made me jump backwards. The door stopped moving. I could hear its breath panting out through red-rimmed nostrils. One cold predator eye fixed on me and, displaying dismaying intelligence, the head wriggled and pushed, seeking to force the door open again. A large, three-fingered clawed hand appeared, scrabbling at the doorframe.

We consistently underestimate the intelligence of everything that isn't human. Either accidentally, or because maybe it had watched me, this thing had worked out how to get through the door. There was no point in me vainly slapping the switch. The sensors wouldn't allow the door to close. Five minutes ago, I'd been grateful for that. And I couldn't override the safety protocols. This pod wasn't programmed with my authorisation.

It wasn't well enough coordinated to get head and hands working together – yet. My best course of action was to persuade it to remove its head and somehow get that door closed.

I flung open the locker doors, frantically looking for something – anything at all – that I could use as a weapon.

The first locker was empty. The second contained only empty boxes and an old blanket. Oh God, there must be something …

The third, however … the third contained the fire extinguisher. I could tell by its weight that it was empty, but never mind. I'd once belted Jack the Ripper with one of these and it hadn't done him any good at all. I couldn't see the fire axe, but this would do.

I heaved it up and turned to the door. Standing to one side so it couldn't see me, I clubbed its hand. You couldn't call it a foot. Or even a forelimb. It definitely looked like, and was being used as, a hand.

Concentrate, Maxwell.

I clubbed again and then lowered the extinguisher and caught its snout on the upswing. Unfortunately, far from this deterring it in any way, it uttered a shriek of pain and redoubled its efforts to get the door open.

There was no help for it. Standing at an angle, I just couldn't do enough damage. I moved in front of the door.

It had tilted its head to one side, furiously wriggling and twisting, trying to widen the gap. A deep, low, bubbling snarl awoke age-old instincts and filled me with the same overwhelming need to scuttle for cover that my own mammalian ancestors would have had. It stood as tall as me and we were eye to eye. It could see me. I'd been identified as its prey and like a shark it wouldn't go away until it had me.

I changed the angle of the extinguisher and instead of swinging at its snout, I jabbed instead.

It really didn't like that, roaring angrily. Maybe it had some sort of scent receptors in its nose that rendered it extra sensitive. I don't know. I just knew I had to finish this soon. I jabbed repeatedly, sweat running down my face. I was screaming words in time with the blows.

'Get. Out. Of. My. Bloody. Pod. You…'

Even over the rank stench of Ronan's pod, I could smell the rotting meat on its breath. See its blood-caked snout and the wicked, cruel intelligence in its eyes. I've often wondered why, even after hundreds of millions of years on this earth, dinosaurs never made the great evolutionary leap. Language, culture, tools, and all the rest of it.

The answer to that, of course, was that they already had everything they needed not just to survive, but to triumph and if the comet hadn't ended everything, they'd be here still. Unchanged. Like sharks. And crocodiles. They didn't need to evolve any further. They already had it all.

In the end, I really don't think it was anything I did that shifted it. I think it could hear the other members of the pack feasting on Clive Ronan – when had he stopped screaming? – and worked out it was getting nothing but a noseful of grief here, with nothing to show for it.

Not without some difficulty, it pulled its head out of the door and with one leap re-joined the others. They snapped and snarled at the newcomer as they perched on the body like giant birds of prey. One had a long strip of flesh dangling from its jaws. I caught a glimpse of Ronan that made me wish I hadn't.

Sobbing with fear, I slapped and slapped at the door

switch and of course nothing happened because I was just confusing it. I shut my ears to what was happening outside, made myself draw a deep breath, gently pressed the pad and finally, the door closed.

I eased myself down to the floor, clutching the fire extinguisher as if my life still depended upon it, panting and sobbing in the dark. After a moment, the dim emergency light flickered on.

I told myself I couldn't have saved him. He was dying anyway. And after what he'd done to Sussman, it was a kind of poetic justice. And justice for Jamie Cameron and Big Dave Murdoch and all the other members of St Mary's, past and present, whom he'd killed over the years. I felt no regret for the end of Clive Ronan.

It was the end of his pod too, sadly. When my hands finally stopped trembling, I removed the front of the console. The first board was almost completely destroyed. And the second. And the third. This puppy was never going anywhere again.

And by extension, neither was I.

So, this was how my life ended. I should have known I'd go to the Cretaceous one time too many. I sat in the chair and stared blindly at the blank screen. There was no hope of rescue. No one even knew I was here. Probably I'd not even been missed yet at St Mary's. I always imagined my final resting place would be in the little St Mary's churchyard, with Tim on the one side, then Kal, then Helen, with Ian on the end to keep us all in order. It had been an oddly comforting thought, spending eternity amongst my friends.

I rubbed my face with my hands and tried to think.

Searching around the pod, I could find no food, no water. The cells were nearly empty. The toilet was unspeakable. Nothing worked. I could die inside the pod or outside the pod. It was just a case of choosing the least unpleasant option.

I sighed.

Taking a deep breath, I hit the manual door switch again. That and the emergency light over the door were the only things in the entire pod that still worked. But not for long. Not once the battery ran out.

The clearing was empty. No sign whatsoever of Clive Ronan. Not even a bloodstain. The Deinonychus had disappeared. Probably because of the weather. Because things just weren't bad enough, were they? I could hear the wind rising and the sky was one, long, endless bruise.

I'd experienced a tropical storm during my first visit to the Cretaceous. It had lasted two days and been pleasantly spectacular when I was snug inside with plenty to eat and drink. This one would be different. I wondered if this was an occasion when I could legitimately feel sorry for myself,

Even as I looked, the sky grew even darker. Clouds boiled. The wind gusted more strongly. Dust, leaves, and small branches whirled past. It was like that scene from the Wizard of Oz. I kept looking for the cow. And then the witch on the bike.

This was going to be a big one. At least I was going out in a blaze of glory.

Fighting down a mounting panic, I made myself remember I was an historian. First and last, I was an historian. Keep busy. There was a job to do here. I found a few pages in a stained and wrinkled scribblepad and started a final report. I worked away, trying hard to lose myself in the task in hand. Not very successfully, because dying alone in the Cretaceous period was not really how I wanted to end my days. I lost my train of thought, couldn't find the right word, gave it up because I couldn't see properly anyway, and laid my head on the battered console. Apart from the odd buffet of wind, the inside of the pod was completely silent.

And then someone knocked at the door.

I didn't move. I'm not sure what I thought. That Ronan was reincarnated? Or regurgitated? That I'd gone mad? That it was debris picked up and slamming against the pod? That I was so desperate I was imagining things? I don't know. But since none of these was good, I didn't move.

The knock came again. A definite rat-a-tat-tat this time. Since things couldn't get any worse, I got up and opened the door.

And there stood Leon Farrell.

There really aren't supposed to be any long-term mental problems with leaping up and down the timeline. Helen says so. We get the odd bit of timelag every now and then, but a stiff drink and a nap usually sorts that out. Occasionally someone mutters about radiation hazards, but, as far as I know, no one has ever reported hallucinations before.

Not that I was complaining. Of all the things in my life that I could be hallucinating, this was top of the list. So shut up, Maxwell, and enjoy the view. You can work out what's going on later.

He was younger than I could ever remember seeing him, and whip-thin. His hair flopped over his forehead in the shaggy, historian style. He wore woodland greens, body armour, and carried one of the big blasters.

There were no words I could say. I just stared. Around me, the sky darkened further and the wind howled. A heavily leafed branch cartwheeled past.

He said politely, 'Can I be of any assistance?'

He didn't know me. He had no idea who I was. I stepped back and let him in. The door jerked closed behind him, abruptly cutting off the noise of the storm outside.

He wrinkled his nose at the smell, but I was still struggling to re-adjust my ideas and not in the least bit inclined to apologise for poor housekeeping. He stood looking around the pod. I had no idea what was going on. An hour ago I was talking to a horse and now here I was, back in the Cretaceous period sixty-seven million years ago, and with a man who'd been dead for nine months. You couldn't make it up. I thought, just for once, I'd shut up and see what happened next.

Nothing happened – that's what happened next. I had forgotten how little he had to say when I first knew him. I could grow old waiting for him to utter something. It was obviously up to me.

'Can I help you?'

He blinked. 'What?'

'Can I help you?'

'What do you mean, "Can I help you?"'

'Well, you knocked at my door. Did you want something? Have you run out of sugar? Can I help you?'

'I don't take sugar.'

There's a sign on my office wall, which reads – *In the event of emergency, bang head here*. Long ago, Peterson had pointed out that it was much too high up on the wall for my head to reach and I had replied that it wasn't *my* bloody head that would be banged against the wall. I would give anything to have that sign now. It would be something to aim at.

We stared at each other in mutual incomprehension. He was being strong and silent and I was already on emotional overload and picking up speed. Deep breath and start again, Maxwell.

286

'Is there some reason you are here?'

'Yes, but there's no time now. We need to get back to my pod before this storm gets any worse. Are you hurt at all? Can you walk?'

'No and yes. Let's go.'

'Do you need to take anything from your pod?'

'It's not my pod.'

'Then what …?' But at that moment, something heavy slammed into us and the pod shuddered. 'There's no time. We need to leave now. Stay behind me and keep close. It's not far.'

We got the door open again and stepped outside. The noise was tremendous and, in my experience, there would be lightning any minute. This was not the place to be.

'Leave the door open,' he shouted over the racket.

He was right. Leaving the door open would hasten the pod's destruction, but I still felt bad. This was a pod. This was Number Nine – it hadn't asked to be stolen and mistreated and used for dishonourable purposes. I patted its side gently to say farewell, and to let it know that an historian was here at its end.

We set off. I trotted behind him, arms up to ward off airborne vegetation and stinging dust, He had a blaster but it wasn't needed. Everything else had far more sense than to be hanging around in weather like this.

It wasn't far. I could see his pod, parked with its back to a low cliff that would provide some shelter from the wind. My hair whipped around my face and dust stung my eyes. Lightning split the sky ahead of us and thunder boomed a reply. The heavens opened. I've been caught in

287

a Cretaceous downpour before. For some reason the water always seems wetter in this period. It took only a few seconds more to get to his pod and then we were safely inside. The door closed against the meteorological mayhem outside.

I took a minute to get my breath back and push my hair back off my face. Since I was the guest, I sat down and unlaced my muddy boots. Historians don't like dirty pods.

Outside, there was a real sound and light show going on. There's something a little unnerving about the ferocity of prehistoric storms. And they're not over quickly, either.

He was peering at the screen. This was his pod so I stood quietly.

'Are you very wet?'

'A little, yes,' I said, over the sound of dripping water.

'I'm sorry, but I don't think I can get you back right now. The lightning rod is deployed but I don't want to take any chances. We don't want two broken pods here. I'm going to power down for an hour or so. Until the worst of it is over.'

He passed me a towel from the toilet and I patted myself dry. My jumpsuit was sodden. In the old days, I would have just whipped it off but this was another time and another place. I hesitated. I had T-shirt and shorts underneath, but even so …

'You should get that off,' he said unemotionally, pulling off his own wet clothes. 'I think I've got an old sweatshirt somewhere.' He passed me an old black thing, but at least it was warm and dry. And my socks were dry, so it could be worse.

He pushed up the trip-switch and I was back in near darkness.

He snapped a lightstick, which sent out a warm glow, and we sat, side by side at the console. This storm was shaping up to be a real doozy. We could be here for at least twenty-four hours, possibly forty-eight. Someone was going to have to say something soon.

I cleared my throat. 'Why exactly are you here?'

'To render assistance. To you, I assume. Why are you here? Are you alone? Should I be looking for anyone else?'

And now it really was crunch time. What exactly did I tell him? The answer, of course, should be – absolutely nothing. If I said or did one tiny thing that changed his future, then that would change my past and then we'd have paradoxes dropping out of the skies like a sumo wrestler whose jetpack has suffered a malfunction. Shortly followed by Mrs Partridge, the Muse of History, resolving the situation in her own very unique and usually terminal style.

'I'm on assignment. Just me. Please don't let the fact that I can't tell you about it make you think I'm not extremely pleased to see you. Do you have a name?'

'Excuse me?'

'Well, you've switched off the power. I've been in the Cretaceous before – it's practically my second home. These storms can go on for days. We can't do anything. We can barely see each other. That just leaves talking. So, what can I call you?'

Reluctantly, he said, 'Leon. What do I call you?'

He'd always called me Lucy. I never knew why.

Whenever I asked, he just said, 'The girl with kaleidoscope eyes.'

'Lucy.'

He looked startled. 'What did you say?'

'Lucy. You know, the girl with kaleidoscope eyes.'

'I do know,' he said slowly, 'I was just thinking … nothing.'

'Well, that's nice.'

Our little conversational well dried up.

I had a hundred thousand words rattling around inside my head, precious few of which I could actually say. It seemed so desperately unfair. How many people in the world have hoped and prayed for a second chance like this one? Yearned for an opportunity to tell someone the things we only realise are important after it's too late? I couldn't let this opportunity go. I just couldn't. This was a gift from the gods. I could talk to him. Explain. Apologise. Make everything right with him. Talk with him one last time.

No, I couldn't. I mustn't. The slightest wrong word could bring catastrophe. Although, looking at the state of him, I suspected he was more than halfway to catastrophe already. The wounds of his family's deaths were still very recent. I could only guess at the effort it must take for him to get up in the mornings. When every day must be even more full of pain than the last.

I stopped thinking about myself.

I could tell him to hold on. That he had a wonderful future ahead of him. That he was loved and would love again. That all this would pass.

No, I couldn't.

I began to wonder if, instead of a golden opportunity – a second chance – this was some sort of punishment.

'Do we have enough power for some tea?'

'I'm afraid not. I can offer you some water, though.'

'Thank you.'

Nearly being killed always makes me thirsty.

He passed me a mug of tepid water.

I sipped and thought. I couldn't be that reckless. If I said or did anything to change his future, the whole of reality might just roll up and disappear. I'd been given a second chance. A chance to say goodbye to the man snatched from me with so much unsaid and I couldn't take it. Life's a bastard.

The wind roared again, or it might have been thunder. It was hard to tell the difference in here. The noise outside only emphasised the silence inside.

Well, if I couldn't talk to him, at least I could look at him. I opened my eyes. He was looking directly at me. To find myself staring into those familiar blue-grey eyes was disconcerting. I tried to smile politely.

'You seem familiar,' he said. 'I haven't seen you at St Mary's. Have we met?'

Not yet.

'I don't recall,' I said, evasively. 'Perhaps we've met in another time. Have you been on many assignments?'

He shook his head. 'One or two. I'm only recently qualified.'

I looked around. 'No wingman?'

'No. I came alone.'

'Well, I'm very grateful.'

'I'm sorry I can't offer you anything better than water.

With luck, this will soon pass.'

'Sorry to have to tell you this, but it probably won't. I've been here before. This could go on for days.'

He looked startled.

'Is that a problem for you – Leon?'

'No, it's just …'

The words, *What am I going to do with you for days?* hung unspoken above our heads.

I didn't dare smile.

I was slowly beginning to get myself back together again. The shock of his sudden appearance was subsiding as training and instinct took over. I told myself it was enough just to see him again. I should just accept whatever gift had been given me and be grateful.

A particularly loud crash of thunder made us both jump.

'So, Leon, tell me about yourself.'

He met this invitation to chat with silence. I should have remembered he wasn't good with open questions. I tried again.

'Have you been qualified long?'

'About six months.'

'What's your speciality? Mine is Ancient Civilisations.'

'Engineering.'

'Oh. That's – unusual.'

He shrugged. 'It doesn't matter. I'm leaving.'

Oh, no. No, no, no. That wasn't good. Never mind me changing his future – it looked as if he was about to do that all by himself.

'Don't you like it?'

292

'When I joined they were full of how important the work was and my vital contribution. So far, all I've done is a bit of bread and butter stuff with Teddy. And this, of course.'

'Well, I'll say it again, Leon. No matter how trivial you think today has been, I'm still grateful. I wouldn't have lasted long out there. If the storm hadn't got me then the indigenous fauna would. Thank you.'

He shrugged again.

I asked, 'So, what's next?'

I meant – what's next now? As in something to eat, maybe, but he misunderstood me.

'The next assignment is even worse. I have to leave something somewhere for some schoolgirl to find. Doesn't matter. I'll be gone by then.'

I stared at him, struck dumb with shock. That schoolgirl was me. I was that schoolgirl and he was saying that the defining event of my life didn't matter? The one event on which my whole future depended and he couldn't be bloody bothered? I felt a surge of fear and anger that surprised me. Delayed shock from Ronan, I guessed.

Years ago, when I was a kid, I was hiding in my wardrobe when I discovered a book about Henry V and the Battle of Agincourt. It changed my life. It probably *saved* my life. I read it until it nearly fell apart. It awoke my love of History. That book set my feet on the path that led to St Mary's. And here was the man who supposedly left it for me saying he couldn't be bloody bothered.

'Well, who's too precious to get down and dirty with the rest of us?'

'What?'

'How long have you been at St Mary's? Long enough, surely, to realise the importance of what we do. Do you seriously think they'd send you on a mission – any mission – that wasn't absolutely vital?'

I was really angry now. I'd sometimes wondered what my life would have been like if I'd never got away. None of the scenarios ended well. The thought of one of them becoming my reality was too much for me to think about calmly. I rushed to speak.

'Get over yourself, Leon. Who are you to say what assignment is or isn't too trivial to undertake?'

Even in the dim light, I could see him flush. Whether with anger or embarrassment, I was unable to determine. But I'd said too much. Shut up, Maxwell.

'You don't understand,' he began.

'Oh yes I do. Historians get down and dirty, Leon. Get used to it. We go where we're told and do what we're told.' Astonishingly, this barefaced lie did not get me struck down by the god of historians. I made a gesture of disgust. 'This is what happens when you give the job to a bloody engineer.'

Much more of this and the engineer was going to open the door and fling the historian back out into the storm. And maybe he should. I was so disappointed in him. We'd never talked much about his early years at St Mary's. I'd always assumed he didn't want to relive that dreadful time after his family died. I'd imagined him struggling on, slowly rebuilding his life with the quiet courage so characteristic of him. I struggled to reconcile this haggard, unhappy, bitter individual with the quiet, gentle man who had made my soul sing.

He was angry. 'Who are you to judge me? What gives you the right? Bloody smug, self-satisfied, better-than-everyone-else historians! May I point out that in this case, the historian would be dead if it wasn't for the engineer?'

True. I sat silent.

'Nothing to say?'

'I don't really know what to say. I thought ... It doesn't matter. I'm just – disappointed.'

I finished the water, swivelled the seat away from him, and contemplated the dark screen. God knows what damage I'd just done. He'd drop me off, storm back to his own St Mary's, stamp straight out of the gates, and drink himself to death, just as he was doing when St Mary's found him.

Perhaps it would have been better if I had died with Ronan. People can live too long. Edward III lived long enough to see his vast French possessions slip from his senile grasp. His great-grandson, Henry V, had the sense to die young. It was too late for me to die young, but I could at least die youngish.

I can't describe the sour taste of disillusionment.

I got up and sat on the floor, in the corner, as far from him as I could get. I'd wait here until the storm ended, go back to St Mary's, give in my notice, and run far and fast from my inevitable fate. It wouldn't work. If he didn't leave that book for me to find then there would be no escape for me.

It was dim inside the pod, but something must have shown in my face, because he got up, paused for a moment, and then crouched beside me.

'Are you all right?'

I'm absolutely fine is the standard St Mary's response to any crisis, ranging from a broken fingernail to decapitation, but not this time. Maybe now was the time for complete truth.

'I'm angry because something similar happened to me. I found something that changed my life and I was just thinking how bad my own life would have been if the person who delivered my – thing – couldn't even be bothered to turn up.'

'Look, I'm sorry, but I think you're over-dramatising this. Anyone from St Mary's could do it. It doesn't have to be me. So long as it does get delivered, it doesn't matter by whom.'

'Oh, Leon, for God's sake. You just don't get it, do you?'

'Get what?'

'That it has to be you. Because you're special.'

Something big clattered against the side of the pod.

He took a deep breath. 'I think you're confusing me with someone else.'

'I don't think so.'

He said bitterly, 'There's nothing special about me.'

'I disagree.'

'I think perhaps gratitude has caused you to exaggerate my abilities, somewhat.'

When you've really screwed something up, the secret is to jump in with both feet and make it worse. It's called The Maxwell Way.

'I don't think so. I can see that at the moment life for you is – not very good. But you'll get past this. There is a possibility you'll go on to have a wonderful life, full of achievement. Respected professionally. Liked by everyone. Loved.'

He sat very still in the darkness. The storm raged outside while I played Russian Roulette with our futures inside.

I went on. 'You maybe haven't been around long enough to realise that cause and effect are interchangeable. If you don't do this thing – this assignment with the book – then you may not have that life. But if you do, if you save this one person, the result could be your own salvation.'

'I didn't say it was a book.'

Shit! Shit, shit, shit!

Shut up, Maxwell. Just shut up now. Never speak again. There is no way you can make this right.

'Yes, you did.'

'I'm pretty sure I didn't.'

'You must have, otherwise how would I have known?'

'What did I say?'

'I don't remember your exact words. Was it supposed to be a secret? I promise not to tell anyone.'

He was just young enough and inexperienced enough for me to get away with this. I could almost hear him running through our conversation in his head, asking himself if maybe he had mentioned a book …

I had to deflect him and what better way than to ask him to talk about himself.

'Leon, tell me what's wrong.'

As I hoped, the question threw him.

'Nothing's wrong. Why should it be?'

297

'Perhaps, when you look in a mirror, you don't see what I see.'

He said, in a quiet, deadly little voice that would have silenced anyone with an ounce of common sense, 'I don't look in mirrors.'

The wind rose to a shriek and the pod trembled.

I could tiptoe around this or jump straight in. Not much of a choice, really. I'm an historian.

'Afraid to look yourself in the eye?'

Even over the racket outside, I could hear the hiss of indrawn breath.

'Who are you?'

Your worst nightmare was the answer to that one. As he was mine, at the moment.

Sitting in the dark, I took a huge gamble.

'I'm the person to whom you are about to tell everything.'

'I don't think so.'

'We'll see.'

I settled back and closed my eyes. He still crouched nearby. If he went back to sit in his seat – if he distanced himself from me, I'd lost.

He lowered himself to the floor and sat alongside me.

I let the silence drift on.

Outside, something shrieked briefly in the storm. He made a slight movement.

'Don't be afraid,' I said, without opening my eyes. 'You're quite safe in here. I won't let anything hurt you,' and held my breath.

'Too late,' he said, bitterly. 'Far, far too late for that.'

I could say something profound, like – 'It's never too

late,' and lead him gently through his maelstrom of grief and rage. Or –

'For God's sake, Leon, stop being such a wuss. I don't know what your problem is but get over it, will you? You've got a job to do.'

A long time ago, he'd once told me that this had been the worst time for him. He'd been continually drunk, picking fights with anyone who would oblige him. It dawned on me now that I was deliberately provoking a man who was not, at present, enjoying the most stable period of his life. A man, moreover, with whom I was trapped in a small space with the world's most hostile environment outside. Good job we historians don't have any sort of death wish.

I tensed my muscles, ready to move quickly, should I have to.

I'd underestimated his self-control. I was going to have to push some more. I assembled every insensitive cliché I could remember and let rip.

Poking his arm, I said, 'You need to lighten up, mate. Stop being such a misery. Pull yourself together, for God's sake. It can't be that bad.'

He said nothing. Damn.

'Look, I don't know what's bothering you, but you need to get over it. It's not fair on other people, you know, to have you trudging round with a face like a slapped arse. Have some consideration for others, will you?'

Still nothing.

I poked him again.

'Come on, give us a smile.'

Finally …

He seized my wrist in a bone-crushing grip. I sat very still and tried not to gasp in pain.

'Shut up, will you. Just – shut up.'

I carried on, apparently clueless.

'There's no need to take that tone. I'm just trying to help. I mean to say, Leon, at the end of the day, sometimes, it does us good to talk, so why don't you tell me. I'm sure you'll find, once you do, that it's not so very bad after all and then –'

'What do you know? What do you know about anything? What do you know of pain? Unbearable pain … that just goes on. And on. And endless grief. That never stops. Because it hurts. Everything hurts. Everything … hurts so much. It never stops. Ever. It never goes away. And I can't bear it. I just can't bear it any longer.'

His voice cracked. 'You've no idea what you're talking about, have you? You're just some empty-headed historian …' His voice broke. 'I lost them. They're gone. How can you understand what it's like to be left behind? To be the one who has to carry on. You don't know. You can't possibly know. You can't possibly …'

He caught hold of my other arm, shaking me in time with his words. 'You can't know … you can't possibly know …'

His heart was breaking.

So was mine.

Something wet splashed on my hand. It might have been his tears – it might have been mine. Too dark to tell.

He caught his breath. 'They're gone. They left me.'

I know, love. You left me.

I remembered I wasn't supposed to know any of this.

'Who's gone? Tell me. Who left you?'

'All of them.' It was a shout. 'They all left me. They – died. That bitch. It was her fault. When I find her ...'

Suddenly, the atmosphere inside the pod curdled. Before, it had been grief. Now grief had turned into something else. Something black and dangerous. All at once, I was more afraid than I had been with Ronan.

He pulled me close in the dark.

'When I find her ... and I will ... she'll pay.'

'Oh, yes,' I said, sarcastically. 'Because that will bring them back, won't it.'

He threw me. Effortlessly. I crashed against the locker doors. He picked me up before I could move and threw me again. This time I crashed into one of the chairs and it hurt.

He grabbed the front of my sweatshirt and hauled me to my feet.

I said nothing. I didn't struggle. I placed all my faith in the good man I knew was in there somewhere.

His face was in mine. Dark and dangerous.

'I can't find her, but I have found you. And you're no innocent, are you? Somewhere along the way, you'll have deceived and lied to some poor sod. It's what women do. And when I've finished, I just throw you outside and tell people you were already dead and no one will ever know.'

He had one hand at my throat and the other under my sweatshirt. I made myself stand very still. He was hurting me, but I had to stand still. His breath came in hot gasps.

I said quietly, 'Oh, Leon, you poor man. You poor, poor man.'

301

At first, I didn't think he'd heard me. Then his hands dropped. He took in a longer, deeper breath. Then another. He stepped back and saw, I think for the first time, what he had become.

He dropped. As if everything in his body had suddenly given way. As if he had just fallen apart. He fell to the floor and I went down with him. I pulled him into my arms, laid his head on my chest, and rested my cheek on the top of his head.

His silence frightened me.

I said softly, 'Leon, let go. Just let go. I promise I'll catch you, but it's time to let go now.'

Much, much later, things had calmed down a little.

I'd ignored his protest, flipped the trip switch, and given us enough power for a cup of tea. There was no alcohol in the pod. First thing I'd checked.

We'd had the lights on only for a minute, but long enough for me to catch a glimpse of his white, worn face and haunted eyes. We weren't out of the woods yet.

I sat alongside him on the floor. I've no idea why we were ignoring the seats. We sipped our tea.

He picked up my wrist.

'Sorry.'

'It wasn't your fault. I deliberately pushed you.'

'I could have hurt you a lot.'

'I knew you wouldn't.'

I felt him turn and look at me. God knows what he thought he could see in this dim light. We'd need to snap another lightstick soon.

'Who are you?'

'Lucy.'

'Not helpful.'

'I never am.'

A pause. 'You helped me.'

And I wasn't done yet.

303

I drained my tea.

'Tell me about it, Leon.'

A longer pause.

'It's not a – good – story.'

I knew that. And no happy ending, either. He'd told me this story, long ago, in a hotel room in Rushford, on a night I would never forget and couldn't tell him about. This time I must listen carefully and not make that stupid 'book' mistake again. Come on, Maxwell, you're supposed to be a professional.

'Tell me.'

He sighed and sat back.

'My mother was a teacher. In France. I never knew my father and probably because of that the two of us were very close. I joined the army, as an engineer. I was posted around the place and served some time on a carrier. I met and married a pilot, Monique. I don't know what she saw in me and, after a while, neither did she. She left, suddenly, leaving me with two small boys. Alex and Stevie. Stevie wasn't much more than a baby.'

He sighed again. 'I did my best, but it wasn't easy. Sometimes, when you have small children, overflowing love is not enough. Anyway, my mother joined us. She gave up her job, but it enabled me to carry on with mine, and life got better for all of us. And Monique had been home so rarely that I don't think the boys really missed her all that much. I took leave whenever I could. We went on trips. We had holidays. We … were a happy family.'

He stopped for a long time. I waited quietly. When he was able to continue, he said, 'And then, one year, there was a big flu epidemic. A really vicious strain this time, that attacked the most vulnerable – the old and the young. My mother was the first. My *maman*. I loved her. When I think of what she sacrificed for me and then just as I was able to make her life more comfortable, she died.'

He drank some tea. I waited.

'Then the boys got it. Alex first. He was ... he was always a quiet boy. He just ... went to sleep. Stevie got it badly. He was only a baby and he suffered so much. I nursed him, but he wanted his *grandmère*. He kept calling for her. He didn't know me. He died not knowing me.'

He put down his mug on the floor and carefully lined up the handle with the locker door, taking his time about it. I waited. I knew there was more.

'While the boys were in hospital, they took blood for all sorts of tests. There was talk of a vaccine ... when the doctor came to see me, God help me, I thought there was a chance ... that we could save them ... that they'd found a cure.

'But it wasn't anything like that. She came to tell me the boys weren't mine. Neither of them. In fact, they weren't even full brothers. Different fathers. My precious, beautiful boys. Only they weren't.'

This was a much more bitter tale than the first time he told me. Time had not yet healed. Not even a little.

'I spent six solid months looking for her. Although I was so drunk most of the time she could have passed me in the street and I wouldn't have known her. Then St Mary's found me. Teddy knocked me out cold and I woke up at St Mary's ...'

He turned the mug around so the handle pointed the other way.

305

'They saved me. I know that. So you could say it's time I paid something back.' He looked at me. 'In fact, knowing you, you probably will.'

I shook my head. 'Don't take any notice of that. I wound you up deliberately.'

'You're a bad woman, Lucy.'

'I certainly hope so. I've put a lot of time and effort into it.'

I felt rather than saw him smile.

'So, what now?'

'Well,' I said. 'You must be knackered. Why don't you get some sleep and I'll keep an eye on things for a bit.'

'No,' he said. 'I'm not tired at all. I want to talk to you. Do you mind?'

'No, not at all,' I said, somewhat surprised. 'What do you want to talk about?'

'You. Tell me about you.'

'There's not a lot actually. As you can see by my battered appearance, I've been an historian for some time. In fact, I've been round the block several times now.'

'It doesn't show.'

'Why, Leon Fa– for heaven's sake, you silver-tongued charmer.'

He looked at me for a moment, and then moved his mug again. Had he caught my slip?

'So, is there anyone in your life?'

Now what did I say?

'Not at present.'

He messed around with the mug a bit more.

'You should find someone. You deserve someone

306

good in your life. Or someone should find you.'

I sighed, deliberately misunderstanding him.

'I'm never around long enough to be found. I'm usually running for my life in any century you care to name. He'd have to catch me first.'

A very, very long silence. Rain drummed hard on the roof.

He turned to me and said quietly, 'I'm a fast runner.'

I couldn't say it was a surprise. I think on some level I'd known, right from the moment I opened the pod door and seen him standing there. And, I think, he'd known it too. The attraction was still there, even if we were now at different points in our lives.

I said in a whisper, 'You'd have to be. I'm not easy to catch.'

He prised my mug from my death-grip.

For some reason the temperature inside the pod had risen considerably. I could hardly hear the ongoing storm over the sound of my own heart.

He sat very still. He was a good man. After his previous behaviour, I could see the first move would have to be mine.

I shouldn't do this. I really shouldn't do this. God knows what sort of problems this could cause. I should smile and let him down as gently as I could. Before this went any further.

But I'd had no chance to set things straight before he died. If we'd parted on amicable terms … If I'd been able to say goodbye … But I'd had none of that. An uncaring universe had ripped him out of my world and now, as far as I was concerned, this same, uncaring universe could just bloody lump it.

I reached out with a hand that wasn't steady and touched his cheek. He touched my fingers with his own. Gently. Hesitantly.

I could still stop this. No harm had been done. I could stop this anytime I wanted.

He closed his fingers over mine and dropped his words into the silence.

'I am on fire with desire for you.'

There was a moment's stillness and then we crashed together. A locker door swung open and deposited its contents on top of us. The fire axe missed his head by inches.

He kissed me, hard and long and I felt my senses begin to slip. He tasted as he always had. He smelled as he always had. I ran my hands under his T-shirt and, as he always had, he made that tiny sound of surprise as my cold hands touched his hot skin. And, as I always had, I laughed under my breath.

His hands were all over me. Those rough-calloused, working-man's hands that always surprised me with their gentleness. Touching, exploring, teasing. Awakening feelings I thought were safely buried. I felt the heat begin to build inside me. I couldn't get enough of him. I was desperate for him.

I have no memory of my clothes coming off. There was just that magical moment when, for the first time, skin touches skin.

The lightstick finally failed and we were in the dark. As if it was a signal, he lowered us to the floor and began to lay himself over me. There was more weight than I was used to and I was already gasping for breath in this thick, heavy, hot darkness. He interlocked our fingers, imprisoning my hands.

'What are you doing?'

He had difficulty getting the words out. 'Giving myself a … fighting chance before those … cold hands push me over the edge of … madness.'

There was no reading his face. He was just a dark mass above me.

I caught my breath. The heat, the weight, the darkness. I couldn't move. A thread of panic …

He pushed his knee between mine. My heart was pounding fit to burst. So was his. His body covered mine. I could feel his mouth on my breast. Oh God …

I might not survive this.

The whisper came out of the darkness. Intimate, painful, unlocking so many memories …

'Lucy …'

I tried to respond, but speech was beyond me.

I could feel him nudging his way inside, hot and very, very hard. And then he was there.

Intense. Exquisite. Excruciating. Golden pain. I groaned and he echoed the sound. I couldn't think properly. I couldn't think at all. I went to push back against him but found instead that I couldn't move. Not a muscle. I was trapped beneath him. Helpless. In the dark …

That faint thread of panic again …

He pushed himself inside again. A great jolt of current ran through me. Every instinct I possessed was screaming at me to push, to move, to do something to shatter this tangled skein of love, fear, heartbreak, desire, and anguish before it destroyed me.

Somehow, I found breath for words. 'Leon, I can't … It's too much. It's too intense. Please …'

'Lucy …'

He slid himself in and out again, leaving chaos everywhere he went.

'Leon, please …' but he covered my mouth with his own, hard and demanding. Now I couldn't move or speak. And running through it all was something I thought long buried. Uncoiling. Responding … I could feel unbearable heat, demanding to be released and I couldn't move. I couldn't do anything except lie helpless, drenched with sensations I never knew existed, dancing on that fine line between overwhelming need and overwhelming fear as he moved inside me. The pod turned red and purple and black. He was hot and heavy. Unstoppable as Time. I gasped, crushed his fingers, and begged and sobbed as the precipice drew ever nearer.

Another whisper in the dark …

'Lucy …'

I was on fire. It was unbearable. It was too much. I could die of this …

'Lucy … let go. Just let go. I've got you …'

I stopped fighting him, sucked in a great breath and tried to let go. To surrender. To open myself up to him. As I had done before …

'Leon …'

He lifted himself slightly. 'Come to me …'

I arched up to meet him. We pushed hard against each other. Moving together at last. Feeling each other. Feeling our need. He lifted himself on his arms. His slight change of position changed something else deep inside and, suddenly, I was hurtling headlong into the unknown.

I screamed.

He cried out. Sharply. Driving himself into me. And again. And again. Shouting my name.

And as if that was the signal, my sight exploded in sheets of light and colour and willingly, I let go, and let him take me wherever he wanted.

He fell heavily asleep, emotionally exhausted. I was determined to remain awake. He had all this to come. It was all ahead of him. But for me – this was the last time I would ever see him, ever hold him, ever feel that strong, steady heartbeat which failed him in the end.

Sooner or later, we would have to part. He would go on to great things. I would face the rest of my life alone. No, I wasn't going to sleep.

When I awoke, he was sitting beside me with a cup of tea. My heart sank. The storm was over. Or had at least subsided sufficiently for him to risk powering up again.

He sat beside me and I leaned against him. He put his arm around me. Neither of us spoke. We would tidy the pod and ourselves. In an hour, we would be gone from here. I was unable to swallow my tea for the lump in my throat. I tried to pull myself together. I'd been given a second chance. I should just be grateful.

He tightened his grip around my shoulders and dropped a kiss in my hair. I snuggled against him. We stayed together for a very long time. Neither of us spoke. There was too much to say and no chance of it being said.

311

One of us had to make a move. I broke free, picked up my still-damp clothes, and disappeared into the shower. He didn't join me.

When I emerged, he was dressed and had cleared away the mess. He'd risked opening the door for a few minutes because the pod smelled fresh and clean. I sat at the console and twisted my hair back into its bun. It would have been easier in the toilet, where there was a mirror, but I'd been doing some thinking and I had coordinates to check. While his back was turned, I pulled out my scratchpad and banged them in.

So there we were – two professionals ready to go. Neither of us spoke. I looked at the screen. The scene outside was unrecognisable. Broken trees, branches, foliage, debris, all piled around the base of the cliff. It was easy to see from which direction the wind had been blowing. There'd been a lot of damage done out there.

There'd been a lot of damage done in here as well. He had that broken look about him again. God knows how I looked.

He shut the last locker door and sat in the other seat. We both stared out of the screen at a hideously bright, fresh, sparkling morning. A new day in the Cretaceous. A new day for both of us.

He said, 'Are you ready?'

I nodded. He was going to make this easy.

'I'll put you down in the woods. Just by the East Gate.'

'Thank you.'

The world went white.

*

312

I peered out into the late afternoon sunshine. I'd only been gone about an hour.

I got up to go.

He checked the proximity alerts and opened the door. Fresh, woodland air flooded in. We walked to the door and looked out.

I didn't dare look at him. I could feel him watching me. I was so desperately envious. He had it all ahead of him. I didn't.

'Well,' I said, finally. 'Nice to have met you, Leon.'

He said nothing.

I put out a hand. 'And again, thank you.'

He took my hand very slowly in a strong, warm clasp, never taking his eyes from mine. I had to look away.

I thought he was going to speak, but he said nothing.

I took my hand back, drew a deep breath, and, still not looking at him, said, 'Look after yourself, Leon.'

Just as I was stepping past him … Just when I thought I might be able to do this after all, he said, 'Come away with me.'

I stopped dead.

'What did you say?'

'Come away with me. I don't want to go back. You don't have to go back. We have a pod. We can choose somewhere peaceful and quiet and make a life for ourselves. You didn't think I was going to let you go, did you?'

I'd survived his death by feeling nothing. By shutting down. It's what I do. And so the huge, hot, jagged pain coming from nowhere just about finished me. I couldn't speak. Which was just as well, since I would have said

313

yes. I had a brief vision of a life together. Laughing. Loving. No need for me to go back to old age and loneliness. We really could have the rest of our lives together.

I stared at the floor and shook my head.

'Lucy …'

I shook my head again. I should have died in the Cretaceous. Nothing could be worse than this.

'Lucy. Please.'

I couldn't do it to him. I couldn't deprive him of his future. I had to walk away and take the chance that he would survive this, stay at St Mary's and – I hate this phrase – fulfil his destiny.

So I shook my head for the third time and stepped out of the pod. Back into my own time.

Without looking back at him, I started across the clearing.

'Don't leave me.'

I couldn't bear the pain in his voice.

I had to do something or he wasn't going to make it. He'd been at the end of his rope when I met him and I'd just made things even worse.

I turned back to him, clutched at his greens, shook him slightly and said harshly, 'Listen to me, Leon. Listen to me now, because this is the most important thing you will ever hear. I will always come for you. No matter how bad things seem, I always come for you. Remember that.'

My words rang around the clearing.

For a long time nothing happened. If he'd heard me, the words hadn't gone in.

He covered my hands with his own and we looked at

each other for a long time.

'You really are the most beautiful thing I've ever seen.'

And that was the moment I took, pinned over my heart and wore like a badge to the end of my days.

Gently, I took back my hands, walked away, and stood at the edge of the clearing with my back to him. After a long while, I heard the door close.

I turned around and stared at the pod, small and squat at the edge of the clearing. The pod stared back. Nothing happened.

I knew what he was doing. He was watching me through the screen. I put one hand on a tree trunk for support and stared back.

Around me, birds sang and golden sunlight filtered through the trees. Still the pod didn't move. Neither would I. I wouldn't leave until he did.

We stared at each other across the clearing.

I woke up. For God's sake, what did I think I was doing? We could be together. Neither of us ever had to be alone again. Sod the time continuum. Sod History. Sod everything. We were two people who'd suffered enough. Let someone else take the strain. I would do it. I would go with him.

And then, just as I took a step towards the pod, just as I raised my arm to wave, just as I drew a breath to call out, to tell him I'd go with him, that I would be with him for ever, the pod blinked out of existence and I was alone.

The next hour was not good.

The evening shadows were lengthening as I made my way back to St Mary's, very carefully not thinking about certain things. I'd made the right decision. I'd nearly made the wrong decision and if he turned up right now and asked me again, I'd probably nearly make the wrong decision again. I've broken shedloads of rules throughout my life, but never come so close to catastrophe before. And who would ever have thought it would have been at Leon's instigation? He was – always had been – so quiet, so law-abiding, so conventional …

I woke up.

No, he wasn't.

He'd helped me cheat in my Outdoor Survival Exam. He'd brought a Maglite to sixteenth-century Edinburgh – which, admittedly, had been a big help, but nevertheless – He'd thrown me across the bonnet of his car and right there and then, in public … And at Troy, he'd tried to break the biggest rule of all. He was quiet, but he was passionate and he'd loved Helios like a son …

I was once in eleventh-century London, observing Westminster Abbey being built and a ten-ton block of stone had dropped out of the sky, missing Peterson and me by inches. I felt exactly the same way now. Something huge had fallen on me. An enormous revelation. How could I ever have missed it?

And now, what was I going to do about it?

I didn't run, because I didn't want to draw attention to myself. I let myself into St Mary's and, using the backstairs, made my way to my room. My instinct was to get to the pub as soon as possible, but that was ridiculous.

I made myself slow down, shower, and change into civvies.

It was a lovely evening and on any other occasion, I would have enjoyed the stroll down to the village.

Reaching The Falconberg Arms, I walked into the bar. There were only a few customers. I got myself a drink and then said to the barmaid, 'Is Joe in?'

She nodded over her shoulder. 'In his office, doing his accounts.'

'Oh.'

'No, go on in. He always welcomes distractions when he's struggling with his spreadsheets.'

I walked slowly down the passageway. His door was slightly ajar. I pushed it open and stood on the threshold.

Joe Nelson was bashing away at a calculator. He looked up.

'Dr Maxwell – good to see you again. Can I help you? Come in.'

I pushed the door shut behind me, crossed to his desk, and sat down.

'Hello, Helios.'

I don't know how I could ever have missed it.

Joe Nelson. Short, stocky, thick dark hair, Dumbo ears and – for heaven's sake – that sickle-shaped scar on his cheekbone. Again, I saw Helios, terrified, traumatised, bleeding, arms and legs clamped around Leon, clinging on for dear life. How could I not have seen it?

He put down his pen and pushed his chair back from his desk. Was he getting ready to run for it?

'Sit tight, Joe,' I said. 'Where would you go?'

'True,' he said.

We stared at each other for a while.

'How long have you known?'

'About thirty-five minutes.'

He regarded me warily. I wondered how much he actually remembered. Did he remember the shouting? Did he remember what I'd said?

'What are you going to do now?'

'Don't say anything. I'm going to tell you a story.'

He nodded. A good start.

'All right. Troy is burning.'

He nodded again, but this time not looking at me. He was looking back down the years. Back to another time and another place. We both were.

319

I relived the scene. Again.

'I've just been rescued by Guthrie. You know I got dragged off with the other Trojan women?'

I was back on the beach again, shuffling towards the ships and surrounded by crying women.

'Guthrie brought me back to the pod.' I had a thought. 'Does he know who you are?'

He shook his head.

'Does anyone know who you are?'

He shook his head again. I know I'd said don't speak, but I don't think he was capable of speech anyway.

'So Guthrie and I are back in the pod. Peterson's waiting for us, fretting as usual. We're getting ourselves together, ready to jump, the door opens, and there's Leon. With you. Do you remember what happens next?'

Not knowing what was the right thing to say, he said nothing. Now that I knew, I could easily see traces of the boy Helios in the man Joe Nelson. The boy I had played jacks with. And dusty hopscotch. I pushed all that aside.

'Well, I'll tell you. I told Chief Farrell to take you back outside and leave you there.'

Silence. On the other side of the door, the world carried on as usual. In here – who knew what was going to happen in here?

'I told him, as his mission commander, that under no circumstances would I permit you to be taken back with us. I assume that now you know why not. That you know why that was such a dangerous thing for him to do. What the consequences could be?'

He nodded. I don't know if he'd taken my instruction to heart or whether he genuinely was too scared to speak.

320

'He pleaded for you.' I said, without emotion, hearing Leon's voice again in my head. Again. 'He begged. He shouted. Do you remember?'

He nodded again and swallowed hard.

'He refused to leave you behind. At one point, I wondered if I was going to have to shoot him. Or you.'

He sat, too frozen now even to nod.

'In the end, he asked for twenty minutes to hide you somewhere. We both knew that was worse than useless. That after the lions had finished with it, Troy would be picked over by the jackals for years afterwards. That it might even be kinder to hand you over to the Greeks. Or kill you there and then.'

I stopped for a moment, because now even I was finding it hard going.

'He took you outside. I watched on the screen. You both disappeared. Twenty minutes later, he was back. Without you.'

But, now I came to think of it, exhausted and with a two-day stubble.

'Shall I tell you what I think happened next?'

No response whatsoever. I carried on anyway.

'I think he had a pod remote control. I think he called up his own pod, bundled you inside, and took you back to the future. To his own St Mary's. I think it wasn't such a risk as I originally thought. I think he was able to remove you from your own time because, if you had stayed, you would have been killed.'

Yes, he would. Probably within minutes. We can remove things from their own time, but only if they're about to be destroyed. Only if they have no future existence in which to influence the timeline. I didn't know we could do it with people. I wished I didn't know we could do it with people. If this ever got out … This might be one of the most dangerous pieces of knowledge ever.

Imagine if a bunch of fanatics tried to lift Hitler in his last hours. Or Caligula. Or the poster boy for compassion and mercy, the Abbot (Kill them all – God will know his own) of Citeaux. Of course, people being what they are, no one would ever want to lift Mother Theresa. Or Francis of Assisi.

I forged on.

'You should be very clear about this. What Chief Farrell did was incredibly dangerous. If you were destined to survive – and he had no way of knowing that – his attempt to remove you could have brought the entire timeline crashing down around us. As it turned out, he got away with it.

'But, if I had had my way, I would have left you in Troy. To die. Quickly, if you were lucky, but you probably wouldn't have been. You need to know this. I would have let you die. To preserve the timeline. I might even have killed you myself. Even now, I'm not sure what damage has been done. What damage you've done just by surviving. Do you have any children?'

He shook his head, white to the lips, eyes huge and dark, just as he'd looked three and a half thousand years ago, back in Troy.

I could see him tensing his muscles. Getting ready to run. I could probably take him with one hand behind my back. In what world was that good?

'All right, Helios. Cards on the table. I was wrong. I

322

apologise. I'm an historian but we should never lose sight of the fact that History is just that – his story, her story, everyone's story. History is about people as well as events. There's a saying, somewhere – *always err on the side of life*. That's what Leon did. That's what I should have done, too. I'm sorry.'

The silence just went on and on.

'I think,' he said hoarsely, 'we could both do with a drink.'

I held up my tonic water.

'No, a real drink.'

He crossed to the door and shouted down the corridor.

He reappeared a minute later with a tray, glasses, and something fiery. I don't know about him, but mine never even touched the sides. I could feel my feet starting to get warm. Always a good sign.

'Do you want to know what happened?' he said, without looking at me.

'Yes.'

He sighed and topped up his glass. 'He carried me around the back, through the smoke, into the olive grove, and out the other side. I didn't want him to put me down because he was warm and safe. He covered my eyes with his hand.

'A few minutes later I felt a hot wind in my face. Dust and smoke swirled around us. When I could see again there was another of your small shacks. I was puzzled because this one hadn't been there before. He put me inside and everything went white.

'When I opened my eyes the whole world had changed. For me, it was terrifying. For two days, I wouldn't let go of him. They were very kind to me but I knew they didn't want me. There was more shouting. In the next room. They decided that taking me back to Troy would do more harm than good.'

'You were at his St Mary's?' I interrupted.

'Yes. Not yours. He – persuaded them to take me in and there I stayed. They looked after me well. There was a lot to learn but I was a kid. Kids are adaptable.

'This next bit is difficult. He was an older man when he took me to St Mary's. When I next saw him, years later, when he joined the unit, he was much younger. He didn't know me. I was hurt. They had to explain it to me several times. I'm not sure I get it even now.

'And then he got his big assignment – to jump back to this time, to your St Mary's, and I came with him. Between us, we took this pub. I've been here ever since. It's in my blood, after all.'

Yes, his father had kept a tavern, back in Troy.

'And, I suppose, I'm a first line of defence down here in the village. A kind of early-warning system.'

'When we first met,' I said, 'when I was a trainee, I used to come down here all the time, with Sussman and Grant. Did you recognise me?'

'Soon as you walked in through the door. You've hardly changed at all.'

'You knew – all these years you've known that I would have left you in Troy? To die?'

He shrugged. 'I survived. The timeline survived. Everyone survived.'

Except Leon. Leon hadn't survived.

He nudged my glass towards me. 'Drink.'

I needed no urging. It had been a pretty shitty day.

'And you never said anything – to anyone?'

'I was just grateful to be alive. I wasn't going to say anything to rock the boat.' He shrugged again.

I drank again.

'I wonder,' he said, hesitantly. 'Can I ask you something?'

Oh, God. Now what?

'Perhaps,' I said, cautiously, not wanting to commit myself in any way.

'Well, I wondered, if it's possible – I'd like to see his memorial stone, you know, in your graveyard. To pay my final respects, if I may. If I'm not breaking any more rules.'

'Of course. What's today?'

I got the 'typical historian' look that he'd obviously inherited from Leon. 'Thursday.'

'Come tomorrow. About ten thirty. Come to the front door and ask for me. We'll go together. If you want that?'

'That sounds fine,' he said. 'Do you want another drink?'

'Thank you, no,' I said, standing up to go. 'I'll see you tomorrow, Mr Nelson.'

'Joe.'

'Joe.'

He nodded. 'Are you all right to get home?'

'Absolutely fine,' I said, shook his hand and staggered out into the night.

I had a very, very careful report to write.

*

I couldn't show Joe the Boards of Honour, on which are inscribed the names of all those who had died in the service of St Mary's, but when he turned up the next day, smartly dressed and still rather pale, I took him into our little churchyard and for a long time he stood looking at Leon's memorial stone. I sat quietly on a nearby bench and looked at all my friends buried there.

He joined me on the bench and we sat for a while in silence.

'You do know he's not here?' I said, at last. 'They sent him back to the future.'

He nodded. 'Do you miss him?'

Now there was a question.

'Yes,' I said, admitting it to myself for the first time. 'Yes, I do.'

We strolled slowly down the path. As always, the place was very quiet. Only the crows cawing in the tall chestnut trees disturbed the peace.

He said suddenly, 'What will happen to me when I die?'

'As far as I'm concerned, Joe, nothing.'

'You're not going to tell anyone who I am?'

'No.'

He swallowed. 'Thank you.'

'Do you miss him?'

'Yes. He was like a father to me. I owe him everything. And now he's gone and I miss him.'

Poor Joe. Uprooted from Troy and then again from the future. And now Leon was gone. And someone else knew his secret. How lonely and afraid must he feel at the moment.

I saw Miss Lee approaching and braced myself to intercept her. Joe Nelson was in no fit shape to encounter the laser-focused hostility and random evil that packaged itself as Rosie Lee.

I got The Look. The one that indicates she's had to perform above and beyond the call of duty. Such as delivering a message to someone who's not at her desk, for example.

She launched into a litany of complaint.

'Why are you all the way out here?'

I opened my mouth to point out that 'out here' was only about two hundred yards from the main building, but there was no chance.

'I am busy this morning, you know.'

This was news to me.

'Sorry to drag you out into the fresh air. I forgot you crumble into dust when sunlight touches you.'

She ignored this.

'And now I've got to go all the way back to Wardrobe because Mrs Enderby wants some files, and you still haven't signed off on next month's duty roster, or approved Mr Clerk's application for leave, or even looked at the pod servicing schedule, or –'

This could go on all morning.

'Why exactly are you here? Is it possible – and I know this is a bit of a new concept for you, but work with me here – is it possible that you have some useful function to perform?'

'Dr Bairstow would like to see your report when you have a moment and there are some urgent –'

I waited for her to finish the sentence, but that seemed

to be it. I was quite accustomed to being told there was an urgent message for me and having to go off and get the details for myself, because she always considered that simply telling me about it completed the job. The actual contents of the message and whom it was from were usually for me to ascertain.

I cleared my throat compellingly and fixed her with the stern eye of an unhappy supervisor. A complete waste of time. She was staring at Joe Nelson. He was staring at her. And both of them were looking as if Stonehenge had dropped on them. Even as I looked, she blushed and dropped her eyes.

What?

A considerable amount of silence passed.

I stared at the pair of them, frozen in time like a pair of mismatched bookends. Surely not …

It dawned on me that something was expected from me. With considerable misgivings, I said, 'Joe, may I introduce Rosie Lee. Miss Lee, this is Joe Nelson.'

'Yes,' they both said together. 'I know,' and fell silent again.

He stared at his feet.

She stared at his feet.

I began to feel as wanted as cholera.

'Well,' I said, backing off down the path. 'I have to go. Perhaps, Miss Lee, you would be kind enough to escort Mr Nelson to the gate. Please don't forget to sign him out.'

I'm not sure why I bothered. She wasn't listening to me. No one was listening to me. Nothing new there. In some confusion, I left them to it.

*

I took my report to Dr Bairstow in person.

Mrs Partridge nodded me through.

He sat behind his desk, writing steadily. I sat on the other side of his desk and waited for him to finish. Silence doesn't bother me. I was quite happy to sit there all day.

Newton says that Time is like an arrow, and can never deviate from its path. Einstein says Time is like a river and meanders, running fast and slow. Maxwell – when she's been up all night thinking too much, says Time is like a circle and ripples in a pool spread out in all directions. Including back into the past.

Leon had appeared at the very time and place I needed him to be. He'd been given the coordinates. Who had told him when and where to go?

I had.

And who had sent him back, alone and broken, to a very uncertain future?

I had.

And who was going to fix that? Right here? Right now?

I was.

For me, he was dead and gone, but I could still save his life.

Eventually, Dr Bairstow capped his pen and looked up.

'May I see my file, please, sir?'

He raised his eyebrows, but pulled open a filing cabinet, rummaged, and produced the battered document that was the story of my life so far.

I flipped it open and took out the photograph again.

I laid it on the desk in front of me and looked at it. Had

I ever been that young?

Yes, was the answer to that one. And I still was. All right, the left knee wasn't up to spec any more, but deep down inside, I was still young. And I always would be.

I turned over the photo, picked up a pen, and wrote across the back:

Leon, come and get me. If you dare. Lucy.

That should do it.

I put the pen down and handed him back the photo. Without even glancing at it, he tucked it back in the file and replaced the whole thing in the cabinet.

'Well,' he said, 'that's solved that little mystery. Let's hear the end of the story.'

I handed him my report and sat back to watch his face.

He read it through, his expression never changing. Laying it on the desk in front of him, he stared at me for a while and then smiled.

'And how was Leon?'

'Not good, actually, sir. Not good when we met and probably slightly worse when we parted.'

Obviously, I hadn't told him all of it. I've always regarded it as my duty not to overburden senior staff with too much information. Their brains can't handle it. It's all that bigger-picture stuff they do. However, I had described, in some detail, the sad end of Number Nine, the less-than-sad end of Clive Ronan, the appearance of Chief Farrell, and my rescue. My subsequent return to St Mary's was covered in half a sentence.

I said nothing about Helios. I would never tell anyone about Helios. Or Joe Nelson, as I must get back into the habit of calling him.

He looked up.

'You did make a note of the coordinates?'

'Of course, sir.'

I took out the most important piece of paper of my life and pushed it across the desk.

He folded his hands and said, 'I was present when my Director pulled out this famous Standing Order. Just one sheet of paper. One named historian to present himself at these co-ordinates to render assistance. This order has, apparently, been handed down from Director to Director until the right historian turned up. Which reminds me – I had better write the damned thing.'

He pulled a sheet of paper towards him.

'Just one more thing, sir. Ronan was an old man when he died. There's absolutely no reason why, as a younger man, he still couldn't come bursting out of the woodwork at any time.'

He nodded. It was true. Something Ronan had done ten years before he died could still be ten years in our future. We would never be completely safe.

'We have defeated him at every encounter, Max. If he has any sense, he'll give us a wide berth in future.'

Neither of us mentioned that he was a desperate fanatic who had long ago kicked common sense and rational thought into touch and had just demonstrated that his hatred remained undimmed right to the end of his life. There was nothing we could do – no way to predict what he might do next. We could never do anything but deal with each threat as it arose.

'Was there anything else, Dr Maxwell?'

I got up. I had more thinking to do.

'No, that's it, I think, sir.'

As I reached the door, he said, 'That photograph saved his life, you know.'

I nodded and left the room.

That photograph saved his life so he could save mine.

The circle was closed.

Time to move on.

Feeling the need to be alone, I saddled up Turk and rode up through the woods and onto the moors. Side-saddle. We stopped at Pen Tor. I sat on the rocks and looked at the distant sea, sparkling on the horizon. Turk got his head down and carried on as if there was going to be some sort of grass shortage in the very near future. At no point did he try to attack me. I wondered if we were both mellowing with old age. It seemed unlikely. I'm an historian. The chances of living long enough to have an old age, mellow or otherwise, are remote.

I sat and thought for ages, sorting things out in my head. Hours passed. I was roused by the old bugger giving me a nudge. He wanted his tea.

I went to see Dr Bairstow that evening and told him I would be honoured to take up the offer of Deputy Director. We had a quick drink and he told me I'd soon come to regret it. I told him I already did.

I put in for my last jump the very next day.

Tim and I were off to Agincourt. It seemed appropriate, somehow.

There are many views of Agincourt. That it was one of Britain's finest hours – right up there with the little ships at Dunkirk, the stirrup charge at Waterloo, and the March Uprisings, when a tiny handful of civilians threw the Fascists out of Cardiff, sparking the nationwide uprising that led to the Battersea Barricades.

And it was. Henry's inspired leadership of his tiny, hopelessly outnumbered army on their increasingly desperate march through France was a triumph of skill and tactics.

On ascending the throne, the fifth Henry took one look at his over-mighty subjects – all the fractious lords who thought they were entitled to a share of the pot simply because they'd joined the rebellion that placed his father on the throne – and said, 'Sod this for a game of soldiers.'

Casting his eyes thoughtfully across the Channel, he revived the age-old Plantagenet claim to the French throne and shunted the whole turbulent bunch of them over to France where they could either get themselves killed or rich. Whichever came first.

They took Harfleur – although not easily, as Henry's 'Once more unto the breach,' speech implies and, with the end of the campaigning season coming up, he had a difficult decision to make. To return home with most of his money gone and only a very moderate victory to show for it, or to intimidate the French with a show of strength and press on to Calais; a march, he estimated, of no more than five days.

He opted for Calais and got it wrong.

Reaching the River Somme, they found the ford held by the French army, leaving Henry and his army with no other option than to head away from Calais and look for another place to cross. The French, for some reason reluctant to force the outcome, followed them on the other side of the river, waiting for Henry to surrender.

By 24th October, the English were in deep trouble, many of them weak and sick and all of them hungry.

The battle of Agincourt was fought the next day – St Crispin's Day – and the rest, as they say, is History.

Tim and I planned to conceal ourselves on the west side of the battleground, near the village of Agincourt to watch the battle from there and, with luck, get the low-down on Henry's controversial order to kill all his French prisoners.

Tim, as a keen bowman himself, wanted to see the English and Welsh archers at their best. Or worst, of course, if you were looking at things from the French point of view. Under Henry, every Sunday (after church, naturally) was devoted to archery practice. Every man and boy took part – even girls got in on the act. It's almost certainly true that a medieval girl could draw a bow better than a young man could today.

And don't think – oh, bows and arrows! A practised archer could easily shoot six arrows a minute. Accurately. That's one every ten seconds. And unlike a man at arms, they didn't have to get close. They could wound at four hundred yards, kill at two hundred, and pierce armour at one hundred. Archers were the shock troops of the age and English and Welsh archers were the best of the best.

Neither Peterson nor I could contain our impatience.

We had a bit of a problem with Dr Bairstow, who complained that St Mary's had invested a very great deal of money in us, all of which would be wasted if we, inevitably as he seemed to think, got ourselves punctured like colanders.

I admit we were going to be a bit close. Closer than we'd told him, actually, but no need to bother him with that now. Normally, we watch this sort of thing from a nearby hilltop or even from the pod itself, but that wasn't possible in this case. Our assurances that we would take every precaution, were, for some reason, met with a derisory snort.

He gave in, however. Mrs Enderby kitted us out in what Wardrobe persisted in referring to as Autumn Tones. I had an ankle-length brown dress, soft boots, a linen scarf to bind my hair, and an old green cloak I was sure I recognised from my very first jump. Tim looked seasonal in russet and grey.

And that was it. I was ready. My last jump. We were going to observe one of the bloodiest battles of the Middle Ages and it was my last jump. What could possibly go wrong?

I'd asked to come off the active list but Dr Bairstow had refused, grumbling it was too much faff to get me back on again, should it ever be necessary. I hadn't argued – just for once – but in my heart I knew this was my last jump.

Tim met me in the Hall and presented me with a single yellow rose.

To hide my emotion, I said, 'This is two in ten years now. At this rate I'll have the full bouquet by the time I'm one hundred and eighty-three.'

'Don't be so ungrateful. This is just the incentive. The rest will be presented to you on your safe return.'

I took the rose. 'Thanks, Tim. And thank you for everything.'

'An honour and a privilege, Max.'

We stood for a bit and then he cleared his throat and said, 'Are you ready?'

He offered me his arm and walked me to Hawking, where I got the traditional round of applause.

I looked around the hangar. The place was packed. Historians hung over the gantry, calling advice and insults. Dr Bairstow nodded. Even Mrs Partridge was there. She looked as if she wanted to say something and I paused, but she just shook her head and stepped back. I waved, smiled, and tried to ignore the lump in my throat.

Techies pulled out the umbilicals and towed them away. I remembered not to look for Leon.

We were in Number Eight. I gave it an affectionate pat as I entered.

Dieter and Peterson checked everything while I stowed our gear.

'Right, you're all set,' said Dieter, stuffing his scratchpad back in his knee pocket. 'Take care, Max. Look after yourself.'

I must have looked surprised at this concern and he laughed.

'Ancient historian tradition. Drinks are on you when you get back.'

First I'd ever heard of that one. I made a rude noise and he let himself out, laughing.

I laid the rose on the console where I could see it.

Tim initiated the jump and the world went white.

We landed on the western side of what would be the battlefield. We found a small hollow and established our equipment and ourselves. Peering through the silent woods, we could make out the French lines. At this moment, we were closer to the French than the English, but Henry would move his troops forward, and then we'd have the best seats in the house.

I breathed deeply, inhaling the smell of wet loam, rotting leaves, mud, and smoke. If I closed my eyes, I could have been back on assignment in 1917, at the Somme. That would be exactly 502 years in the future, but nothing ever seems to change. I know they must have seasons in France, but in my memories it's always autumn. Always cold and damp, with the smell of wet earth and bonfires and the memory of conflict.

The long night was ending. The French camp blazed with lights and cooking fires. Music and laughter drifted through the dripping woods. The French, confident of tomorrow's outcome, were shouting, laughing, and dicing, dividing up the prisoners they were confident of capturing the next day. Their only concern was that, because the odds were so overwhelmingly in their favour, the battle would be over before they all got a chance

337

to display their prowess.

For most of them it was their last night on earth.

The English camp, in contrast, was nearly silent. Men gathered quietly around such small fires as they had been able to put together. They were cold, hungry, and exhausted. Many of them were sick. All of them were far from a home they never thought they would see again.

According to Shakespeare – and it was probably true because Henry was an inspired leader – the King spent the night walking from one miserable campfire to another, making an effort to talk to everyone, forgetting no one, spreading such good cheer and encouragement as he could. Putting the heart back into his troops. Shakespeare calls it 'a little touch of Harry in the night'.

Dawn came silently. The day was mild and damp. Clouds hung low in the sky. The English rose first, probably glad to have the night behind them.

The French assembled themselves with a colossal racket. There were thousands of them. Richly decorated tents and pavilions stretched as far as the eye could see. Brilliantly coloured pennants and flags hung limply.

The knights arrayed themselves in three mounted lines. The first was led by the two big-hitters, the Constable and the Marshall of France, both of whom would have difficulty controlling the over-enthusiastic French forces.

The second line was commanded by the Dukes of Bar and Alençon.

And, as if these two massive lines weren't enough, a third, led by the Counts of Dammartin and Fauconberg waited impatiently in the rear. I took a moment to wonder if the latter was in any way related to our local pub – The Falconberg Arms. I'd look it up when we got back.

All three lines jostled each other impatiently. Discipline was minimal. As far as I could see, no sort of strategy had been devised. Their plan was simply to charge the English and overwhelm them by sheer numbers. They probably thought it would all be over by lunchtime.

In contrast to all this raucous clamour, the English slipped quietly into place as the early morning mist uncurled about them.

A mere knight, Sir Thomas Erpingham, led the bowmen. Unlike the French, Henry promoted by merit, not rank. They deployed themselves on each flank, digging in the sharpened stake every man had been ordered to cut, shape, and carry with him since they started out from Harfleur, all those long days ago.

Once the stakes were in place, they strung their bows and waited.

Compared with the French they were a sorry-looking lot. Few of them wore any sort of armour. Most wore a simple, mud-splattered leather jerkin over a short tunic with boots and a hood. They carried waist-quivers, stuffed full of arrows and either an axe or hammer in their belts. And that was all they had. They relied on the men-at-arms to protect them. And the men-at-arms relied on the archers to protect them.

Edward, Duke of York, led the vanguard. He would be the only noble English casualty, sharing the same fate as many of his French opponents – smothered to death in the mud.

The King himself commanded the main body. Henry had been fighting since he was fourteen. He'd won his spurs in the Welsh Marches, fighting Owen Glendower and the rebel Percys. This was not a king who skulked at the back. He wore a golden crown on his helmet, which would make him instantly recognisable to friend and foe alike. Over his head hung the Royal Standard of England – the golden Lions of England on their red background, quartered with the blue and gold Fleur-de-Lys of France, which must have pissed off the French no end. Alongside the standard, the banner of St George hung limply. There was no wind today and the heavy air was damp.

I could hear Peterson calculating numbers. He estimated the English forces at between eight or nine thousand. He glanced at me for confirmation and I nodded. The French forces were more difficult to compute. Behind the three lines of mounted knights and the ranks of men-at-arms behind them, the French camp seethed in chaos.

Thousands milled around in the rear. Servants, spare horses, commoners, grooms, pages, camp-followers. And the archers. Regarding them as inferior troops, they left their archers behind the lines. What were the French commanders thinking? Henry had no such qualms and his archers would win the day.

We settled eventually on between thirty and forty thousand French troops. Which made the English, playing away, outnumbered by about four to one.

The English waited patiently as the French got themselves sorted out. Around us, the day lightened a little, although thick clouds still obscured the sun. The woods around us were completely silent. I could just hear an occasional drip of water rolling off a leaf somewhere and splatting onto the carpet of wet leaves.

From where we lay we could see part of the English force and the massive French lines drawn up against them.

They were ready.

We checked our equipment again.

We were ready.

Everyone was ready.

And nothing happened. Both sides stared at each other across the muddy fields. Sounds carried clearly in the still air. I could hear the chink of horses' bits, the scrape of metal on metal, and the creak of leather.

Time passed.

Henry now had a problem. He knew the French were unwilling to fight. They were waiting for reinforcements. Although where they would put them was anyone's guess. Already their ranks were packed so tightly they could barely move their sword-arms.

The English, on the other hand, couldn't afford to wait. The men were weary. Weary unto death, as the saying goes. They had no lines of supply. The last thing they needed was to wait endlessly on foreign soil feeling their courage ebb away while the enemy gathered strength.

The military manuals of the time were very clear. He who moves is lost. The accepted wisdom was to stay put and let your enemy come to you.

Henry, typically, took a calculated risk. Orders were shouted. Horns blew and the archers ripped out their stakes. The whole army was on the move. He marched them towards the French, reached the place where the woods formed a narrow waist, and halted there.

Peterson and I, lost in the moment – again – inched our way closer, wriggling through drifts of wet leaves, desperate for a closer look.

This was the most dangerous moment of all. Until they could hammer their stakes into the ground, his archers were completely unprotected. If the French moved now, all was lost.

But they didn't. Inexplicably, they stayed put. Who knows why. They hesitated long enough for the English archers to dig themselves in behind their stakes again and suddenly, it was a whole new ball game.

Suddenly, the English were only three hundred yards away from the French lines. Whether the French were aware, at that moment, that this despised rabble was actually a well-trained, well-led, disciplined, almost professional army, they certainly would be in several hours' time.

Their own ranks consisted of the flower of French nobility, mounted knights – the football stars of the medieval age – behind them, large numbers of men-at-arms; and behind them, conscripted peasants. Because, yes, having ten or fifteen thousand ignorant, reluctant, undisciplined, untrained, unpaid, resentful serfs to back you up was such a good idea. Leonidas the Spartan, berated for arriving at Thermopylae with only three hundred troops pointed out that he'd brought three hundred professional soldiers and while everyone else may have brought thousands, they were only farmers and stable boys. The French should have paid more attention to the classics.

A small group of unarmoured heralds detached themselves from the French ranks, picking their way disdainfully through the mud. They halted and waited under their blue and gold banner – the Fleur-de-Lys of France.

'There,' said Peterson, pointing, as Henry, bareheaded, rode out with his entourage to meet them. The great banner of St George streamed out behind him. 'There he is.'

The two parties spoke together, a little patch of brilliant colour in the dull landscape around us.

We could hear their voices, clear in the cold air, but were unable to make out the words. The meaning was clear however. Henry shook his head and spoke briefly. The French spoke again. They were urging him to surrender. Henry responded.

Come on, come on. Just turn your head this way. Just a little. I really wanted to see his face.

'Are you getting this?'

Peterson nodded, not taking his eyes from the scene. I didn't blame him.

Finally, the heralds turned back. As did Henry and his entourage and I finally got to see the mighty Henry V. The hero of his age. And yes, he really did have that bloody awful pudding-bowl haircut. They all did. Whether Henry was a royal trendsetter or it was practical under their helmets, I didn't know. I certainly couldn't think of any other reason for having the most hideous hairstyle in a History that includes Donald Trump.

His face was very long and badly scarred down one side. He'd caught an arrow in the cheek at Shrewsbury in 1403 and had been lucky to survive.

The king was on his way back to his own lines which were already opening up to receive him when a great cry of outrage rose up from the English ranks.

He wheeled his horse. Swords were drawn.

One of the French heralds, secure in his immunity, was standing in his stirrups. He held his right arm above his head, the first two fingers extended. With his other hand, he made a chopping gesture.

It was true! It was true after all! It's moments like this make me realise why I don't have an office job.

Legend says that the French, secure in their assumption of triumphant victory had threatened to chop off the first two fingers of every captured archer, thus ensuring he could never again draw a bow. The truth of this had always been hotly debated. Not least because the more normal fate of captured commoners was death rather than mutilation. Plain and simple.

As one man, the English roared defiance and Henry galloped back to his own lines, flourishing his sword over his head.

Preliminaries over. Time for the main event.

Trumpets sounded. Orders were shouted. Someone was banging a drum.

The French cavalry lined up, each beneath his own banner. Horses reared and plunged, impatient to be off. I heard no orders given, no trumpets sounded, but suddenly, like thunder, they were on the move. Lying prone, I could feel the earth tremble beneath me.

They weren't fast, but they were unstoppable. A giant wall of men and horses bearing down on the tiny English force.

Amongst the English, the order was given and seven thousand archers let fly.

I've pulled a bow myself and I'm not bad. Nowhere near as good as Peterson, but I'm not bad. I was watching the English archers now and I've never seen anything like it.

I know you don't just pull with your arms – all your back muscles come into play, as well. These archers pulled with their entire bodies – backs arched with the strain as they aimed high into the air. The force generated was such that on shooting the arrow, their feet actually left the ground.

And they were fast. Five or six arrows pulled from waist quivers in less than a minute. The air was thick with the sight and sound of arrows, shot high into the air. We could hear screams and shouts as they fell amongst the advancing ranks.

For the cavalry, it all started to go wrong from this moment. Unable to outflank the archers because of the trees, and forced forwards by the pressure behind them, they were pushed onto the pointed stakes. Their horses, unarmoured except for their heads and bleeding from numerous arrow wounds, milled around, screaming and panic-stricken. Knights crashed to the ground. Many never rose again. The English archers poured arrows into them at point-blank range. Injured and riderless horses tried to barge their way back out of the conflict, trampling the fallen and hindering those attempting, and failing, to retreat in good order.

It was no longer possible to hear any commands given from where we lay, but suddenly the first rank of French men-at-arms was on the move towards the English lines. Squeezed tightly together as they were, any movement other than forwards was almost impossible. The unending hail of arrows from above meant they not only had their visors down, but also actually had to lower their heads as they marched. They couldn't see. They couldn't hear. They couldn't breathe. And thanks to the French horses having chopped up the ground so badly, they could barely move, either. Unable to avoid the suddenly retreating cavalry, many were ridden over by their own countrymen who were fleeing for their lives.

I could see the Constable's thinking. If he could get his men-at-arms to the English front line then they'd outnumber the enemy at least three to one and it would all be over very quickly.

Except that they couldn't get to the English front line. They struggled, knee-deep in liquid mud. They had to find their way around piles of dead or wounded men and horses. Their own cavalry were trampling them into the ground. Again, many fell and couldn't get up again. They struggled feebly, drowning in the mud inside their own helmets.

They were pressed together so tightly that the forces behind them were unable to move forward in support. And their archers, so far back behind the lines, were powerless.

Not so the English, shooting volley after volley into the flailing mass. They never stopped. They were pitiless.

Some military leader once said: 'Always leave your enemy a golden bridge to retreat by.' The English had no golden bridge. They were fighting for their lives in a foreign country and they showed no mercy. There was no hope for anyone out there in the mud.

It got worse.

When their arrows were expended, and with the entire French army at a virtual standstill, the English archers picked up their mallets and poleaxes, exploded out from behind their stakes, and waded in.

These were powerful men. It takes a lot of strength to pull a bow. Unarmoured and unencumbered, they skipped neatly over the dead and laid about them. French men-at-arms, trapped in the mud, went down like trees.

And then it got even worse.

Not having any clear idea of what was happening, the second line, now eager to get to grips with the foe themselves, advanced, pushing the remains of the first line directly into the arms of the English and their stakes.

I'd been to the Somme in 1917. I'd briefly served there in a French hospital. The sight of men, screaming, impaled on stakes or barbed wire is not something anyone should see once. Let alone twice.

There was nothing anyone could do. Unable even to raise their weapons in the crush, unable to advance, unable to retreat, the first rank were just sitting – or standing – targets.

The second rank of French men-at-arms, eager for their share of what they perceived as the day's glory, clambered over their fallen comrades and straight into the English, who were fighting like madmen.

Hundreds, possibly thousands, of Frenchmen were passed back down the line as prisoners of war. After all, it was every man for himself. Every man had the right to return home laden with booty and ransomeable prisoners. For them, that was the whole point. Who cared who sat on the French throne so long as they went home rich?

I could hear the cries and pleas of the fallen all around, the screams of injured and terrified horses, and shouted orders as French commanders desperately tried to restore order and organise a controlled retreat. And, rising above everything, the triumphant shouts of the English as they slaughtered very nearly an entire generation of the French nobility.

It was only when I moved to change a disk that I realised how stiff and cramped I had become. Hours had passed and we'd been completely lost in what was happening around us.

'We should move,' said Peterson, hoarsely. 'Look at all these prisoners. Let's get down to the baggage train. We really need to see what's happening there.'

I was torn. Half of me wanted to see what was happening at the baggage train. The other half wanted to see the triumphant English archers standing on heaps of dead men and sticking their unamputated fingers up at the French.

But Henry's order to kill the French prisoners is controversial to this day and needed to be investigated.

We wriggled back to the pod and dumped what we had so far. He handed me a fresh recorder and pulled on a small sword. 'You record. I'll keep an eye out.'

He was as good with a sword as a bow. I nodded.

We inched our way through the woods. The baggage-train was at the rear, hidden, to some extent among, the trees.

The English had circled the wagons long before American settlers made that popular and placed their wounded – of whom there were remarkably few – in the middle.

A few women were present. Camp followers, maybe a wife or two, maybe even a French girlfriend. Who knows? At any rate, I wouldn't be too out of place.

Young boys ran hither and thither, bearing messages and slopping water in buckets too heavy for them. Off to one side, sitting in the mud, the captured French nobility awaited the outcome of the battle. Hundreds of them. Hundreds and hundreds of them. Contemporary estimates put the final number at around seventeen hundred. All guarded, as far as I could see, by two men and a small dog.

'My God,' said Peterson, softly. 'No wonder.'

I knew what he meant. There was a second army sitting here. Defeated and exhausted for the moment but that could change in an instant. If this lot armed themselves and fell on Henry from the rear, it would all be over in minutes. No wonder Henry gave the order.

'Come on,' he said. 'This is no place for prudent and sensible historians. Or us.'

I agreed. For once.

Then, suddenly, it was too late.

Figures moved among the trees.

A shout rang out. Those who could grabbed their swords. A woman screamed.

The trees were suddenly alive with men – not men-at-arms, but French peasants, poorly dressed and barefoot but clutching knives, scythes, and clubs.

Whether they were under the instructions of the main French force or simply engaging in a bit of private enterprise has never been clear. Even as I watched, three of them turned on a small boy and hacked him down. An elderly chaplain approached them, holding out his arms in protest, and he was stabbed too.

People scattered, screaming, trying to escape into the trees. One woman seized an old pike and stood defiantly over her unconscious man. Not everyone was running.

She jabbed and swung. Like most women of her age, she knew how to defend herself.

No one deserves to die. But some people deserve to live. I said, 'Go,' to Peterson, who leaped across the space, roaring like a bull. He thumped two of them with the flat of his blade. Painful, but not fatal. The rest fled.

I picked up a piece of wood and swung at them as they passed, making contact with at least one of them.

I wanted to see what the prisoners were doing. They'd surrendered; taken themselves out the fight. Everyone knew the drill. The rules of war. What would they do? Would they join in?

Of course they would. They must have been convinced Henry and his rabble army were, at that moment, being cut to pieces by their countrymen. They weren't going to sit around and wait for humiliating rescue.

Suddenly, Henry really did have another army at his back. This was the moment when it could have gone either way.

We should have gone. We should have left them to get on with it. But most of the people in the baggage train weren't soldiers, or warriors, or noblemen – they were the little people. Just like me.

I laid about me as hard as I could. Others were fighting back as well.

The attackers were greedy, fortunately. They'd come for whatever they could scavenge. Most of them were more interested in the contents of the wagons or making off with the spare horses than massacring old men, small boys, and women. Someone pulled out a pack. The contents tipped all over the ground and suddenly they were fighting each other and not us.

Peterson pushed me against a wagon and stood in front of me, sword raised. He looked big enough and ugly enough to be avoided for the minute.

French peasants were overrunning the whole camp. Later estimates put their numbers at several hundred. That was a lot – and if you added the seventeen hundred odd prisoners – this was no place to be.

'This is no place to be,' shouted Peterson. 'Move. Do not stop to save anyone or subvert the course of History in any way. Just move.'

And immediately disobeyed his own orders.

A man lay dead, his guts spilling everywhere. Lying amongst a tangle of bloody intestines was a horn. Peterson grabbed it and blew.

The first sound was just a bubbly squeak, but he tried again. The second attempt was better and the third had the whole Robin Hood thing going for it. Faintly, in the distance, I heard a reply.

He tossed the horn to someone else. Help would come. Henry would despatch some two hundred desperately needed archers from the front to quell whatever was happening at the rear – and order the execution of French hostages. Most of me didn't want to see that, but part of me did.

His actions were understandable. He was fighting for his life. He couldn't afford to have over two thousand hostiles behind him. Some reports say the order was obeyed. Some say it wasn't. Some say a few were killed, but not many. This was my own theory – it would take two hundred men a very long time to kill two thousand other men. And the French would hardly sit still and wait to be slaughtered. I was desperate to know what would happen next, but Peterson had hold of my arm. He was just pulling me around the side of a wagon, when, from nowhere – I swear I never saw him until he was right in front of us – some stunted peasant swung his rusty scythe at Peterson, partially severing his arm.

It went deep. I could tell. A great gout of blood sprayed through the air, all over both of us. I grabbed Peterson's sword as he dropped it, but the peasant was gone. I never saw him go, either.

Peterson collapsed against me, unable to stifle his cry of pain.

Now we were in trouble.

We had to get out of here.

Now.

He was almost a dead weight. I dragged his good arm around my shoulders and tried to take his weight on my hip. Thank the god of historians he'd always been skinny.

He was conscious. He knew what was going on. He tried to help.

I got him just far enough away from the baggage train and into the trees before he collapsed. I ripped the linen scarf off my head and tied it around the wound. He barely made a sound. I suddenly became aware of tears running down my cheeks.

'Come on, Tim. Stay with me. Stay with me, now.'

He said, between clenched teeth, 'Oh, Jesus, Max. It hurts.'

'I know, love. I know. Can you walk?'

'Yes.' He squinted up at me, his face unrecognisable with pain. 'Love?'

I tried to grin at him. 'You'll never remember this tomorrow. I can say whatever I like. Can you lend me a lot of money?'

He grunted as I tightened the bandage. 'Not a problem. As much as you like. We've both ... got the life expectancy ... of a mayfly, anyway.'

I finished bandaging and looked at him properly. He was white, cold, and shaking with shock. Any minute now, he'd lose consciousness.

'I need to get you back to the pod. It's not safe here.'

Indeed, it wasn't. I could hear people crashing through the undergrowth all around us. Shrieks and screams echoed through the trees, although who was killing whom was anyone's guess. In the heat of battle, it would very much be a case of stab first and ask questions later.

I got him to his feet somehow. His arm dangled uselessly. I suspected he'd never have full use of it again. At least I'd slowed the bleeding. I tucked his cold hand inside his tunic to try to ease the weight.

He was so good. So brave. He never made a sound as we limped along the path. Behind us, the noise of battle grew more muted. On the other hand, the sounds of pursuit and sudden death were all around us.

Two big advantages, though. Our clothing blended well – thank you Wardrobe – and our move to investigate events at the baggage train had actually brought us nearer to Number Eight. If I craned my neck, I could see it. I began to entertain a hope we might get away, after all.

Wrong.

We were never going to get out of this.

I heard a shout behind us and looked around. A group of four or five men were heading towards us, swords drawn, but still some distance away. If Tim had not been wounded, we could have strolled to the pod, waved them a casual goodbye, and easily made our escape.

But Tim could barely move.

'Go,' he said. 'Leave me.'

I was barely conscious of making the decision. In fact, the word decision implies choice. There was no choice to make. No difficult decision to wrestle with.

I pushed him off the path into a small hollow. Bushes overhung the far side. He fell, fortunately cushioned by drifts of still dry leaves. I jumped down after him.

There was so much I wanted to say to him. Well, it would never be said now. Even as he rolled over and said, 'What …?' I was fishing around for what I wanted. A nice smooth rock. Definitely no sharp edges.

I found one and said, 'Listen to me, Dr Peterson. Wait here for the rescue party. They will come. Make it back safely. Have a good life. That's a command,' and tightened my grip on the rock.

Still not quite sure what was happening, he said, 'What ...?'

I slugged him with the rock.

Not too hard – oh God, not too hard.

He fell back soundlessly on to the soft ground. I rolled him under the bushes with his sword and covered him with leaves as best I could.

No time for goodbyes.

No time for ... anything.

There was a time in my life when I never thought I would have any friends. Actually there was a time when I never thought I'd have a life, either.

I'd had both, against all the odds. But everything has to be paid for and my time to pay had arrived.

I scrambled out of the hollow, lifting my head cautiously over a fallen log. There were three of them that I could see, working their way slowly towards us. We had a minute, maybe less.

I pulled myself over the top, took one last look at where Tim lay hidden, and drew a deep breath. And ran. Away from Tim. Away from the pod. As fast as I could.

You can't cry and run. One or the other. So I ran.

It seemed to me I'd been running all my life. The Somme, Whitechapel, Nineveh, Troy, Cambridge, the Cretaceous – you name it, I've raced through it.

This was my last run. Make it count, Maxwell.

I flew through that wood. I pounded along the path, jumping over logs, half-blinded by branches whipping across my face. I felt no fear. No fatigue. I flew. I could hear shouts and pounding footsteps behind me. They'd catch me eventually – and it wouldn't be pleasant – but it wouldn't last long. It would soon be over, and my friend Tim would be safe.

In the meantime …

I tucked in my chin, pumped my elbows, and went for it. Major Guthrie would have been so proud.

I ran and ran, twisting and turning, never once looking behind me, all my attention on drawing them away from Tim and the pod.

I was going so fast that I never saw the one who stepped out from behind the tree. I cannoned into him. He staggered but remained on his feet.

I kicked him hard, poked his eyes, and tried to pull his ear off. He roared in anger, but I had only one aim now – to get this over with as soon as possible. I heard his friends behind me.

They'd forgotten all about Peterson. My job was done.

I yanked again on his ear and, as I tore free of his grasp, I heard the ring of steel as he drew his sword.

The world went very quiet and still.

21

'I see you,
Golden-eyed girl.
Watcher of time's brave pageant.
Beloved of Kleio.
Weep for your dreams
For today they die.
Your heart will grow cold.
And as the leaves fall
The golden-eyed girl
Will leave this world.
Never to return.'

I stared uncomprehendingly at the red, wet thing protruding from my chest.

I should do something, but I was already drifting away.

I should scream, but the need to breathe had left me.

Time – finally – stood still for me. I looked up at the tracery of black branches dramatically etched against the milk-white sky. I looked down at the sodden, once golden leaves. I should move. Run. Do something.

I closed my eyes and fell forwards into the pile of wet, soft …

… hard, hairy carpet.

*

Sometimes, it's best to leap to your feet, armed and ready to tackle anything, and sometimes, it's best just to lie still and wonder what the hell's going on. My nostrils were full of carpet dust. I could feel the bristly texture of Axminster against my cheek.

A familiar voice said, 'Breathe.'

That was not going to happen. My chest was on fire. Huge, pulsing, red-hot, agonising fire. Breathing in could only make it worse. Besides, I was dead. I must be. No one could survive a wound like that.

My stupid body took over and I took a deep, carpet-dust laden gulp of air, coughed blood, and doubled up in a pain no words of mine could describe.

I don't know how long I lay, taking tiny, shallow breaths and bleeding all over someone's carpet.

Since I obviously wasn't dead, I eventually opened one cautious eye.

I could see carpet, the lower half of an armchair, and elegantly sandaled feet.

I closed my eyes again. I knew those feet. They never boded well.

The silence went on. I knew she was waiting. Dear God, was there no respite? Even in death …?

In a painful whisper, I said, 'I'm not dead, am I?'

'No.'

That would do for the time being. Just let me rest. In peace, preferably.

'Open your eyes.'

It was a command and my eyes opened of their own accord.

'Can you get up?'

'No.'

'I think you should try.'

Well, she would think that, wouldn't she?

I put my forearms on the floor and tried to push myself up. Pain sleeted through every last inch of me. Everything hurt. For God's sake, I had taken a sword through the heart. Why couldn't she let me be?

'Try again. The sooner you are able to move, the sooner your pain will dissipate.'

A likely story. But again, independent of anything I wanted to do – which was just lie still and die all over again – I pushed myself a few inches off the carpet and tried to look around.

Nothing I recognised here. Early- to mid-twenty-first-century furnishings. Solid. Dull. Clean. Conventional. I fell back again with a groan.

'Come along, Dr Maxwell. Time is short.'

'Go away,' I said, brave because I was already dying. What else could she do to me?

'I shall, as soon as I see you on your feet and functioning.'

I got one knee underneath me this time, then the other, a forearm on the coffee table, another on the sofa. And that was it. I hung, quivering with the strain.

Someone lifted me up and dropped me onto the sofa. I lay back, waiting for the waves of pain to subside.

'Please drink this.'

God knows what it was. Some ancient corpse-reviver from the groves of Mount Ida, probably. It tasted like someone's discarded washing-up water. Hot liquid burned its way down my throat and mingled with the other, larger, still-present and definitely-not-going-away pain.

I closed my eyes, still unwilling to participate in current events.

'Dr Maxwell, open your eyes, please, and listen to me.'

I sighed. I'd deliberately asked no questions or shown any interest in anything in the vain hope she would just go away and leave me alone.

As if what I wanted was of any importance.

The silence lengthened as she waited for me to utter the traditional, 'When am I?' followed by the equally traditional, 'Where am I?' and followed, in this case, by the very justified, 'What the hell is going on?'

I refused to cooperate. 'Any chance of a cup of tea?'

'None whatsoever.' I sighed. Of course there wasn't.

'What do you want, Mrs Partridge?'

Do you ever wonder if there was a Mr Partridge?

'I want you to open your eyes and pay close attention. This is important.'

'Am I dead?'

'As I told you, no.'

'Is this the Elysian Fields?'

'You are in Rushford. Please try and pull yourself together.'

I opened my eyes and squinted down at myself. 'The sword's gone.'

'The wound is closed.'

'The wound still hurts like hell.'

'I said the wound is closed, not healed.'

'Why not?'

'I'm not a healer.'

'Could you fetch one?'

'You're young and strong. Heal yourself.'

I suppose, if you're thousands of years old, even I must seem young.

'What do you want, Mrs Partridge?

'I need you to concentrate.'

I sighed. She was never, ever going away.

'All right, tell me.'

'Look around you.'

I looked around me.

I was in a small living room in a small flat. I gave it a careless glance and then, forgetting my closed but unhealed chest wound, tried to sit up. I saw an unfamiliar but conventional living room with a fire laid and ready, but the picture over the mantelpiece was one of mine. A Mediterranean landscape, with apple-green pine trees marching down to a sparkling turquoise sea. A painting of a special place for me. Leon and I used to go there, secretly, to spend time together. Special time. I'd painted my favourite view and Leon had loved it and snatched it off my easel before even the paint was dry, and now it was here.

When I looked more closely, I saw other familiar objects scattered around the room.

On the mantelpiece stood the small model of the Trojan Horse, made for me by Leon himself and my most treasured possession. And a framed photograph of him and me, laughing together. I remembered the day Dieter had taken it.

Battered pine bookcases stood on each side of the

fireplace. The right-hand one was full of my books. I recognised the titles. They were all here. Even the little book about Agincourt he would leave for me all those years ago. A stuffed scarlet snake hung from the top shelf.

The left-hand case was full of his own stuff. Books with the words 'Quantum' or 'Temporal Dynamics' in the title and the occasional thriller.

I looked around the room. On my right, a door led into a small kitchen from which the smells of something delicious wafted. A closed door ahead of me probably led to a bathroom. On my left, two bedroom doors.

I lurched to my feet and wobbled off to investigate further.

The bigger bedroom was his. A pair of jeans lay across a chair. I opened a wardrobe. Men's clothes. I recognised some of them. On the bedside table stood another copy of our photograph. In fact, the two of them were placed in such a way that wherever you stood in this tiny flat, you could see at least one of them. I began to have yet another bad feeling.

I limped slowly into the other bedroom. My things were laid out on the dressing-table. My clothes hung in the wardrobe. A book I had been reading stood on the bedside-table. I looked under the pillow with growing unease. My yellow and white spotted PJs …

The room looked as if I'd just walked out of it. How was this possible? Had I lived here?

If you want to know who lives in a house, look in the bathroom.

A man lived in this house.

One toothbrush. Shaving gear. No hair conditioner.

I lurched back to Mrs Partridge, still in her alter ego as Kleio, Muse of History, and waiting for me. I sat heavily.

She looked at me for a long time and then said, 'In this world, it was you who died.'

I took a moment or two to sort through the implications of 'in this world,' and 'it was you who died.' Suddenly, many things made sense. I waited.

'He did not handle it well.'

No, he wouldn't. He'd lost too many people in his life.

'Against the advice of Dr Bairstow, he left St Mary's and came here. Apparently, you had once had a plan to set up home together.'

I nodded.

'He has built a shrine to you. Your clothes, your books, all your belongings. He brought them all here. He cooks meals for two. He lays the table for two. He discusses his day with you. He talks to you continually. His grief is overwhelming him.'

'Is that why you have brought me here? To talk to him?'

'No. I have brought you here to live with him. Here. In this other world. This must be your world now.'

'No,' I said, firmly. 'Absolutely not. I'll talk to him. I'll even stay for a while until he's better, but I have a job to do. I have to get back to Peterson. He's wounded. He needs help.'

'Dr Peterson is safe. The rescue party has found him. They will not find you. Because you are here. In this world.'

'No. I have to go back. Tim …'

'Is safe. He does not need you. Leon Farrell does. It is

363

very important that you remain in this world. There is a job to be done and only you can do it.'

'No, I have to go back.'

'If I send you back, you will die. You were only seconds from death when I brought you here. You will not live long enough to see Mr Peterson.'

'I want to see Tim Peterson. Afterwards, I'll do whatever you want, but if I don't see Peterson then you'll get nothing from me.'

My God, I was defying Mrs Partridge, the immortal daughter of Zeus. If I hadn't been seconds from death before, I was now.

We stared stubbornly at each other.

'Very well,' she said. 'I can find you a few minutes in your old world. But it will not be long. And it will have to be paid for, one day.'

'Agreed.'

'Stand up.'

I did, and was suddenly back in Sick Bay. The change was so abrupt, I rocked on my feet to get my balance.

I was in the men's ward. Tim lay in the bed by the window, head turned, looking at the dark world outside, his arm heavily bandaged. A single battered yellow rose lay on his bedside table.

I said, softly, 'Tim?'

He turned his head.

I have no memory of getting across the room, but suddenly I was on the bed. He got his good arm round me. I hugged him as tightly as I could.

'Tim ...'

364

'Max! Oh, my God, Max. They found you. You're alive.'

'And you. You made it. I knew you would. How are you?'

'Absolutely fine. Even better knowing you're here. What happened? When did they find you?'

I sat back. 'They didn't.'

He took in my blood-soaked dress and my tangled hair. I probably didn't look good.

'Then how did you get back? How did you get away?'

'I didn't.'

He lay back on the pillows. I could see him trying to work through the implications and not understanding any of them.

'Max?'

'I've been allowed back, Tim. Just for a few minutes. I've been given a chance to say goodbye. Don't let's waste time with questions.'

'Goodbye? Are you – are you leaving St Mary's? Where are you going? What is happening?

'There's something I have to do and it's important. But I only agreed to do it if I got a chance to say goodbye to you. That's why I'm here.'

My voice wobbled horribly because I'd suddenly realised I would never see him again. Ever.

'I've come to say goodbye.'

He wouldn't accept it.

'No. No. You can't leave.'

'I can't stay, Tim. This is a fatal wound. I can't come back.'

I was crying now and so was he.

365

'Please, Tim, don't. Be happy for me.'

'I thought you were dead. That you'd given your life for me. I'm happy you're not. I'm crying for me. You can't leave.'

'I must. I made my choice at Agincourt and I don't regret it. Not for a moment. Please don't you regret it either.'

He was silent a moment and then said, quietly, 'There won't be any more adventures, will there?'

'Yes, of course there will, Tim. For us, there will always be adventures. Just not together any more.'

He shook his head. 'This arm is probably never going to be the same. And even if it is – I'm not sure I want to do this without you.'

'Tim …'

'It was always you and me, Max, wasn't it?'

I smiled through my tears, 'Ever since you peed on me. I think it left some sort of imprint.'

'I'm off the active list. Probably for good. Apparently, I'm going to be Deputy Director. Can you believe that?'

'You'll be superb.'

'Yes,' he said, with a touch of the old Tim. 'I probably will. But you won't be here.'

'You'll have Helen, who loves you more than she's prepared to admit. And Kal. And everyone here. You'll do great things, Tim.'

Someone tapped on the door.

He tightened his grip.

'People are upset. Can I tell them you're not dead?'

'Tell the Boss.' I couldn't bear the thought of him sitting in silent grief when there was no need. He'd lost

Leon and now me. 'Give him my love. Tell him I'll think of him every day. And now, I don't want to, but I have to go.'

'No. Please. Can't you stay a little longer. This is all the time we'll ever have.'

'I can't. I'm sorry, Tim.'

He said, desperately, 'Do you remember – that night at Rushford when I gave you that golden rose? *For my golden friend, Max.*'

I swallowed. 'I do. I kept it for ages. Do you remember our night at Nineveh?'

'I remember you yanking us out of the Cretaceous period. You were as pissed as a newt.'

I laughed through my tears. 'I remember how bad you smelled.'

'I don't think you have any idea how much I'll miss you.'

I stopped laughing. 'Yes, I do know. I know exactly how much.'

I tightened my grip. So did he. We might only have three good arms between us, but we were holding on to each other like two people who knew they'd never, ever, see each other again.

'I wish we could begin it all again, Max.'

I touched his face and we kissed, very gently and sweetly. Such a lot was said but not spoken. A lifetime of memories with him kaleidoscoped through my head. I could feel his tears running down my face.

'Max ...'

'Tim, my dearest friend ...'

I held his face between my hands, we looked at each

other for the last time, and then I was back in the little living room.

She gave me a minute while I blew my nose on my sleeve.

Finally, I was able to say, 'Thank you.'

She inclined her head. 'I shall leave you, now.'

'Wait. You can't go yet.'

'You have a task to perform. I should let you get on with it.'

'At least give me some information before you go. What is this task? What must I do? Should I go back to St Mary's? How did I die? I can't just come back to life, surely?'

She stood. 'Events will play out. You will do whatever is required. Try not to fret too much about the future.'

'Well, I don't have to, do I? I'm dead.'

The familiar expression of exasperation crossed her face. 'I keep telling you, Dr Maxwell, you are not dead. Why you have this persistent obsession with your own death is a mystery to me.'

'But what do you want me to do?'

'Your best.'

And she was gone, because God forbid she should ever make things easy for me.

I stood alone, in a strange room in a strange world, wondering what on earth to do next.

The sensible answer would be to change out of my bloodstained garments, have a shower, and tidy myself up a little.

I went out into the kitchen instead and stared at a tiny

kitchen table laid for two, found the back door, and let myself out.

I knew where this was. I was in Rushford and this was one of those units down by the river. The derelict ones that the council had reclaimed. Living space over a downstairs workshop. Very popular with artists and such. A small courtyard held parking for two cars. To my right, a tiny garden. In the back left-hand corner stood a familiar, small, stone shack. He'd tied a clothesline to one corner and the clothes prop leaned against it. I swallowed a huge lump.

I made my way carefully down some stone steps into the courtyard. The workshop doors were open to let in the summer sunshine. From inside I could hear a radio playing quietly, some chinky tool noises, and someone talking.

I oozed quietly through the doors and stood on the threshold, looking around.

He stood with his back to me, moving around a work area he'd created by pushing three tables together in a U shape. The surfaces were littered with items that meant nothing to me.

The far end of the workshop had two big windows and between these, he'd made a corner with two tables and set up my easel. My paints were laid out neatly, my brushes in a jar and canvases stacked against the wall.

Mrs Partridge had been right. He'd made a shrine. I would not have thought my heart could break any more.

He was speaking. To himself.

'So, one of us is going to have to speak to Mrs Foreman about the precise relationship between electricity

369

and water. When the instructions say to clean with warm, soapy water, they really don't mean her to shove the entire grill into the dishwasher. And since you yourself are even hazier about the precise relationship between electricity and water than she is, it's going to have to be me again, isn't it?'

He groped along the bench for some implement or other.

I stood perfectly still, while the blood thumped in my head. He was here. Not five paces away. It was Leon. Leon was here. Not dead. I could walk towards him. I could touch him. Feel his arms around me. Look into his amazing eyes. Feel his hands on me again. Hear his voice. Smell his smell. I tried to remember to breathe. I swear I never made a sound, but some instinct must have warned him.

He turned slowly.

I stood in the entrance, dark against the bright sunshine.

He put down whatever it was he was working on and took two steps forward.

I drew a deep breath.

He stopped.

He peered uncertainly.

His face cleared.

He smiled, stretched out a welcoming hand, and said, 'Isabella?'

And everything inside me screamed.

They say that should you ever be unfortunate enough to meet yourself, you won't like what you see. That you won't like yourself at all.

I'd never met myself – in my job that would be a bit of a catastrophe. The closest I'd ever come was meeting Isabella Barclay. Who looked very much like me. Bitchface Barclay. Former head of IT at St Mary's. And I hadn't liked her. Not one little bit. In fact, I'd hated her so much I'd killed her. Everyone needs to be clear about this – I deliberately killed Isabella Barclay.

And now, now I'd waded through blood and death – mine – to be here. I'd abandoned my old life and my best friend to be here. To be here with him. And for him. And what did he say?

Isabella?

Isabella fucking Barclay?

My recently damaged heart nearly erupted through my recently punctured chest as a massive wave of searing, red-hot, uncontrollable rage …

I'd died in this world. Mrs Partridge said I'd died in this world and here he was … *Isabella? … Fucking Isabella Barclay?*

My hand closed on something. I had no idea what it

was, but at that moment I was so head-burstingly furious that I could have fashioned something lethal from a ball of wet cotton wool. He was dead in my world. Well, now he was about to bloody die in this one as well.

The radio played "Staying Alive".

I stepped forward out of the sunlight to let him have a good look at me before I ended his life.

Despite everything, I was shocked. He looked both younger and older. Younger, because he wore casual clothes – old jeans and a baggy black sweater with holes in the elbows – and older, because he was suffering. His pallor accentuated the browny-purple shadows around his eyes. His lips were thin and bloodless. Even as we stared at each other, colour surged across his face and then receded, leaving him even paler than before.

He reeled. Literally reeled – falling back against his workbench and knocking equipment to the floor.

A battered old sofa was set against one wall. I helped him across the workshop, a small spark of resentment adding itself to the bonfire of my fury. I was the one who was dead. Well, nearly dead. So why was he the one wobbling about like a fainting schoolgirl? On the other hand, I could see he'd been suffering for a very long time. At least I'd only been dead for an afternoon. He sat for a while with his eyes closed, breathing heavily.

I sat down myself. It had been another long day.

He opened his eyes.

I know he said, 'Max,' because his lips moved, but no sound came out. I nodded. Not in encouragement, but so that he would know who was about to splatter him all over his own workshop.

'Yes,' I said, tightly. 'Max. *Not* Isabella.'

He closed his eyes again.

'That won't save you. Open your eyes.'

He did. Still dazed, he ran his eyes over my face. His lips moved and again, he said, 'Max?'

I said nothing this time.

'I … How? …' I think it was all too much for him. He closed his eyes again.

I poked him. 'Don't go to sleep.'

That jolted his eyes open. He blinked a little, made a huge effort to pull himself together, and said, because in a crisis, the mind tends to fix on trivia, 'What are you holding?'

I discovered I had been about to gut him from groin to gizzard with an old plastic dustpan. Blue.

'Never mind that. *Isabella*?'

'What?'

'You said, "Isabella".'

He was still confused.

'Did I?'

I couldn't keep it in any longer. 'You couldn't wait, could you? "Oh, my redhead's dead. Never mind, I know where I can lay my hands on another. All cats look the same at night." '

He slapped me.

I hit him with the dustpan.

This was going well.

He sat up. 'How could you think …? How could you think even for one minute that I …? What is the matter with you?'

'The matter with me? I'm not the one shouting my

373

current girlfriend's name at my ex.'

'She's not my girlfriend. How could you think that? And who are you, anyway? What do you want?'

I was reaching boiling point.

'You're pretending you don't know who I am? Well, I'm not bloody Isabella.'

'Yes, I think we've established that. Do you want to continue through a list of people you're not?'

'Don't you know me? Or don't you want to know me?'

'I know who you look like, but she's dead. So just tell me. Who are you? What do you want?'

I suddenly saw things through his eyes. A stranger in his workshop. Actually, a blood-drenched madwoman clutching a blue dustpan.

The radio broke into "Things Can Only Get Better."

I struggled, discarding words, phrases, explanations.

'In my world, you died.'

It was the best I could do.

He said again, 'Who are you?' But this time in a completely different voice.

'My name is Max.'

He seized both my arms and dragged me round to face him.

'No. No, it's not. She's dead. Who are you?'

'My name is Madeleine Maxwell. I work for St Mary's. I was on assignment at Agincourt with Peterson. Everything went tits-up. I was stabbed. With a sword. I fell down. When I opened my eyes, I was in your flat upstairs. I'm sorry but I've made an awful mess on your carpet. If the blood doesn't come out then you're going to lose your deposit.'

He dragged his eyes away from my face and finally took in the fifteenth-century costume, which managed to be both stiff and soggy with blood.

'That looks bad. Should I get an ambulance? Ring St Mary's?'

I shook my head. 'The wound is closed. I just need a bit of peace to recover.'

He dropped my arms and now moved to the far end of the sofa, distancing himself from me. I hadn't expected jubilation, but horror, shock, disbelief, and fear were written all over his face. He didn't know what to do. I didn't know what to do. My temper was subsiding. This really hadn't been a good day and its events were beginning to catch up with me. I didn't know what to do next. It had never occurred to me he might not be as pleased to see me as I was to see him. Once again, I was lost in an unfamiliar emotional maelstrom.

However, there's a St Mary's ritual for dealing with this sort of thing.

'Any chance of a cup of tea?'

He got up, switched on the kettle, and pulled two mugs off a shelf.

I don't like milk much. If I can, I always have lemon in my tea. He had a little saucer with slices of lemon already prepared. I had a throat-closing vision of him carefully slicing a fresh lemon every morning. For someone who was dead. Who would never …

He really was in a bad way.

I remembered again what Mrs Partridge had said. Remembered the books, the snake, and my picture – all my stuff carefully placed and dusted. Laying the table for two. The slices of lemon. There was no way he was with Izzie Barclay. I'm an idiot.

I felt suddenly cold and tired.

He came and perched on the edge of the sofa and looked at me.

I said again, 'In my world, you died.'

He seemed calm, so I continued. 'I was in my office, laying out next year's schedule.'

No need to tell him we were estranged. Not now, anyway. And definitely no need to tell him why. There might be a Joe Nelson in this world who would need protecting, too.

'The phone rang. I was heavily into twelfth-century France. It was you. You were in Hawking but you sounded miles away. I thought at the time ...' I stopped.

I thought at the time that he had sounded as if he was on the other side of the universe. Suddenly, for the first time it struck me – I'd spoken to him not ten minutes before I saw his body, but his hands were cold. He'd been dead a long time. And I'd spoken to him on the telephone ...

He said, hoarsely, 'I called you. You were late for lunch. Again. I said ...'

'You said, "Where are you?" and I said, "In my office..."'

'And I said, "Lunch?" And you said, "What?" And I said, "I'm waiting ..." And you never came.'

I shivered.

'I should get a doctor. Take you to St Mary's.'

'No. I'm fine. The wound is closed.' I swallowed.

'They found you in Hawking. In Number Eight. The Boss sent you back. In your pod. There's a memorial stone in the churchyard.'

He said, hoarsely. 'They found you in your office. You still had an assignment in your hand. Julius Caesar. The Boss had to shut down St Mary's for two days. People were in a state. Peterson was just ... Markham too. And Izzie. Kal had to be driven over from Thirsk. She was in no condition to bring herself.'

He stopped.

'Tell me, Leon. What happened next? What did you do?' Where was Bitchface Barclay in all this?'

'I buried you.'

I tried not to catch my breath.

'And then ...?'

'I tried. I tried to carry on. People tried to help. But you weren't there. Ian was amazing. So was Izzie. I don't know why you said what you did. She was one of your best friends. You surely don't think ... She drops by, sometimes, just to talk. That's what I thought when I saw you. Everyone tried so hard, but you weren't there. You just weren't there, Max. Everywhere I looked, you weren't there. So in the end, I left. I couldn't handle it. We'd been going to leave; to set up home together. So that's what I did. I left and started a new life.'

No, he hadn't. He'd built himself a false construct – a fantasy world in which nothing was real.

'And Dr Bairstow let you go?'

'Not willingly. Not willingly at all. He made me serve a six-month notice, hoping all the time, I think, that I would change my mind. He still visits once or twice a month, although there's no need. Sometimes Ian comes too.'

'Why didn't you go back to your own time?'

'You would have been even further away ...'

I nodded, taking all this in.

'What about you, Max? What did you ...? I mean, how did you ...?'

'I stayed at St Mary's. You were there. You were everywhere. Everywhere I looked, there was some place where we'd had a conversation, or sat together, or kissed. Every time I looked up and saw a door closing, it was as if you'd just left the room. The whole place was permeated with memories and I couldn't leave them.'

Silence.

'Why are you here? How did you get here?

'The answer to both those questions is that I don't know. As I said, I was stabbed. It hurt. I fell forwards onto a pile of leaves and found myself on your carpet. As to why I'm here, I have no idea. Only half an hour ago, I was dead. Or as good as. I'm struggling a little with the events of today.'

He sat still, staring at his hands, nodding.

'So, what's next, Leon?'

'What do you mean?'

'Well, do you want me to leave? In which case, can you ring St Mary's and see if they'll take me in? I can't go to hospital. I'm dead in this world. I don't know how I'm going to get around that. I don't really know anything at the moment.'

'I think you should stay here. I'd like you to stay here. At least for a little while. But ...'

378

This had to be said and it had to be said now.

'Leon, you must get your head around this. I'm Max, but I'm not your Max. We might look alike but be very different in character. Your Max might have been quiet, calm, patient, and able to cook and didn't stuff herself on chocolate and …'

'No, my Max wasn't any of that, but I take your point. And I'm not your Leon, either.'

'In fact, we're complete strangers. We're strangers with familiar faces. We don't know each other at all.'

'Yes. I understand that. Even so, I would like to extend an invitation for you to stay for a while. If this really isn't your world then you have a lot of catching up to do. Decisions to make. But all that's for the future. For the time being, until you're better, I think you should stay. I really would like you to stay.'

I took a breath. 'Thank you. I really would like to stay.'

He put out a hand. 'Hello. My name's Leon.'

The years rolled back. I was standing on the staircase at St Mary's, meeting a man in an orange jumpsuit … and the whole incredible adventure was about to begin, all over again.

I held it tightly. 'Hello, Leon. Nice to meet you.'

The silence lengthened.

I gently pulled my hand free before the tears started to fall. This was no time to get all soppy and sentimental.

I staggered to my feet and went to investigate my painting area. It was all very neat and tidy. I'd soon put a stop to that.

I bent painfully, placed a canvas on the easel, and

379

stroked it gently, while I waited for it to tell me what it wanted to be.

The silence was overwhelming.

I reached up and began to twist my hair back into its bun. That done, I pulled my brushes towards me, looked at him over my shoulder, threw him a bit of a wobbly smile, and said, 'Where's that tea, then?'

EPILOGUE

I'd had a good night's sleep, a very long, hot bath, several mugs of tea, and was now feeling very much more on top of things.

In an effort to overcome the slight social awkwardness occasioned by the two of us not knowing where to begin, he was fussing around the kitchen doing me some tea and toast since I'd missed breakfast. I was busy at the kitchen table.

'What are you doing?' he said, plonking a mug of tea in front of me.

'Writing my obituary.'

'What on earth for?'

'Well, you can't do it, can you? I never met you before yesterday.'

'My surprise was based less on the fact that we've hardly met and more because you're not actually dead.'

'No, but I was. Maybe I'm a zombie. Brains ... must have brains ...'

'No brains. Only Marmite.'

'A very acceptable alternative.'

There was a slight pause. I wondered if perhaps his Max hadn't liked Marmite. Was this how it was always going to be, with each of us silently comparing this new version of ourselves to the old one. I liked Marmite – maybe his Max hadn't. This Leon wore black socks – my Leon hadn't. My Leon had been dynamite in bed. We were good together. Suppose now ... we weren't?

I looked up and he was watching me, following my every thought. That hadn't changed, anyway.

'It's not going to be a problem,' he said softly. 'We don't have to rush anything. We have our whole lives ahead of us and we'll just take each day as it comes. The first priority is to get you fit and well again. I don't like women running around the flat with big holes in their chests. It makes the place look untidy.'

'All closed up now,' I said. 'It just hurts a bit every now and then.'

Actually, it still hurt a lot. Mrs Partridge had known what she was doing. I had no choice but to remain here and take things slowly. For a week, at least.

A lot can happen in a week.

And it was about to.

The telephone rang.

Busy buttering toast, Leon ignored it and the machine cut in.

I heard his voice. 'Please leave a message.'

A pause.

A beep.

Then Dr Bairstow, his voice harsh with urgency said, 'Leon. Get out. They're here. *Run!*'

THE END

382

ACKNOWLEDGMENTS

My thanks to all the marvellous people at Accent Press for their patience and encouragement.

And, as always, special thanks to Connie and Martin. And to Mike and Jan for their hospitality. And to Aly and the yoga group who never laugh at my downward facing dog.

And finally, huge thanks to everyone who has bought this book.

Want to know what happens next?
Catch up with Max and the disaster magnets in

Sometimes, surviving is all you have left.

Max and Leon are safe at last. Or so they think.

Snatched from her own world and dumped into a new one,
Max is soon running for her life. Again.

From a 17th-century Frost Fair to Ancient Egypt; from
Pompeii to 8th-century Scandinavia; Max and Leon are
pursued up and down the timeline, playing a dangerous
game of hide-and-seek, until finally they're forced to take
refuge at St Mary's where a new danger awaits them.

Max's happily ever after
is going to have to wait a while . . .

HEADLINE

NO TIME LIKE THE PAST

A fete worse than death.

The St Mary's Institute of Historical Research has finally recovered from its wounds and it's business as usual for those rascals in the History Department.

From being trapped in the Great Fire of London to an unfortunately timed comfort break at Thermopylae, which leaves the fate of the western world hanging in the balance, Max must struggle to get History back on track.

But first, they must get through the St Mary's Fete – which is sure to end badly for everyone.

Only one thing is certain, life at St Mary's is never dull.

HEADLINE

'To do what I do – go where I go – see what I see – it's a wonderful, unique, never-to-be-taken-for-granted privilege.'

With great privilege comes great responsibility, something Max knows only too well, and as newly appointed Chief Training Officer at the St Mary's Institute of Historical Research, it's up to her to drum this guiding principle into her five new recruits.

With a training programme that includes Joan of Arc, an illegal mammoth, a duplicitous Father of History, a bombed rat, Stone Age hunters and Dick the Turd, the question everyone is asking themselves is – what could possibly go wrong?

HEADLINE